Fresh News Straight From Heaven

A Novel based upon the True Mythology of Johnny Appleseed

Gregg Sapp

FRESH NEWS STRAIGHT FROM HEAVEN
A Novel based upon the True Mythology of Johnny Appleseed

FIRST EDITION SOFTCOVER
ISBN: 1622535073
ISBN-13: 978-1-62253-507-1

Editor: Lane Diamond
Interior Designer: Lane Diamond

www.EvolvedPub.com
Evolved Publishing LLC
Butler, Wisconsin, USA

Printed in Book Antiqua font.

DEDICATION

To Gene and Punkin,
love that always "delivered."

PART ONE – 1801

"From all we can learn, we are of the opinion that contemporaneous with [Andy Craig] was the oddest character in our history, Johnny Chapman, alias Appleseed."

Banning Norton, "A History of Knox County, Ohio"

Chapter 1 – August 1801

Owl Creek, the Ohio Country

Dead Mary squinted and sucked hard on her breath as she took lethal aim. She felt the draw tension of the bow in her forearms, and the taut, deer-tendon string hummed as if begging for release. When she'd gotten up that morning, killing somebody had been the furthest thing from her mind. She still didn't feel much like doing it, but, if she listened to her own common sense, she had no better choice than to slay this rambling half-wit who'd trespassed into her woods. He was a white man, thus worthy of death, even if he was a bit peculiar and possibly harmless.

Will I regret it if I let him live? Won't it be simpler just to snuff him out now, and end the whole story?

She'd tracked this gnarly, gangly frontiersman for several hundred yards along the riverbank, waiting for a clear kill shot, but also, almost despite her better intentions, studying him. He was weird just to look at. His eyes bulged like a catfish's beneath a high brow, and his face twitched as if his cheeks were stuffed with ants. Clad in tatters, barefoot, swinging his arms, he skipped like a child through the weeds and brambles, carrying a walking stick and singing in a cheery voice:

"The tree of life, my soul hath seen,
laden with fruit and always green.
The trees of nature, fruitless be
compar'd with Christ, the Apple Tree."

His swift stride conveyed purpose and conviction, as if he knew where he was going... which Dead Mary figured to be impossible, because ahead of him lay only thousands of acres of primitive forest, the great Black Swamp, and isolated Indian villages. Furthermore, this solitary white man, traveling where very few of those were brave enough to venture, was unarmed. He carried something bundled in a kerchief tied to his stick, and nothing more. It didn't seem possible that he could've made it so far.

Despite all of these oddities, the beaming grin he sported, as if he'd just gotten away with something, struck Dead Mary as the queerest thing about him. Maybe he was drunk, or more likely just feeble-minded. Either case presented excellent justification for killing him. Much as she resisted the notion, though, she couldn't help but wonder if this beggarly character was really as happy as he seemed to be.

She'd never killed a happy man before. It didn't seem right.

The wayfarer stepped into a clearing, loosened his trouser cords, and allowed his pants to drop. He then squatted above a large skunk cabbage and began grunting to encourage the evacuation of his bowels.

"Thank ye, Lord," he howled at the sky, "for what comes out as much as what goes in."

Now, Dead Mary felt like killing him would be doing him a favor, since he was probably destined to become some hungry bear's snack—the meat on his bones being insufficient for a full meal. Still, taking a man's life in the middle of his pinching a shit seemed a rotten thing to do.

She waited, anchoring her bow against her jaw, ready to let the arrow fly....

"I know that ye'd be a-watching me," the man shouted over his shoulder. "What is it a-going to be? Are ye fixing to kill me?"

Dead Mary lowered her weapon. Was he actually calling her out while she had him trained in her kill sights, and at the same time squatting over his heels, shitting pellets? That was beyond just peculiar; more like the far side of crazy.

The man continued. "I first saw ye gathering sassafras roots upstream half a mile. I considered stepping out of the woods to introduce me-self, but I did not mean to spook ye. Instead, I reasoned that a woman alone in the wilderness would not be a-feared of any man while he is bent over in the act of moving his bowels. So here I squat. T'would be easy to kill me, although I do prefer that ye not to do that." Bare from the waist down, he faced her, lifted his shirt, and puffed his chest to give her a clear target. "But if ye aim to kill this earthly body anyhow, I beg of ye to strike your arrow into me heart, the better to free me soul when the blood gushes out."

In this moment, Dead Mary got her first clear view of this man—more of an eyeful than she personally would have preferred, but so strange to behold that she couldn't make herself look away.

Although nude and as hairless as a suckling piglet from belly to ankles, he displayed himself with absolutely no modesty, which seemed even stranger in that he possessed a rather dwarfish manhood. His sandy hair draped uneven across his brow, as though it had been hacked through by a dull knife, while in the back it hung long and matted, containing twigs, burs, small pine cones, and probably all sorts of bugs that he'd picked up along the trail. His patchy beard looked like the tail of a diseased fox. Bony shoulders jutted out like plough blades from under his gray linsey shirt. His legs stretched too tall for his body, but his calves and thighs were sinewy—the only real muscle on his whole frame—and his feet appeared flat as canoe oars.

Dead Mary scanned up and down his body, and then instinctively returned her gaze to his eyes, which seemed to be shining gently, as if lit by a candle inside his skull. She blinked hard, for she worried that looking into those turquoise eyes dead-on might be a trap.

"Pull up yo' britches. I cain't kill no man what ain't got 'nuff dignity to wear pants."

"Clothing is not for dignity, but for pride. If I am to die today, let it be as a humble man."

Dead Mary grinded her teeth and released the arrow. It shrieked through the air and lodged in the trunk of a poplar tree inches from the man's ear.

"Thank ye, sister, for using the free will that God gave ye to leave me alive." He saluted her, twisted the arrow loose from the tree, inspected it, and nodded. "Tis a Delaware arrow."

Dead Mary's first thought was to scold herself for having gone soft and let him live. *"Killing abides no doubts,"* Fog Mother had once said to her, but whether that meant it was right or wrong to kill somebody, she wasn't sure.

She steeled herself against useless sympathy. "Shut up, or I'll kill yo' fo' real."

"Forgive my effrontery, dear woman, for the Lord has cursed me with more curiosity than is always in me best interests. Rather than occupy any more of your time, I shall bid fare-thee-well." The stranger pointed upriver with one hand while lifting his trousers with the other, and pivoted to leave.

"Wait!" Dead Mary shouted after him. "Who're yo'?"

"Thank ye for asking me to speak about me-self," he chimed. "Me name is John Chapman, a sower of seeds. I would be pleased if ye chose to call me Johnny. I am a Yankee from Massachusetts by birth, more recently a resident of Western Pennsylvania and the Ohio Valley, but as of this moment, I feel like I have discovered a new home, here in this splendid wilderness."

"What're yo' doin' so deep in d' woods?"

"I got here by following the beauty. A month ago, I left Pittsburgh with no particular thought of where I might go. I was attracted by the ripples of sunshine on the river, by the shadows of the hills, the colors and the fragrances of the forest, the soughing of the breeze through big maple leaves, the merry chatter of songbirds, and the lonesome howl of wolves. I followed the Ohio to the Muskingum, upriver to the Walhonding, to where I am now, which I presume to be Owl Creek. Just this morning, though, I heard a Voice telling me this is where God wants me to be."

"Huh? Yo' heard a voice?"

"Indeed. It was my own mother's sweet voice."

"Yo' momma? Where?"

Johnny made a grand gesture encompassing everything. "Right here in this place. She exists in the beauty that God has spent here."

Dead Mary had stood in that exact spot many times, but never once saw anything that God might especially favor in it, so she took another look. When she opened her eyes wider, she spotted needles of light blinking through the maple and oak leaf canopies. They seemed to dance on Johnny's shoulders as he wiggled a finger, inviting her to follow.

He led her to a narrow clearing over a washed-out ridge at a bend in Owl Creek. The water ran wide and shallow over a sandy bottom, with a small waterfall in the middle where the flow dropped down over several, step-like sheets of mica. Johnny put his hand to his ear and encouraged Dead Mary to listen to the rhythmic flow of water.

It murmured in the shallows, burbled in the little circular eddies around side currents, and simultaneously plunged and tumbled over the miniature falls in the main channel. Something popped in her head, and the landscape then resolved into discrete details of brilliant, intricate clarity: a praying mantis camouflaged on a poplar branch, a bumblebee hovering above a patch of purple milkweed, a pair of spadefoot toads humping in a puddle covered with river foam. Dead Mary usually filtered these things out of her awareness, distractions from the labors of hunting and gathering herbs. But, come to actually notice them, they seemed pretty amazing.

"Look over yonder." Johnny directed Dead Mary's attention to the other side of the river.

The flat shoreline and an expansive floodplain were covered with big bluestem, Indian grass, and switchgrass, along with flowers like wild hyacinths, prairie coneflowers, sawtooth sunflowers, and a whole mess of yellow dandelions.

Johnny laughed. "My mother spoke to me in her eternal Voice, telling me that this was a place chosen by God for me to plant an apple orchard. Can ye not just imagine it?"

"Say wut? Yo' momma ain't really here, is she?"

"In body, no."

"So she's a like a ghost?

"A spirit, yes. The poor woman was too frail for this world. She died giving birth to my only brother, who died soon thereafter, too. My father later married Lucy Cooley, and together they sired a fine brood of half-siblings for me. But my mother continued coming to me in her spirit form, just to me-self alone. She often speaks to me."

That, Dead Mary couldn't quite imagine.

"And she tells yo' to plant apples heah? "What fo'? Who's gonna eat all dem apples?"

"Settlers," Johnny replied. "They are a-coming. Civilization is destined for Ohio. When those settlers get here, they will want apples, which I will provide, with God's help.

"If white folks be comin', I'll shoot dem full of arrows. White folks be devils."

"I believe that all souls can be saved," Johnny disagreed. He stepped between Dead Mary and the riverbank, intercepting her gaze. "Ye must have suffered greatly, to bear such hostility."

"Oh yeah."

"If ye don't mind me inquiring, dear woman.... Obviously, the only explanation for a young negresse like yourself being alone in this unmapped territory is that ye are a runaway slave. But how did ye arrive here?"

"Why yo' askin'?"

"Because I care."

It had been a long time since anybody had asked Dead Mary about herself. Her shoulders heaved in exasperation, but once she started talking, it felt good.

"I was a slave fo' d' most vile man in all western Virginia. His name was Granger Stone, and he done kilt a man in Baltimo', den run away. He settled a piece of land along d' Little Kanawha. Hogs was his business, but drinkin' and gamblin' and fuckin' was what mattered most to him. He won my momma in a game of faro cards, an' I got tossed into d' deal when dey found me hidin' 'neath her skirts. Stone took my momma fo' his bed slave. Me, he gave to be d' wife of anotha' slave, named of Dolt Stone, who was a growed man and a good handler with hogs, but a dummy an' a toady fo' his master. I was jus' eleven years old.

"My job was to bear children with Dolt, but he didn't rightly know what to do with a woman, so he leaved me alone. I think Dolt jus' plain preferred hogs to women. He shoveled out dey sty and spread down wood chips fo' dem. He'd groom dem hogs usin' a horse hair brush, and he'd pick out nits and mites from dey fur with his own fingers. When he had to notch one's ear, he rubbed it with lard first, so's it wouldn't hurt so bad. He claimed dat d' hogs loved him back.

"Dey was one ol' swine Dolt loved most o' all. He called it Daddy Hog. He used to take walks with it, and when he'd talk, it'd grunt right back to him, like dey was speakin' real words. Daddy Hog was a razorback Granger Stone took from a litter o' wild boars, with his intent bein' to mate it with his Yorkshire hogs, but Daddy Hog was mean an' ornery with everybody 'cept Dolt, and he'd sooner fight a sow than hump on her. Finally, Granger Stone decided instead to slash off Daddy Hog's nuts and fatten him fo' market. He told Dolt to do d' dirty work. Dolt blubbered, 'Please don't make me nut dat boar, Master Stone,' but seein' Dolt's weakness jus' made Stone harder in his soul. 'Yo' balls ain't never done *you* no good,' he said to Dolt, 'so why's should yo' care what dat hog loses his nuts, too?' Dolt finally did like he was told, but he told me dat jus' befo' he slit Daddy Hog's balls, he promised dat one day he'd make it up to him.

"It was four years befo' I busted free from Granger Stone. He decided to take his hogs to market in Marietta, where he'd heard dey'd fetch $2.50 per hund'rd weight. He needed Dolt to herd d' hogs to market, an' Dolt begged him to bring me, too. Why, I don't know, nor do I know why dat horrible man agreed, 'cept maybe by dat time he'd done used up all'a my momma and was now gettin' ready fo' me. So I took a vow t' myself that once we ferried int' Ohio, I'd not go back t' Virginia. I didn't tell Dolt, 'cause I was feared he'd snitch t' his master.

"From d' moment we landed in Marietta, Granger Stone left all d' work mindin' d' hogs up t' Dolt, while he conducted his busy-ness with men in taverns an' gamblin' halls. Last night befo' d' hog sale, Dolt slept in d' sty with Daddy Hog, like he was sayin' goodbye. I thought it was disgustin' an' shameful, but now I know he had a plan.

"Next day, at d' hog market, with Granger Stone an all d' white men gathered at a table drinkin' an' signin' dey papers, Dolt rounded up d' swine into a chute dat led dem to a butcher's wagon. Daddy Hog was last, and I noticed how, jus' befo' he got into d' chute, Dolt gave him a whack o' his switch. Dat made Daddy Hog go berserk, breakin' loose into d' open market. He rammed a merchant's table full of flour bags, which busted open like a snowstorm, den he barreled towards d' table where Granger Stone sat. Stone grabbed his long rifle, but was too drunk to shoot straight. Next, Daddy Hog knocked over a whiskey barrel, spillin' sweet mash everywhere. By dis time, Dolt had reached Granger Stone's side to help him up, but Stone slapped him away an' shouted 'Kill that hog, you dickless nigger!' He handed over his long rifle to Dolt.

"Dolt had not fired a musket in his life, but he took dat rifle, centered it so's he was lookin' straight down its shaft at Granger Stone, and Dolt den shot his own master right smack in d' middle o' his skull. Blood 'n' brains spewed everywhere. Dere was a half second when I caught Dolt's eye, befo' white men realized what had happened, an' he winked at me, which I took fo' a message to run like hell, so I did. Dey kilt Dolt an' fed his corpse to d' dogs.

"Fo' days 'n' nights, I followed d' river north. I ate what I could find, which weren't much, 'cause I didn't know what plants was food and what wasn't. I got real weak, sore, an' dizzy in my thoughts. When I started despairin' fo' myself, though, I called back thoughts of Granger Stone, an' I knew that if he caught me, he'd rape me or kill me, or both. Dat gave me 'nuff courage to keep ploddin' ahead. Finally, I crawled into a hollow sycamore trunk and went to sleep, not carin' no more if I woke up or not.

"Next thing I knew, I was in a Delaware Indian camp. I was nursed back to health by a woman named Fog Mother, who was a powerful medicine woman, but was shunned as a witch by most o' d' tribe, 'cause dey'd converted to Christian religion. Me and Fog Mother kept our distance from d' Christian Indians, an' dey did d' same with us. Dat's how it was."

Dead Mary clenched her fists, declaring, "I became Fog Mother's daughter. Dis land is ours, an' ain't no cowards' treaty can tell us we got to leave."

Johnny clapped his hands. "Hooray! I, too, believe that God of Infinite Compassion means for ye to live here in peace. This glorious land—" He flung both arms from his chest to his sides. "—is God's gift to all free, peace-loving people."

That sounded too reasonable to be true. "Where white folks go, peace don't last long. Get yo' goin' now," she ordered, once again drawing her bow. "Don't come back."

Johnny bowed and turned upstream. Before moving out of range of her arrow, though, he paused and called back, "Are there any other white men living in this land?"

The question made Dead Mary think of a way by which she might relieve herself of any potential nuisance that Johnny might cause in the future, without having to kill him herself. "Yeah, Andy Craig. He lives a couple o' miles upstream."

"Oh, him.... Well, *adieu* ma'am." Johnny nodded his appreciation and, seemingly without taking another step, disappeared into the brush.

There was no doubt in Dead Mary's mind that she'd seen the last of this Johnny, because that nasty weasel Andy Craig wouldn't have a second thought about killing a trespasser.

Johnny knew that some folks became afflicted with "woods madness" if they wandered off the beaten track anywhere in the Ohio back country. Most everybody had heard and told the grim story of the young girl who chased a hare into the forest behind her family's cabin near Big Bottom, only to disappear, as if swallowed whole by some fearsome demon. The men of the village had formed a search party, and for a week they combed the woods, but not even the hounds could sniff the girl's scent. Long after the rest of the community had abandoned hope, the girl's disconsolate father kept searching alone, day-by-day, ignoring the pleas of his family, his neighbors, and his church. Then, one evening, he didn't return either.

Johnny shivered whenever he heard a strange call in the woods at night, recalling how folks said that the girl and her father's tormented ghosts wailed in the dark because they knew their bodies would never be given a Christian burial.

For Johnny, not getting lost was more a matter of intuition than technique. As everyone knew, the scouts from Western Virginia could navigate by studying the angles of shadows at noon, the thickness of tree bark, the growth of lichens on stones, and the bend of ash branches. He had learned these skills from some of the most knowledgeable woodsmen of the Northwest Territory, like Dan McQuay, who legend had it had hiked all the way from Pittsburgh to New Orleans, and from old Simon Kenton, who'd scouted for George Rogers Clark. Still, when Johnny tried to apply their methods, he only got disoriented.

Instead, he'd discovered that by emptying his mind, he could see nature exactly as the wildcat saw it, smell it as keenly as any wolf, and hear its every snap and shudder as clearly as a bat. He could imagine the vegetable consciousness in the great, knowing oaks.

Nothing in nature ever got lost. Neither did Johnny.

Whenever it happened that Johnny misplaced his bearings, he just stopped, sat down, and remained still until he received guidance from his Voices. Sometimes they came as inner shouts so urgent that he couldn't believe nobody else could hear them. Most of the time, though, they manifested as subtle music drifting to him from outside, in the murmuring of the breeze, the plinking of raindrops, the swaying of tall grasses, or in the amalgamated chirps, croaks, caws, drones, busses, honks, humming, growls, snorts, grunts, pants, gasps, chortles, heehaws, and howls that, when he listened carefully, resolved themselves into human Voices speaking plain English. He figured that God had used these kinds of Voices when speaking to the prophets of the Old Testament.

Johnny didn't believe he possessed any special spiritual virtue that enabled him to hear them—except, possibly, his mother's voice. Indeed, he remained convinced that anybody patient enough to listen would be able to hear the Voices. He wasn't surprised so few actually heard, though, because most people didn't even listen to each other when they spoke straight from one person's mouth to another's ear.

Johnny didn't need any help from the Voices to find Andy Craig's residence. As it turned out, tracking the madman of Owl Creek was as easy as following the path of rampaging bull. He knew that he was getting close when he found foot traps set under a persimmon tree, one of which had been sprung but without a catch. He easily sidetracked a pit trap, rather sloppily camouflaged with a thatch of ash switches and clumps of grass. It was deep enough to hold a person, which might've been its intended prey.

Not much farther, he encountered a patch of sumac shrubs that looked to have been flattened at the point where a chase had commenced. He found some powder residue on fern leaves, where someone had fired a shot, and booted footprints in the mud. Around a bend, Johnny smelled death, and following the odor he came upon what was left of a white tail buck's carcass. Andy had slaughtered it on the spot where it had died, then discarded the leavings for the beetles, the maggots, and the turkey vultures.

From there, the route to Andy's cabin was easy to follow by its wanton hacking of limbs and foliage, footprints preserved in moss, and indiscriminate litter left behind, from nails and hammering stones, to hand spikes and an axe wedged into a beech trunk, and lots of broken moonshine bottles. The path spilled into an open corridor strewn with stumps, boulders rolled into heaps, and several trees with girdled bark, around which had been strung a rope to demarcate a property boundary. In the center of this tract sat Andy Craig's single-pen chestnut cabin, with a bark-thatched roof, a stick-and-mud chimney, and a lean-to shed on the side. It had no windows, although some of the unfilled chinks were wide enough to look through. A full bearskin hung across the open doorjamb. Above the threshold, the bear's stuffed head was mounted, its mouth open, roaring. Beneath it, a scrawled sign read, "Do Not Entry."

"Hallooo," Johnny sang out.

After a tense pause, Johnny heard the sound of a flintlock hammer being pulled back, and acting upon an impulse he could only attribute to divine intervention, he jumped. A half second later, a bullet whizzed beneath him, splitting his legs, through the exact spot where his groin had just been.

The indignant Andy thrashed aside the bearskin and bumped his head against the door frame. Musket rifle on his shoulder, he screamed, "Thief! Scoundrel!," and fired again into the space that Johnny had just vacated. "Ass-lickin' surveyor!"

Johnny had moved twenty yards downwind before his feet touched ground. He dashed toward the river, compelled by an instinct that he'd be safe if he could reach the other side. Splashing across the shallows, he vaulted the narrow channel and landed halfway up the embankment on the opposite shore just as another shot blasted overhead—close enough to part his hair. He bolted across a grassy meadow into the shelter of deep woods.

Andy fired two more shots, but these carried more message than menace.

Johnny climbed a sugar maple tree and sat comfortably in the crook of several branches. The orange sun was already angling low and rippling off the canopy. To pass time, he snapped off a dead twig and rubbed it down to get a feel for it, then took out his buck knife and started whittling. He carved the bough into a thin cylinder, rubbed smooth with spit in his palm, and, using the tip of a porcupine quill that he kept in his kerchief, he hollowed it out until he could see from one side to the other. On one end, he whittled a sloping fipple, and along the shaft he punched holes.

He then blew into it and played a passable scale. It sounded like a lullaby to him.

That night, Johnny slept as solid as if he were part of the tree, and when he woke, an albino squirrel fidgeted in his lap. It sat on its haunches, folding its paws and barking as if in skittish prayer.

"Good morning, blessed creature," Johnny cheered.

The white squirrel ran off, leaving behind a handful of nuts and seeds, for which Johnny thanked God, then consumed them as his breakfast. The day dawned soggy, leaves and grasses soaked with dew, infusing the air with a mildew smell that reminded Johnny of foot fungus—which he believed was an affliction only of persons with an unhealthy dependence on shoes.

He descended the tree, stretched, and faced the sunshine to absorb its direct heat. "Hallelujah! I cannot wait to see what God has planned for me today."

He hoped to avoid the previous day's contretemps by giving Andy Craig plenty of advance notice that he was coming. Across Owl Creek, around the bend but within earshot of Andy's cabin, Johnny began playing *Over the Hills and Far Away* on the whistle. Skipping along as if he were leading a parade, he stepped into view of Andy's home.

Andy faced him with a musket on his shoulder. "Is yah'll a goddamned lunatic or jest fuckin' crazy?"

Johnny played a little flourish before lowering his whistle. "I am not a goddamned anything, that much I know, as I have done nothing to earn eternal damnation. So by your reckoning, that would make me just fucking crazy."

Andy cocked his head for a better view. "Yah'll don't look like one of them degenerated cunt-faced surveyors, so ah'll allow yah to 'splain what yah're doin' here."

"Thank ye for not killing me."

"Tha' don't mean ah won't kill yah."

"Of course not. Ye are but the instrument of God's will."

He huffed. "Don't yah'll forget, neither!"

The notion that God's will had anything to do with his life had always struck Andy as dubious, although he did feel flattered to be thought of as the host of divine providence. That morning, he had awakened in a rare good mood. He didn't know why. He'd rolled off his sleep mat and bound right onto his feet, as if he had something important to do, and most unusual, he awoke without a bourbon-fired headache. Even more odd was that his first piss of the morning was bright yellow and free from the normal urethral burning. Afterwards, he still felt so good that he thought he might spend the morning splitting clapboards for the loft that he'd long intended to add to his cabin. Maybe he'd even postpone the first drink of the day until after noon.

When, while chopping wood, Andy picked up the airy treble of a distant whistle, he thought at first that it sounded like a black-throated warbler. But once he spied that same ratty intruder from the day before on the opposite bank of Owl Creek, blowing into a toy wooden whistle, he rushed to retrieve his weapon.

"Do yah'll have any money?" Andy called out.

"Sir, I am as poor as a church mouse."

"If'n ah ain't gonna kill yah, ah gotta at least rob yah. What'cha got that ah can steal?"

"In my kerchief, I carry just a few simple tools." Johnny still held the whistle in front of his chin. "But if ye would accept it, I would be pleased to give ye this instrument as a token of friendship."

"Bah. Ah'll take it, but if'n anybody e'er asks, let's jest say that ah'm robbin' it from yah." Andy leaned his musket against the cabin. "Well, come'n o'er here an' give it to me."

Johnny played a few bars of *Yankee Doodle,* lifting his knees in a marching fashion as he waded across the creek.

Andy kept his palm on the butt of a tomahawk in his belt, his eyes slanted in what might've been a scowl, except it was hard for Johnny to discern any expression beneath the unkempt beard that covered his face from his neck to just below his eye sockets, and a mustache so thick that his mouth wasn't visible when he spoke. He wore an open frock, buckskin pants, and moccasins trimmed in beaver fur. Mayflies lighted around his head and shoulders.

Johnny stopped in front of and presented the whistle to him. "Here is your gift... that is to say, your plunder."

Andy took the whistle and tooted in it once so hard that slobber dribbled out the other end. He shook his head, spit off to the side, and tossed it into a pile of kindling wood. Without a word, he went into his cabin.

Johnny followed him in.

Andy began sorting through piles of animal pelts laid on a table, as if searching for something in particular. Most every wild beast that roamed the Ohio territory was represented among the inventory: coon, mink, squirrel, raccoon, fisher fox, otter, beaver, muskrat, deer, and of course, the big black bearskin that covered the portal to his abode. Finally, he settled upon a rather sparse piece of fur, not much more than a man could use to wipe his nose. This, he tucked under his belt.

He then returned his attention to Johnny. "Yah'll got anythin' to eat?"

"I am sorry, but I have no food that ye can rob from me."

Andy scoffed. "Ah might kill a man, but ah wouldn't leave him to starve." He pointed to the lean-to adjacent to the cabin. "If'n yah'll're hungered, ah got a jar of dried venison in the shed. Help your self."

"I thank ye anyway, but I me-self do not eat animal flesh."

"Won't eat meat?" He shook his head in disbelief. "If'n God don't mean fer us to eat animals, why'd he make them outta food?"

Johnny decided to start over. "Sir, I presume that ye are Andy Craig?"

"How d'yah know mah name?"

"A charming negresse whom I encountered downriver told me that I might find ye here."

"Dead Mary? She and Fog Mother are witches, yah know. Did she might to put a curse on your soul?"

"The Lord protects me from such deviltry."

For the first time, Andy looked Johnny in the eye. "Ah don't much like it when strangers know who ah am, but ah don't know who they'd be."

"Thank ye for asking me to speak about me-self. Me name is John Chapman, a sower of seeds. I would be pleased if ye chose to call me Johnny."

Andy made a slicing gesture across his throat. "Ah don't want to know nothin' 'bout yah, 'cept one thing. What're yah'll doin' *here*?"

"I am seeking paradise."

Andy mulled those words. "Paradise, huh? Not many men see paradise in this brutish country. It's a cruel land, a killin' place, desolation...." He flashed a rotten-toothed grin. "But it do kinda suit me. If'n all what yah want is to be left alone, this here's somewhar near paradise. Ah don't much like people. Ah ain't never had a problem that wasn't caused by some other person, 'specially my brother, cornhole-suckin' horse-faced bastard that he is. Tell him that ah said so, if'n yah see him."

"So ye live alone in this paradise?"

"Oh, ah ain't completely alone, 'cause Injuns roam the hills and valleys. They don't bother me none. Fact is, ah do some business wit' one Wyandot, named of Toby. He's one honest Injun, who brings mah skins fer sellin' at Fort Detroit, an' he brings me back whiskey, powder, flour, salt, cheese, more whiskey, an' this 'n' that. Toby is purt much the only companion ah need. Well, 'cept fer a woman. Ah'll buy one, when ah can afford her, to do mah cleanin' and cookin', and to make me some baby boys. Gimme a strong woman an' ah'll be right happy here fer the rest of mah life." He caught his voice beginning to drift, so he cleared his throat and concluded. "So yah see, I generally kill any folks what venture into mah land, 'cause once they start, surveyors follow. The first sign that good country is 'bout to go to hell is when some surveyor starts peepin' through his eyepiece thereabouts. Surveyors plot the land into little boxes. It ain't natural. A man what lives in a box cain't be really free."

"Bravo," Johnny cheered. "I agree."

"Don't yah be soft-soapin' me none. Wha'd yah mean that yah're lookin' fer paradise? Ah live to tell yah that it ain't here!"

"No, certainly not. True paradise exists only in the presence of our Lord in heaven. But I do believe that we can create an Earthly paradise where people live together in love, truth, beauty, peace... and it can start with *apples!*"

"Well, yah got a point thar, ah reckon. Any proper paradise would to include a bounty of apples—ripe and juicy, as big as your fist."

"Then ye agree, this land could be improved upon with a living orchard of God's most precious fruit—apples?"

"Ah do sometimes hanker fer a jar of hard cider."

Johnny reached into his kerchief and showed Andy a handful of crusty seeds. "Through fruit, grace, my friend. In the Bible, the Word of God consecrates 'the apple of your eye' as something to be cherished. There is no more righteous way to nourish your body than to take a healthy bite from a crisp apple. It crunches when ye chew, engaging your jaws in a most satisfying way, while fiber and pulp burst like delicious waterfalls in your mouth. An apple is as nourishing to the body as God's love is to the soul. I believe that every man should own an apple tree from which he can pluck delicious fruit at will. If it is within human power to create such a life, are we not obliged to do so?"

"Say huh?"

"The Eastern lands that I left behind have been scarred by greed and violence. Many people wish to leave, and they will come here looking for a better life. Today, this savage territory is beyond the care of civilization, so settlers must be prepared to endure great trials, but I can make things easier. There is yet time, in advance of the newcomers, to prepare a pomaceous garden for them. From these seeds, I will plant orchards, and these trees will nurture God's peace in a new place innocent of sin—Ohio."

Andy stared at him as if Johnny were a one-winged bird. "Are yah pullin' mah leg?"

"No sir. I never lie."

"Too bad." He grabbed his musket and took aim. "'Cause now ah gotta reconsider whether to kill yah or not."

Being prepared to die wasn't the same thing as being willing. Saddened, Johnny closed his eyes and banished timid thoughts from his head. Several moments passed before he thought it safe to peek.

The musket was still on Andy's shoulder, but his trigger finger was dangling limp. "Thar's three reasons that ah ain't gonna kill yah. First, yah ain't no shit-snortin' surveyor, in which case ah'd've put your head on a pole without thinkin' twice. Second, 'cause ah do believe that yah ain't right in the brain, so it ain't your fault fer saying such stupid things. And, third, most important, yah can do somethin' fer me."

Andy tossed the nappy pelt that was hanging from his belt to Johnny. It was scarcely as much fur as a mangy squirrel's, but something about it gave Johnny the chills. He ran his fingers over its sutures, until he realized what it was and cried, "God have mercy."

"It's the scalp of the last surveyor what dared come peepin' 'round hereabouts."

"Andy, no! 'Tis not a Christian thing."

"For fuckin' sure, it ain't!" he yelled proudly. "It's evil and wicked, not to mention a bloody awful way to die. But tha's the fate what awaits any cow-fuckin' trespassers. Go show folks tha' scalp an' warn 'em that if'n they don't want their own skulls scraped clean, they'd best stay from away from Andy Craig. Tell 'em. Warn 'em. Scare 'em. Now go!"

Johnny swallowed his revulsion, but handling the scalp for a few seconds caused a transference to begin within him. In it, he felt the lingering residue of its previous owner's soul. He gently folded the piece and tucked it into his kerchief.

"I bid ye farewell, Andy Craig."

As he departed, Johnny felt Andy's gaze on his shoulders. Once he cleared what he judged to be the extent of Andy's territory, he scanned the surroundings for some sign that would provide guidance for what he had to do next. Johnny carried the desecrated scalp in both hands, with reverence, for he believed that God had delivered it into his hands for a reason. Ahead, on the trunk of a black-barked oak tree, an albino squirrel—surely, the same one—scampered halfway down, cocked its head to look at Johnny, wiggled its whiskers, then zipped into the dense upper branches.

"Here?" Johnny inquired out loud.

The words that entered his head were so lucid, they made his ears pop. His mother's voice almost whispered, "*Yes, here.*"

Johnny removed the scalp from his kerchief and flattened it on a fallen log. He rubbed bear grease through the hair and raked it with his own haw comb, until it looked ready for Sunday church.

With a hand spade, he dug a rectangular hole large enough for a whole head, and gently placed the fully-extended scalp in its diminutive grave. He whispered the Lord's Prayer, then pushed dirt back on top of it.

Last of all, he snapped off two twigs, one long and one short, and tied them into a cross with a length of creeper vine. This he planted into the center of the grave.

He made the sign of the cross And sang out, "Rejoice, pilgrim, for now ye are in heaven."

Chapter 2 – September 1801

Deer Creek, the Scioto and the Little Miami Rivers

After his encounter with Andy Craig, Johnny followed Owl Creek another twenty or so miles, past a couple of tributaries and through a narrow gap. Branches of cottonwoods on each side reached so far across, they nearly met in the middle. He reached the stagnant bog that was the creek's source, and paused to watch a pair of frolicsome black bears feasting on pawpaws.

He yielded the bears their fill before sampling the fruit himself. Halving a specimen with his knife, he used his index and middle fingers like a spoon to scoop a bite. The custard-like pulp had a woodsy flavor that was also tart enough to make him pucker. The delight of this taste inspired him to sing out loud:

"Where, oh where is dear little Nellie?
Where, oh where is dear little Nellie?
Way down yonder in the pawpaw patch...."

His singing must not have been very good, because white tail deer scattered, chipmunks dived into their burrows, and even the bears covered their ears with their paws. He hoped God didn't mind his singing half as much as the animals.

Johnny could make a single pawpaw into a meal, so with his new supply, along with chestnuts and cattail roots, he had all he needed to gorge himself contentedly for the next couple days.

He slept in a hollow log on a bed of moss. In his solitude, he often did nothing at all, or whatever he pleased. Still, Johnny knew that, sooner or later, a scout, or a soldier, or another squatter like Andy Craig would discover this place, and once that happened, it'd be Eden no more. The best that he could do was plant his seeds, so that when civilization finally got here, there'd be something growing that people would want to leave as is.

Given a choice, Johnny never liked to travel the same route twice, but the safest course out of the Ohio back country would be to return the way he'd come, downriver by Owl Creek. Furthermore, he estimated that he'd wandered north of the Greenville Treaty Line, into Indian lands, so continuing in any direction other than south entailed the risk of getting tomahawked. Johnny got along with most Indians. He believed they too had immortal souls, unlike what many white folks—including clergy—claimed. Even so, some young brave looking to bolster his reputation for brutality might kill him just to prove he was wicked enough. Discretion clearly favored a southern retreat. Still, discretion showed less than complete faith in God's providence, and where faith is supported by desire, decisions are easy.

Johnny headed west.

He traversed a genuine no-man's land, but he knew a network of south-flowing creeks lay to the west, which he could follow until they connected to the Scioto, and downriver to civilization—to the degree that Chillicothe qualified as such. Ancient forests covered the terrain, a hilly, piedmont landscape so damp and shadowy that they soaked Johnny's senses. He had a feeling he was being followed, until he came to a familiar landmark a second time.

"I'm following me-own self."

The first night, he slept in a bat cave and dreamed in echoes.

He started the next day at dawn, following the early morning sun wherever glimmers filtered through to the ground. Those brief flashes had often vanished by the time that he got to them, though. Once, pausing to rest, he leaned so heavily against a tree he thought he heard it say "ouch." The talking tree—a hemlock over a hundred feet—stood taller than any others around, and something compelled him to climb it.

On the highest branch, he peered at the horizon from above the canopy, and the seamless, rolling green of treetops suggested infinity. He was then startled by a honking and, so close that he could've plucked one of their feathers, a "v" of migrating Canadian geese passing overhead, their formation spanning the entire sky. They couldn't have pointed his direction more clearly if they'd put up a sign.

The following day, he found Big Lick Creek by falling into it. This close to its source, the Big Lick existed as little more than a dribble, and Johnny thought he was stepping down an escarpment, which turned out to be the soft, crumbling bank of the creek. The next thing Johnny knew, he plunked onto his backside in the drink.

"Falling down is God's way of telling ye to pay attention." Johnny laughed at himself as he rolled up his pants legs, then waded downstream.

Time passed quickly because Johnny forgot what was he was thinking before he'd even finished thinking it, then started thinking about something else. The moon being full that night, he kept on journeying in the darkness. After some miles, the creek built in width and volume, and eventually, Johnny came upon a verdant meadow where the Big Lick merged with two other creeks, creating what he'd heard scouts refer to as the Big Walnut, a tributary of the Scioto.

Here, for the first time in days, he detected signs of recent human presence. At first he spotted tracks and little cairns left behind to mark a direction, but it wasn't long before he found evidence of predation, where kills had been made and fire pits left behind.

Johnny looked back to say goodbye to the wilderness, wondering how much longer it'd last.

Then hs mother scolded him.

'Stop blubbering! God didn't create all of this just for you.'

At the confluence with the Scioto, Johnny picked up the pace—no reason to linger any longer, since he was back on human time. Overnight, a heavy fog had saturated the river valley. As the seasons turned in the vast Northwest Territories, the dewy, sultry mornings became foggy and chilly, and when the afternoon sun finally did burn through, it cast long shadows that seemed to reach out and grab you. In just a matter of days, the first leaves, usually birch and gum, would start turning colors. Autumn in Ohio was both the most colorful season, in its brilliant foliage, and also the most colorless, in the all-too-common ghost fog.

By midday, Johnny guessed that he must be thirty or so miles north of Chillicothe. On the opposite bank, a tributary flowed into the Scioto, and he watched as three canoes piloted by Shawnees entered the current and began crossing.

Two men sat in each canoe, and five of the six were painted Indian braves with feathers dangling from bands tied across their hair. The sixth man was white, and while dressed in native buckskin with bone pendants hanging from his earlobes, he also wore a Christian cross on a chain around his neck.

Johnny walked to the point at which he estimated they'd reach shore, and skipped stones while waiting.

When the canoes pushed into sand, the braves remained inside, while the white man stepped out and stood ankle deep in the river. "Who are yah?" he asked.

"Thank ye for asking me to speak about me-self." Johnny wiped his hands on a clean part of the inside of his trousers, and extended his right one to shake. "Me name is John Chapman, a sower of seeds. I would be pleased if ye chose to call me Johnny.

"If'n I shake yer hand, it don't make us friends."

"But it's a good start."

The two exchanged a handshake, which Johnny let linger, the better to underscore his amicable intentions.

"Mister Chapman, I'm right sorry to bust up yer day like this, but our big chief wants to have some words with yah."

"'Tis God's will."

The man bid Johnny to enter a canoe between himself and a brave who wore a bone-handled knife in his belt.

Although not how he'd planned the day, Johnny considered it a pleasant morning for a paddle. He trailed his hand in the water and said, "I was of the impression that there were no more Indians south of the treaty line."

The white man glanced at his Indian companion, as if checking to see if he'd understood the question, then answered. "This is Shawnee homeland."

"That is so, but ye are not Shawnee, sir."

"My name is Stephen Ruddell," he said. "But amongst my Shawnee brothers, I'm called Big Fish. That's because once I caught the biggest walleye pike whatever swam in this river, probably forty pounds and as long as my reach. I worked him all day and night with just a poplar branch pole, a line made of bear gut, and a hook carved from a cougar's sternum. That fish fought so hard that he pulled me ten miles upstream. When I finally dragged him onto a sandbar, he just rolled over, and his eyes bugged out both sides of his head so he could look straight at me. Then he spat out the hook and swam away."

Johnny whistled. "That's some story."

The brave in the canoe with them said something in his native language, which made Stephen Ruddell laugh. He translated for Johnny. "My friend Battle Panther says that he worries having somebody to speak English with will make me talk too much. So he suggests that I cut out yer tongue to keep yah from answering back."

"I hope not." Johnny stuck out his tongue. "But while I still have a tongue, do ye mind if I ask, Mr. Ruddell, did ye get taken, or did ye go wild of your own free will?"

"Oh, I got kidnapped with my brother when we was just little grunts. The Indians killed our parents for revenge, because somebody from our village killed an Indian who stole his horse. My parents had nothin' to do with neither the killin' nor the horse stealin', but that was how justice worked in Kentucky. The Indians had mercy on me and my brother, though, so they took us and raised us like their own. Today, I live among the Kispoko Shawnee. Our main settlement is along White River in the Indiana territories, but some of us still live here, on Deer Creek. That's where we're taking yah."

The voyage lasted over an hour, upstream on Deer Creek and past some large tracts of land that had been recently cleared, with huge butts and slag piled for burning. Johnny knew this land was part of the Virginia Military District, which, in accordance with the new Frontier Land Act, sold at two dollars an acre. But with a minimum purchase of 320 acres, that price was beyond the means of anybody Johnny had ever met, so it surprised and somewhat irked him to see that moneyed landowners were already staking claims to pieces of the back country.

The Shawnees' Deer Creek village rested several miles farther, at a bend in the rivulet, which formed a natural pool. There, they pulled their canoes aground. The delegation led Johnny into a concourse surrounded by ten animal skin huts of recent construction, four domed *wigwams* with bark roofs in need of repair, and, at the border between the compound and the woods, a longhouse that had collapsed at one end. Beyond the camp's perimeter, a clearing provided evidence of a once much-larger village, now overgrown.

Johnny reckoned this party consisted of around fifty members, about half of which were squaws. The women occupied themselves with a variety of domestic tasks, like working clay into pottery, staking out hides to dry them, and weaving baskets out of ash splints, all the while carrying on glib conversation that reminded Johnny of the way that young women interacted while waiting for gentlemen to ask them to dance at a New England society ball.

"Wait here," Ruddell instructed Johnny.

A flabby and somewhat jaundiced Indian rolled over on his blanket on the ground, thrashing his arms to either side, all the while moaning like a sick cow. He had a face like a splotchy brown cowbird egg, with one eye glazed by a milky cataract.

"What's wrong with that man?" Johnny asked Ruddell.

"He says that a snake in his liver is eatin' him from the inside, but what that really means is that he's got the whisky yips."

Johnny made a move toward the man, intending to offer him a drink of water, but his attention was diverted when the village women's conversation halted and their heads all turned in one direction.

The Shawnee chief emerged from his *wegiwa* and stood, hands on his hips and his chin perpendicular to the ground, in the pose of a man allowing himself to be gazed upon. The breeze gusted behind him, as if at his command. His face was rugged, but contemplative, with sharp cheekbones and pitted temples framing a brow so taut that it looked like a piece of clear sky had settled on his forehead. He had a thin red line painted across the bridge of his nose, and wore a woven scarf high upon his crown, tied behind his neck, with two raven feathers dangling in the train of long black hair between his shoulders. The whites of his eyes shined brilliantly around intensely black irises and pupils, so that looking into them created a sense of peering over a great ledge. Dressed in a leather breech, shirtless with deerskin arm dressings, he stretched, and the bands of muscles in his forearms, chest, and shoulders stiffened. The chief nodded his head, and the rest of the tribe breathed.

He then pointed at Johnny, and turned to Stephen Ruddell to say something to him.

Ruddell, in turn, translated. "Our chief wants me to introduce him. His name is Tecumseh, which means Shooting Star. This here is the land of where he was born, and he loves it better than any other place. He says it was stolen from him by Americans, who he calls Long Tongues."

"Long Tongues?"

"Yeah, yah see, most Indians call white men Long Knives because of their bayonets. Tecumseh, though, he says they ain't worthy of a warrior's name. So he calls them Long Tongues, because all they do is flap their tongues and lie, lie, lie."

This clarification satisfied Johnny, but made him nervous. "Well, thank Chief Shooting Star for inviting me to speak about me-self. Tell him that me name is John Chapman, a sower of seeds. I would be pleased if he chose to call me Johnny."

Tecumseh spoke, and Ruddell explained. "He says that he knows who you are. Some days ago, you were on upper Owl Creek. This made our chief curious, and he wanted to see you for himself."

"How does he know where I was?"

Tecumseh spoke directly to Johnny, and then froze his expression while waiting for Ruddell to translate.

"The chief says that last night a witch's fog fell over this valley, covering everything with knowledge. He says that a vision can travel for many miles through the fog."

"I like that idea." Johnny nodded and smiled. "It would sure save a lot of unnecessary talking if people could send messages through the air like that. What else does Chief Shooting Star know about me?"

Tecumseh said something that made the other Indians laugh, and Stephen Ruddell, too, although he was timid about translating it.

"Well," he finally began, "our chief says that he knows that you don't shit stones like a normal man. Instead, you shit pellets like a doe. We should call you Shits Like Deer."

"I cannot say that would be much to me liking," Johnny declared. "But all that I ask is that whatever ye call me, ye also say that I am a man of God, a man of peace, and unlike those so-called Long Tongues, I will never lie to ye."

Tecumseh cut off Stephen Ruddell in mid-translation. He curled his lips, then spoke in English. "You look to be a fool, but you do not speak like one."

Johnny chuckled, as if hearing these words confirmed a suspicion. "So you *do* speak English."

"Yes. Ruddell taught to me your language, but speaking your English makes my mouth taste foul. English is for naming things, but Shawnee language is for describing things by sound. There are many Shawnee sounds that English does not know." On a stump next to him rested a long-stemmed pipe carved out of antler. He lifted it and showed it to Johnny. "Consider... you use a word for this thing, *pipe*. That is a childish word. It sounds like a weepy girl. P*uh--ayayayay-puh*. This word for you means just a tube to suck smoke. We, Shawnee people, call it *hobocan*, pipe of peace, which was given to our people by Waashaa Monetoo so that we might burn sacred *ksha'te* to heal our hearts and souls. The *hobocan* lifts our dreams to heaven. You feeble Long Tongues cough when smoking *ksha'te*, like boys who cannot stomach men's medicine." Blowing into the pipe, Tecumseh added, "Now, let us smoke."

Battle Panther took the pipe from Tecumseh and filled it with k*sha'te*, mixed with sumac leaves and some dogwood bark, lit it, and passed it around a circle.

Breathing it in triggered a sensation like lightning striking between Johnny's eyes. "Have mercy!" He wheezed and passed the pipe.

The next Indian in the circle, the chubby one-eyed man, had maneuvered himself upright by leaning his belly against a stump. He snatched the pipe from Johnny, burped as he sucked on it, and blew the smoke back directly into Johnny's face.

"That's Lalawethika," whispered Stephen Ruddell. "His name means Noisemaker, and he's our chief's drunk, half-blind brother."

"Why that poor man," Johnny said. He reached into his kerchief. "I have some dried trillium flowers. The tea is good for a gut-ache."

While Johnny was rummaging through his possessions, though, Tecumseh tossed a bottle of whiskey to Lalawethika, who opened it with his teeth, spat out the stopper, and quaffed all in one motion. Tecumseh made a remark in Shawnee that Johnny didn't have to understand to know was supremely insulting. Not only did he not take offense, but Lalawethika roared, suddenly fortified, and chugged liquor through of one side of his mouth while he smoked *ksha'te* through the other side.

Tecumseh unfurled a mat and sat in silent reflection for a moment. Soon he began to sing in a poignant baritone.

Half a dozen young women fanned around him, listening intently. One of them brought a pitcher of water and began washing his feet with her hair.

The chief held a note for longer than seemed possible, as if waiting for an answer from the sky. When at length he took a breath, the rest of the tribe cut loose.

Battle Panther slapped a hollow log with the blunt end of a tomahawk, while other braves contributed to the percussion with hand drums and turtle shell rattles. Several squaws rose and began dancing in synch with the drumming, while Tecumseh sang as if he was trying to start a fire with just his voice.

Lalawethika contributed a sputtering fart to the celebration and stomped both feet to announce that he was feeling better and ready to dance. No partners volunteered.

Amid the festivities, Johnny wished he hadn't given away his whistle, so he might join them. Although he didn't know the words to their song, he shouted "Hallelujah!" where it seemed appropriate. A couple of the squaws favored him with their attention, but he didn't understand their behavior, laughing boisterously and making squatting motions. Then he understood: they were joking about him shitting pellets.

Eventually, Stephen Ruddell seemed to take pity on Johnny, and pulled him aside. They sat down together and finished the pipe.

"Where yah headed next?" Ruddell asked.

"I am a-heading back east, to the cider mills in the Allegheny and Mongehela valleys, where I will gather apple seeds. Tomorrow, I should reach Chillicothe, and then I will cut across the Belpre Trail to Marietta. From there, I can catch a keelboat upriver to Pittsburgh."

"If yah'd be goin' thataway, yah might want to talk to my friend James Galloway, who lives just southeast of here. Yesterday, he told me that he wanted to hire somebody to carry a message for him to Marietta."

"I'd be pleased to be of assistance." Johnny wasn't inclined to chat, though, for with all the excitement surrounding him, he just couldn't remain seated any longer. He bounced onto his feet, slapped his hip, and started dancing like a native.

That night, Johnny slumbered on a sandbar by Deer Creek, having moved farther and farther from the encampment during the night to escape the thunder of Lalawethika's drunken snoring. Finally, he solved the problem by plugging his ears with balls of black rock moss. Even with his ears plugged, though, he still heard the voice of his mother call him in the morning:

'Johnny, wake yourself up.
This day won't ever happen again, so don't waste it.'

He returned to the Shawnee village just as sunrise colors leaked over the horizon. While waiting for the tribe to rise, he rubbed ashes from the campfire onto his feet, to toughen them up.

Four squaws lay sleeping outside of Tecumseh's *wegiwa,* side-by-side in a fashion that suggested a sequence in which each, in turn, had waited to be summoned into the Great Indian's quarters.

When Tecumseh emerged, he gently nudged them aside with an expression of benign exasperation, as if their overtures were inconvenient to him. He faced the sunrise, holding his knife in front of him so that its tip glinted, and let out a hearty whoop.

"I see that ye are feeling mighty frisky today, Chief Tecumseh," Johnny remarked.

Tecumseh said, *"Ne wes hela shamamo,"* not so much in response as to make it clear that he did not wish to ruin his good mood by speaking English.

Stephen Ruddell, who'd volunteered to escort Johnny to his next destination, did not rise early as promised. Instead, he was among the last in the community to stir, surpassed only by the still-snoring Lalawethika.

By the time that Ruddell appeared rubbing his eyes, he'd already missed breakfast of beaver tail and corn hominy, but he was content to sip a cup of dandelion tea and munch on hickory nuts. While all around him the Shawnee busied themselves with preparations for the day—the men for a hunting party, and the women sewing, weaving, and boiling hides—Ruddell took his time, blowing his nose and picking his teeth.

"I ain't the most industrious man in this tribe," he admitted to Johnny, "but so long as the chief's brother is here, I'll never be its most useless neither."

"A drunkard is only as harmful as he tries to be helpful," Johnny said.

After tending to his morning hygiene, Ruddell announced that he was ready to leave. The previous night, when he'd told Johnny that James Galloway's farm was about a six-hour journey, he'd meant on horseback. Accordingly, he'd planned to let Johnny ride one of the tribe's nags.

Johnny declined that offer, stating his preference to travel by foot.

Ruddell threw up hands in the air. "Yah're a queer one, that's for sure. Don't eat meat! Would rather walk than ride! What else don't you do that normal men do?"

This was hardly the first time that Johnny had been told he wasn't normal. Still, hearing this always mystified him. Everything he did seemed perfectly normal to him. "Have ye ever paused to consider that I might be the normal one, and everybody else is living in an unnatural way?"

Ruddell's dismissive reply—"Sure, if yah say so."—disappointed Johnny. As many times as he had asked that question, nobody ever took it seriously. Someday, Johnny hoped, somebody would answer him. He really wanted to know.

With Ruddell riding bareback upon an old cow pony, and Johnny half-running, half-walking, they traversed a rutted trail through a gently rolling, sylvan terrain, heading southwest into the upper Little Miami River valley. Wild turkey, abundant in the woods, followed Ruddell's pony and picked at its scat. The men passed a few cabins, some fields that had been cleared but not yet planted, and a couple of abandoned Indian villages, which Ruddell explained had not been taken over by whites because before they'd departed, the Indians had placed a curse upon the land.

"Ain't nobody who'll admit he believes in no Indian curses," Ruddell said. "But, still...."

A spur off the main trail led to James Galloway's homestead. In the four years that his family had lived there, Galloway and his sons had cleared considerable acreage, although they'd tilled and planted just a few plots, and the limp corn was barely shoulder high at harvest time. In the center of the estate was a dusty yard, with a corral encircled by a post and rail fence, where two rather feeble cows browsed in a field of desiccated grass.

However, Galloway's poplar-planked cabin—set on granite stones, with a two-room loft, double stone chimneys, and oiled paper windows on the front and back—was among the grandest domiciles Johnny had seen in the Northwest back country. He even appreciated how Galloway had left two sprawling oak trees on either side of the cabin, as if out of respect to the erstwhile forest.

A freckled ragamuffin wearing a short-dress, with her orange hair stuffed loosely under a bonnet, saw the two men approaching and, recognizing Ruddell, dashed to meet them.

Ruddell dropped to his knees to catch her. "How're yah twistin' today, Messy Becky?"

Little Rebecca Galloway squirmed out of Ruddell's embrace and gazed over his shoulder. "Where's Chief Te-cum-see?" she squealed. "Oh, please do say that he came."

"Sorry, li'l girl. The chief ain't here. I did bring somebody else, though. This here is Mister John Chapman."

Hearing of the great Indian's absence, the girl frowned and grunted. "Ohhhhh...."

Johnny reached into his kerchief and pulled out a piece of sorghum taffy, which he offered her.

She snatched it but did not meet his eye.

"Where's yer daddy?" Ruddell asked.

Rebecca led them around the cabin and to the front of a woodshed, where the brawny, shirtless James Galloway swung an axe over his shoulder and brought it down hard on a chopping block, severing the head from a plump chicken.

Johnny forced himself to swallow—the only way that he could keep from puking.

The chicken's head dropped into a pile of chicken heads, rabbit heads, squirrel heads, and raccoon heads. Meanwhile, its body rolled onto the ground, landed on its feet, and scampered for freedom, until it realized it was dead.

"Pick that up and clean it, would'ya honey?" Galloway said to his daughter. He spit into his palms, rubbed the bloody spray off his forearms, and turned to Ruddell. "What brings an Indian-lover like you onto my property?"

"This is only your property 'cause the Indians done got pushed off'n it."

"True enough," Galloway agreed, plugging one nostril and blowing out of the other. "But today I want no less than to be a friend to them Indians."

Ruddell nodded. "Tecumseh sends his greetings."

Johnny stepped forward and stuck out his hand. "And inasmuch as we have not been introduced, sir, let me take this moment to say that me name is John Chapman, a sower of seeds. I would be pleased if ye chose to call me Johnny."

Galloway possessed an axeman's handshake, with a grip that could splinter a man's forearm bones, and he squinted with steely, seen-it-all eyes as he sized up Johnny. "I've heard tell of you, Chapman. Last spring, settlers traveling upriver saw you by Cox's Ripple, where the word is that you planted fruit orchards from seed. They say you aim to sell the seedlings to settlers. It ain't the dumbest idea I've ever heard, but even so, most people seem to think that you're crazier than a loon. No offense. They say that you put every seed in your mouth, fill your cheeks with spit, and swish it all around before planting it. Is that true?"

Johnny chuckled. "No sir. I might lick a seed or two, sometimes, if it looks dry, but as for soaking it in me own spit... t'would be plain foolishness!"

"Yes, indeed, but seed apples are a risky business, because they never grow true. Now, if you select trees for grafting—"

"Never!" Johnny stiffened. "'Tis wicked to cut up trees that way. Natural apples are God's work and cannot be improved. Those who graft trees are guilty of the sin of pride!"

"This country'd still be wild, if not for prideful men."

Ruddell intervened. "Mister Chapman is bound for Marietta. I recollected that the other day yah were lookin' to hire a courier to take a message to someone there, so I figured that yah'll might work out some arrangement."

"Ah hah," Galloway said. "Gentlemen, let's go inside and discuss this thing."

"Maybe we might could stay for supper?" Ruddell asked hopefully.

Inside Galloway's cabin, his comely wife Rebecca—born Rebecca Junkin—tended a kettle simmering over a low fire in the hearth.

Johnny surmised that it was a hospitable abode, but a bit gloomy. At first, he wondered why they'd covered all the windows on such a clear, fresh afternoon, but momentarily he picked up a subtle scent of distress in the air, and he soon realized that upstairs in the loft, a brooding presence lay, somebody whose sadness was stronger than the light of day. He listened to the sound of a woman inhaling deep thoughts, but exhaling in a thin, despondent sigh, and Johnny shivered the entire length of his body with an empathetic pain.

He shook himself and turned to Galloway. "Ye say that ye have heard of me, Mr. Galloway, but I too have heard about ye."

"About me?"

"Stories get told. I have heard that back in your ranger days, ye were shot by that renegade Simon Girty for no good reason at all. The story goes that the bullet blew through your shoulder and lodged in your neck, where it has stuck ever since, doing no harm except that sometimes when the weather is a-fixing to turn bad, it can cause cramps. Therefore, folks far and wide come asking ye for a weather consultation."

Galloway winked at his wife, who shook her head. "There might be some morsel of truth to that. Even though I had that bullet cut outta me years ago, people still ask if it's gonna rain, when's the first frost coming, how much snow is gonna fall in winter, whether there'll be flooding in the spring...." He lowered his collar and turned to show the men his scar. "That shot almost done me in, all right, but I'm content to leave my fighting days behind me. Today, I'm just a farmer who wants to live in peace."

"Even peace ain't safe these days," Ruddell proclaimed. "More'n once, I've been shot at by some fool who thought that I was Indian. Some newcomers to these lands seem to shoot first, ask questions later."

"The only way to keep from getting shot is to stay away from people with weapons," Johnny said.

Galloway scratched his ear, as if trying to decide if what he'd just heard was wisdom or foolishness. He called across the table to his wife. "Rebecca, Mr. Chapman here is bound for Marietta. He has offered to carry a post for us. Perhaps this is a chance for you to—" He glanced upstairs at the loft. "—deliver that letter of yours."

Mrs. Galloway gestured with her palm for her husband to speak more quietly. "Yes, that would be superb. We can pay you twenty cents if you get it there by Friday."

"I can deliver it personally by Thursday," Johnny promised.

While Mrs. Galloway retired to the front porch to compose her missive, the men chatted about James Galloway's erstwhile adventures as a member of George Rogers Clark's raiders during the Indian wars of the 1780s.

"Those were savage and malicious times," Galloway recalled. "The troops raided Indian villages in Old Chillicothe and Piqua, burning the Indian cornfields, plundering their graves, defiling their women, and executing any prisoners who did not swear allegiance to the Lord Jesus Christ and the President of the United States. I am truly remorseful for any misdeeds, though. Whenever I recall those days, and my own brutality, I wonder why it took me so long to grow a conscience."

Johnny nodded in understanding. "Thank God almighty that we finally have a chance at peace with our native neighbors."

Mrs. Galloway returned to the room carrying a folded letter sealed with a drop of candle wax and pressed with her own ring. She handed it to Johnny as if, by doing so, she was relieving herself of great stress. "Please, deliver this message personally to the man whose name is on the front of the envelope." She leaned closer to him and whispered, "He can be found at Picketed Point."

Johnny read the name on the envelope: *Lieutenant Frank P. Bantzer.*

"I will make this me own personal mission," he assured Mrs. Galloway.

The color returned to her cheeks. "Now, my dear Mr. Chapman, would you honor us by dining with us tonight? We are having boiled turnips with a nice pigeon pie."

Johnny envisioned a flock of beautiful gray sentinel pigeons getting decapitated, dismembered, and eviscerated, then rolled into a pie with gravy, carrots, and potatoes—and his stomach took a sudden dip. He was careful not to let it show on his face, though, for meat-eaters tended not to be rational about the subject of their diet.

"No thank you." Johnny bowed and begged her pardon. "I would prefer to be on me way, the sooner to deliver your very important letter."

"But wait a minute," Stephen Ruddell protested. "Just 'cause he's leaving don't mean that I couldn't stay for supper. Ain't nothin' I love more than a good pigeon pie!"

Chapter 3 – September 1801

Marietta, the Ohio Country

Frank Penobscot Bantzer taught his only acknowledged son, Frank Junior, at least one thing: a man with no dignity was... well, undignified. This was not an intentional lesson from the senior Bantzer, a cad and a charlatan who wound up tarred, feathered, and run out of town by collaborative effort from a cuckolded husband, an aggrieved creditor, a scorned woman, and other parties who simply did not like him. As a young man, Frank Junior almost wished his father would do something wicked enough to warrant a public hanging, thereby saving a modicum of dignity.

Thus, dignity mattered a great deal to Lieutenant Frank P. Bantzer, Junior, and the most conspicuous statement any man made about his character was the manner in which he presented himself to the public. So, even when riding hard miles with his rough-and-tumble militia through gnarly forest or mucky quagmire, Lieutenant Bantzer always kept his goatee trimmed, his belt buckle polished, and the epaulets on his greatcoat combed. He retained a small mirror in his pocket, for spot-checking.

From horseback, Lieutenant Bantzer monitored his regiment's march and concluded that, unless they picked up the pace, they'd never get back to Marietta by nightfall. These men were hardly the most durable or courageous in Governor St. Clair's militia, and Bantzer wished that he could trade every single one of them for half as many sober regulars. The problem was that if these men drank too much, they became lethargic and recalcitrant, but if they drank too little, they grew surly and belligerent. Bantzer already had several in mind for flogging once they got back to Picketed Point... but first he had to get them there.

"Sound off!" the lieutenant barked.

Following some mumbling and grumbling, one man returned with a call of, "Left, Left, Left," and the troops fell into a sloppy marching cadence of:

"Right, left. Left, right.
Fight by day. Fuck by night.
Hit 'em low. Hit 'em high.
Scalp 'em raw,
Rape their squaws.
Sound off:
Kill, kill, kill, kill,
Injuns!"

The drill gave the men a second wind for a couple rounds, but when they came to a marshy patch of ground, they got stuck. With boots sucked right off their feet, the entire regiment stood milling around in knee-deep slop, waiting for instructions about what to do next.

"Sergeant Work, get these men out of the mud!" Bantzer ordered.

"Yessir," Sergeant Clayton Work chirped, knocking his hat askew as he saluted.

The marsh was a semi-liquid peat fed by a brook meandering down a wooded hillside. Bantzer guided his horse around the bog, and noticed a tree had been felled near a bend upstream. He left his men to follow the brook along a narrow path, around to the far side of high ground, where a large, vertical outcropping scoured the hillside. Atop this plateau sat the unfinished frame of an off-kilter log cabin.

Squatters, Lieutenant Bantzer realized. He thought first of duty, which was clear and non-negotiable in the case of squatters. Then he thought, *Oh, bother, now I'll never get home for supper.*

Bantzer's ruminations were interrupted by a shot, which rustled leaves over his head, and he glimpsed the flash of musket fire from behind a woodpile. He unsheathed his sword and waved it in the direction of his assailant. "Beware, squatter!"

In response, he received a second shot, no closer than the first, though whether by intent or by poor aim, he couldn't tell. In either case, this situation counted as a hostile resistance to an officer in the performance of his duty, and thus justified aggressive measures in response. He turned his horse and galloped back to his regiment.

Not all of the men had yet extricated themselves from the filth; in fact, some had settled into reclining positions and seemed to enjoy the opportunity to wallow. The reappearance of Lieutenant Bantzer was thus met with a groan of dismay.

"Sergeant Work!" Bantzer bellowed. "Why are the men sitting in the mud?"

Work, sunk to his calves, could only shrug. "This here's some extra sloppy mud," he explained. "The more ya struggle in it, the deeper ya sink."

"Never mind, imbecile." Bantzer raised his chin and commanded, "Soldiers, fall in! We have work to do!"

When confronted by incompetence or laziness, Bantzer reminded himself, *"Duty is dignity put into action."* Those words, spoken with conviction by the eminent General Anthony Wayne to his brigades the evening before the Battle of Fallen Timbers, had made an indelible impression upon him as a young infantryman. Just seventeen and eager to prove his mettle, Frank went on to distinguish himself in that penultimate conflict of the Ohio Indian Wars, where he personally shot and killed six savages—albeit while they were in full retreat—and thereby earned his first military commendation. "Just doing my duty," he'd said later, downplaying his heroism, for he'd learned that false modesty was a career-building virtue in the army.

The lieutenant allowed Sergeant Work to organize the troops and lead their march, while he guarded the rear against defection. He presumed that the only thing most of them cared about was the daily liquor allowance. Given constant supervision, supplemented judiciously by the occasional flagellation, he could coerce them into performing most of the simple custodial tasks of the armed services profession, like watching sentry, peeling potatoes, or cleaning stables. When it came to doing any job that involved even remote chances of danger, however, every man in the troop would run if he thought he could get away with it. Accordingly, Bantzer followed closely on their heels as they marched, and supplied an occasional nudge of the bayonet to keep them moving. He knew this made him unpopular among the men, but he was rather proud of being disliked—although sometimes he bristled at the disrespect. Behind his back—he overheard them once—the men called him "Lieutenant Bugger," and joked that he had a bunny rabbit-sized penis. Every time one of them saw a rabbit, it precipitated widespread comedy, to the lieutenant's chagrin.

When the men came into view of the squatter's cabin, Bantzer called them to stand at attention. He rode to the front of the formation, considering his next move. Sometimes, a squatter would surrender upon sight of the forces marshaled against him. Still, most felt obliged to at least put on a show of resistance. Bantzer's fondest hope was that this squatter would panic and flee into the woods, thereby leaving the soldiers free to torch his domicile and be on their way. That wish was dashed with another shot in the lieutenant's general direction.

"Git off mah property! Or ah'll kill ever' damn one of yahr'll daid!"

Bantzer ordered his riflemen to ready themselves, then tugged on his sleeves and cupped his hands over his mouth, and yelled, "On behalf of the government of the United States of America and the sovereign territory of Ohio, it is my duty to inform you that you are unlawfully occupying this land and must vacate immediately, or I shall remove you forcibly."

The squatter screamed, "Up mah cherry red arse!" and fired again, this shot landing in the dirt close to the lieutenant's feet.

The squatter was drawing a bead, and Lieutenant Bantzer wasn't willing to risk that he might truly mean to kill. "Marksmen," he commanded. "Take aim!"

Behind the woodpile, two voices became involved in some kind of dispute. Finally, a female shrieked "Naaaaawww!" and a young woman sprinted toward Bantzer.

It stunned him to see that such a shrill, tooth-chilling sound had come out of the mouth of a mere girl, who, although dressed in an old woman's drab housedress, looked to be around fourteen years of age.

She prostrated herself at the officer's feet. "I'm a-beggin' you, please don't kill us!"

Stepping around the woodpile, the male squatter revealed himself to be a skinny, freckled lad, shorter than his rifle by a foot. "Awww, Millie... yah cain't do that ever' blame time that ah git in a faght," he complained.

Still on her knees, Millie shouted back. "Ain't worth gettin' your fool self killed over, Otto."

The lad stomped his feet. "Sweetie pie, this here's our home, an' if that ain't worth gettin' kilt o'er, ah don't know what is."

Lieutenant Bantzer gestured at his men to lower their weapons. If this situation had involved just one solitary squatter, it'd have been easy to dispatch with no witnesses and no questions asked. A paired couple presented complications. Especially troubling was that Otto and Millie were of such youthful age, more suited for school than for the strife, privation, and danger of homesteading a harsh land. What the lieutenant wanted to do was spank them and return them home to their parents.

"Son...." he began.

"Ah ain't yahr son," the lad protested. "Mah name is Otto Blubaugh. Tha's mah wife, Millie. C'mon, Sweetness, git up off th' ground."

Millie sprang onto her feet and scurried back to her husband, wrapping her arms around him and sobbing.

"Now lookit what yahr'll done gott'n her upset," Otto griped. "Cut it out, Hon. Yah know ah cain't stand it when yah cry."

Millie bawled even louder.

"Young man," the lieutenant resumed, "you are a squatter, so in accordance with the Harrison Land Act you must vacate this land and all structures on its premises forthwith. I will allow you five minutes to pack your belongings."

Otto stomped his feet. "Well ain't that jest fine! Whar d'yahr think we oughta go?"

"Back to your mam and pap, I would suggest." Bantzer took an earnest tone. "This isn't a safe country for two fledglings like yourselves."

"We ain't no children! We're married!" Otto insisted.

"An' we are in *love*, too," Millie added.

Lieutenant Bantzer hardened his cheeks. "So be it." He descended from his saddle and walked between the two young lovers and their cabin. "Sergeant Work," he barked. "Burn this structure to the ground."

Otto hoisted his rifle, ready to take a shot, had Millie not put her head on his shoulder and whimpered, "Let's just move on. We still got each other."

"Ah got yah, baby lover."

"I got you, too, lover boy."

"Baby lover."

"Lover boy."

These endearments annoyed Bantzer. He made a slicing gesture to Sergeant Work, reaffirming his orders to torch the young couple's abode.

Millie's weeping hit notes so strident that they seemed to add fuel to the fire. Otto picked up a rock and squeezed it, clearly suffering to watch the flames consume his work, the symbol of their love. , perhaps his hopes and dreams. In defiance, he hurled the rock into the fire, then slipped his hand into Millie's.

"Ever'thin 's-a gonna be a'right," he told her. "We ain't gonna admit failure 'n go crawlin' back with hat in hand. We'll rebuild, 'n prove ever'one wrong."

Bantzer suffered no sympathy for lawbreakers. Still, not beyond offering some helpful advice, where warranted, he sidled close to Otto so that none of his reports could hear, and said, "Young man, if I were you, I'd join the army. It will make a man out of you."

Millie reared back and slapped Lieutenant Bantzer across his face. "How dare you? My Otto is more 'f a man than you'll ever be!"

Quaking, Lieutenant Bantzer stifled a violent impulse.

Millie held his gaze, as if inviting him to slap her back.

Ultimately, what tempered the lieutenant's response was not any scruple against striking a woman, but the awareness that his men were watching him. He imagined them already taking wagers on whether he'd slap her back. He dared not dignify their worst assumptions.

"I wash my hands of you," he pronounced. "You will never survive a year." He didn't speak those words tentatively, as if expressing an opinion, or directly, as if stating a fact, but he enunciated them sarcastically, with evident relish, as if making a wish that he hoped would come true.

In 1878, when the gentlemen of the Ohio Company of Associates met at the Bunch-of-Grapes Tavern in Boston to discuss their vision for colonizing the terra incognito north of the Ohio River, they had big, big plans. They were all going to get rich. After the creation of the Northwest Territory by an act of Congress, those in the know about the land business saw clearly that the next virgin frontier ripe for settlement was the vast Ohio Territory, with its fertile soil, plentiful game, and fair climate. It would have been paradise except that there remained a pesky—but manageable—Indian infestation. So, confident of the success of their venture, this genteel group of speculators, entrepreneurs, and developers purchased 1,500,000 acres near the confluence of the Ohio and Muskingum Rivers, and the call went out for men to join their crusade.

When the first flatboat, christened the *Adventure Galley*, reached the camp at Marietta and Fort Harmar, the thick fog caused its crew to continue downriver, over-shooting their destination.

Captain Pipe of the Delaware Indians watched and hoped that this misdirection was a good sign. Pipe looked them over and called the settlers "Buckeyes," which in his native tongue meant, approximately, big dumb galoots.

If the village of Marietta—named after her graciousness, Marie Antoinette of France—had evolved according to the fondest visions of its founding fathers, it would have become the Paris of the Northwest Territory. The Associates conceived of a spacious municipality, laid out on a grid of avenues perpendicular to the Muskingum, with sections demarcated for business, schools, churches, and common grounds. Shady mulberry trees would line grand boulevards, and a central square would host public events sponsored for the cultivation of civic pride. The Associates would name the streets after themselves. Overlooking this community was the Campus Martius stockade, a magnificent edifice built on a hilltop and consisting of four corner blockhouses, enclosed by plank-walled offices and private residences.

These grand plans, though, fell short due to a variety of mishaps and hardships. Spring floods, dry summers, and early frosts had conspired against them. Far less game existed than they'd expected, too, and far more melees with restive Indians. Living there meant barely scraping by, and the population came to be dominated not by refined New Englanders, but by rangers and trappers from Western Virginia. By 1801, Marietta had become a rowdy, transient river town, where everybody going downriver stopped for provisions, news, and to tie on a good drunk before pushing onward to better places.

Marietta's fate did not surprise Johnny, who was dubious about most real estate boondoggles. The only part of the land grab that he approved of was the legal requirement for settlers to cultivate their property by planting fifty fruit trees within three years. These people became Johnny's customers.

The Picketed Point Stockade, the last of three forts built around Marietta during the Indian Wars, was an unwelcoming enclosure with three sides of upright timber palisades connecting three blockhouses. One side faced the Muskingum, the second faced the Ohio, and on the third, a gate opened toward the low-lying section of town. Soon after its construction in 1791, the Ohio Company of Associates went bankrupt. Campus Martius was dismantled and Fort Harmar was vacated, and most river commerce passed straight downstream to the growing town of Cincinnati.

By 1801, Picketed Point was no longer of any strategic importance, and the small numbers of citizen-soldiers assigned there were given mop-up and domestic peace-keeping assignments. The lack of meaningful labor suited them; it just seemed fair, since these men all understood that in the event of armed conflict anywhere, they'd be among the first shipped off to the front-line, wherever that happened to be, probably to die. For men such as these, this was the best deal available.

Upon reaching Marietta, Johnny made haste to Picketed Point. It looked abandoned, with a frayed flag hanging above the gate. He called out.

Eventually, a sentry peered down from a lookout and growled, "Go sleep it off, yah slovenly beggar."

Johnny protested that he was neither drunk nor indigent, and insisted that he had to see Lieutenant Frank P. Bantzer.

"Lieutenant ain't here," the sentry said. "He's away leading his troops on field maneuvers."

"In that case, I reckon that I shall wait." Johnny sat with his back to the gate and closed his eyes.

After a few hours, the militia came plodding to the fort's gate like a parade of the wounded damned. They jostled into a halfhearted formation, which they held only until the second that their lieutenant dismissed them, and then scrambled en masse for the Adelphia Public House.

The lieutenant looked away in apparent disgust, and turned to stand eyeball to eyeball with Johnny. "Be gone, you venal drunkard," he snarled.

"Oh, I am not drunk, but thank ye for your concern. Are ye Frank Bantzer?"

"Who asks?"

"Thank ye for asking me to speak about me-self. Me name is John Chapman, a sower of seeds. I'd be pleased if ye chose to call me Johnny."

"Oh, you are, are you? A sower, eh? A regular *appleseed*. Ha! What possible business could you have with me, Mr. Appleseed?"

"I have a letter." He produced the envelope from his kerchief. "Per agreement with Mr. and Mrs. James Galloway, I am here to convey to ye an epistle, written no more than 48 hours anon."

Bantzer sighed. "Galloway, huh? Very well. Follow me." He led Johnny through the heavy, creaking doors of the fortification. "But keep your distance, you vile supplicant. And do not ask me for food or money. You'll get none from me."

"I ask for nothing from any man, except his respect."

He followed to the lieutenant's private room in the corner blockhouse facing the Muskingum. Other than the sentry, Johnny counted just himself and Lieutenant Bantzer in the entire fortification.

In his quarters, the lieutenant hung his tri-corner hat on a nail, removed his gloves and set them on a table, and laid his coat across the back of a wooden chair. He then sat and began unlacing his boots. "Wipe your shoes before entering," he instructed Johnny.

"Pray, do what?"

It was only then that Lieutenant Bantzer noticed that Johnny was barefoot. "I've encountered many vagrants in my time, but never one who did not shoe himself."

"Bare feet keep a man honest."

Bantzer rubbed his chin and mused: "Honest? Of more worth is one honest man than all of the ruffians that ever lived."

"'Tis a wise thought. One might even say 'common sense,' as in the famous book by Thomas Paine."

"Indeed!" Lieutenant Bantzer snapped, seemingly taken aback by Johnny's reference. "What do you know of Thomas Paine?"

"A wandering man learns a lot by just listening. I have never read any whole book from start to finish except the Bible, but that does not mean I am not well versed. People tell stories. People have opinions. I listen to them all. I think that Mr. Paine would agree: that is the most common of sense."

Bantzer shook his head dismissively. "May I have the letter?"

Johnny smoothed the letter and handed it to Bantzer, who remained seated.

The lieutenant slid a knife under its seal. His eyes traveled down the page as he read, and he rubbed his temples as of to ward off a headache. When he reached the bottom of the page, he closed his eyes and whispered, "Ah, duty... where a woman is concerned, what good are you?"

"Sir?"

Lieutenant Bantzer started. "My god, you cretin! Why are you still infecting me with your presence?"

"I merely wanted to suggest, sir, that if ye have troubles, ye could do worse than to pray."

"I pray, then, that you take leave of me."

Johnny breathed in the insult, flinching, then breathed it out. "Fare thee well, Lieutenant."

Now Johnny had a decision to make: to retire for the night in some accommodating haystack or hollow tree, or to hit the road forthwith for Pittsburgh. He looked around trying to decide, walking as he did so.

On the town square, the doors to the Aldelphia Public House swung as rowdy brutes staggered in and out, while string band music mixed with hee-haws, hollers, and assorted booze-fueled rants. Johnny was not averse to an occasional draught of hard cider or a dram of distilled spirits, and on more than a few occasions he'd patronized a friendly saloon, but taverns such as this one, which provided haven for naught but the drunken revelry of freebooters, brought a plague upon the Ohio Territory.

The din of the debauch was like hornets buzzing between Johnny's ears. He felt the need for quiet.

He walked to the bank of the Ohio, where he intended to sit, skip stones—he always kept a few good skipping stones in his kerchief—and listen to the fish.

A bullish man with muscular long arms, toting a jug in one hand and a riverman's pole in the other, while sitting with his legs dangling over the side of a keelboat, yelled, "Hey, brotha! Goin' upriv'r?"

"Why, yes."

"C'mon. I uh'm quittin' this hyar town. T'at pisser barkeep won't serve me no more whiskey, e'en tho' I uh could drink 'nother gallon, an' I uh'd still be sober 'nuff t' shoot th' curly tail off'n a pig at ninety paces."

"That's remarkable skill."

"Damn my motha f'r givin' birth t' me if'n t'ain't true. Goin' upriv'r? I uh'll give yer a ride."

Although he had misgivings, Johnny was loath to refuse kindness from any stranger. He jumped onto the ship just as the man reached forward with the pole and began pulling away from the docks.

Puffing his chest, the man shouted, "Hyar we go!"

Now, they belonged to the river.

"Mah name is Mike Fink," he said. "And in case yer ain't heard, I uh can out-run, out-shoot, out-jump, throw down, drag out and lick any man in th' country."

Indeed, Johnny *had* heard of him—specifically, he'd heard that Mike Fink was in jail for assault and public drunkenness after a bloody brawl in a Wheeling brothel. Since this was clearly not the case, Johnny decided to allow him benefit of the doubt and assume that reports of his misdeeds were exaggerated.

Furthermore, Mike Fink explained that he'd heard of Johnny, too, and according to what he'd been told, John Chapman lived in a tree and ate only bugs.

Both men agreed that it was fairly astonishing the kinds of tall tales that got told about people. For that entire night, while Mike Fink drank and single-handedly poled that boat up the mighty Ohio, he and Johnny told stories that each of them had heard about the other, and just for fun they made up a few more.

PART TWO – 1804-1805

"There is in the western country a very extraordinary missionary of New Jerusalem. A man appeared who seems to be almost independent of corporeal wants and sufferings. He goes barefoot, can sleep anywhere... and live upon the coarsest and most scanty fare. He has actually thawed ice with his bare feet.

"He procures what books he can of the New Church; travels into remote settlements, and lends them wherever he can find readers, and sometimes divides a book in two or three parts for more extensive distribution and usefulness.

"This man for years past has been in the employment of bringing into cultivation, in numberless places in the wilderness, small patches (two or three acres) of ground, and then sowing apple seeds and rearing nurseries."

From a report of the Manchester (England) Society for Printing, Publishing, and Circulating the Writings of Emmanuel Swedenborg

Chapter 4 – July 1804

Owl Creek

"Dey'z comin', like a stinkin' bloody pox, dey'z comin'," Dead Mary fumed as she tossed aside the folds to Fog Mother's wegiwa.

Fog Mother sat on a blanket, her long dress bunched over her knees, and worked a pestle to pulverize black cohosh in a bowl on her lap. Two cats slept at her feet. She did not look up, but, speaking in Algonquian, raised her voice. "Daughter, you know better than to waste your life's sacred breath speaking the language of those who enslaved you. English is a weak language for lazy thinkers who must write their words to remember them. Slap yourself!"

Sometimes, when Dead Mary got excited, she lapsed into English. It was a crude and raunchy language, which was probably why it came off her tongue easily when she wasn't thinking straight. Dutifully, Dead Mary slapped herself across the cheek, then responded in the words Fog Mother had taught her. "Forgive me."

Fog Mother rolled upon her heels in a fluid motion, her dress and all its colorful ribbons and beads tumbling around her body. Taller than most men, she could only stand fully upright near the center of the *wegiwa,* where the smoke from a slow fire wafted through an opening in the roof. The depths in her eyes made it seem like she regarded everything from a vanishing perspective. Her long gray hair, the lines on her brow, and the faded scar on her left cheek endowed her features with a grim wisdom.

Fog Mother pressed her finger against Dead Mary's lips. "Listen," she said.

Dead Mary did not abide silence naturally. Eager to speak, her mind continued to ramble, but after a moment she realized that she was still thinking in English, and that was the whole problem. She disengaged from her thoughts, the better to command them. From the treetops, She heard the song of a cardinal coming from the treetops— *hmukwinunt,* the blood-colored bird. Her thoughts shifted as if from prose into poetry, and she commenced in the language of her higher self.

"It is as you yourself prophesized, Mother. For days, I have sensed troubles coming. There's been a disturbance among the spirits in the forest—leaves that fluttered without a breeze, rivers and streams that ran darker than normal, deer that have never been timid keeping their distance, and solid stones cracking in the still of the night. I could tell that our woods were fearful and stressed. The Long Knives do not see nature as we do—its names and feelings are lost on them, such that they never pause to consider the blossoms on the dogwood tree before they cut it down.

"Although I despise him, I inquired of Andy Craig as to whether he'd encountered any scouts prowling the country. He replied that he and his Wyandot friend, Toby, had spotted hunters near Black Bear Crossing. These men, he feared, were from the new settlement along the Lick-Licking River, near the Great Circle earthworks of our ancestors. They call their village the New Ark. Then, today, while gathering red sumac berries past the sandstone cliffs where the Ko-ko-sing spreads into the lower valley, I happened upon a cabin just above the floodplain. Several tall beech trees along the ridge had been stripped and felled. The ground was cratered with pits where roots had been pulled, and as I walked among this foul debris, I myself could imagine the pains of Earth Mother's body being ripped asunder. Beside the cabin was a grinding wheel, and spread next to it were sharp tools for tearing the soil—shovels and spades, axes, adzes, and froes, a hoe and a moldboard plow, and a crosscut saw. These men are not hermit squatters like Andy Craig, or wandering hunters or scouts. They are here to stay.

"Although I myself have dreaded this day, I was still not prepared for the rage that boiled inside of me. I let go of a bitter, hateful scream, shrieking into the sky, *'Show yo'selves, yo scabby cunts, yo hog fuckers, yo' pus-suckin' maggots, yo dickless diddlers... stop wankin' an' stand up to me, unless yo' got goose eggs 'stead o' balls 'tween yo legs!'* But nobody answered.

"Furious, I struck flint against their own grinding wheel to create sparks, and lit a torch. I then ignited the roof of their cabin. I gathered all of their tools into a pile and set those aflame, too. A breeze stirred, which I took to be a sign from Nanapush that He favored my deeds. In minutes, the entire camp was cleansed by conflagration. Before I left, I shot a single arrow into a tree trunk at the boundary of the clearing, as a warning for them to proceed no farther.

"But now that I've calmed myself, I am worried, Mother, that my actions may provoke retaliation. I do not know how many of them there are. I do not know anything of their intentions. Yet, I can only expect the worst. What are we to do, oh wisest of women?"

Fog Mother sighed, which had a chilling effect on Dead Mary, and added sweet-smelling birch bark into the fire. She stared at it as she spoke. "When my people, the Lenape, come to any new place, we bring only what we can carry and we take only what is needed. But when the Long Knives enter new lands, they bring all of their sins and burdens loaded into their wagons. They hide their flaws behind pride and a will to conquer. This is, of course, ultimately futile, for it is better for people to adapt to the land than to try to re-make it to serve unnatural purposes. But Long Knives believe that their god has blessed only them, and all other gods are false. In truth, however, their mangod, Jesus, and our great hero Nanapush, are brothers, separated in youth and raised by different mothers. Jesus does not speak Algonquian, so he does not possess its imagery and eloquence, and is thus reduced to base English, which is not much evolved from animals snorting. If the Long Knives could but glimpse the visions that spring from our language, maybe they would act more like human beings."

"But how can we communicate with brutes whose minds are so feeble?" Dead Mary wondered.

"Despite their vocabulary of lust and hatred, and although they pass every thought through a filter of vanity, they themselves do, still, harbor the same spark of love that the great spirit Kishelemukong bestowed upon all sentient creatures. When they act upon their better instincts, without thinking, they are sometimes capable of moments of compassion. They know no better than what they do, but they can occasionally do better than what they know."

"I have seen no mercy among them. How can you say?"

Fog Mother picked up one her cats and began stroking it soothingly. "Before I found you, my daughter, when I was just a young woman, I lived near a Lenape community that numbered in hundreds, a village that the robed Jesus missionaries called Gnadenhutten. I kept apart from the larger tribe living there, as they feared me. I had known from the time that I reached womanhood that I was destined never to marry, nor ever for a man to touch me, and so my path was to become a medicine woman. When I accepted this as my calling, I was reborn in the winds of the four directions, to live bodily within the community, but for my soul to dwell among the spirits. For that reason, some called me a witch.

"One year, a plague of bilious fever afflicted the tribe, and although I prayed, worked potions, and tended the sick as best I could, many Lenape died. The missionaries were miraculously unaffected, and many members of the tribe converted to Jesus. I warned them that they were entrusting their lives and the legacies of our ancestors to a religion that scorned them. 'But the Long Knives' god is stronger!' they argued. Perhaps, I agreed. He may be stronger, but he is also jealous and demands fearful obedience, on pain of death. None listened to me.

"The Long Knives know no other way than war, and their conflict is a curse upon Indians, too. Innocent Lenape often find themselves in the middle of disputes about which they know nothing, but even so are held accountable as scapegoats and surrogates. Such is what happened in Gnadenhutten. Our chief, White Eyes, curried the favor of the Americans, and he signed a treaty granting them permission to travel through Lenape territory so they could launch attacks upon their British enemies. These skirmishes settled nothing, though, as every attack triggered greater retaliation. The Christian Indians wanted nothing more than to be left alone to tend their crops and live in peace. But this desire for peace was like a wish made upon a bad moon. Although professing faith in Jesus, the Indians at Gnadenhutten were distrusted. Passive blood is almost always the first to be shed.

"We were starving in the middle of a long winter of scarcity. I told my brothers and sisters that their only hope was to recant their false Christian convictions, to repent and burn offerings to Kishelemukong and the *manitowak.* But they dared not, for they feared Jesus. On the blackest night of the coldest month, a regiment of Long Knives from Pennsylvania occupied our village. They blamed us for raiding outposts in their state. The accusations were preposterous, which their colonel surely knew, but on the frontier, bloodlust often defeats justice, and those soldiers found the Christian Indians guilty in a sham trial. The soldiers decided to destroy Gnadenhutten and execute all of the Indians living there, at dawn of the next day.

"A few of the Christian Lenape escaped and fled to my camp, crying, 'We reject the Christian God, truly. Please cast a spell over the Long Knives, that we might be spared.' We knew that we were doomed, but for an intervention from the spirits. All that night, we gathered in a circle, prayed, repented, and sang stories of our ancestors and our gods, while I burned herbs, feathers, wampum, and prayer sticks pleasing to Kishelemukong, to Nanapush, to Mother Corn, and to all the loving spirits of our people.

"Meanwhile, the desperate Christian Indians back in the village made a show of praying to their Jesus, hoping for him to soften the militia's hearts. At dawn, though, they were herded into the center of town, bound by their hands and feet, then one by one smashed with a mallet across the head and scalped screaming. The Long Knives piled bodies in the mission church and burned everything to the ground.

"Thus might the story have ended, just another brutal example of the Long Knives' barbarism. However, there is another part to the story, which astonishes me, still, of how a handful of us survived. It revealed to me my purpose in this world.

"From my camp, we heard the cries of the dying. We all knew that we'd soon be found and slain, too. A mother in our group embraced her children, sobbing, and while she huddled over them, a book fell from under her shawl. It was a Christian Bible. I took it into my hands, cautious of its unknown powers. I understood nothing of the symbols scribbled onto its pages, but I did know some of its words from having listened to the missionaries. I am loath to trifle with another person's gods, but this was a desperate moment, so I ripped a page out of that book and placed it in the sacred fire, adding it to my conjuration, and I chanted a passage in English as it burned."

> *"Let the wicked forsake their ways and the unrighteous their thoughts. Let them turn to the LORD, and he will have mercy on them, and to our God, for He will freely pardon them."*

"What it meant, I did not know. I shouted those as if to challenge the Christian mangod, whom I blamed for all of this wickedness. I knew that those might be the last words that ever I spoke in this life.

"At that moment, three men from the militia scrambled into our camp. They were winded, as if they had been running, and seemed surprised when they happened upon us. One of them waved his arms, urging us to 'Come!' I realized that these men were fleeing the savagery of their companions, and that they could lead us to safety. Everybody scurried onto their feet and followed the soldiers, while I remained behind long enough to extinguish the sacred fire and thank all of the spirits who had provided us with deliverance, including Jesus.

"I gained new powers on that day. Through my act of desperation, I had happened upon a spell that could convince the gods to cooperate. It is a fearsome incantation, though, and I am wary of using it... but I now wonder if this might not be a proper time to petition all of the gods, in their own languages. If the gods can be persuaded to be civil with each other, those who believe in them can do no less."

Fog Mother bent over to retrieve a woven bag next to her bedroll. As she faced Dead Mary across the fire, the pupils in her eyes reflected the red glow of the coals. "Tonight, we shall bring down a cleansing fog."

Dead Mary shivered. "Is that not dangerous?"

"Every spell risks evil consequences. Prayer normally goes from one person to one spirit. This prayer goes from all people, to all gods. The gravest danger is that the essence of the wrong god will enter the heart and soul of a human who is unfit to receive it. I need for you, daughter, to witness and learn this ritual, for one day you may be required to practice these arts, when I am no longer here."

"Me? I could never...."

Fog Mother cupped her hands and blew powder of black cohosh into Dead Mary's eyes. "Say nothing. Just do what I ask."

"As you wish," Dead Mary agreed, but added, in English, for effect, "But still, I want to kill dem ass-faced hogs with turds 'stead of brains."

A faint smile curled in the corners of Fog Mother's lips as she put down her cat. "Shit eaters," she added, also in English.

Chapter 5 - September 1804

Chillicothe, Ohio

When Reverend James Copus rode into Chillicothe, he saw a whole mess of souls in need of being saved. He didn't blame them. It seemed to him that good choices just as often led to bad outcomes as bad choices led to good ones. People who admitted to being sinners generally weren't as bad as they thought, and those who insisted they were doing God's will were usually just doing their own. Frontier folks didn't trouble themselves with the moral niceties that fueled those interminable debates at theological conferences. Nowhere was this more evident than in the barely settled territories of the brand new state of Ohio, which meant keeping things simple fell high in the frontier preacher's job description.

At the end of his second season riding the southern Ohio Methodist circuit, Reverend Copus knew that he, too, had probably picked up a few new sins along the way. He was possibly the least methodical Methodist there could be. He had more habits than methods, which by their very nature tended to reinforce a person's laziest tendencies—sins, even. He was not an early riser; he kept a liquor flask in the deep pocket of his linen trousers; his vocabulary included profanities that sometimes slipped off his tongue—in this way, he was no different from the hardscrabble pioneers to whom he preached, so he was inclined to forgive their occasional lapses.

The Word of God didn't often take with these folks on the first try.

James Copus hadn't been looking to get "saved" when he became a Methodist. It started with taking a bath. In May of 1801, he'd ridden into Bourbon County, Kentucky and, with just enough money to either fill his flask or take a bath, he decided, uncharacteristically, to do the latter. It'd been so long since he'd been genuinely clean that he figured it'd feel better than getting drunk. So he rented a tub at the only hotel/tavern/general store in town and scrubbed himself with lye soap until his skin tingled. Thinking to himself that he might never be so clean again in his entire life, it occurred to him that his soul could use some polishing up, too, and he went looking for a church.

Coincidentally, just outside of town on Cane Ridge, hundreds of Presbyterians, Methodists, Baptists, and other excitable revivalists had gathered in a great camp meeting, all praying, shouting, prophesying, and engaging in laughter, spasms, rants, gibberish, and ejaculations. None of that stuff appealed to Copus, so he wandered over the ridge and found a Methodist preacher by the name of John Strange standing knee-deep in Stoner Creek, baptizing a group of shackled slaves one by one. It seemed like a more appealing expression of spirituality than all of the hollering and passing of snakes at the camp, so he accepted Reverend Strange's invitation to get himself baptized, too.

Conversion came easily, but not frivolously to James Copus. For a traveling man like himself, who often occupied himself on long trips by pondering the whys and what-ifs of existence, it wasn't a stretch to go from getting baptized to becoming a full-fledged preacher. By attending the Methodist Conference in Baltimore later that year, he acquired ministerial status and, thus ordained, committed himself to carrying the gospel across a circuit from Marietta to Cincinnati, and numerous backwater settlements along Zane's Trace.

At first, he journeyed as the junior accompanist to Otis McDonald, a fiery exhorter with a knack for spellbinding large audiences. Eventually, given Copus's more subdued style of preaching, the two decided they could more effectively serve God if they divided the workload. While McDonald worked the countryside organizing love feasts and camp meetings, Copus drifted from one cabin or farm to another, sometimes pausing only long enough to water his horse, but if invited he'd stay for supper, followed sometimes by prayers and scripture.

Reverend Copus was always willing to impart a blessing, which he'd never known any settler to refuse. "May God make you equal to your challenges," was his favorite.

Chillicothe had grown too big for Reverend Copus's liking. Established as Ohio's capital when statehood had been granted, it was now home to around a thousand folks, and even more cattle. Significant numbers of cattle served as a turning point in any community's growth. When civilization moved forward, first people cleared the land, then they built upon it, and then they cultivated it, all before bringing the first cow into a settlement. A cow, although dumb, trusting, and born to be slaughtered, was also at peace for all its life, so when a town grew to the point where it was safe for cattle, Copus reasoned it was ready for preaching, too.

Apropos of that, the reverend headed out for the cattle farm of Mr. George Rennick, which that weekend would host a "grand jamboree Methodist revival and crusade in the name of Jesus Christ" – according to the bills Otis McDonald had posted all over town.

When Copus arrived on Saturday morning, the camp had already reached a level of bedlam suggesting that, in addition to the natural enthusiasm of religious zealots, there were probably more than a few bottles being passed. That was no doubt due to the influence of Baptists, who commonly crashed Methodist camps demanding equal time, bringing along with them their own army of whiskey-emboldened yokels. Furthermore, with harvest complete across most of the land, homesteaders who hadn't been to church all summer felt at once grateful to God, and also ready for some rip-snorting celebration.

None of this conflicted with the preacher's goal of winning souls. He not only welcomed backsliders, but considered them necessary in order to meet quotas. Indeed, some men repented and got baptized several times during the course of a good camp meeting.

Clean manure and fresh cut hay scented the air that fine afternoon in Rennick's pasture, an open expanse that could accommodate vociferous multitudes, while also providing an idyllic setting where more contemplative folks could wander off to pray. The grounds sloped around a meandering brook that spilled into a pond that was serviceable for baptismal immersions, never mind the copperbelly snakes. Along the forest margins, the foliage had just begun to turn, with the yellows of poplars and cottonwoods tossing in a light breeze, like sunshine in motion.

Workers had erected the main stage beneath a sprawling tent in a field previously cleared of cow chips by black servants – technically, not slaves, although that particularly unpleasant task was reserved for them alone. In front of it, tree stumps or boulders supported rows and rows of seating in the form of cross-laid boards.

Throughout the day, speakers took turns on the stage, each beginning by thanking God for His great goodness, then proceeding to warn listeners of the fire and brimstone that awaited them, if they didn't shape up.

Reverend Copus tethered his horse and began working the crowd. His strategy at camp meetings was to mosey around, making personal contacts and kindly suggesting to folks that the Lord was watching and hoping that they'd become Methodists. Hardly anybody ever declined to do so, but the reverend doubted that half as many ever made it to the baptizing pond.

Copus had taken just a few steps into the mob when he spotted a young man waving and whistling through his fingers to attract attention.

"O'er here, parson!" the lad shouted, nearly jumping out of his pants. Next to him, on a blanket in the grass, lay a conspicuously pregnant girl in a black and white calico dress.

At first glance, the reverend could have mistaken her for a tipped Holstein. He shook that image out of his mind and accosted the young man. "How may I help you?"

"Yahr'll a preacher man, ain't yah? Ah wanna ask fer a blessin."

"A blessing?"

"Yahr'll do that thing, don't yah?"

"Well, yes, you might say that blessings are my business." All this time, he'd been looking at the pregnant girl, who was nibbling on a dandelion.

"It's mah wife what needs the blessin'. She's not afar from havin' our'n baby, an' we wanna be sure tha' God 'll send some 'a His grace."

"Uh huh." Reverend Copus knew this story all too well. In Ohio, girls got planked and planted with child almost before they'd even gotten wet. At least in this case the father wasn't some old coot who'd traded livestock for her. "What's your name, son?"

"Otto Blubaugh. This here's mah wife, Millie, the mother of mah baby son—"

Millie kicked Otto's ankles. "It might could jest as likely be a girl."

"Baby Lover, ah done nail'd a rattlesnake to an oak tree, an' that all-ways brings a boy."

"Shucks, I'd just be teasin' you, lover boy."

"Baby lover."

"Lover boy."

"Ahem," Reverend Copus interrupted. "Are you from hereabouts?"

"Yeah," Otto asserted, while Millie simultaneously replied, "No sir." They looked at each other, as if unsure who was right and who was wrong. Finally, Otto resumed. "See, we've been followin' the work, where'r it leads. Most lately, ah done worked with Mr. Rennick on bringin' in harvest. What we want, though, is our'n own home, up north, whar land can get gotten fer cheap. Tha's whar we'll raise us our children."

"Children!" Millie exclaimed. "How many you got in mind?"

"Lots, baby lover. Ah cain't stop."

"I don't want you to, lover boy."

"Baby lover."

"Lover boy."

The reverend shook his head, glad they could only make one baby at a time, or else they might just get started on a second one right there and then. "Are you Methodists?"

Otto said, "Mah pappy n'er went to no church, but he did find Jesus 'fore he got hanged."

Millie added, "I think that I might jest be a Methodist. I was raised by my aunt, and she weren't nothing, but I think either mam or pap must've been. What does a Methodist do, anyhow?"

Reverend Copus had always thought of being a Methodist as something that a person just *was*, not something one *did*. On the spot, the best that he could come up with was, "Get baptized. Go to a Methodist church on Sundays. Pray when you need to."

Otto chirped, "We can do them things."

"Start by getting baptized. The line forms over yonder... but not right immediately, because that there is a Baptist preacher. You'll want to wait 'till after supper, when the Methodists are doing the baptizing."

Millie was confused. "Are you saying that there Baptist ain't a proper baptizer?"

This raised a point of rather arcane theology about which the reverend was unprepared to discuss. He continued. "After Reverend McDonald has delivered his sermon, we Methodists shall gather at the pond to anoint new converts." He took his Bible and held it in front of him. "But in the meanwhile, why don't I make that blessing you requested?"

Millie pushed herself up and, wobbling, presented herself belly-first to Reverend Copus.

With his Bible in his right hand and pressing his left against her protuberance, the reverend imparted a standard blessing.

> *"May the Lord, Mighty God*
> *bless and keep you forever.*
> *Grant you peace, perfect peace,*
> *courage in every endeavor."*

He added, "And may your child be healthy and thrive with the love of Jesus Christ."

"Amen," Otto and Millie chimed in unison.

Upon hearing about the great Christian camp meeting in Chillicothe, Colonel Frank P. Bantzer had considered it his duty to attend, for the public would expect the newly-promoted field commander of their local militia to be present to demonstrate his piety and good standing with God. It was not, however, the kind of crowd with which Bantzer generally liked to associate. He tended to be suspicious about people prone to radical exhibitions of religious conviction, which he saw as breakdowns of discipline. By contrast, a man in his position of authority had to maintain high standards for decorum. He figured God would be watching to confirm that he was there, but at the same time He'd surely understand that the lieutenant's attendance was more a matter of civic duty, rather than to pant, chant, whoop, and holler like the rest of the rabble.

Bantzer traversed the assembly, nodding "good day" to the women and thanking well-wishers, while quietly sizing up the men for their fitness for military duty. Above all, he kept moving, the better to be seen by the largest number of people. In full uniform, he enjoyed wearing the symbols of his status and how people saluted him. Thus focused on the crowd and not the people in it, he was prejudiced against recognizing anybody, so when he linked eyes with a passing gentleman, that person's identity did not instantly register. He kept walking.

"Stop, you worm!" an angry voice called.

Bantzer turned and stood face-to-face with James Galloway, who wagged a stiff finger at him. Given time to steel himself, Bantzer could be resolute in the face of confrontation, but whenever called out by surprise, his first instinct was to hide. Bantzer pretended like he didn't see him.

Galloway, with his wife on his arm, had stopped and turned so abruptly that he'd nearly twisted the poor woman's shoulder out of socket. "Ouch," she complained, punching her husband in the ribs. She then saw Bantzer and squealed, "You humbug!" The Galloways were accompanied by their daughter, Rebecca, who peeked from under a parasol to witness the commotion.

Colonel Bantzer conjured an affable demeanor. "Well, if it isn't James and Missus Galloway, not to mention pretty young Miss Rebecca. Ho, I have a piece of hard candy in my pocket. May I give it to the young 'un?"

"Uhhh," Galloway choked. "Are you serious, man?"

"Quite. It is good candy, from Philadelphia no less."

"Gawd, Bantzer, have you forgotten the last time we spoke?

"I cannot say that I recall the occasion," he lied.

"Incredible! Let me help you to remember—the subject was honoring the promise you made to my sister-in-law, Mona."

Indeed, as Bantzer further recollected, that encounter had taken place at gunpoint, and in the company of several of Galloway's thug friends. The only thing that he could think to say was the same thing he'd said then. "I made her no promises."

"You're a real horndawg, ain't you?" Galloway's tone was attracting the attention of folks nearby. "Did'ja think you could dishonor her, then just leave?"

"I did truly care for her," Bantzer mumbled.

"Oh ho! You *cared* for her, did'ja now? If you cared for her so dang much, why'd you slink off under cover of darkness the eve before your wedding? You done broke her heart. For months she moped until, finally, she up and quit the normal world and joined some kind of nunnery in Pennyslvania. Now she says she's 'a married to Jesus Christ. Ain't that a fine thing! But I reckon that ain't your fault... since you *cared* for her so much?"

Colonel Bantzer placed his hand over his heart, which he hoped would not only represent sincerity, but also call attention to the medals upon his chest. "On my word, sir, I prayed long and hard to God for guidance on that matter, and in the end I had no choice but to yield to His will. God has other tasks for me. I command one of the largest militia in Ohio. That makes me as good as married to my duty. I could scarce impose a soldier's life upon any woman."

"Bah."

"Perhaps you think you are safe because we have treaties, but I swear to you that the red savage Indians are instruments of Satan himself, and they're sworn to scalp our men, kidnap our women, rape our virgins, and burn down our churches. Not to mention that they are likewise in cahoots with the British, who plot to steal Ohio for their king."

"So you say. When I look at you, I don't see a real soldier—I see a snooty officer who thinks his shit don't stink."

"I'm sworn to protecting good people like you... albeit at great personal sacrifice."

"No, it's men like you that I fear most. I personally know the Shawnee chief, Tecumseh, well enough to call him my friend. When I settled in the Little Miami valley, he greeted me. We smoked a pipe and promised to live our own lives and to do no evil to each other. Why, I'd trust him wit' my own daughter."

"Her? Are you a fool? A savage cannot be appeased."

Galloway grunted and knelt next to his twelve-year old daughter, gently lifted her chin, and turned it toward Bantzer. "Study this man's face, Becky. Do you see the vanity in how he lifts his chin, in the slant of his eyes, and in the way he poses in his uniform? Soon, you'll become a maiden, and should you ever be courted by a man so full of arrogance, I want you to spit right in his eye."

With that, Galloway and his family turned and receded into the crowd.

Bantzer stiffened his back and aimed his sights above the glances of passersby who had been privy to the exchange of words. To his relief, at the center of the concourse, a new preacher hopped onto the stage, and in the general drift of bodies toward the front of the camp, he was able to retreat without taking a single step backwards. This allowed him a discreet avenue of escape, as if God had chosen that very moment to divert the crowd's attention—and who knew, maybe that's what had actually happened.

"Thy will be done," he whispered, sipping discreetly from his pocket flask.

In the early evening, time for the final sermon of the day, a lamplighter with a long pole proceeded from one lantern to the next around the entire conclave, and the flickering of so many candles were like countless tiny epiphanies. To either side of the stage, men stoked blazing fire stands with a mixture of dried hardwoods, producing a scent that evoked nuances of frankincense and myrrh to noses that didn't know any better. With the fading sunset on one horizon and the spreading nightfall on the other, the passage of worldly time seemed accelerated.

Beckoned forward by Reverend Copus, the entire assemblage focused on the speaker approaching the main stage. Except for the front row, populated by gimps and cripples hoping for a cure, everybody stood. Hundreds of bodies pressed against each other—a boon to the juvenile pickpockets sneaking about—so that when one person shuddered, it triggered a wave through the entire population. It felt as though Jesus himself were elbowing his way through their midst.

When Reverend Otis McDonald leapt onto the stage and pumped his arms, such a roar erupted that it scared birds out of trees. McDonald moved as if skating on lightning, with twitchy gestures that seemed to cast sparks into the crowd. His gray jacket was too large for him, lending the appearance of his being a marionette whose strings were being pulled by God Himself. His long beard exploded sideways as much as down as he stomped from one side of the stage to the other, urging the worshippers on either side to cheer louder than those on the opposite side.

Finally, he stopped next to the rostrum, kissed his Bible, and began to pontificate. "The Lord sayeth unto Moses, 'For behold, this is my work and my glory—to give the gift of eternal happiness to mankind.' Well, I say hally-looo-yah to that!"

This invocation elicited a thunderous ovation. Some of the women swooned into the arms of whoever stood next to them.

"But Moses ain't here! Nuh uh, noooooo! Neither is David or Daniel or John the Baptist! Fact of the matter is that all I see here is a whole slew of sinners! It looks like God done opened up the sky and dumped a huge bucket of greasy, oozing sin down on top of all yaw'll."

The crowd responded to the insult with rousing affirmation. Shouts of "Yes sir!" and "Praise the Lord!" rang out.

"The problem with sinners is that they are stupid. They forget that they are *sinners*—wretched wrongdoers, fallen souls, abominations in the eye of our loving Father. Don't never ever doubt, each, every, and all of you, that God knows what you do and what you think before you do or think anything. It's just like the Prophet Isaiah sayeth, 'When we display our righteous deeds, they are nothing but filthy rags. Like autumn leaves, we wither and fall, and our sins sweep us away like the wind.' And the blessed Paul wrote in a letter to the Galatians that when a person gives in to sinful desires, the results are:

"Sexual immorality!
Lust!
Idolatry!
Sorcery!
Hostility!
Quarreling!
Jealousy!
Anger!
Selfishness!
Dissension!

Envy!
Drunkenness!
Wild parties!
And other evils too many to count!"

"So, let me say it again, until it rings in your ears, that any person who chooses to give in to the temptations of the flesh will spend all of the days of eternity in the screaming agony of hellfire.

"Yaw'll have got a choice to make, ain't that so? You can do what you please in this world, and then pay the consequences of suffering for endless time. Or, you can live right and spend all of eternity basking in God's love. What's it going to be, people? Heaven or hell?"

"Heaven!," the chorus returned with the obvious choice. Having just been made aware of the sinful corrosion presently devouring their souls, some in the mob began to thrash about as if trying to get it off. The most agitated among them jumped up and down, and thus an ecstatic and desperate tumult broke out, like a mass of people trying to stomp out a wildfire.

Similarly, during his sermon, Reverend Otis McDonald was in constant motion. His face was dominated by his mouth, which seemed to come unhinged when making an especially emphatic point. Surrounded by his erratic beard, that gaping mouth reminded Reverend Copus of a bear getting ready to take a big bite. For even greater dramatic effect, he removed a whip from beneath the podium, unfurled it, and snapped it several times.

He continued. "Let me tell you what sin looks like to God. Envision in your mind's eye a soul smeared with sin as black as tar, as sticky as syrup, and as heavy as a coat drenched in molasses. If you die with sin stuck on your soul, it stays on you for all time. It burns blue hot, but is never consumed, and it scorches from every pore, inside and out, and even your guts bake and throb with excroooociating pain, forever and ever without a moment's rest or any hope for relief. Eyeballs melt and hang from their sockets. Tongues glow red hot like coals in their mouths. So be warned, sinners: Thou shalt fear the LORD thy God."

"Fear is love!" somebody shouted. A woman removed a squawking baby from her breast and passed it to the person in front of her, urging him to forward the infant to the stage for the Reverend McDonald to bless it.

A melee broke out in the crowd where several men took off their belts and began to flagellate each other.

Meanwhile, a wiry figure sifted through minute creases in the packed crowd, advancing toward the rostrum.

"So seeing as how every one of you would drop straight to hell if you died right now, what's to be done? Why... repent, of course! R-E-P-E-N-T! It's like the apostle John promised when he wrote, 'If we walk in light, we have fellowship with one another, and the blood of Jesus, His son, purifies us all from sin.' Too many people nowadays fail to follow the example of the first apostles, of Paul and Peter and John, not to mention Matthew, Mark, and Luke, and all of the primitive Christians in Galilee. What you must do is follow in their paths, to liiiiive like they liiiiiiived, to belieeeeeve like they belieeeeeved. Be like the primitive Christians, if you want to go to heaven...

"Show me just one person among you who lives righteously, like a primitive Christian."

As if from thin air, a lanky, disheveled man wearing a torn shirt open at the chest and a pair of trousers cut off at unequal lengths loped onto the stage. At first, Reverend McDonald did not notice him, for this was a moment in his sermon when he paused and lowered his brow, so as to allow listeners to absorb the profundity of his words. Gradually, he became aware of the turning of heads among the crowd, and he followed their gaze to where a man was standing next to him.

"Who are you?" he demanded.

This scrawny man spoke in a surprisingly hale voice. "Me name is John Chapman, a sower of seeds. I would be pleased if ye chose to call me Johnny. But I am a-standing here to say, look at me, sir. Here I am. *Here* is your primitive Christian!"

That being all he had to say, apparently, Johnny Chapman hopped down from the rear of the stage and, not looking back, marched toward the darkening woods.

Reverend James Copus jogged to catch up. "Hey, stranger," he called out.

Johnny kept walking.

"Excuse me, my good man."

Either Johnny didn't hear, or he didn't think that the summons applied to him.

"Mister Chapman—*Johnny*—could I have a word with you?"

Johnny turned around but kept walking backwards.

Reverend Copus realized that if he wanted to speak to him, he was going to have to hustle. By the time he reached Johnny's side, the reverend was breathing so hard that his words came out in gusts. "Where're you off to in such a hurry?"

"I have in mind more of a direction than a destination."

Reverend Copus cringed when he saw Johnny backing straight toward a low hanging branch, but at the last moment, the man ducked, as if he had eyes in the back of his head.

"Are you the one that they call Appleseed?" Copus panted.

"Appleseed, eh? I me-self would prefer to be called the Apple-Proclaimer, the Pomaceous Prophet, or the Fructifier of the Wilderness. But I can accept being called Appleseed."

"Whatever you're called, folks are talking about you far 'n' wide. They say you've planted seedling orchards throughout the Seven Ranges, as far as the Licking River."

"True enough, but 'tis not all. I intend to push still farther, ahead of the tide of settlements. The people will need apples once they get there."

Reverend Copus felt his calves starting to cramp. "They say you do a bit of preaching, too."

"Preaching? Not really. I do more asking than telling. When I get good answers, I feel like it is my obligation to share them."

"Answers from whom?"

"Spirits."

"Spirits?"

"'Course, they are God's answers, ultimately. He does not speak directly to the likes of me-self. So I listen to spirits, who are nearer to me."

Baffled, Reverend Copus decided to get right to the point. "Then, what religion are you?"

"Like I said back yonder, I am just a primitive Christian."

"But what kind? A Methodist, I hope?"

"Somewhat, sort of."

"You ain't a flippin' Baptist, are you?"

"What is the difference? Do not Methodists baptize and do not Baptists have methods? For that matter, Shakers are not the only ones that shake, and Quakers are not the only ones that have Friends, and Presbyterians are not the only ones that... well, I do not know what, exactly, they do, but I will wager that others do the same, too. Even the Indians pray, in their own way, and God cannot help but hear them, too."

By now, Reverend Copus was huffing and puffing so laboriously that he couldn't summon air sufficient to comment, only to ask for clarification. "God listens to Indians?"

"Certainly," Johnny affirmed. He'd reached a tangle of chokeberry shrubs, which to the reverend looked impenetrable, but Johnny

Appleseed looked up, down, and sideways, then reached up, took hold of a branch, and swung to the other side. Continuing, he called back, "Take care, though, reverend, for there is a party of Shawnee braves hiding on top of the next rise. Fare-thee-well."

Shawnee! The reverend stopped in his tracks, his first thought to curse the Pompous Fruit Fryer, or whatever he wanted to be called, for having led him into an ambush. Copus hadn't heard, seen, or even sniffed any Indians nearby, but he'd ridden enough backcountry circuits to know that is precisely when they were most dangerous. Instinctively, he crossed himself.

Still, Johnny's comments set him to wondering: Did Indians kneel when they prayed? Did they fold their hands together like regular Christians? It was something to think about. Copus whispered, "God, I am no longer my own, but thine," wondering if a Shawnee would agree.

Tecumseh wanted to howl, to release the coiled torment in his soul, to launch forth with all of the agony and outrage that he bore on behalf of the entire Shawnee nation. Instead, he grunted and muttered, "Fools."

From his hidden vantage, the chief had been observing the camp meeting with mounting scorn for that entire day. He was in one of his brooding moods, and needed to be left alone. Even the eager women that always followed him kept their distance. He hadn't told the small party why they had journeyed from Deer Creek to this place; he'd merely announced his intent to go, so they'd followed.

He knew that the farther they ventured into territory forbidden by treaty, the more uneasy his men became. So near to a massive gathering of Christians, they were outnumbered by hundreds for each one. If discovered, they'd surely be butchered and their heads staked upon poles, Jesus be praised. Thus, they clustered in the shelter of dense sycamores, hoping that Tecumseh could get them home safely.

The only exception to this general foreboding was expressed by Lalawethika, who sucked his fortitude straight out of the bottle and laughed. "Christians worship a god hanging dead and naked from a tree." Every time he opened his mouth, the other Indians shushed him.

Tecumseh knew that if Lalawethika weren't his brother, the others would have rolled him down the bluff and left him to be devoured by the beasts or Christians, whichever got to him first.

When Tecumseh had spoken, the group nodded in hopeful agreement.

Battle Panther rose and said, "Yes, they are fools."

Tecumseh replied without so much as glancing at Battle Panther. "These Long Tongues, they worship their mangod with such baying and yelping that it would be an offense to any god with dignity. Their religion is their sin. Their Jesus is a bloody god, a criminal tortured, hung from a stick, and left to bleed out in front of vultures. They know nothing of sacred ceremonies, of ancient rituals, or of the discipline that is rewarded by grace. I cannot fathom why Waashaa Monetoo permits such blasphemy to exist."

"To test us?" Battle Panther hazarded.

"If so, why? For how long? The Long Tongues are as many as mosquitoes, and as hungry. Waashaa Monetoo created this homeland for the Shawnee, just as he created the air for birds, the water for fish, and the soil for plants. I was born here. Now, on this very land, I see fat cattle grazing and shitting. This is where, as a young man, I hunted with my father, Pukeshinwau, and my noble brother, Cheeseekau—both slain by Long Tongues. Seeing this land desecrated feels like having my heart ripped from my chest."

As Tecumseh spoke, his coterie of infatuated squaws wept at his pain, burying their faces in each other's shoulders, wiping their eyes with each other's sleeves, until one of them broke from the others and prostrated herself at Tecumseh's feet. "Please accept my body to soothe your distress," she wailed.

Tecumseh rolled his eyes and sighed. "Do not patronize me, woman." At the same time, he noticed Battle Panther gazing at the woman's rear end while his hands groped under his breech cloth. "Instead, please me by taking this man," he instructed her.

A cheek-splitting grin broke across Battle Panther's visage. Instantly, the other men in the party also perked up, concerns for betraying their camouflage abruptly banished from their minds. The women looked at each other, using winks and nods to assign appropriate pairings for themselves. However, nobody moved until Tecumseh released them with a slash of his hand, at which point they all enthusiastically commenced intimacies.

"What about me myself, oh brother?" Lalawethika complained.

Tecumseh tasted disgust. "As always, you see everything with one eye, and I don't mean the one on your head. Take a woman, if one will lower herself to lay with a diseased anus like yourself."

"Oh, you are very eloquent, my brother. You may well be more handsome, articulate, and intelligent than myself, but I have skills of mine own."

"Which are?"

Lalawethika grabbed the medicine bundle tied to his belt and shook it. "I am a healer!" With this sudden gesture, though, he knocked over his bottle, and as the brown liquor gurgled from its mouth, he dove for it, tongue fully extended to lap up every drop.

That ignominy was more than Tecumseh could endure. While all around him his followers unabashedly copulated and his dipsomaniac brother tipped the bottle with one hand and fondled himself with the other, the great chief retreated to a meditative distance.

On that night, wisps of enchantment mixed with madness in the air. When he was a young man on his vision quest, on this very site, he'd sat with his back against the trunk of a tall oak, stretched his arms to extend the range of his senses, and tossed back his head, exposing his throat to the Great Spirit... and in the next vision, Waashaa Monetoo slashed Tecumseh's jugular, and the gushing blood soaked that same patch of earth, so that the things that grew naturally there were of his own being. Whatever the Long Tongues planted there, though, was the product of their false gods. It was like a spell that had gone wrong. Tecumseh knew very well that whenever religion got out of control, bloodshed was inevitable.

Probably, his.

Chapter 6 – February 1805

Butler County, Pennsylvania

Not until his toes started to tingle did Johnny pay any mind to the cold. Only after sloshing through slush and sliding over ice all day, when his digits began itching with frostbite, did he ever dress his feet—with shoes, if he could scrounge some, but any kind of wrappings would suffice. In the harshest winter weather, when frost seeped through his foot covering and his toes started to go numb, he knew that he didn't have long before the rest of him would shut down, too.

The thought occurred to Johnny that if hell was cold, instead of hot, this current spell of brutal weather must be close to hell. The thin rays of the setting sun looked like yellow icicles, casting frozen shadows onto the ground. For all his years in the backcountry, Johnny had never experienced snowflakes so sharp they cut... until now. He wondered if it was true that, in extreme cold, even flames could freeze solid. More ominous, the high mackerel clouds blowing overhead indicated a storm was coming. With night falling fast and conditions bound to get worse, he wouldn't be able to push all the way to Pittsburgh. He needed to seek shelter—immediately.

Just one problem: he didn't know exactly where he was. It'd been a month since he'd visited with his brother and sister-in-law at their cabin on French Creek. Since then, he'd moved between several camps in the interior plateau north of Pittsburgh, sometimes borrowing a trapper's lean-to, but mostly making do with rock shelters or hollow logs. His best guess was that he'd descended into the valley of a slow creek that the Iroquois called the Connoquenessing.

Night was sweeping down fast, so he accelerated his pace. He took a shortcut around a bend in the creek, where he happened upon a cross that somebody had nailed to a tree. It wasn't much of a cross, just a couple of slats hammered together, but somebody had taken the time to carve the letters "INRI" into the bark above it. As it was Johnny's practice to never pass a cross without saying a prayer, he whispered, "Praise God," then proceeded along a path that took him deeper into the forest.

Now fully dark, he could see nothing but shapes, so Johnny followed the path by listening. God sent him a favor in the form of a gust of wind, which whooshed and swirled in a way that he recognized as pointing the direction to a clearing. He continued about a quarter mile before bumping into a huge woodpile. Around the pile, niched into the rocky moraine at the bottom of a hill, there was a dwelling with a single candle burning in an upstairs window. Johnny concluded that the Lord had intended for him to stop here for the night.

This was no lone woodsman's cabin, longer than wide, two floors, with a brick foundation, hewn board siding, and lattice windows—all shuddered except the one with the candle. Strangely, it had no door on the front, but it had a door with a porch on each side.

Shivering, Johnny considered the protocol for approaching this peculiar residence. He never knew what kind of a reception to expect from knocking on a stranger's door at night, especially in the middle of a storm. This, combined with his uncertainty as to which door to approach, gave him pause. Then he discovered a crescent-mooned outhouse on the far side.

Praise the Lord, I've found me shelter for the night.

Inside, next to a squat box with a single hole above a pit, sat a bucket of leaves for wiping. The overwhelming stench passed for a kind of warmth, for which Johnny was thankful. He inhaled deeply, detecting scents of deconstructed grains and the gaseous byproducts of digested starches, as well as traces of brined game meat—these folks sure weren't starving. He noticed a crooked panel under the pitched roof, higher than most people could reach, behind which someone had hidden a bottle of corn liquor. On such a night, with his very survival at stake, surely he could be excused for warming his innards with a taste.

This immediately made him sleepy. Sitting sideways, he made himself passably comfortable and commenced to doze.

Johnny was in the midst of a lilac-scented dream when he felt himself being poked in the ribs. His alarm mechanism triggered abruptly—he wasn't used to being touched—and his first instinct was to kick. The random blow caught a stranger in the groin.

A man doubled over, squealing, "I s'pected that yer was dead!"

"Forgive me, sir. Are ye damaged?"

The man scooped a handful of snow, dropped it down the front of his trousers, and rubbed vigorously. "Curses and damnation. Not tha' I got any use for my chestnuts 'round here, but it still hurts." He looked Johnny up and down. "What in the name of Martha Washington's bloomers are yer doing asleep in our shitter?"

"I'm a traveler, and needed a place to bide the storm."

"In here?" the man hooted. "It stinks bad 'nuff to choke a hog. Yer dang lucky I happened to have business to do this evenin', 'cause in here, if the cold didn'a kill yer, the fumes would. Look, mister, give me a moment while I attend to my needs, then I'll take yer inside."

As commanded, Johnny waited while the man repaired into the privy. He didn't mean to eavesdrop, but he couldn't help but notice that the sounds from within were not of tinkling or bodily evacuations. Rather, he heard swallowing, followed by a gasp, more swallowing, and a long, satisfied belch.

The man re-emerged with shiny eyes. "Follow me," he said to Johnny.

They walked past the first door, all the way to the entrance on the other side, and went in. Johnny wiped his feet.

"Hang yer coat," the man said as he took off his own, revealing himself to be wiry and jut-boned underneath.

Pegs lined the walls in the antechamber, from which hang such things as hats, coats, and scarves, but also baskets and buckets, a broom and dust pan, a broad axe and claw hammer, and a bouquet of dried flowers bound in twine. The room was empty save for a comb-backed Windsor settee, a three-legged table upon which sat a Bible and a burning candle, and a maple-faced cabinet built right into the wall.

The man blew out the candle before continuing into an adjacent room.

Six people sat in a spacious hall around a long, trestle table—four women on one side, two men on the other. Two empty chairs sat on the masculine side. The women wore butternut bark-dyed dresses, with narrow sleeves to the wrists, accessorized with white, triangular kerchiefs that covered their shoulders and breasts. Two of the women had their gray hair wrapped in tight buns, and with the oil lamp illuminating the left half of one's face and the right half of the other's, together they looked like one person. A third woman, conspicuously younger than the others, had her head entirely covered with a gray scoop bonnet, drawn and tied so tight beneath her neck that it made her chin stick out. The two men—one a bald gentleman with flaring mutton chops, and the other a negro with hot, yellowish eyes—wore identical tan shirts, brown vests and jackets, and round straw hats.

The women all turned to stare at Johnny, but the men just glanced and shrugged.

The fourth woman gathered her skirts and rose from the table. Her hair was like stickler thorns, with streaks of white over each temple. "What manner of wretch has thee brought us, Mister Rope?" she demanded.

"Sister Say, this man here was passed out in the crapper. If I'd not found him, he'd have froze solid dead by dawn. Uh, praise Jesus, that is."

Sister Say leaned forward, fists on the table. "Passed out? What kind of man be thee?"

"Pleased to meet ye, ma'am. Me name is John Chapman, a sower of seeds. I would be pleased if ye chose to call me Johnny."

"In this church, no one has a name until earning the right to be called a brother or a sister. Thus, thou shall be nameless until I decide otherwise. Be silent and heedful, or thou can leave this place and perish in the storm."

Johnny bowed, silently and heedfully.

Sister Say sniffed. "I detect Satanic fumes on thy breath! Hard liquor is forbidden in this house. Does thou have any more?"

Behind him, Mister Rope kicked Johnny in the back of the leg.

"No ma'am," Johnny replied.

Sister Say glared at him and declared, "I doubt that thee can be saved. Because we are the true church of last chances, however, Christian charity compels us to give thee the benefit of doubt. So I propose this compact: in exchange for saving thy life, thou must remain amongst us for one week, to live as we do, to pray and worship with us, and to honor our ways. If after one week, either thou does not wish to remain as our brother, or if we do not wish to extend membership in our community, then thou must leave... and God have mercy on thy pitiful soul."

That sounded better than freezing to death in a stinking outhouse. "Very well so," Johnny agreed, "and I thank ye graciously for the hospitality."

"T'aint hospitality. 'Tis the Lord's work. Every person at this table joined our Millennium Church of United Believers under that same agreement. By staying, they chose to endure scorn and hardship in hope of winning a seat in the glorious hereafter. But many others who tried our ways found themselves unfit and unworthy, so after a week they fled to the comforts of their sinful ways. I pity them, but bear them no ill."

"That is a fair deal, says I."

Sister say waved a hand dismissively. "T'ain't neither fair nor not. 'Tis just how God wants it."

The secret to getting along with the United Believers was to always be doing something. Orchestrating the group's activities was Sister Say's primary function. First thing in the morning, she waited in the common room, having placed a Bible in front of every seat around the table. Before breakfast, everybody took turns reading from Scriptures—except for the negro, Heck, who let Sister Say read for him, then repeated exactly what she said.

Afterwards, the two elder women—who in the light of day, Johnny saw, were, in fact, almost identical twins, though one was shorter due to a humpback—hastened to the kitchen and milled corn for grits. Meanwhile, the men returned to their quarters and made their beds, swept the floor, dusted every level surface, and picked up anything out of place.

In an hour or so, the twins served breakfast, preceded and followed by more prayers.

Next, the Believers waited for Sister Say to delegate their chores, which, although pretty much the same from day to day, nobody would have presumed to start before receiving permission. The twins cleared the table, scraped the plates, and tidied the kitchen. The youngest woman was responsible for washing, mending, and sewing the wardrobe for the entire group. The men performed various jobs involving manual labor or manufacture. Heck split wood and stacked it outside the cellar. The gentleman with the mutton chops spent his days assembling small oval boxes out of thin bands of maple wood. Anybody with nothing better to do between meals or prayers knew to pick up a broom and start sweeping.

For her part, when not overseeing everybody else's work, Sister Say would sit at the long table in the common room, to write her autobiography.

On Johnny's first day with the Believers, Sister Say paired him with the thin man who had rescued him from the outhouse.

"My name is Philander Rope," he said as they descended into the cellar. "My job is to bottom chairs."

The cellar contained hundreds of stacked chairs. "Have ye not got enough chairs already?" Johnny asked.

"More'n enough fer every arse in Butler County," Mister Rope admitted. "But that ain't the point." He removed a pipe and tobacco pouch from his vest. "Smoke?"

"No thank ye. What, then, *is* the point?"

"The point is tha' when the day is done, you got somethin' to show for yer day's labor." He exhaled a puff of smoke. "I reckon we all must seem like a peculiar church."

"Just somewhat more so than most."

"Tha's fairly charitable fer yer to put it like that. But lookee here, Mister Chapman, let's yer 'n' me be straight wit' each another. I ain't really one of them odd folks. Like yerself, I was on the outs wit' winter settin' in, so I ciphered tha' stickin' here, warm and well fed, was better'n freezin', starvin', or gittin' et by wolves in the wild. Still, I'll be hightailin' outta here roundabout PawPawing Day.

"I ain't saying tha' life here is easy, tho'. Sister Say is like a demon bitch with fangs 'round her cunt. Her story goes tha' when she was younger, she miscarried four babies and had two husbands drop dead, so she finally swore off men altogether. She fell in wit' Mother Ann Lee an' the Shaking Quakers in Albany, where she lived fer a time. Sister Say claims tha' she left the Shakers to go on her own faith mission, but I think she got kicked out. She really wants to start her own church. In her mind, she figures tha', come Judgment Day—which'll be soon, she says—only those tha' believe in what she teaches will git saved. The others'll burn in hell.

"The twins, Mary Rose and Rose Mary, came wit' her from Albany. The crippled sister got kicked by a horse when she's a girl, but somehow both of 'em wound up feebleminded. If yer ask one of them a question, the other will answer, and versa vicey. I don' e'en think they know tha' there's two of themselves.

"This house belongs to ol' Fritz the German—he's the one wit' the crazy whiskers. Back in his homeland, he was a lawyer, but also a childless widower who got to followin' some radical Lutheran preacher named of Johann Rapp. Ol' Fritz was sent to blaze a trail fer the religion in America, so he came here, bought this land, built this house, and waited fer the rest of the Rappites to show up. I guess he got tired of waitin', 'cause when he heard Sister Say preachin' down Pittsburgh way, he became her firs' convert. Fritz's got 'nuff money tha' he coulda picked any religion, but my opinion is tha' he likes havin' a woman tell him what to do. Heck is the ol' man's hired hand, who ran from Kentucky, so he'll believe whatsoever he's told to believe. He works too damn hard, tho', 'n makes me look bad.

"Ahh, but I know what yer'd be thinkin'.... The young, purty one, eh? Tha's Mona Junkin, formerly of Chillicothe. I don' rightly know what she's doin' here, 'cept there's a story 'bout gettin' her heart broked by some soldier what had his way wit' her, then skedaddled. She says tha' Jesus is her new husband. Once, when she came down to the cellar to call me fer dinner, I tried to foist my hand up her petticoat... but she commenced to havin' the shiverin' fits so bad tha' it scared me soft. If yer got an eye for tha' one, you'd be better advised to acquaint yerself wit' yer right hand."

Johnny thanked him for the information. Anxious to earn his keep, and since he'd learned to weave a chair from his father, he began assembling the frames and fixing the bottoms with poplar strips.

"Take yer time," Mister Rope urged, looking unhappy at Johnny's skill and enterprise. At length, he decided to equalize their combined output by doing nothing at all. "I gotta pay a visit to the crapper," he announced, and was gone until lunch.

The members of the congregation assembled at the long table, and waited for Sister Say to bless their luncheon of johnnycakes, calico beans, and salted venison.

Upon entering the room, Sister Say paused, sniffed disdainfully, and twisted her brow in a pained expression. Spasms rose in her throat as she declared, "Mister Chapman, thou reek like the devil's bottom hole!"

Johnny had been told he stank on more than one occasion, although he'd never heard it put in such pagan terms. "Pardon me?"

"Thou art unfit to consume this food that the Lord has provided. To the washroom with thee! Do not presume a place at this table until scrubbing thy body."

Johnny wasn't particularly averse to washing; he just figured that, to discerning nostrils, most everybody wore some manner of odor. It was a sign of good health. Still, a bath wouldn't hurt him none.

A rusty washtub sat in the middle of the men's quarters, barely big enough to squat in.

Heck lugged in two buckets of lukewarm water, took one look at Johnny, and said "Boss, yo' gonna need mo' some water." He handed Johnny a cake of lye soap.

Sitting in the tub with his knees against his chin, Johnny not so much scrubbed as chiseled the dirt off his body. The strata of filth came off in layers of different colors, from dark peat to red clay, and floated on the surface like river scum.

Heck kept bringing more water, and when the last bucket arrived, Johnny dunked his whole head, then began working soap into his hair and beard. He was surprised by some of the things he found in there, including bugs, burrs, hardened sap, and a haw comb that he'd put behind his ear and forgot.

On his last trip, Heck brought a freshly pressed suit, a tan linen shirt, and brown wool jacket and trousers, identical to the attire worn by the other men. He then scooped up Johnny's discarded clothes, commenting that they weren't worth saving even as rags.

Refreshed, Johnny presented himself to Sister Say.

"Thou art nearly suitable to sit amongst us," she said. "Thou may dine now, but after the meal, Sister Mona will barber thy hair and whiskers."

Given a heaping plate, Johnny pushed aside the venison, but devoured the rest with delight.

Mister Rope's eyes shot wide. "He's eatin' like he's been livin' off dirt fer so long that he done forgot wha' food tastes like."

After the repast, while the others returned to work, Sister Mona led Johnny into the laundry closet adjacent to the kitchen. He sat on a stool there, watching while she laid out shears, clippers, a straight razor, a hard bristle brush, a stick of shaving soap, and a bowl of herbs and vinegar.

Nervous, Johnny started talking. "I hear that ye hail from Chillicothe."

The scornful expression that Sister Mona returned caused Johnny to worry that she had access to so many sharp tools. She said, "If you so much as brush the back of your little finger against the hem of my dress, I will scream to Sister Say that you tried to rape me, and she will crown your head with a frying pan, grab and twist your testicles until you beg for mercy."

Johnny pressed his finger to his lips to indicate his compliance, but sitting still didn't come naturally to him. He didn't like the sensation of fingers in his hair—too much like being scalped.

Attempting to brush through the tangled mess, Sister Mona pulled and pulled, and the harder she yanked, the wider Johnny's eyes bulged. Finally, she just started hacking away, all the while chiding him to, "Sit still!" The more hair that she cut away, the gentler her touch became, as if her task was getting easier.

When she wrapped a towel over his head and began rubbing vigorously, Johnny felt a static sensation in his follicles.

She stepped back, examined her work between the blades of the open scissors, and nodded. "That's better."

Johnny started to stand, but she flattened her palm against his shoulder. "We aren't done. Now, the whiskers have to go."

Sister Mona went to work on the beard, snipping the ends on one side, then the other, as if it were important to maintain balance. When she got to his mustache, she placed her finger against the tip of his nose and tilted his head backwards.

Johnny smelled vinegar on the shears.

After a time, she sighed and said, "I am not *from* Chillicothe, despite whatever that despicable Mister Rope told you. I did, however, live near there with my sister's family for a spell, while I was ill."

Forgetting his vow of silence, Johnny couldn't help but respond. "I do hope that ye are feeling better now."

"Not really." She gazed down toward the floor and shook her head. "But the Lord does not reward us in *this* world."

"That is exactly what I tell folks, too."

"You're a drifter, aren't you?"

"The Lord's service calls me to many faraway places."

"What's your business?"

"I am a sower of seeds—apple seeds, to be precise. I have planted trees up and down the Ohio valley. I have ventured into new territory, ahead of the settlers, so that when they arrive in the country, I shall have seedlings ready to sell them."

Sister Mona dipped the shaving brush into a mug of water and began whipping up a foam. "So, you're a squatter."

"No, I'm not a squatter, since I don't live on the lands where I sow, and whenever possible, I get permission before planting. Also, one fine day, I plan to buy some land of me very own, but not for living on."

"What for, then?"

"To leave it alone."

"Like as wilderness?"

"To the wolves and the bears, 'tis not wilderness—'tis home. They need some land set aside for themselves, too."

Sister Mona's face scrunched up in a puzzled look. "Well I have never heard of such a thing. What good is land that isn't settled?"

"'Tis land that will always be there."

"So, then, you intend to remain a wanderer all your days? Don't you think that the Lord wants you to marry and raise children?"

"My calling is not to be a family man. I do not love women the way most men do."

Sister Mona gasped, and whispered, "Are you a *sodomite*?"

"No, not that. I just don't have the same appetites as most men. I don't know why-for. When most boys reach an age, their lusts grow hungry, but those feelings just never kicked in for me. That is perchance why I plant apple seeds. The trees are my children."

"Are you being truthful with me, Mister Chapman?"

"I have never been otherwise with anybody."

She paused to regard Johnny, and finally said, "I believe you."

The shave took longer than Johnny had expected. With every slash of the blade, though, a tingly sensation spread across his cheeks.

When Sister Mona trimmed the fuzz under his nose, she leaned almost close enough to kiss him. Finally, wiping a towel across his face and splashing his cheeks with the herbs and vinegar mixture, she proclaimed that, "Underneath, you're a right fair-looking man, Mister Chapman."

He knew that it was arrogance, but he liked being told. He felt like he had taken off his old face and put on a new one.

"Would you like to see?" She offered a vanity glass to him.

It had been a while since Johnny last looked into a mirror. As a rule, he avoided them, on the grounds of the old church women's tale that every second a person spends looking into a mirror is taken off his lifespan. Still, if he never looked at himself again in his entire life, he just had to see what he looked like at that moment.

"Glory," he gasped. "If I was not holding this mirror in front of meself, I would not believe this face was me own."

Sister Mona looked over her shoulder and sighed. "I may be married to Jesus Christ, but I do know a handsome man when I see one."

Johnny's seventh day with the United Believers was their Sabbath. The prior day, the members spent all of their waking hours cleaning and cooking, so that on the Sabbath they could devote themselves entirely to prayer, thanksgiving, and purgation. Johnny did whatever he was told cheerfully—he even took another bath!—although he'd quietly begun to suspect that he was doing things just for the sake of doing them, rather than to get something done. He'd never swept the floor so many times in his life.

"Sweep so thou shalt be clean from all thy uncleanness," Sister Say would pronounce.

That was a helpful notion, Johnny agreed, but he thought that just because something was dirty didn't mean it was unclean. To him, that was an important distinction.

Each day that week, Sister Say quizzed Johnny as to whether he yet felt inspired to confess his sins and join the Believers.

Not wanting to disappoint her, he'd replied, "I have not felt so moved just yet."

She'd glare at him and *tsk* with subdued dismay, but Johnny still suspected that she liked him, if for no other reason than because she didn't berate him the way that she did Mister Rope, whom she referred to as a "slobbering swine."

In fact, Johnny felt rather welcome among the misfits of this church. He'd already gained a couple of pounds, thanks to the Rose and Mary sisters' potato and turnip soup.

Meanwhile, Brother Fritz seemed pleased at how Johnny took an interest in his box-making techniques. When Johnny observed that those small boxes would be useful for storing seeds, Fritz gratefully proclaimed, "Yah, good for der seeds!" as if it had never occurred to him that his boxes might actually be used for anything.

Also, Brother Heck was a guitar player, and with Johnny accompanying him on the whistle, the two of them worked out some fairly melodic versions of spiritual tunes with names like "Judgment Day is a-Rollin' 'Round," "I'm Glad There's No Dyin' in Heaven," and "Massa Gonna Sell Me to Jesus Tomorrow." All in all, Johnny figured there was nowhere more hospitable for him to go and nothing more pressing for him to do.

Still, while he sincerely left his mind open to the possibility of conversion, that notion troubled his sleep at night. He listened for Voices in the darkness, but heard none.

Johnny allowed Sister Mona to shave him a second time.

This time, when she greeted him, she asked if he'd like her to trim his eyelashes, along with the shave, free of charge. She flattered him by complimenting the firmness of his jaws, and repeatedly during the shave, she lifted his chin and looked directly into his eyes, as if she were reading his mind.

That impression didn't bother Johnny as much as he felt it ought.

"Your beard is quite thick," she observed. "You should shave every day."

Johnny's very first thought was, *'no, never, what an indulgence and a waste of time'*; however, he said to her that he'd be okay with that, if she was willing.

On the morning of the next Sabbath, with everybody gathered in the common room, Sister Say instructed the men to move the meal table aside, to allow them freedom to move across the floor as the spirit beckoned them. It thus seemed strange to Johnny that the next thing she bade them to do was kneel, while she read and commented upon The Book of Job:

> *"Then answered the LORD unto Job out of the whirlwind, and said, Gird up thy loins now like a man: I will demand of thee, and declare thou unto me. Wilt thou also disannul my judgment? Wilt thou condemn me, that thou mayest be righteous? Hast thou an arm like God? Or canst thou thunder with a voice like him?"*

This passage agitated the Rose and Mary sisters, who began bowing with their arms extended in prostration. They staggered these movements, so that one went down when the other went up, and kept it going for the duration of the reading, until Sister Say closed her Bible. The sisters then bounced onto their feet and began to sing:

> *"Come life, oh good Shaker life,*
> *Come to better life eternal.*
> *Shake, shake right out of me,*
> *All that is carnal."*

As if he'd been waiting for the opportunity, Brother Heck dashed for his guitar and began strumming a rhythm.

The sisters sang louder:

> *"I'll dance a nimble step,*
> *Like great David.*
> *I'll show Michael twice,*
> *How Shakers behave."*

At which point, Heck belted out, "Oh yeah, oh say it, Lord, *woohoo*, shake it now."

Humpbacked Mary Rose gave a ribbon to Rose Mary, who started clapping and began skipping in circles, wrapping the ribbon around her sister tighter with every revolution.

"Shake me, shake me good, oh yeah."

Letting loose her hair, Sister Say took a massive breath and exploded: "Work, brothers and sisters! Make thy bodies work! Work to purge sin from thy bodies!"

Mister Rope hollered, "I gotta shake myself now!" and dashed out the door toward the outhouse.

Hopping onto his feet, Brother Fritz inadvertently passed gas loud enough to carry over the din. "Acch," he grunted. "*Mein schließmuskel freut sich der stimme Gottes,*" he elucidated. Strutting to the hearth, he bent over the flames and, gathering his inner gasses, let loose another fart prodigious enough to cause a flare. Unburdened, he twirled around Rose Mary and started reciting:

"Vater unser im Himmel,
geheiligt werde dein Name."

Heck sang and began dancing with his guitar as if it was a girl. "Get offa that thing, and shake till yah feel better."

"Dein Reich komme;
dein Wille geschehe,
wie im Himmel so auf Erden."

"The spirit of the Lord has possessed Brother Fritz," Sister Say proclaimed. "He is speaking in tongues. Hearken...."

"Unser tägliches Brot gib uns heute.
Und vergib uns unsere Schuld,
wie auch wir vergeben unsern Schuldigern...."

"I do believe that's German he's speaking," Johnny begged to differ.

Heck picked up a pair of spoons from the kitchen and began rattling percussion against the wall. "Get offa dat thing, an' shake it till yah sing."

"Do you feel it, brothers and sisters? Tis the Holy Spirit!"

"...und führe uns nicht in Versuchung,
sondern erlöse uns von dem Bösen.
Denn dein ist das Reich und die Kraft
und die Herrlichkeit in Ewigkeit."

Mister Rope returned, howling, "Yeehaw!" He broke into a clumsy, heel-to-toe clog dance, cavorting around the room. His feet landed so hard they shook the floorboards, and his jaw bounced as if it were about to drop loose from his face.

The Rose and Mary sisters kicked up their heels next to him.

Mister Rope grinned and whistled at them, but kept sidestepping in the direction of Sister Mona, who throughout had remained kneeling impassively in the center of the room. In an effort to gain her favor, Mister Rope performed some high-kicking, knee-slapping, hips-thrusting gyrations, inviting her to join him in his divinely-inspired revelry. When he attempted to impress her with an acrobatic twist-and-lunge maneuver, though, he stumbled and landed in Sister Mona's lap.

They tussled, and she emerged from the fray with her foot suspended above his head, poised to grind it into his face.

Sister Say deflected the tension by calling out, "Brothers and sisters, form a purity circle!"

All the while, Johnny had stood aside watching, not so much unmoved as simply confused. He searched inward for any whim of religious fervor, but just didn't feel it. Nevertheless, when the group organized into a "purity circle," he tentatively stepped forward.

The congregation formed a line, led by Sister Say, and began marching around the room clapping hands, singing, whooping, squawking, or blabbering as they were so moved.

Sister Say spun into the middle and, rolling her arms, doubled over, lower and lower, and then jumped as high as she could, arms and legs outstretched. "Fly away, lusts and vices!"

The others flailed their arms in a similar fashion, as if casting handfuls of sin into the air.

Next, Brother Fritz took a turn in the center of the circle, pantomiming that he was carrying a cross, and moaning as though under the sting of a lash. He sobbed, *"Heile mich mit schmerzen."*

In turn, the Rose and Mary sisters wrapped their arms around each other's shoulders, pressed their foreheads together, and each chanted one word at a time.

Rose Mary: "Shake!"

Mary Rose: "These!"

Rose Mary: "Wicked!"

Mary Rose: "Sins!"

And then together: "Awaaaaay!"

Heck dropped to the floor in a 180-degree split.

It made Johnny wince; *That had to hurt.*

Then Heck sprang, pirouetted, and bowed. This performance drew a boisterous ovation from the other worshippers, and Heck wailed, "Get offa dat thing, an' shake it till yah sing."

Brother Fritz delighted. *"Brüder! Schwestern! Schau! Ich tanze mit Gott."*

About this time, Johnny started worrying about what he'd do, if called upon to take a turn in the center of the circle. He'd never learned to dance proper steps, and although he often liked to join the fracas at a barn dance, he needed to feel sincerely moved to do so. Having to think about it made it hard for him to want to do it.

Mister Rope broke loose from the purity circle. He staggered and teetered, all the while laughing so hard that he flung spittle and chunks from his mouth. Every time that Sister Mona passed, he gestured for her to join him, and finally he lunged for her.

She dodged him, and then suddenly stood alone in the center. She dropped her shoulders and tilted her head backwards.

"Become an instrument for the Lord!" Sister Say urged.

For two full rotations of the circle, Sister Mona remained rooted to her place. Slowly, she began nodding her head sideways, and her eyes swelled as if they were being cranked out of their sockets. At once, she stepped into a shaft of light beaming through the window, catching it full in the face. Her expression mixed agony and joy, her lashes rising while her unblinking eyes filled with tears. She seemed to be gazing into the eyes of a ghost, as if it were right in front of her. At once, as if frightened, she slashed her head sideways, then backwards so hard that it looked like her neck was going to snap. "Noooooo!," she erupted. "Please, noooooo!"

"Let the Lord make thee His instrument!" Sister Say pleaded.

Sister Mona collapsed to her knees onto the floor, pounding her fists so hard, it seemed she might break the bones in her hands. Then she rolled onto her back and arched her whole body, raising herself on her heels and her shoulders, while convulsions ravaged her limbs and her face contorted as if something larger than her head was trying to exit through her mouth. Her complexion turned bluish.

While Sister Mona seized, the members of the purity circle kept spinning around....

...except for Johnny. He stepped aside, bent over Sister Mona, and gently turned her onto her side. He ignored Sister Say's command to "Leave her be!" and cushioned her head with one hand, while massaging her shoulders and collarbone with the other.

Gradually, Sister Mona resumed breathing normally and her eyes descended back into knowingness.

The purity circle screeched to a standstill.

Sister Mona glanced at Johnny and raised her head feebly, just enough so that she could kiss his hand. Then she closed her eyes and fell unconscious.

Johnny carried her across the forbidden barrier into the women's quarters, where he lowered her into bed and covered her. He could hear the voices in the other room; the word "blasphemy" came up once or twice. He lingered, looking down at Mona and wondering what to do next, when a sound came from the door.

Sister Say stood in the doorway with her arms akimbo. "Mister Chapman?"

"I think that I know what ye have to say."

"No, I think not." She sighed. "Thou probably believe that I am going to tell thee to leave, and that is true. Clearly, thou hast not taken to our ways. But there's something else that I want for thee to know."

"Is it important for me to know, or can I get along just the same without knowing?"

"It is important for *me* to tell thee. Thou art a kind man, Mr. Chapman, a God-fearing man in thine own way. Under other circumstances, I would welcome thee to stay as our brother. However... there is clearly a sparking between thee and Sister Mona. This, I cannot allow in our community."

That was the last thing Johnny had expected to hear. He looked at the sleeping Sister Mona and wished that she'd awaken to deny it. "I swear to ye, Sister Say, that I have nothing more than brotherly intentions toward this woman."

She nodded and said, "It's not *your* intentions that concern me."

"I see," Johnny answered, even though he did not. Without a fare-the-well, and taking nothing except the clothes on his back, he went straight through the door and departed into the still-raging winter outside.

Chapter 7 – April 1805

Greensburg and Pittsburgh, Pennsylvania

"May God strike me blind!" John Young rubbed his eyes. "Is that verily you, Mister Chapman?"

Being smartly coiffed and clean-shaven had some disadvantages, including that even folks who knew Johnny well didn't recognize him. Throughout his travels, he'd made many acquaintances from Lake Erie to the Ohio River, so that only a few places remained where his reputation didn't precede him. He was well aware that one attribute of his reputation related to a certain distinctive untidiness, offset, he hoped, by a clear conscience and genial disposition. Not caring what one looked like was its own kind of fashion statement. Many people liked him anyway, and he appreciated being liked by those kinds of people. It therefore irked him a bit when those same people—among them, John Young—expressed such amazement at his new, dapper appearance.

"Ye should not jump to false notions about me looks," Johnny said. "I am not turning into a dandy. As soon as I drift back into the county, I shall let me-self grow back to normal."

"Perhaps so," John Young allowed. "But right now you look as fine as any of the fancy lawyers in Philadelphia. You might do well to give up apples and consider a career in the law, instead."

If he'd intended that to be a jest, Johnny didn't see any humor in it. "There is less chance of that than there is of the sun rising in the west."

"Now, that sounds more like the Johnny Chapman I know."

John Young had known Johnny since 1797, when they'd met while traveling westbound into the Allegheny Valley. With his new wife, Marcia, Young had been en route to a spacious homestead they'd purchased in Westmoreland County. Johnny had helped Mr. and Mrs. Young replace a broken wheel on their wagon, and from that act of generosity they'd developed a bond and occasional business relationship.

Johnny was a swift, reliable courier who knew the land well, and John Young had frequent need to dispatch and receive missives between his home in Greensburg and business associates in outlying areas.

Later, when Johnny began planting his orchards, every fall he returned to the nearby cider mills to collect seeds from the apple pumice, which he then stored in grain sacks in Young's cellar until the following spring. With a new growing season now getting underway, Johnny had returned for his seed stock.

The two men lunched on cornbread biscuits and boiled eggs, catching up on each other's news in between bites. According to John Young, due to a surge in keel boat traffic for all manner of goods to destinations downstream, Pittsburgh was rapidly becoming the Athens of the inland empire. The city's first branch of the Bank of Pennsylvania had opened recently, and with it had come new demands for legal services managing sales, loans, contracts, and disputes. Still, Young preferred to conduct business from his home in Greensburg, where he could escape the vices and iniquities of the three rivers waterfront.

"In certain circles," Young lamented, "'tis becoming so foul that you cannot always depend upon another man's faith in God to ensure his honesty."

Unfortunately, Johnny agreed that some men seemed not to care about their own salvation. Thinking about his recent experiences with the United Believers, he added, "And yet, there are a good many folks around these parts with some fairly peculiar beliefs."

Young snapped his fingers. "That's why I choose to base my faith upon reliable authority..." He pushed aside his plate. "...which brings me to a matter I wish to discuss. I'd like to hire you for a service."

"Whatever it is, I would do it for free."

"I know that you would, my friend." He reached into the hearth with a pair of tongs, retrieved a glowing ember, and used it to light his clay pipe. "But what kind of a lawyer would I be, were I to accept unwarranted gratuities?"

"I agree, for 'tis obvious that any good lawyer loves and honors the law like his own child."

He followed Young into the cellar, thrashing aside smoke and wondering what it was about pipe-smoking that cultured men like John Young found attractive. Unlike Indians smoking their pipes of peace, white men actually inhaled fumes into their lungs. It was just one of the many things about polite society that mystified him.

"Here are your seeds," Young indicated. "Kept cool, moist, and at a constant temperature, ready to sprout and bear blessed fruit." He then pivoted and pointed at a hardtack crate on a table next to the seed sacks. "And this is some cargo that I'd like for you to deliver to a certain party residing on an island in the Ohio River, not far downriver from Marietta."

"'I am going that-a-way," Johnny volunteered. He lifted one corner of the crate. "'Tis a wee size heavy, is it not?"

"As well it should be, for it contains twenty brand new, cloth-bound copies of the most amazing book, *The True Christian Religion*, by the great servant of our Lord, Emmanuel Swedenborg."

"Is it for that reading religion of yours?"

"Indeed. The works of Swedenborg contain nothing less than divine revelation, so we who call ourselves 'Readers' consider it a sacrament when we gather to recite and discuss them. These writings will literally take you to heaven."

"I trust the Bible to do that."

"Prophecy did not end with the Bible."

"But the Bible is complete, nevertheless."

"From God's perspective, yes. Swedenborg completes it from that of mankind."

Johnny didn't quite understand what his friend was talking about. The idea of worshipping by sitting around a table and taking turns reading from a book—a book other than the Bible—didn't seem quite on the up and up to him. Still, John Young was a good, moral Christian, so it hadn't done him any harm.

Young continued. "Load your seeds and my books onto my old pack mule and go to Pittsburgh. From there you can commission a keelboat downriver. Belpre Island is a mile beyond the confluence of the Ohio and Little Kanawha. You'll recognize it by the beautiful white Palladian mansion on its eastern shore. There dwell Harmann and Margaret Blennerhassett, the grandest couple in all of the Ohio Valley. Please deliver these books to Madame Blennerhassett personally. She's a Reader, like myself. After you've done that, you will have fulfilled your obligation to me."

"That I will surely do for ye, friend."

John Young turned his pipe around and poked its stem toward Johnny. "And if along the way you feel inspired to read Swedenborg's wonderful news, it surely couldn't do you any harm."

"I reckon not," Johnny replied.

Johnny led John Young's shaggy, long-eared pack mule down Liberty Street in Pittsburgh, stroking her and even shouldering part of her load himself, for the beast seemed spooked by the hubbub. Horse-drawn carts and wagons raced past them, dogs barked at them, and along either side of the avenue, pedestrians bustled over stone walkways. Everybody seemed to be in a hurry.

In just the eight years since he'd first drifted into Pittsburgh, the city had swollen with activity and population. Where there'd previously been just a fort, a land office, and a few trading posts, such a proliferation of commerce and construction had occurred that nearly the only part of town he recognized was the three rivers. Mercantile establishments sold everything from cutlery to firearms to hats, and new shops had sprouted for craftsmen like blacksmiths, glass cutters, and tanners. Small industries had formed, like a lumber mill and a blast furnace foundry, and of course taverns now seemed to occupy every street, with fanciful names like the "Green Tree," the "Harp and Crown," and the "Whale and the Monkey." With it all came an incessant, insect-like buzzing in the background, broken only by the occasional ferry horn.

On either side of the main road ran parallel residential streets, where a hodgepodge of log, brick, stone, and frame houses stood side-by-side. Domestic refuse, including waste from pigsties, chicken coops, slaughterhouses, and other feculent leavings, lay heaped along the streets in festering piles. Johnny took a wide path around those—the smell of disintegrating tripe too much to bear. More subtle, but just as disorienting, was the slight but pervasive acidity in the air, and the blur of dry soot that hung over the core of the city and drained it of its colors. A thin veneer of ash covered the ground in Pittsburgh.

John Young had likened Pittsburgh to the gloried city of Athens, but to Johnny, if that's what the Greek capital looked like, then Plato could keep it. Maybe, he conjectured, if only there'd been somebody ahead of the migration planting apple trees, more of the land would have been spared, and people would seem happier.

He planned to charter passage downriver on the next available keelboat. At the shipyard, the only person he could find was a ferry keeper, who explained to him that a crew of keelboaters had just arrived yesterday, and he presumed that they were presently spending their wages in the Pittsburgh Point Brewery, where they typically congregated between jobs.

Johnny hated to hear this, as leelboaters tended to be a coarse rabble, especially when in their cups. Still, he whispered to heaven, "Thy will, not mine, be done," and led his forlorn mule down Water Street. He followed the noise to the brewery, and found its doors wide open.

Inside, in just a single sweeping glance, Johnny observed that a number of sins in both mortal and venial categories were being wantonly committed. Each of the room's four corners seemed to have been zoned for some specific form of depravity. To his left, gamblers had gathered around gaming tables. They rolled dice, dealt cards, placed wagers, and displayed short tempers.

Behind them, in a darkened niche with quick access to a curtained hallway leading up a staircase, slack-jawed men bought drinks for cavorting wenches in exchange for their attentions, including the occasional digression into those upstairs quarters.

Up front to Johnny's right, drunkards sloshed their glasses and bottles with exaggerated gestures while swapping cock-and-bull tales of their personal adventures, each trying to top everybody else's.

In a distant, smoky corner, businessmen wearing frock coats, brocade vests, and top hats convened to negotiate deals involving acquisitions of assets, distribution of contraband, and maximization of profits by all means available to them under, or in spite of, the law.

On a makeshift stage next to the bar, a fiddler and a banjoist played as fast and as hard as they could, as if being chased.

Amid all the bacchanalia, though, the central and most commanding figure was Mike Fink. Standing in front of the bar, with a jug in one hand and a wench under his other arm, he regaled everybody within earshot with a rollicking song:

"Polly, pretty Polly, come and go along with me.
Polly, pretty Polly, come and go along with me.
Before we get married some pleasure to seek."

After finishing, he waited for applause, and when it was not immediately forthcoming, he growled, "Cain't yer bunghole gougers hear?"

In response, the bartender rang a bell, which triggered a round of applause among those closest to Fink and thus most afraid of getting smashed over the head by a barstool.

The singer took his bow.

Weighing his options, none of which seemed particularly auspicious, Johnny decided to approach Mike Fink. "Hello, friend, I see ye are in high spirits."

Fink squinted dubiously. "Yer don't look lahk no friend 'o mine."

"'Tis none other than I, Johnny Chapman, a sower of seeds. Once, I was a passenger on your boat."

"Ah hah!" Fink hollered. "Yer don't look none lahk yerself. I uh took yer fer one uh those thievin' bankers. Wha' happen'd to yer?"

"Just a shave and some new clothes."

"Well it don't suit yer none," Fink judged. "Buy me a drink."

Johnny signaled the bartender, who served Mike Fink's usual drink, a mug of stout with a shot of rum mixed in.

The keelboater nodded at his wench to grab the mug and pour it down his throat for him. The faster he drank, the more she tilted it, until there was none left. She then licked the foam off his lips.

"Cock-a-doodle-doo!" Fink exclaimed. "Wha' ken I uh to do fer yer, Chapman?"

"I would like to book passage on the next boat downriver. I have a load to deliver to a Madame Blennerhassett, who lives on Belpre Island."

"Bennerhassett! Well, lah-dee-dah, Chapman, ain't yer a grand feller, hobnobbin' wit' dem ahrist-o-crats. Well, me 'n' mah crew leave at six bells. Fer a dollar, yer can squeeze on mah boat. But yer gotta pay up front."

Johnny removed a bill from his pocket and tried to hand it to Mike Fink, who instead nodded at him to give it to his wench.

"It'll be hers soon 'nuff anyhow," he explained. "Look, Chapman, I uh'm raght busy at the moment. Go find a place to wait, 'til I uh've had mah fill 'o drinkin' an' whorin'."

It pained Johnny to think of his money being used for sin, but the price was reasonable, the hour of departure acceptable, and his chances of finding a more sober keelboater nil. It seemed the best deal he was likely to get. Still, not trusting Mike Fink to abide by the agreement, Johnny determined that he'd better not let him out of his sight. With four hours until six bells, that left him with some time on his hands.

Usually, Johnny occupied idle time with prayer, but in present circumstances he did not particularly wish to call God's attention to his whereabouts. Then, he recollected how John Young had encouraged him to invest any spare time reading from that big, thick book by....

What was his name? Switzerburger? Luxembourg? Swedenborg?

He fetched a book from the crate and returned to the bar, where he sat on the floor with his back to the wall. The book felt like a brick on his lap. Its title, *The True Christian Religion*, sounded rather vain to him, so he was more skeptical than curious when he opened it.

'Listen, Johnny.'

His mother's voice slashed through the din like an angelic trumpet.

Johnny raised his head, searching with his ears. The clamor of the brewery receded to a murmur, as the audible space around Johnny drained to receive further revelations.

Listen to what? he wondered. He averted his eyes, the more thoroughly to concentrate, and they settled upon the open pages of the book on his lap. Johnny read:

> *Once while I was talking with angels, certain spirits that had recently arrived from the natural world were present. Seeing them, I bade them welcome to heaven, and I told them many things they had not known before about the spirit world....*

Johnny blinked in consideration of this passage—the author, a living man, was writing about being in heaven and meeting with newly arriving souls. That proposition seemed audacious, even a bit absurd, and yet he wrote about it as if it were as common as chatting with a friend over tea and biscuits. Johnny read some more:

> *I replied that for nothing in nature is nature of itself the operative power, but God through nature. And when they asked for proof, I said, 'Those who believe the divine operation to be in every least thing of nature find in very many things they see in the world much more evidence in favor of God than in favor of nature. For those who find evidences of favor of the divine operation in every least thing of nature observe attentively the wonderful things that are seen in the production of plants and animals.'*

"True, indeed," Johnny mused. Then he noticed that when he paused in his reading, the stillness surrounding him contained an echo. He tugged on his earlobes, and the echo resolved into a stentorian, slightly accented voice, which continued:

> *'They observe that from a little seed sown in the ground there grows forth a root, and from the root a stem, and successively branches, buds, leaves, flowers, and fruits, even to new seeds, just as if the seed knew the order of succession or development by which to renew itself.'*

Johnny was no longer reading, but listening:

'Moreover, to any mind that thinks deeply, things that excite wonder are presented wherever creatures in general are observed; as that both the smallest and the largest of them, both the invisible and the visible, that is both minute insects and great birds and beasts, possess organs of sense, namely, sight, smell, taste, and touch; also organs of motion, which are muscles, for they fly and walk; also viscera connected with heart and lungs which are moved by their brains. What man of sound reason does not see that the natural world cannot be the source of all this?'

"Not me!" Johnny jumped in, for he now felt that he was a participant in animated conversation with the Philosopher. "I testify that what ye say is clearly true and obvious to anybody with eyes, ears, and an open mind."

The Philosopher replied:

'Then you are ready to learn more. I have visited heaven and shared the company of innumerable spirits, angels, saints, and prophets, and these are the things they've told me. Listen....'

And he commenced to expound upon how, through personal visits to heaven and extensive face-to-face conversations with angels, he had become privy to the universal theology for a new church.

'There is a correspondence in heaven with everything Earthly. It only made good common sense that if God intended for the human world to be a training ground for eternal life, then heaven should represent the perfection of this mortal sphere. The kindness and goodness that we show to others on Earth is like practice for the eternal benevolence in heaven. Since angels are people and live together the way people do on Earth, they have clothes and homes and a great many other things; the difference, however, being that everything is more perfect for them.'

"Just as I thought!" Johnny concurred, for he had always believed in his heart that the beauty and bounty in this world, if made permanent, were akin to paradise. Whatever wasn't perfect in this world was the fault of people, who despite their best efforts were still, ultimately, sinners. Given infinite love, though, purified spirits could perfect any Earthly community—even Pittsburgh, maybe.

The Philosopher went on:

'It is not so hard to lead a heaven-bound life as people think it is. It is simply a matter of recognizing, when something attractive comes up that he know is dishonest or unfair, that it is not to be done because it is against the Divine commandments.'

"Nothing could be truer," Johnny agreed, for so far as he'd seen in life, everybody—without exception—really did know right from wrong, if only they heeded their inborn consciences.

'People who have led a life withdrawn from worldly concerns are aflame with a sense of their own worth, and constantly crave heaven.'

Hearing that, Johnny understood, all at once, why he lived the way that he did. He didn't want to be in this world nearly as much as he felt like he belonged in heaven.

'All the power good has is by means of the Truth.'

And in that instant, the *Truth* entered Johnny's body. His epiphany didn't feel anything like he'd supposed it would. He'd always imagined it would happen like hot energy bursting through his skin, with flames of the Holy Spirit surging skyward. Instead of trying to break his soul loose from his body, though, what he'd needed all along was to open himself up, to allow the *Truth* to enter him like a seed in the soil. In this case, it came in through his ears, via the Philosopher's voice, as if he were absorbing something pure, the very air that angels breathed.

That day, Nature entered Johnny, and Johnny became Nature.

The Philosopher cleared his throat, and then addressed Johnny personally, one Christian to another.

'And now you, my friend, must choose whether to believe, and if so, to join me in spreading the word of the New Church wherever you go.'

"I do so choose!" Johnny sang out. Never before had he heard words more in accord with his personal view of the world. It was now so obvious that he wondered how he'd missed it. The Voices that he heard were the voices of spirits, who occupied the same space as he, but in a perfected realm. He was drawn to nature, not because of its beauty or tranquility, but because that's where God was waiting for him.

The next thing Johnny knew, Mike Fink poured a mug of stout onto Johnny's head, and laughed. "Ho, thar, Chapman. Wake up. Yer talkin' in yer sleep."

Johnny emerged from his stupor totally alert and certain about what he had to do next. "I must go," he said. "The Lord's work cannot wait."

There was no time to waste. Johnny burned with the passion of revelation. He could not dither or dawdle until the keelboaters were ready to leave, nor did he wish to pollute the purity of his spiritual condition through further association with them. Dashing out of the Pittsburgh Point Brewery, he grabbed the long-eared mule's tether and hastened to the shipyard.

A refuse heap sat just beyond the docks on the waterfront, where parts, pieces, and scraps from various nautical vessels had been discarded and left for rot or rummage. Among the junk, Johnny found a half barrel that floated, a canoe that leaked just slowly enough to make bailing a navigable option, and a couple of planks that he could stretch between the two. Reusing salvaged nails and not-yet threadbare rope, Johnny assembled a craft in shallow waters.

The ferry keeper scoffed. "You ain't fixin' to float that heap, are you?"

Beaming, Johnny replied, "Not only will it float, it will *glide*."

The last thing Johnny did before disembarking was to leave the ferry keeper with instructions to stable the mule in town, and gave him payment sufficient for that service.

The ferry keeper looked left and right, and pocketed the cash.

Then, loading his cargo into the barrel and kneeling in the canoe, Johnny pushed his makeshift catamaran into the spring runoff of the Ohio River. Once in the current, he knew that he had little control over where it took him.

"But God does," a Voice assured him.

Chapter 8 - April 1805

Blennerhassett Island

Most folks who migrated into the Ohio Country dreamed of getting rich, an ambition symptomatic of "Ohio Fever," which afflicted a vast number of wishful citizens. They dreamed that if they worked hard enough and managed to save a little money, they could snatch up abundant, fertile land in Ohio on the cheap. These folks imagined that through hard labor, and a little divine providence, they could one day acquire their own magnificent estates where they'd build mansions, hire servants, and pass their days in leisure.

To some others, though, even that sounded like too much work.

Also afflicted by Ohio Fever were freebooters, lured to the wilderness in hopes of finding treasure. There might be gold, they speculated, in some hidden trove of ancient Indian fortunes. They ransacked Shawnee villages up and down the Muskingum, searching for the legendary bonanza of precious artifacts left by prehistoric mound builders. However, whispered rumors also suggested that heathen devils guarded those sites—man-eating serpents, giant spiders with Indian faces, and multi-headed monsters who would devour any white man who so much as dug the tip of a bayonet into an Indian burial ground. While the fear of being swallowed whole by a demon from hell was a powerful deterrent, still, if so much as a single golden nose ring had ever been found, every Indian mound in the country would've been flattened. The most common attitude among folks with Ohio Fever was that they were entitled to whatever they found, or took.

Despite all the people who dreamt of wealth, Johnny didn't figure he'd ever met a genuinely rich person—until he laid eyes upon the Blennerhassetts' mansion, that is. Set on the upriver side of its little island, the edifice gleamed like some European nobleman's castle, by far the largest home Johnny had ever seen. The white frontage of the mansion spanned three buildings—a lofty main residence with a pillared entrance, connected by curved walkways to two separate wings, one of which was a kitchen and the other the master's private bureau. From the moment that it came into view around the river's bend, Johnny could only stare, as if no matter how wide he opened his eyes, it still wasn't wide enough to take in so much grandeur.

He'd drifted halfway past the dock before he snapped out of it, then commenced poling frantically against the current to get back to the landing. There, Johnny disembarked and unloaded, wondering what to do next.

A maid scurried out of the kitchen wing, wrapping a shawl over her shoulders. "Stop yo' thar! Wha's yo' bus'ness?"

"I have an important delivery for Madame Blennerhassett."

"Slap mah haid if she didn't say it'd come t'day," the maid said. "Ma'am sho' got a way 'o knowin' things."

She bent over to drag the crate, but Johnny nudged her aside and lifted it himself.

"Mistah, I can't let no gen'l man t' haul his own load," she objected.

A gentleman? "I insist," he said.

Johnny hefted the crate onto his shoulder and followed the maid up the stone path to the Blennerhassetts' mansion. The sight of several negro laborers toiling, bent over in the lawns and gardens, reminded him that he was in Western Virginia—technically, the "South." The palpable loss of freedom struck him hard, like a heavy sigh.

Never in his life had Johnny passed through such an ornate doorway—solid walnut with silver knobs and hinges, set under an arched porch suspended by twin pillars. It opened on two sides into a hall with a welcoming hearth beneath a domed ceiling. While the maid dashed up the twisting staircase to fetch Madame Blennerhassett, Johnny peeked into the parlor to his right, furnished with upholstered armchairs and fine cabinetry, end tables holding alabaster vases, and the largest object in the room, a mahogany grand pianoforte. Oil paintings of pastoral scenes hung on the wall, but the largest painting, hanging in the center of the room, depicted a handsome, fair-skinned, aristocratic couple whom he presumed to be the Blennerhassetts. He stood examining the woman in the picture, how her sideways glance seemed knowing.

"How may I help you?"

Johnny turned and beheld the very likeness that had inspired the portrait.

Margaret Blennerhassett stood in a shaft of light in the threshold between the entrance and the parlor. Her auburn hair hung loose over her shoulders, curled but not unruly, lending depth to her soft features. Her darting eyes seemed curious, and her billowing, cream-colored gown enhanced the ethereal quality of her presence. "Are you the courier that I've awaited from John Young?"

Johnny recollected that when making the acquaintance of a woman of culture and status, it was customary to kiss her hand. "Yes, indeed," he said, reaching for it. "Me name is John Chapman, a sower of seeds. I would be pleased if ye chose to call me Johnny."

Margaret giggled. "Are you the one they call the Appleseed?"

"Some do so, I suppose."

"I've always believed that fruit is the food of paradise."

"I agree." He'd said that many times, but hearing it from somebody else felt validating. "The merchandise from Mr. Young is in the box next to the hearth."

With no less excitement than a child at Christmas, Margaret slid onto one knee and used a fire poker to pry the lid off the crate. She removed the topmost book and pressed it against her breast, and gasped. "Glory! This book is my calling."

"Mine, as well."

"Sir?"

Johnny had hoped to have a conversation with Madame Blennerhassett about this book, but he hadn't planned on blurting it out so abruptly. Since leaving Pittsburgh, while drifting downriver, he'd carried on long conversations with the Philosopher, but he'd uttered not a word to a flesh and blood human being. He remembered, though, that John Young had said that Madame Blennerhassett was a Reader, and it occurred to him that the two of them had some things to talk about.

"You've read this book, haven't you?" Margaret stated in the form of a question.

"I did not so much read it, as it was read to me."

"By whom?"

"By the Philosopher, Dr. Swedenborg himself."

"Do you mean by the angelic spirit of Dr. Swedenborg?"

"I reckon so."

Margaret blinked as she looked him up and down, and nodded as if verifying something to herself. "Won't you walk with me in the garden?" She extended her forearm.

He figured it for a welcoming gesture, and thought he should take it. While traversing the walkway, he noticed movement by a window in the east building.

Inside, two men stood in front of a desk, examining some document—a map, perhaps—and they were too engrossed in their activity to observe the passersby.

"That would be my husband, Harman, and a distinguished gentleman from Washington, Mr. Aaron Burr," Margaret explained. "Those men... they have such ambitious plans."

Johnny waited for her to elaborate, but she shook her head, as if to scatter her thoughts, and shut her eyes. With eyes closed, she kept walking.

This was disconcerting to Johnny, for she began veering into the path of a muddy puddle.

One step short of landing in the muck, just before Johnny would have drawn back on her arm, she stopped and held her foot in the air. Slowly, she lowered her foot, toe-first, and re-directed around the puddle—all without once opening her eyes.

They left the path and strolled through grass so lush that Johnny couldn't wait to take off his shoes and dig his toes into it. They moved in the direction of a wooden bench beneath a drooping willow.

Margaret sat and raised her forehead so that her lashes could catch the breeze, and in this manner, parted her eyelids. "When you trust the angels to lead, you can never take a wrong turn. You do understand, don't you Mr. Chapman?"

"Johnny, if ye please, ma'am. And yes, I do tend to wander a far way, and while I cannot say that I always know just whereabouts I am, I have never felt like I was lost."

"Why so?"

"On the cause that even in the wilds, far from any other human being, I have never once felt that if I called out, I would not be answered."

"By whom?"

"Voices, ma'am. Whenever I listen with a clear mind, I hear them—some familiar, some not, but all of them friendly and helpful, with good advice for me to follow. I didn't realize for a long time that only I, meself, can hear them."

Margaret placed one hand on each side of Johnny's head, the pulses in her fingertips synching to that in his temples. "You are truly one of us, Johnny! Rejoice!"

"I do rejoice, almost every day," he said. "But I still have questions. First of all, who do ye mean when ye say *us*?"

"Why, we Readers, of course. We have all been touched with some special blessing by the Lord. The greatest among us, our founder Emmanuel Swedenborg, was able to see and speak with angels, and to move freely through heaven and hell. He was chosen by God to bear witness to the Last Judgment and Second Coming of Jesus Christ, and to found a New Church to spread the news of what he'd learned. Likewise, some of us who have been called to be Readers have special sensitivities that distinguish us as carriers of a deeper faith. Some have divine visions. Others are prone to falling into revelatory trances. Yours is the gift of hearing heavenly Voices. Myself, I can feel the presence of spirits, who walk right into my body just as if they were putting me on like a coat. Sometimes they sweep my senses out from under me, into their eternal realm. It feels like...."

"Like joy?"

"Precisely!" She picked up a dandelion puffball and blew its spores into the air. "Would you do me a kindness before you leave this island, Johnny? I'd be most grateful if you'd plant an orchard. To me, this island is as near to Eden as any place on Earth, so it makes only makes sense that apple trees should grow here."

Johnny reached into his pocket and produced a handful of seeds. "I am ready to start right now. Just show me the place, ma'am."

"Follow me. The spirits have shown me a most delicious spot for an orchard."

Johnny wasted no time tilling and planting his orchard on Margaret Blennerhassett's island. It felt good to get dirty again. When he took off the wool jacket that he'd worn since he accepted the gift from the United Believers, he felt remarkably lighter. He rolled up his shirtsleeves, flexed his forearms, then opened and closed his fists to restore their vigor. Best of all, he removed the buckled shoes that had confined his feet for three months, pulled off his stockings, and groped his toes into fresh soil.

Soon he was on his hands and knees, peeling aside sod, turning the ground with a flat stone and raking it with his fingers. The spot that Margaret's spirits had selected was indeed perfect for a nursery—rich soil, clear drainage, ample sunlight, and adjacent to a grove of flowering hyacinths for added beauty. Johnny inserted each seed into its own damp nest, adding a prayer, a handful of crumbled leaves for compost, and gently patting the soil above it.

While he worked, Margaret sat in tall grass, making a daisy chain while answering Johnny's questions.

"How was it that ye became a Reader in the New Church of Swedenborg?" he asked.

"It's often painful for me to recall my life before I discovered Swedenborg. As a child, my parents worried about me. They said I lived in my dreams, and that I was given to sudden spells and flights of fancy, where I'd speak in strange voices and say things they didn't understand. In my native land, I belonged to the Church of England. When I was sixteen, the vicar in our parish gave me the Book of Common Prayer, and told me that if I prayed every prayer, I would earn some grace, which would cure me of my capriciousness. Alas, I did as he beckoned, but I was unchanged. To the dismay of my family and the church, my reveries became more frequent and profound. They considered sending me to live with a community of Carmelite nuns, but I escaped."

"Escaped? How so?"

"During those times, the only person to offer any sympathy to me was my dear, dear Harman. Though he was my uncle, he cherished me as a woman. He said my visions made me special, and that I was 'touched by a miracle.' We were deeply enamored of each other, but forbidden to marry in England because of our relation, so we plotted to start a new life together in America. Harman was hier to the Castle Conway in Ireland. In secret, he sold his estate and, with the profits, we sailed for America. Harman had friends and business associates in Philadelphia, so we settled there, in a red brick home on Quince Street. It was liberating, to be surrounded by so many creative and enlightened people. We entertained often. Harman loved to gather with his fellows and talk politics until all hours of the night. One of those gentlemen was John Young."

"John Young!" Johnny perked up, excited to have finally gotten an answer to his question. "Surely, the Lord guided each of us to make his acquaintance. 'Tis Mister Young who did me the service of introducing me to Swedenborg's great book, *The True Christian Religion*."

"Mister Young recognized that I had a calling, but did not yet understand its purpose. He invited me to my first Reading. As soon as I began reciting its words, I embraced the book, *Heaven and Hell*, as if it had been written only for me. Finally, the nature of my mystical experiences made sense. All my life, I'd felt as though my soul and body were rather loosely coupled. Now, I understood why."

Still on his hands and knees, Johnny kept digging while he told the story of how he achieved a similar epiphany while dozing in the Pittsburgh Point Brewery. At the story's conclusion, he looked over his shoulder at Margaret and said, "And now I me-self have determined to practice the faith of the New Church, and to share this faith with others where'er I go."

"I applaud your conviction. You are, indeed, a worthy vehicle for Swedenborg. May you plant seeds of faith as well as of fruit. This land will honor you for doing both."

"May I inquire why you left the company of your friends and moved so far, to such an uncivilized land?"

Magaret tied the daisy chain around her neck, drew a deep breath, and spoke as she let it go. "Moving to this tiny island was Harman's wish. He's possessed of an ardor and energy for revolution. Just as he opposed the government in Ireland, and in England, so has he found the political system of America to be corrupt beyond repair. He believes that here, where most people live beyond the reach of any state, he has an opportunity, indeed, an obligation to work to establish a civil and benevolent rule, for the good of all citizens. I suppose that's the reason that Mister Burr is here. I leave the men to their schemes, for politics bores me.

"Mind you, I do not protest. All I ask from Harman is his love, which he supplies in abundance. This is a healthful place to raise our two boys. Here, I have the freedom and leisure to pursue my passions for art, poetry, and the study of New Church doctrine. Swedenborg wrote, *'Our nature after death depends on the kind of life we lead in this work.'* I have thus devoted myself to nurturing my spirit and cultivating the beauties that I hope will surrounded me in heaven. I yearn for perfect beauty."

The island looked pretty close to perfection, all right, although in his mind, Johnny flashed back to the image of slaves working in their gardens. While he hadn't thought it through entirely, it didn't make quick sense that there ought to be slaves in paradise.

"Is your husband also a Reader?"

"Harman was baptized in the New Church, but he isn't blessed with any special psychic abilities, so he exercises a more this-worldly version of the faith. I comfort myself believing that Harman's ambitions are God's will."

While Margaret had been talking, Johnny kept working, and she seemed to be fatigued on his behalf.

"Surely, you can finish tomorrow," she called in a slightly pleading voice. "In the meantime, we'd be honored if you were to dine at our table this evening."

"The honor would be mine."

"In that case, you will probably wish to wash yourself and shave your face before dinner. I'll fetch a servant to draw you a bath."

Johnny was caked with mud and figured he probably smelt rancid, too. It felt good. Still, he'd acquired enough vanity over the last couple of months to realize that he had only to pay a bit of attention to his hygiene to make himself fit to dine at a wealthy man's table. That felt better than being shunned as a vagrant, to be sure.

By his silence, and with a polite nod, he conceded.

Political news from Washington D.C. was slow to reach the Ohio Country, less because of the distance than due to the indifference of the people toward it. When news did get passed on, it had generally been distorted beyond any semblance of fact. According to various reports that Johnny had heard, Mr. Aaron Burr was either the vice-president of the United States, a mere heartbeat from the height of national power, or he was a craven coward on the run because he had shot a political rival in the back.

It was a paradox, for sure.

On one hand, Mr. Burr was traveling in luxury—his flotilla consisted of three flatboats tied together, the middle one housing his private chambers—accompanied by a retinue of uniformed soldiers, as well as two personal servants, a nurse, and a small but feisty pug dog named Merry, which nipped at Mr. Burr's heels as he walked. On the other hand, the flotilla was parked on the far side of the island, where it could not be seen by approaching river traffic, as if to both ensure secrecy and allow for a hasty departure.

It didn't quite add up to Johnny, for it conflicted with his suppositions about the moral character of men who aspired to public service.

Burr was cordial to Johnny when introduced in the Blennerhassett's dining hall. Dressed in gray trousers, a double-breasted waistcoat, and a white linen shirt with pleated cuffs and a high collar, he wore his hair waxed and brushed back so as to emphasize his prominent forehead.

As they shook hands, Burr listened as Johnny explained that he was a sower of seeds, and further queried, "So you are a horticulturist?"

"That I am," Johnny acknowledged.

"I, too, consider myself of planter of seeds," Burr continued. "They are called ideas."

"Bravo!" Harman Blennerhassett cried, elbowing between Johnny and Burr. "I trust that your ideas will bear glorious fruit."

The men chatted in the parlor on subjects about which Johnny had scant interest—the fickle nature of political fortunes, the perfidy of the Federalists, and the outrageous presumptions of President Jefferson. Harman sympathized with Burr's opinions, almost before he spoke them. Burr, in turn, flattered Harman as "a brave and true friend of freedom." The whole time, Burr's insistent dog, Merry, repeatedly tried to hump Harman's ankles. Since Burr just laughed, Harman agreed that it was funny.

With no particular viewpoints on those matters, Johnny drifted toward Margaret, who played a baroque sonata on the pianoforte. She wasn't a very masterful musician, and Johnny steeled his face against the occasional discordant note that she plunked without seeming to notice. Still, he preferred it to talking about politics.

At length, they were summoned to the dining room by the same maid who had met Johnny at the dock. Much more tidily attired now, she wore a floor-length dress, a clean apron with an embroidered bib, and a scarf covering her hair.

Inside the dining room, one corner of the long table was set, with four black and gold painted chairs situated in front of settings of Queen's ware china and silver flatware, offset by a blue porcelain vase filled with spring irises. A dressed goose roast crowned the center of the table, flanked by bowls of mashed potatoes and boiled cabbage, a boat of rich gravy, and a loaf of freshly baked cornbread.

A male servant wearing a cashmere tweed suit pulled back the guests' chairs for them.

Also scampering into the room was the little dog Merry, which Burr informed the servant should be provisioned with a small bowl for table scraps.

Only Johnny seemed to have noticed how the servant rolled his eyes upon being thus instructed.

The maid carved slices of the bird and served Burr, then Harman, but before she could cut another piece, Johnny stayed her hand and proffered that he would be content to eat just the bread and vegetables.

"What d'yo say?" she asked.

At this, Margaret, herself an aspiring vegetarian, warranted that she, too, wished to refrain from eating meat on that evening.

Burr trimmed a piece of the roast and forked it into his mouth while handing the grizzle to Merry. "My opinion is that religion feeds a man's soul, but *meat* feeds a man's body," he proclaimed.

Harman, waving a gravy-soaked chunk of goose meat, added, "Oh, I agree, sir. God would not have provided such ample game had He not intended for us to consume it. Sometimes, though, for health purposes, my wife likes to fast. Isn't that the case, my dear?"

"I suppose," Margaret relented.

"To each his own," Johnny said, and shrugged.

Burr primed the conversation by asking questions of the Blennerhassetts. "How did you build your fortunes? What are your current business enterprises?"

Flattered by being asked to speak of himself, Harman recounted his and Margaret's trials against repressive authorities in their homeland, their perilous voyage across the Atlantic, and their vision of bringing civility and liberal values to a benighted land.

Burr chewed loudly while Harman spoke, then swallowed and cut him off. "I congratulate you for your courage, resolve, and the perspicacity to realize that this island is of strategic importance to westward migration. The next revolution will pass right by your doorstep."

"Revolution?" Margaret interrupted. "Will it be... noisy?"

Harman kicked his wife under the table. "We have always regarded ourselves as revolutionaries, haven't we, dear?"

"Of course you have," Burr reassured him. "Already, it has begun. Daily, cargo boats pass bound all the way to New Orleans. Thus it happens that I am going to that bayou city, so that I might assess political conditions there. The south is ripe for revolution, with the Creoles feeling betrayed by the Louisiana Purchase, the Spanish in West Florida looking to spread their territory, and lawless renegades populating the farther lands of Texas and Mexico. There is turmoil, but also enormous opportunity for a sufficiently capable statesman to fashion a new empire bordered by the Gulf of Mexico."

Harman announced, "You are that very man, Mr. Burr!"

Burr struck a pose with his jaw square and his brow elevated, like a bust of Julius Caesar. "Your words, not mine," he offered magnanimously.

Johnny set down his fork; he wasn't quite sure, but it sounded like they were talking about starting a war. People who stood to gain the most from war were also those who risked the least. Regular folks, whose lives were already hard enough, always bore the burdens. Most folks were loath to start a fight, but they could easily be persuaded that their enemies were unscrupulous enough to attack without provocation, so the prudent thing to do was to strike first, even though that made them as bad as their enemies. The more a person tried to make sense of it, the more circuitous the logic of war became.

While looking at a fork full of mashed potatoes, Johnny heard, whispering into his ear, the voice of the Philosopher:

> *'There were certain spirits who, while living in the world, did not believe the Lord to be the God of heaven. For this reason, they were permitted to wander about and inquire wherever they wished whether there were any other heaven than the heaven of the Lord. As they were told that heaven does not consist in such things, they became indignant, and wished for a heaven where they could lord it over others, and be eminent in glory like that in the world.'*

While listening to the Philosopher, Johnny watched Burr's lips moving. He hadn't heard a word the man said, but felt compelled to comment nonetheless. "If ye want to create a new empire, I think that ye could do a whole lot worse than to begin by planting apple trees."

Burr had to stop chewing to think through what Johnny had said.

Harman tried to explain. "Mr. Chapman foresees a vast agricultural empire based upon apple cultivation, similar to that which exists in the South with cotton."

Burr swallowed, then murmured, "Ah, so... I see."

"No, 'tis not exactly what I'm a-talking about," Johnny said. "I envision the entire Ohio Country more like a garden than a plantation. Every family will plant an apple tree on its property. As the tree grows, so does the family, so does the community, so does the territory, and so does the nation. Everybody has an equal share in everybody else's well-being. For example, every autumn, when the fruit is ripe for picking, neighbors will work side-by-side to pluck the blessings of another gainful season. Each person shares equally in the beauty and the bounty. That is the key to keeping peace in any empire, so says I."

Burr twirled his fork. "Are you serious, sir? Peace is never achieved so simply."

From his pocket, Johnny unearthed a handful of seeds. "Take these, Mister Burr. If ye please, plant them in New Orleans, when ye get there. Ye may be surprised by what grows."

The joke had apparently gone quite far enough for Burr. "Apples are poor sustenance for a nation. They can be bitter and sour. Feed them to the people, and I promise you that they will revolt."

"I disagree, sir."

"Leave the politics to me." Burr's nostrils flared as he snorted. "And I'll leave you to plant your trees."

"Some more wine?" Harman broke in.

Returning his attention to the fork, Burr looked at the morsel of goose skewed thereon as if it suddenly seemed unappetizing to him. He flicked it into Merry's bowl, and seemed surprised that the dog did not pounce upon it immediately. "Merry! Where are you?" he called out.

Everybody looked under the table at once.

Burr's furry little pug lay curled around Johnny's ankle, its head upon his foot, sound asleep.

That night, Johnny declined the Blennerhassett's kind offer to sleep in a guest room, explaining that he preferred to repose under the stars on the riverbank. In truth, he knew there'd be no sleeping on that night. By the time the servants had cleared the dinner table, Johnny's head swarmed with a melee of inner Voices, like the clamor of an anxious crowd, and he needed space and privacy to sort them out.

He couldn't be sure, but maybe this is what a prophecy sounded like—urgent, but unclear.

It helped to keep busy, so Johnny resumed his work on the orchard under the moon. He worked at a faster than normal pace, which had the opposite effect of calming him. Blood rushed to his head, so that the sound of his heartbeat provided a rhythm to the babble of the Voices. All at once, a thought bubble burst in his brain and sent waves throbbing through his sinuses and ear canals. When the sensation subsided, he felt literally empty-headed, as though nothing but air remained in there.

From that void emanated the Voice of the Philosopher. Swedenborg told Johnny that many angels and spirits were anxious to meet him. In heaven, however, astral beings communicated by thought, so by attempting to broadcast their messages to him, they had unintentionally overwhelmed his mortal capacities. Thus, the Philosopher had decided to facilitate the dialog in a manner appropriate to Johnny's limited abilities, by introducing them one at a time.

The first person Swedenborg presented was the prophet Jeremiah, who repeated to Johnny the same thing that God Almighty had said to him:

'Get thyself ready!'

Next, Johnny talked awhile with Job, who reminded him that hardship was inflicted upon a man in direct proportion to his faith.

"True," Johnny agreed, "the Lord giveth and the Lord taketh away, but it likewise follows that if a man keeps nothing, he can't lose anything."

Next, John the Baptist reassured Johnny:

'The authorities believed that I was crazy, too, because I wore clothing of camel hair and ate locusts and wild honey.'

A new Voice, speaking with a slight lisp, introduced himself as Giovanni Francesco. That name meant nothing to Johnny until, with a sly inflection, the Voice added:

'But you perhaps know me better as Francis of Assisi.'

"My favorite saint!"

'Preach always, but speak only when necessary.'

Johnny made no reply, thereby proving that he got the point.

One after another, a procession of divine beings, some familiar names and some less so, addressed Johnny over that long night. A hermit named Enoch from Canaan joked that in life he didn't speak a word to another person for sixty years, but in heaven he was married and sang in the heavenly choir. Ingrid, a pilgrim wife who'd come to America on the Mayflower, said that when they landed at Plymouth Rock, Moses himself was waiting there to greet them.

It shocked Johnny when old Dan McQuay shouted out, "Halloooo, Johnny," because he hadn't known he was dead. Although he felt like he ought to say he was sorry to learn of Dan's passing, that didn't seem quite right, seeing as how his friend was now in heaven.

And there were others....

The pleasant filibuster continued for so long that when a moment of silence finally arrived, he figured it was over. Suddenly, though, a real sound from this world rose from the far side of the island—a piercing howl. He first though it might be a wolf, but it sounded more like a human wailing, part in pain and part in defiance. No matter in which direction Johnny turned, the sound was always behind him, but getting closer.

Finally, it resolved into a screeching cry.

'I am the Door. Meet me on the other side.'

Johnny couldn't remember the last time he'd been truly afraid of anything, but that voice spooked him.

All the while, he'd kept working, not once pausing, until the last Voice, his mother's, came to him with the first mellowing of dawn:

'It is time,'

"It is time," Johnny repeated. He knew what he had to do.

Overnight, a fog had draped the river, so that he couldn't see the other side. He skipped a stone on the water and watched it disappear after three hops. Johnny knew that Ohio was just over yonder, but he could imagine that water might just as well be the River Jordan.

"Sir? Are yo' feelin' awraght?"

The male servant who had attended their table the night before was standing next to Johnny. In contrast to the neat tweed suit he'd sported for the dinner party, he now wore a pair of tattered trousers of hemp cloth, a coarse shirt with cutoff sleeves, and a pair of brogan boots with his toes showing through.

An inspiration seized Johnny. "Friend, take off ye clothing!"

"Say huh?"

"I will trade me own clothes for yours. 'Tis a fair swap. These are fine clothes, but they are not suited for the work I must do."

"It wouldn't be raght fo' me t' take no white man's britches."

To expedite the exchange, Johnny began to strip. "'Tis as right as can be." He chuckled when he kicked off his pants.

With a naked white man standing in front of him, the servant looked worried, as if he might get into some kind of trouble over this. He seemed even more disconcerted when Johnny kept talking.

"Apologize to Madame Blennerhassett that I am leaving without saying fare-thee-well, but tell her I finished me planting and decided to get an early start. I'm headed far into Ohio. Tell her I shall return to tend this orchard next year, and I look forward to future conversations with her. Will ye tell her these things?"

"Awraght."

The raft on which Johnny had floated to the island remained tied to the dock, half full of water but solid enough to make one last river crossing. He tossed in the servant's clothes and his sacks of seeds, as well as a single copy of *The True Christian Religion*, and pulled the boat into the shallows. He waded as far as he could, then began swimming.

"God be with ye," he called out.

In midstream, where the fog hung so heavy that he could see neither side, Johnny ducked his head under the water. Then came a familiar Voice.

'I baptize thee, friend, in the name of God.'

Johnny wept, for it wasn't every fellow in Ohio who could say that he'd been baptized by John the Baptist himself.

Chapter 9 – July 1805

Newark, Ohio

Every morning that week, Otto Blubaugh arrived at the stable to find that, overnight, somebody had nailed a different notice on top of the one that had been nailed to the flogging tree the previous day. It was like a game of child's tag. On Monday, Mrs. Bonita Danner, the wife of Samuel Danner, who operated the mill at Ramp Creek, posted an announcement that the renowned Methodist preacher, Otis McDonald, would lead an open-air church service on the Newark town commons next Sunday. Overnight, though, some anonymous vandal had nailed another notice on top the first. This one read: "Horse Race Sunday. Prize for Winner."

Mrs. Danner, upon discovering that her handbill had been vandalized, responded by hammering another directly on top of the offending notice. Come the next morning, though, it was covered again by another that read: "Horse Race Sunday. Swell Prize for Winner." This pattern repeated every day that week, and each time the magnitude of the promised jackpot increased, from "Swell Prize" to "Big Prize" to "Huge Prize" to "Rip-Roaring Prize" to "Richest Prize Ever in Ohio." Consequently, Mrs. Danner successively described the preacher as "The Honorable Otis McDonald," "The Righteous Otis McDonald," "The Blessed Otis McDonald," "The Venerable Otis McDonald," and finally, "His Holiness Otis McDonald."

Otto had heard rumors that it was Samuel Danner himself sneaking out at night to upstage his wife's daily handiwork.

On the streets, though, the citizens of Newark chattered almost exclusively about the horse race. As a stable hand, Otto heard it coming and going. Folks came from as far as Zanesville and Lancaster to wager on the contest. By the end of the week, there were so many horses from out-of-town in the livery that Otto could barely shovel fast enough to keep up with all the turds dropping. He enjoyed the company of horses, though—some folks joked that he spoke their language better than English. Someday, he hoped to save enough money to buy a horse of his own.

Jim Craig had enlisted Otto to jockey his horse, a rambunctious two-year-old quarter horse named Horny. Craig, who hailed from parts unknown, claimed that he was "jest passin' throo," but decided to stick around awhile when he learned about the great race. He boasted that he himself would ride Horny to victory, but Otto, observing how temperamental it became whenever Jim Craig hopped onto his back, couldn't bear the animal's pain.

"Let me ride yahr Horny horse, Mist'r Craig," Otto had pleaded, "Ah'll do it fer free, and yahr'll can keep the prize, too."

Jim Craig had congratulated Otto for being such an ambitious young man, and accepted his offer upon the sole condition that they seal the deal over drinks, which, he said, business etiquette dictated that Otto should buy. Since Otto had declined to drink, on the grounds that he had too much work to do, Jim Craig drank his share, too.

On Saturday morning before the race, Otto arrived at the stable and found three men hunkered asleep in the straw. One was Jim Craig, with an empty bottle cradled against his chest. Next to him, a stranger lay flat on his back, with both hands covering his crotch. The third man, dressed in the same gray shirt and brown jacket as the other, was a negro about Otto's age, hugging a guitar while asleep.

The guitarist stirred first. "Hey, yo." He waved to Otto, then rolled over and sang into his partner's ear, "*Get on up!*"

The man grumbled and scratched his groin.

"*Yo, Mister Rope, get on up! Time to do yore thing!*"

"Heck, cain't yer never just speak in a normal voice?" the man protested. He opened his eyes to see Otto standing over him with a pitchfork in hand, and jumped onto his feet. "Where's my horse?" he cried, looking around.

"Weren't no horse nowhar near whar yahr'll was sleepin'," Otto replied, a bit insulted. After all, these men *were* trespassers and ought to show more respect.

"I gotta git my horse."

In the meantime, the other man wandered into the woods behind the stable, calling sweetly, "Mojo?" while strumming his guitar. Within a couple of minutes, he returned tethering a spotted paint horse which seemed to have a mischievous smirk on its upper lip.

"Curses and damnation, Heck, stop yer tomfoolery. Tha' horse is our meal ticket."

"I reckon yahr here fer the derby," Otto said.

"Is there any oth'r reason fer bein' in this here backwater town?" The man rose, steadying himself against the wall. "My name is Philander Rope, the owner of tha' fine horse, Mojo, an' tha's my rider, named o' Heck. I don't much mean to brag, but, but yer might as well hand over the prize money now, 'cause we aim to win it all."

"Don't be so plumb cocksure."

"I don't mean no insult. I jest state plain facts. I bought this horse in Pittsburgh fer the cost o' twenty poplar armchairs, an' e'er since me 'n Heck 've been travellin' the horse race circuit far and yonder, an' we've been winnin' more oftener than not."

"Ah maght jest could have somethin' to say 'bout tha'!" Otto snapped. "On the 'cause that ah'm ridin' Mist'r Jim Craig's horse in tha' same race, an' we don' gallop second to nobody."

"*That Jim Craig?*" Mister Rope asked, pointing at the man still slumbering in the hay. "He can't hold his liquor. Anyhow, we'll settle the issue come Sunday. So, how do I get registered fer the race?"

"The entry fee is twenty-five cents. Thar's a Mist'r John Chapman who's keepin' all the money 'til race day."

"John Chapman? Be he the same fool what plants apple trees?"

"One 'n' the same. He maght be a sure fool, but he's the only man what everybody agrees can be trusted with the money."

"Where can I find Chapman?"

"Ain't no way to find him. If he could be found, he'd git robbed. But he'll be 'round by an' by."

Otto bent over the horse trough and scooped a bucketful of water. "Now, if'n yahr'll don' mind, ah got work to do."

Reverend James Copus was not optimistic about his prospects for winning converts in Newark. Situated at the edge of civilization in the interior of the Ohio Country, the town attracted motley vagrants, outcasts, mercenaries, charlatans, refugees, and fugitives. Maybe forty families lived in the settlement at the confluence of two forks of the Licking River, but numerous rascals occupied temporary huts built upstream from town, close enough so they could ride to Black's Tavern, but far enough to ensure privacy for whoring, distilling, fighting, or burying their dead. Consequently, Newark's reputation for bawdiness and hooliganism distinguished it even by the rough standards of the frontier.

For example, Copus had heard the story about a Newark marksmanship contest where participants were *required* to drink a dram of whiskey before every shot, and which ended in a brawl when Elias Smucker hit a target dead-center, but on the wrong tree, then claimed that he should be declared the winner because it was a more difficult shot. Another story involved a pig roast at the Easter celebration on the town square, which got out of hand when John Larabee and Richard Pitzer, both so full of cider that they sloshed when they walked, decided that the swine would taste better if marinated in a salty and fruity broth. So they pissed onto it as it roasted, and from there, of course, a brawl broke out.

Yep, Reverend Copus figured that convincing the citizens of Newark with the good news about the gospel of Jesus Christ was going to be difficult. What would start as a sermon could just as easily end in another brawl.

Despite those concerns, his partner Otis McDonald vowed, "We shall march boldly into the den of iniquity!"

That was easy for him to say. He had the simpler task of just showing up on Sunday morning and leading a church service. Copus had to do the advance work of mingling with the citizens to drum up some religious fervor. That was a hard sell under any circumstances, but especially when there was a horse race scheduled for the same day. Although that was arguably a sacrilege, Copus knew he'd get nowhere by pressing the point.

Thus, with his Bible under his arm, Reverend Copus marched into the "den of iniquity"—Black's Tavern.

At midday, thirsty legions of horse racing enthusiasts already packed the establishment. The revelers all had their favorite horses, and they shouted over each other arguing why theirs would win, claiming all other horses weren't good for anything but dog food.

Jim Craig, recovered from his morning hangover, raised a mug of hard cider and boasted, "My boy Blumbaugh'll ride Horny hard an' fas' straight to the finish line! Ain't no other nag in the race worth ev'n mountin' or whippin'."

A newcomer named Dan Sapp stomped his feet and retorted, "I got the winner, and she's a prime filly named Lulu. She'll finish quicker than a drunk keelboater with a high class whore."

"Gentlemen, place your bets right here," the proprietor, Joseph Black, called out.

Reverend Copus sensed that this was an inauspicious time to bear witness to the glory of Christ.

While he surveyed the premises, a cheerful bar wench accosted him with a boisterous, "Hallooo there, reverend. D'you 'member me?"

Reverend Copus considered it bad news whenever a strange woman—a bar wench, no less—accosted him in that way. This lass was girlish, with bright eyes and an infectious smile, but she also moved in the breezy, seductive manner by which bar wenches earned big tips. She did look familiar, but he was loath to think too hard about why.

"I'm Millie Blubaugh. Back at that camp meetin' in Chillicothe, you done gave a blessin' on my baby. 'Member?"

"Why, yes, I do. Pray, how is your child?"

"Oh, the poor l'il baby never took one breath in this world."

Reverend Copus felt his face go numb. "I... I'm so... sorry, my dear."

"I cried and cried, but no woman can 'xpect that *every* baby born in this country will live. My Otto and me can make some more children, in our own time."

"Still, I am sorry."

"Ain't no need, Reverend. 'Tweren't your blessin' that was at fault." Millie put her hand on his shoulder. "Are you here to do some preachin'?"

Reverend Copus was grateful for the opportunity to get back onto script. "Yes. Have you heard that there's to be a church service on Sunday?"

"Oh, I done heard, all right. But what 'bout the race? Ain't no man that will miss a horse race for a church service." Millie cupped her mouth and whispered. "My Otto is ridin' in the race. Could you maybe say a prayer for him?"

"Well, that wouldn't be..."

"Fair?"

Reverend Copus was going to say that it wouldn't be *appropriate*, but he was flattered that Millie thought so highly of his powers.

"However, I will pray for his well-being," the Reverend consented.

"Thankee. Now, what can I getcha for drink?"

Reverend Copus ordered a glass of cider, reasoning that if he had a drink in hand, it'd be easier to strike up conversation with folks. Unlike most preachers who spoke in declarative sentences—it is written, the Lord sayeth, thou shall not, etc.—Copus had more success mixing with people by asking easy questions.

"What brings you to Newark?" he asked several folks.

Nearly everybody responded, "The horse race, of course," then elaborated about which horse they preferred, how much money they had at stake, and what they'd do if the Lord blessed them by hitting the jackpot.

Reverend Copus suggested they pray together, for he knew that most folks dared not offend God by refusing prayer. Copus counted on everybody believing in God, even if they occasionally forgot that they did.

As the afternoon wore on, more and more folks kept coming into Black's Tavern, but nobody ever seemed to leave. People waited in a line that stretched out the door to place bets with Joseph Black. He wrote down their wagers, counted their money, gave them their receipts, and then dropped the cash into a mush pot on top of the bar.

Judging by the size of the pile of bills, Copus estimated that the purse easily exceeded any amount of tithes that he and Otis McDonald had ever gathered. The reverend was tempted to stake a small amount of his own funds on a particular pony about which he had a hunch. That might be a conflict of interest, he supposed, but the more that he thought about it, the less wrong it seemed.

Around dinner time, when the tavern was so full that it didn't seem like there was room for one more person, the doors swung open and a voice shouted above the din, "Hello, friends and fellow sinners. I meself have arrived, bringing fresh news straight from heaven!"

It was Chapman, the Appleseed—or Johnny, as the reverend recollected the man preferred.

"Hey, Mister Appleseed," Elias Smucker snorted. "What'd God say to ya'll to-day?"

Johnny held a large book above his head, opened it with a flourish, and began tearing out random pages and handing them to people.

"'Tis all written here, friends. Every word direct from angels' mouths."

At every table, folks heartily greeted Johnny. Everybody wanted to buy him a drink, but he refused, explaining that he was too busy.

"What's yer hurry?" John Larrabee challenged him.

"I have much to do with the time that God has allotted me in this life," Johnny replied, tearing another page from the book and giving it to him.

Richard Pitzer laughed and said, "Yah can do God's work fer the both of us, an' ah'll do all the drinkin' fer both of us."

"I am a-drinking from God's everlasting cup!" Johnny testified.

"Wha's in that thar cup? Beer, cider, whiskey, or wine?"

Johnny mimed as if drinking from an invisible bottle.

"Why, the most intoxicating beverage of all—the blood of Jesus Christ!"

That inspired a chorus of chortles and hee-haws. The harder they laughed, though, the more people extended their hands to receive the pages that Johnny was now distributing as fast as he could tear them out of the book.

Reverend Copus nudged through the crowd to meet Johnny, who, seeing him, whistled and said, "Well, how-dee-doo, Reverend Copus. Are ye in town for the race?"

"Uh, no sir."

"Just having a drink or two, then, are ye?"

Reverend Copus disliked having his tactic of asking questions turned back upon him.

Johnny continued. "This is not a bad gang of folks here, although I do suspect that most of them are bound for eternal hell. Only the Lord can say. But I do believe that any soul can be turned."

"That is the truth."

"The Truth, indeed, is hard to find. I say that a man is more likely to stumble over it by mistake than if he searches for it his whole life. God's plan is mysterious like that. Do ye not agree?"

"I reckon so...."

"We see things alike, reverend," Johnny said. He took the corner of a page in his book and snapped it out crisply.

"Read this page. The words come some straight from heaven."

Reverend Copus tilted his head to read the title on the book's spine, *The True Christian Religion*. He had never heard of such a book, although it seemed like he should've. Johnny handed him the page facing forward, so when he took it, he started reading:

> *"The natural man is not capable of any perception of God, but only of the world and adapting this to himself. Consequently, it is among the canons of the Christian Church that the natural man is opposed to the spiritual, and that they contend against each other...."*

Revered Copus thought those words pretty accurately described the present scene inside of Black's Tavern. "Thank you," he said. He wanted to know more, but was cautious about inviting further discussion on the subject.

"Ye are most welcome, sir." Johnny closed the book. "But, if ye don't mind me asking.... If ye are not here for the race, why *are* ye here?"

"To preach, of course. Have you not heard? There will be an open-air Methodist church service on the town square, Sunday afternoon."

"Sunday afternoon?" Johnny repeated quizzically. "During the race?"

"Sunday *is* the Lord's Day, after all."

"But the whole town will be at the earthworks racetrack."

"Alas, I do fear that it will be difficult to sway some people from their gambling and debauchery."

Johnny's eyes burst with sudden insight. "I see no reason why ye could not combine a race and a church service, all at once."

Upon first thought, Reverend Copus was not as offended by that remark as he figured he should be, so he indulged himself to think about it some more.

Joseph Black interrupted the two by calling Johnny over to where he was counting the money.

"There's our banker, now," Black said, dumping all the cash and receipts into the mush pot in front of him. "Mister Chapman, this here pot contains th'entire kitty for the morrow's race. Bein' as how yah'll've been elected the keeper of the funds, I do hereby give everything o'er to yah. But be warned, if so much as one fippenny goes missin', yah'll git murdered in ten different ways."

Johnny laughed. "This money is as safe with me as with Jesus Christ himself." With that, he emptied the cash into his kerchief, knotted it and tied it to his walking stick, then put the empty mush pot upon his head and departed via the back door.

Reverend Otis McDonald pitched a venon-spitting conniption when he learned that there was going to be a horse race concurrent with his sermon. "Blasphemers and infidels!" he raged. "A plague of gnats and locusts upon them!"

"Perhaps we should pray for them," Reverend Copus hazarded.

"Bah. 'Tis the same as when Moses asked of God in the burning bush, '*What shall I do unto this people? They be almost ready to stone me?*' Do you recall, Mr. Copus, how the Lord answered Moses?"

"I do not."

"You should! His Holiest God Almighty answered Moses, *'Go before the people, and take in thy hand the rod wherewith thou didst strike the river.'* I do not have a rod, but I have my whip, and I shall snap it as if lashing Satan himself. Let those venal sinners flock to their horse race, if they value eternal life so little. They are gambling with their very souls!"

The men talked on the porch outside of Samuel and Bonita Danner's cabin, where they had invited Reverend McDonald to spend the night. Mrs. Danner had insisted it was the least that Christian hospitality required, since all the boarding rooms in the town were occupied. There was only room for one person, though, so McDonald, as the senior exhorter of the two, asserted his priority. When he bade farewell to Copus that evening, he wished him a restful night's sleep, without bothering to ask where, exactly, he was going to take his repose.

There being no other doors open to him so late, Copus returned to Black's Tavern. At that hour, on a day when everybody had started drinking early, the establishment's only remaining patrons were passed out, except, every few minutes, when one or another would revive long enough to take another sip of their drink, then pass out again. He sat at the bar and remembered what it was like to live that way, and debated with himself.

What good is free will, if everything that you do is wrong?

"Rum?" Joseph Black asked, waving an empty glass.

Copus downed the drink in one swallow, and in that moment, he felt at peace, as if he'd been forgiven for something that he hadn't known he'd done. He recollected something that Appleseed had said to him earlier that day, as well as the words of Scripture that Otis McDonald had just quoted: *Go before the people.* That gave him an idea, which might have been divinely inspired—who could say not?

"Mr. Black," Reverend Copus said, "Do you think that God allows horse racing in heaven?"

Joseph Black was skilled in ignoring drunks, but something about that question, coming from a man of faith, intrigued him. "I don't see what harm it could be? It'd be jus' fer sport, right? I suspect that e'en angels like recreation."

"I agree," Copus decided. "It would, in fact, glorify God, don't you think? Listen, tomorrow, let's put on a horse race that will please God Himself."

In advance of the race, workers had cleared and leveled the quarter-mile horse racing track in Newark. A circular earthen mound surrounded the park, which, according to popular lore, was the ring of debris around a hole in the ground that, in ancient times, marked the entrance to the underworld, where half-human, half-wolf Shawnee monsters dwelt in darkness and devoured each other's young. Occasionally, folks still worried that racing horses upon a bedeviled landscape risked provoking the hungry damned. Other than that, though, it was a flat, green prairie, where racing spectators could sit anywhere along the perimeter and have an unobstructed view of the entire course. Until somebody actually saw one of those baby-eating gargoyles, the races would continue. Besides, by the night before the big race, so many fans gathered at the site that they figured they had the demons outnumbered.

Come dawn, the grounds looked something like a battlefield, with bodies strewn among a field of debauched wreckage.

Reverend Copus cringed, reflecting to himself that an Indian curse could not have done more damage. "I'll make some coffee," he said to Joseph Black. "It will help get folks onto their feet."

Black snapped off a coneflower blossom. "Mix some of these in wit' the grounds. It'll purge their guts good as new."

Reverend Copus complied, even though he was none too certain that he wanted to see what would happen if these ruffians felt an urge to purge their guts all at once. After thinking about it all night, he didn't feel entirely right about what he was doing, but still more right than wrong. After riding the Ohio circuit with Reverend Otis McDonald for three years, he knew that no matter how he explained what he was doing, McDonald would scream "Judas!" and threaten him with an eternal damnation, where goat-headed harpies would flay him with red hot meat hooks. There could be no peace between them in separation, so it was best that they split, without goodbyes. Reverend Copus had made up his mind that, for once, he was going to preach *to* the people, rather than *at* the people.

The riders and their horses for the day's event arrived well before the scheduled starting pistol. The late registration of Mister Rope's horse, Mojo, resulted in a field of nine. Since the original plan had been to sponsor a series of two-horse match races leading to a final pairing, the race organizers labored to recalculate the seedings to accommodate an odd number.

"Cain't we git another horse?" Joseph Black lamented, "to make it an e'en number?"

That appeal failing, they eventually decided to run three separate three-horse heats, with the winners galloping against each other for the grand prize. This alteration of plans also triggered a flurry of late betting, so Black turned over a barrel and used that as his desktop for conducting transactions. A line formed in front of him.

At about that time, Johnny Appleseed appeared, strolling along the rim of the Indian mound, stepping gingerly over slumbering bodies in his path. He cut to the front of the betting line and presented himself to Joseph Black, who remarked, "I was gettin' ready to send out a posse to fetch yah."

Johnny laughed, untied his kerchief, and delivered the purse money to Black, along with his personal guarantee that every last red cent of it was accounted for. Then Johnny took a straw whisk broom out of the kerchief and asked, "Do ye mind if I tidy up the track a wee bit?"

Joseph Black chortled, "I don't care if yer lick it clean."

"That will not be necessary. This small broom will suffice."

And Johnny set about sweeping pebbles off the entire quarter-mile length of the dirt track, so that none of the horses might land upon one and twist a leg.

Watching Johnny work prompted Reverend Copus into action. As per the agreement that he and Joseph Black had hashed out the previous night, the reverend was going to be the master of ceremonies for the races. He went to inspect the three horse stalls and the makeshift starting gate; the structure was rather rickety, but he figured that it would hold together for the day. To one side of the gate, he rolled a couple of large stones together and placed a plank between them to serve as his podium.

Copus stepped up and composed himself, not so much having second thoughts as realizing that there was no turning back. A sign from God would've been welcome, though.

"This coffee tastes like black tar mixed with bitch-in-heat piss," one man near him complained, then poured whiskey into his cup. When he recognized the reverend, he added, "But hallelujah anyhow."

By noon, when the first heat was scheduled, Reverend Copus surmised that the entire population of the Licking River valley, and half of the towns along the upper Muskingum, had all turned out. He couldn't help but wonder, also, how many folks were simultaneously congregating at the town square to hear Otis McDonald preach.

Early arrivals sat in tiered rows along the earthwork mounds, while stragglers spread out in the grass flats wherever they could unfurl a blanket.

Johnny Appleseed paced along the sidelines of the track, attempting to preserve clear pathways for the horses, even though the leading edge of the crowd kept elbowing closer and closer to the racing lanes.

Still, with bottles already being passed and spirits high, everybody's outlook was pleasant, and their energies, while restless, were mostly positive.

Three riders led their horses into the starting gates. "Let the races begin!" Joseph Black screamed at the top of his lungs, inciting cheers, foot stomping, and chest pounding.

"But first," Black continued, "this being the Lord's Day an' such, we're gonna start with a right proper prayer. Reverend...."

This was Reverend Copus's moment. He'd never spoken to so many people at once in his life. "Brothers and sisters in Christ," he began, then, reconsidering, toned it down a notch. "Ladies and gentlemen, and horse racing fans everywhere, welcome to this glorious day that the Lord has given us.

"Some would say that a horse race ain't a fit place for a church sermon. I disagree. There're many valuable lessons that we can learn here. First, I'd argue that any purpose that brings so many people together in fellowship must be right and good, ordained by God, because He knows that life here can be downright brutal, and folks pioneering this land deserve some honest entertainment. God wants every one of you to enjoy this day. Just don't forget that He is watching.

"Life is a race, after all. It's a race against death. Victory in this kind of race doesn't always go to the swiftest. In fact, those who live fastest, usually lose. In life, you win not by finishing first, but finishing strong. Along the way, you may get sidetracked, or you may trip and fall, or you may find yourself running backwards... but the heavenly prize goes to those who pick themselves up, mend their ways, get themselves on the right path, and stick with it all the way to the finish line, which is at Saint Peter's pearly gate.

"There's another way that life is like a race. Some of you all have a wager or two on these horse races, and that's okay with God, too, because there's a lesson to be learned. Life is a gamble. When you decide to live according to the commandments of God, you place the biggest bet that you ever can. Your immortal soul is at stake. If you win, the payoff is eternal life in paradise. Or, you have the free will to live as you please, in defiance of God's plan. But when you die, your soul belongs not to God, but to Satan. I'm asking you just to use your common sense to decide. Which is the smarter bet? To live a life of sinful pleasure, then pay for it with infinite suffering? Or to live a righteous life that pleases God, then spend eternity with Him in paradise? Nobody gets out of this world without making that wager.

"So, let's all say the Lord's prayer." Reverend Copus started the prayer, and was gratified when folks joined in, so that by the time that they got to "amen," the reverberations of the assembled voices felt like a scene straight out of the gospels. All that was missing were the loaves and fish.

Afterwards, the reverend remained atop his podium as Joseph Black handed him the starter's pistol.

A rope drawn tight in front of the starting gate held back the snorting horses. At the side of the gate, Millie Blubaugh was ready to yank the rope aside when Reverend Copus fired the pistol. The riders mounted their horses, making fists around the reigns. Way down at the end of the track, Johnny Appleseed, the spotter, had cleared enough space so as to have an unobstructed line of sight at the finish line.

Copus rammed the powder and lead shot in his pistol, aimed it into the treetops, and fired.

The first race was effectively over before the echo of the starting pistol faded. A jittery Palamino owned and ridden by a lawyer named Portius Miller spooked at the get-go and reared on its hind legs, then charged through the crowd and disappeared over the mounds.

"And good riddance to lawyers," some folks called after him.

Meanwhile, the favorite, an Indian horse owned by Jim Danner and ridden by a bare-chested Potawatomi wearing eye black, started from the center gate and may have been nudged or distracted by the commotion, so that it got off to a slow start and never gained traction.

The victor by a couple of lengths was Mojo, whose jockey named Heck was heard to be singing for the entire duration of the ride.

"Re-do! Re-do!" cried those who had stakes on the losing horses.

"Ain't no re-dos," Joseph Black pronounced decisively.

The second race was closer, but less dramatic than the first, for within the first twenty yards of the race, all three horses settled into the precise positions in which they ran the entire course and in the order that they finished, not one of them gaining or losing a single step on the others. The winner was Dan Sapp, a newcomer to the community, who guided his chestnut filly, Lulu, as efficiently as if she were an extension of his own legs.

At the end, Johnny Appleseed spotted the precise margin of Lulu's win and measured it to be the length from the tip of his middle finger on his right hand to a knob on his shoulder bone. That being pretty even-on to what everybody had seen, nobody questioned the accuracy of his calculation.

That set up the third heat, which was the most eagerly anticipated of the qualifying races, as indicated by the number of wagers placed and the amount of money on the table. In lane one, a soldier who was absent-without-leave from the Kentucky militia was riding a powerful cavalry horse; he'd bragged that he escaped by outrunning the entire brigade on that same horse's back. Bristling in the center lane was a gray stallion from George Rennick's farm, supposedly bred of stock from the famous Godolphin Arabian, being ridden by Rennick's full time jockey. Finally, Horny Horse, the longshot in this race, was Jim Craig's sleek animal, which had gained popularity in the late betting because many people had hunches that its rider, Otto Blubaugh, just seemed to have a way of getting the most out of any horse.

While the riders in the first two stalls braced for the start, Otto sat on Horny's back as casually as if they were preparing for a leisurely trot along a murmuring creek on a spring day. The last thing Otto did before Reverend Copus fired the starter's gun was wink at Millie, for luck, and folks were shocked that Horny Horse winked at her, too.

The horses launched at full steam and kept galloping harder and faster with every foot strike. Whenever one horse began to pull ahead by even the slightest distance, another surged suddenly, and then the third would get inspired, so that they were neck and neck and neck, accelerating, the entire length of the track. The cavalry horse chugged on the inside as if being pursued by the entire Bluegrass State militia. Early in the race it gained half a head lead, but the thoroughbred, sprinting as if generating its own wind, surged ahead about halfway from the finish line.

With the end in sight, though, Otto Blubaugh crouched flat on his horse's back, wrapped his legs around its ribs, and screamed, "Go git Horny boy!"

The finish was breathlessly close, but Horny's charge beat the thoroughbred by a nose, or as Johnny Appleseed declared, by the exact distance between the lobe of his left ear and the corner of his right eye. Otto fell off Horny into Millie's arms. Horny neighed happily.

This turn of events unleashed another round of frenetic wagering on the outcome of the final race between Dan Sapp's Lulu, Mister Rope and Heck's Mojo, and Jim Craig's Horny, ably ridden by Otto Blubaugh.

Winners were eager to parlay their profits into even greater revenues. Losers took heart from the surprising outcomes in the semi-final races as reason for hope that they were just one shrewd bet away from recovering their fortunes.

Joseph Black, unable to manage the volume of transactions by himself, deputized a handful of men that he hoped he could trust to function as bookmakers on his behalf. Once the likes of Smucker, Pitzer, and Larabee started accepting people's ventures, they expanded the scope of wagering to include side bets on such things as if Reverend Copus was going to make them all pray again, which horse would drop the most shit before the next race, and what were the chances that at any point Millie Blubaugh would get so excited jumping up and down that her bosoms would pop out of her smock. If there was a chance that anything might happen, somebody was willing to put money on it.

Meanwhile, the break left the riders, the owners, and their horses with time to prepare. While Mister Rope strutted around bragging, Heck led Mojo into a clearing, where he strummed his guitar and serenaded the animal.

> *"I've got me a crown in the Kingdom*
> *Ain't that good news*
> *I've got me a harp up in the Kingdom*
> *Ain't that good news...."*

He sounded good enough that some folks paused to listen, and a few even tossed coins into his hat.

Nearby, Otto and Millie Blubaugh stood on opposite sides of Horny, petting and brushing the horse while blowing kisses to each other. Horny tossed back his head and nickered with what looked like a big grin on his face.

And at the same time, Dan Sapp wandered down to a brook with Lulu, where the horse drank while he sat on a mossy rock. Dan pulled a rosary out of his pocket and commenced reciting Hail Mary, one bead at a time.

"Lookit, Dan Sapp is a damnable Popish Cat'lick," somebody pointed out. People gathered to watch in awe and dread.

Reverend Copus wandered amid the crowd just to be seen, for the sake of whatever moderating effect his presence might exert upon people's rambunctiousness. Once, he thought he heard a distant echo in the breeze that sounded like Otis McDonald crying, "Doom and perdition!" It was soon shouted down by a slow, but building refrain of, "Start the race. Start the race! Start the race!"

Meanwhile, Joseph Black seemed content to take people's money all night, as long as there was one more person with a nickel to plunk down. When the reverend tugged at his sleeve, he finally declared that the betting was officially closed by shouting, "It's show time!"

All around, bodies swarmed the track, every person on his or her feet, some standing on chairs or sitting on friends' shoulders, and gawkers clung to even the most tenuous branches in every tree along the route. The late afternoon sun angled behind the starting gate, with three columns of light shining through, so that when the horses stepped into it, they cast elongated shadows onto the track.

As the riders mounted their beasts, Reverend Copus hopped onto his platform, whispered, "Jesus have mercy," and raised the starter's pistol. The silent suspense felt like waiting for the Second Coming.

The shot unleashed a riot of cheering, a mob wave of body heat, and the thunder of marauding horseflesh. The horses ran like a three-headed Biblical beast in one body, racing to pull itself apart. Their strikes pummeled the dirt track, trailed by a cloud of dust and gravel. The animals streaked by so fast that the only thing anybody could see was a muscular blur, as if the air itself were warped in the backdrafts.

It knocked some people over. Others panted for breath.

Around ten seconds into the race, the horses stormed by the post marking the halfway point, but nobody could separate them clearly enough with naked eyes to tell which, if any, was in the lead. Mojo, Horny, and Lulu struck their leading legs in seemingly synchronized unison, and except for slight variations in when each tipped its muzzle, there was no discernible space between them. Even the jockeys rode in identical compressed postures, pinned back by the force of the velocity. They gained speed as they sprinted toward the finale, like three boulders rambling down a steep hill toward a cliff.

Folks with the prime viewing positions along the side of the track backed off, concerned that they might get trampled.

All except Johnny Appleseed, that is, who centered himself, dug in his feet, intertwined his fingers, and squinted so that all he could see was the plane marking the precise finish line.

In a flash, the horses galloped past it and kept going. People clustered behind the end of the track scattered to get out of the way, while the horses kept on chugging, as if they intended to race all the way to the horizon.

It was over, but nobody knew what had happened. Everybody looked at somebody else for an answer.

Meanwhile, though, Johnny Appleseed leaped into the center of the track and promulgated, "The winner is Lulu, by a whisker!"

"Noooooooo!" erupted a cacophony of voices.

"Yessssssss!" exploded a chorus of others.

Joseph Black expressed the majority opinion, though, when he stomped his foot and insisted, "I don't believe it's possible to say so!"

"I am certain. I saw it me-self, as clear as if that moment was frozen in time. Bring the horses to me. I will prove it to ye."

It took a few minutes to turn around the horses, during which time people started recovering their senses of either indignation or triumph, whichever was the case.

Sensing unrest, Reverend Copus stood next to Johnny, offering his visible support... even though he, too, doubted if it was possible that any mortal eye could've truly seen what happened at the race's conclusion.

Johnny waved at Dan Sapp. "Bring your Lulu horse over here. Stand her up straight. Lift her head. There...." Johnny pointed. "Do ye all see that long whisker a-poking out from her left nostril? 'Tis the very one that crossed the finish line ahead of every other horse. That would be the exact margin of victory."

It was true that Lulu had a stray whisker sticking straight out of her nostril, but it was only visible upon looking closely, almost certainly impossible to discern at full gallop. Some began taunting: "Appleseed ain't right of mind," "Maybe John the Baptist told him so," and, "He eats so many carrots, he thinks he can see better than everybody else."

Joseph Black said, "That ain't proof fer nothin', Chapman."

"I could be wrong, but I do not ever lie. I know what I saw," Johnny calmly reaffirmed. Sensing that his words were less than convincing, however, he added, "If ye do not believe me, ask the horses."

Shaking his head, Joseph Black lamented, "Appleseed, I'm a-feared that you *are* mad."

Undaunted, Johnny tsk-ed and walked to where Mister Rope, Heck, and Mojo were standing. Johnny rubbed the horse's muzzle, looked it in the eye, and asked, "Did ye win that race, Mojo?"

Mojo snorted and shook its head from side to side.

Next, Johnny went to Horny, who was flanked on one side by Otto and Millie, and on the other by Jim Craig. In the same manner as before, he posed the question, "Did ye win that race, Horny boy?"

Horny blew air from both nostrils, shaking his head from side to side.

Finally, Johnny marched to Lulu and looked the beast in the eye. "Now, Miss Lulu, did ye win that race?"

Lulu jerked her head up and down proudly and whinnied in a way that sounded to everybody like she was saying, "Yeaaaaaahhh."

"There you go," Johnny said.

Thus, there being no person among the mob brazen enough to question a horse's own word of honor, that settled the matter.

That night, at Black's Tavern, Dan Sapp graciously offered to buy a round for his rivals in the great race. That gesture helped to soothe feelings, as did the decision to split second place winnings evenly between the other two finalists, so Jim Craig and Mister Rope both felt better about how they'd fared. Otto and Heck were also at the table, as well as Johnny Appleseed.

When everybody had a full mug glass of cider, Dan Sapp raised his and proposed a toast. "To amity," he said.

"To what?" Jim Craig asked.

"Where's Amity?" Mister Rope wanted to know.

"Amity means friendship," Johnny explained.

"And peace," Dan Sapp added.

Jim Craig pondered that sentiment for a moment. "Ah guess thar ain't no harm in drinkin' fer peace an' friendship."

Everybody quaffed, while Johnny sipped. It seemed there was nothing left to say.

Dan Sapp was in a loquacious mood, however, and he wasn't averse to talking about himself, since he viewed his personal story as being quite interesting. He told the men about how he'd recently migrated into the Ohio Country from Kentucky by way of Maryland, where his proud family of Sapps had originally journeyed to America on board the Dove with Lord Baltimore. He planned to buy some cheap land in the sparsely settled region northwest of Newark, where he intended to establish a new town and name it after himself.

"Sappville?" Johnny asked.

"No sir. *Dan*-ville."

"Ain't it still dangerous up there, what wit' Injuns and wolves?" Mister Rope inquired.

"Not to mention criminals," Jim Craig added. "Like mah broth'r, who's a vile murderer. He lives way up 'n Owl Creek north of the gap. He hates ever'body. He'll try to kill yah, but fortunately, he's a poor shot."

Johnny perked up. "Andy Craig? I have made his acquaintance. He is a bit raw, 'tis true, but not so bad once ye get onto his good side."

Jim Craig grunted. "Mah broth'r don't got any *good* side."

Otto, who'd been listening with interest to Dan Sapp's plans, said, "Me 'n' mah wife likewise talk 'bout makin' our homestead up the riv'r. When we save ourselves 'nuff money, we'll buy us some land, build a cabin, and have ourselves a mess o' children."

"A young man with your horse skills could do well for himself in Danville," Dan Sapp said. "Look me up when you get there."

Mister Rope jumped in. "What the hey? Maybe me 'n' Heck'll buy some cheap land up yonder, too. Heck has a plan to start a big ol' hemp farm."

"Haw. Tha's rich—*Rope* growin' a crop o' hemp. What good else is hemp, oth'r than fer rope-makin', anyway?" Jim Craig asked.

"It'd be healthful, when smoked," Heck said.

"Perchance, then, I shall see all of ye thereabouts," Johnny added, "for I have planted orchards in those parts, and I can sell ye apple tree seedlings for two and one half cents apiece."

Johnny pushed back his chair and retrieved a whistle from his kerchief.

Heck also stood, grabbing his guitar.

"Now, if ye will excuse us, gentlemen, Mr. Heck and I have a history of playing tunes together, and we figured that folks might appreciate hearing some music here tonight."

Heck picked a couple of chords, grinned, and sang out, "*Get on up, yah. Time to get up, do yore thing.*"

Chapter 10 - October 1805

West Fork of the White River, the Indiana Territory

"Battle Panther has been stricken by the nightmare witch's fever," Tecumseh said, kicking his brother in the back. "You must now go to him."

Lalawethika had just fallen asleep and, in his normal course of sobering up, would have remained unconscious for another twelve hours. Barely sentient, he felt himself being hoisted into a sitting position, his mouth pried open, and the neck of a bottle inserted therein. The liquor that his brother poured down his gullet made him gag. Tecumseh kept tipping the bottle until Lalawethika voided his stomach contents onto his sleeping mat.

"Come now to your senses. Bring your medicine bag. Battle Panther needs a physician. Unfortunately, we have none but you."

Lalawethika tried to think through the severe throbbing in his head. This is what he hated about being a healer: it was such a bother when his patients got sick, even more when they were dying. They sometimes lingered for days, which was a complete waste of his time.

"Nothing can I do for him," he grumbled.

Tecumseh lifted his brother's head by the earlobes and snarled, "Even if nothing can be done, you must do something!"

"As so you wish," Lalawethika conceded. These were trying times for a medicine man. Winter's first frost had just fallen, and already a burning influenza ravaged the nearby Lenape villages at Woapimininschi and Woapicamikunk. Now it had reached the Shawnee settlement on the White River. Being a healer during a time of plague was a thankless burden, with the job's incessant stress and demands, not to mention the exposure hazards that he risked every time he treated another soon-to-be-deceased patient.

Reluctantly, Lalawethika assembled herbs, tinctures, talismans, and relics of spirit animals for his medicine bag. He also took a bottle of

British rum, explaining, "This will help to preserve my own self from the disease."

"The alcohol preserves only so that it can kill you more slowly."

"Bah. You know nothing of my medicine. To you, I gladly leave matters of war and politics. Please, to me leave the arts of healing."

"Battle Panther is my friend. Give him some comfort, if nothing else."

The tribe had built a thatched *wegiwa* at a far corner of the village, away from the common areas and the water source, to serve as a sick house. Outside of it, Battle Panther's parents, brothers and sisters, and wives wept, sang prayers, and burned offerings.

"Look at these fools," Lalawethika whispered to Tecumseh, "making such an unruly noise, as if they could appease the spirits with their whimpering."

"Because they love Battle Panther, they can do no less."

When Battle Panther's father saw Lalawethika coming, he protested. "This man has himself been drinking the Long Knives' fool juice. He is unfit to perform a cure."

Battle Panther's family blocked the entrance to the sick house.

Lalawethika stopped and prepared to back away, even to run if necessary.

Tecumseh placed one hand on Battle Panther's father's shoulder, and gestured with the other for Lalawethika to come forward. "Keep to your prayers, my friends," he told the family, "and leave our medicine man to work what cures he is able."

Lalawethika passed through the gauntlet, consciously stepping as straight as he could despite the blur all around him. Once inside, he bumped his head as he grabbed onto a post. A miasma of briny sweat, putrid bile, and the beginnings of a rancid death stench saturated the sick room. Battle Panther lay flat on a mat with his eyes open and his lips trembling, but unconscious. That was fortunate. Conscious patients only interfered with his ministrations. Lalawethika knelt next to Battle Panther, gazing at him and wondering what to do. The warrior's face was so pale and stretched, it seemed as if his skull was breaking through the skin. Blood trickled from his nostrils.

Lalawethika surmised that his disease was too far advanced to treat by incantation alone. For this patient, he was going to have to get his hands dirty. First, he soaked a poultice in wild ginger tea and placed it across his forehead. Next, he plumped a vein in Battle Panther's forearm and lashed it with his knife, collecting the hot red blood in a bowl. Finally, while the bloodletting continued, he massaged ground milfoil leaves into his gums.

The rest was up to Battle Panther, or to the spirits, if either was up to the task.

This was going to be a long night. Even though Lalawethika believed that remaining with the patient served no useful purpose, the reality was that if he did not stay the night, and the patient died, he'd be viewed as negligent for leaving, as if he could have done more. If Battle Panther happened to survive, however, Lalawethika would have a greater claim to the credit if he was on hand to announce the miracle. So he was stuck.

Liquor made the waiting almost pleasant, though. It rather amused him to listen to the fervent invocations of the patient's kin just outside of the sick house, where they kept a desperate but undaunted vigil.

The men chanted to their guardian spirits, while the squaws wailed profusely. "Have mercy," his first wife bawled. "Despite our unworthiness," his second wife finished.

Lalawethika mocked them by mouthing their words while swilling rum. He masked his belches with exclamations of "Heal this soul!", or "Shed thy mercy upon our warrior!", so that the relatives outside would hear and imagine that he was busily administering advanced shamanistic therapies.

The moon was full that night, which unnerved Lalawethika. Sometimes, he worried that his drinking behavior might offend his tutelary spirit, *Tepeki,* the face on the moon. He often felt as though the full moon judged him, but Lalawethika likewise judged *Tepeki,* who had done a poor job of guiding him through his life's challenges. What good was a god that you couldn't trust? When, as a youth, Lalawethika had gone into the wilds on his solitary quest for manhood, *Tepeki* had helped him by casting light into the forest. At the same time, when Lalawethika tried to kill a sacrificial deer with bow and arrow, *Tepeki* failed to give him the strength and confidence that he needed to shoot straight, so the arrow misfired, and he shot himself in the eye instead. Bleeding and half blind, he'd staggered back to camp, having shamed himself and his family by failing his rite of passage.

When he thought about these things in a sober mind, Lalawethika wondered how he had affronted his spiritual guardian, and what he might do to win back his favor. Pleasing *Tepeki* seemed impossible, though. When drinking, Lalawethika could convince himself that he wasn't a failure, but *Tepeki* was. It was all *his* fault.

Rum was good. Unlike the caustic moonshine whiskey that he sometimes acquired from the Americans, this British rum, traded down from Canada, had a smooth, grainy taste with just a slight backlash. It quickly transported him into that fanciful state between falling asleep and starting to dream, where he drifted contentedly, aware only of his desire to remain exactly as drunk as he was at that moment. Every time he felt the tug of gravity pulling him down, he took another quaff of rum, which sustained his tipsy equilibrium a bit longer.

Upon draining the last drop from the bottle, Lalawethika wrapped his legs into his chest and braced himself against a sudden plunge. A volatile substance swelled within his body and triggered seizures in the pit of his stomach, which spread and fissured along cracks in his bones and across the raw nerves on the surface of his skin. With nausea came a sensation of eruptive bloating, as if he were being inflated with molten vomit. This churning in all quarters of his body resolved into a funnel, and as he spun into it, he sank faster, as if gaining mass during collapse. His whole body felt like broken bone fragments within a bag of flesh and viscera. The Earth opened into a receding abyss, while visions of everything that he'd ever hated, dreaded or feared lashed against him in the whirlwind. His last thought was that he wasn't ready to die, but he deserved it, anyway.

Just before dawn, while Battle Panther's relatives slept outside of his sick house, the sound of rustling and feeble moaning stirred from within. Tecumseh, the earliest riser in the tribe, heard it from the riverbank. Thinking that it must be his brother's inebriated babbling, Tecumseh dashed into the sick house to shut him up.

Battle Panther had rolled onto his stomach, raised his head and chest, and braced himself by the tips of his elbows. His eyes were cloudy, and his jaw dangled sideways with his tongue hanging like a slab of salted bacon. He made a fish-out-of-water gesture with his lips.

While looking for the water bladder, Tecumseh nearly tripped over Lalawethika, whom he rolled aside as if he were a log in the way. He snatched the bladder and tilted it above Battle Panther's mouth.

Battle Panther's father entered the hut and, seeing that his son was conscious, beat his chest and cheered. "Like the risen thunderbird, my son lives!"

This summoned the rest of the relatives. His wives swooped to either side of their stricken husband, one taking the water bladder and the other feeling his forehead, announcing, "His fever has broken." They all huddled around him to gaze in joy and awe at what they immediately proclaimed to be "a miracle!"

Tecumseh retreated to allow the family to share this happy moment. Then he thought about Lalawethika, who was lying prostrate in pooled blood and bodily filth, his face locked in a grimace that captured a moment of excruciating pain. Gradually, Tecumseh's disgust abated, giving way to curiosity. He grabbed his brother's limp arm and felt for a pulse. He thought he felt a beat, but then lost it, if it had ever been there at all.

"Is our great healer dead?" Battle Panther's father asked.

Tecumseh had always believed that his brother would die drunk, but never imagined it under circumstances quite like these.

"Yes, so I fear."

"His own life he sacrificed, that Battle Panther might live," one of the wives asserted. "Great be the name of Lalawethika!" the other added.

Tecumseh knew that sacrifice was the last thing his brother would ever do for anybody. Still, he quickly calculated that it might serve his interests to have a martyred brother. He had to lower his head to say it, but managed to croak, "Sing praise to Lalawethika."

Meanwhile, one of Battle Panther's brothers checked Lalawethika for vital signs. "I feel a faint pulse."

This was typical: Lalawethika could not even die properly.

"I will have the body cleansed and dressed. We shall leave it here until death is confirmed," Tecumseh said. "But, come, let us share the glad news of Battle Panther's rebirth with the tribe, so that we might all sing and pray together. Leave my brother to his fate."

But for the first time since he'd become their chief, Tecumseh's people did not hasten to obey his instructions. None had ever seen a miracle before—it was a wondrous event, but it was also fearful, and they all felt as if they were being watched from on high by Lalawethika's spirit. They dared not risk incurring the disfavor of so powerful a sorcerer.

Shrugging, Tecumseh relented. "But first let us pray."

For two days, nobody knew for certain whether Lalawethika was alive or dead. Evidence one way or the other was inconclusive. Tecumseh had confirmed an exceedingly feeble pulse, but it only beat at irregular intervals, which he contended was just a cardiac reflex. When he held a blade beneath Lalawethika's nose, drops of moisture formed on it, but not enough to prove that he was breathing; it could be just vapors, which meant he'd started to rot.

Being both un-dead and non-living was a great boon to his reputation as a shaman, though. The people's widely-held explanation for Battle Panther's amazing recovery was that Lalawethika had vacated his body and hazarded into the realm of the storms to battle the demon Mothsee Monetoo over the fate of his friend's soul. Ultimately, Lalawethika had triumphed, and so Battle Panther returned to the world of living; but had he won that victory at the cost of his own life? Folks said that his spirit had taken up residence in the moon, where some claimed they saw Lalawethika's one good eye looking down at them.

In consideration of these circumstances, tribal members regretted having held Lalawethika in such low regard when he was alive. Day and night, contrite well-wishers maintained continuous traffic visiting the sick house to kneel by his side, kiss his forehead, and pray for his mercy. Devotees gathered strands of his hair and clippings of his nails. Word of Lalawethika's miracle reached the neighboring Lenape communities, and pilgrims seeking their own cures came to bask in his salubrious aura. Some conjectured that the great healer had chosen to remain suspended between the mortal and immortal realms, channeling his grace to serve as a portal for future miracles. Some even dared to wonder aloud: was Lalawethika the Prophet who'd been promised?

Tecumseh heard this speculation, and it made him think that, perhaps in death, his brother had finally figured out a way to make himself useful.

By the third day, though, Tecumseh began to worry that this public spectacle was reaching the point of diminishing returns. Precise confirmation of Lalawethika's demise was still uncertain, but meanwhile he was beginning to stink. At the same time, his legend was growing as tales of his supernatural powers spread to Ojibwas, Wyandots, and Potawatomis, who kept coming to glimpse this marvel for themselves. By way of a solution, Tecumseh announced that Lalawethika's spirit was no longer in need of its worldly body. Therefore, come sundown, there would be a great, intertribal ceremony to celebrate his life and give thanks for the blessings that he'd bestowed upon Indian peoples. Following the benediction, the tribe would burn his corpse upon a pyre with flames reaching to the sky so that his inner energies might be released into the heavens, and afterwards, the mourners could collect and keep some of his ashes.

Tecumseh claimed that his brother had come to him in a dream and told him to do these exact things. "Our great healer will protect us from beyond," he said.

That day, the entire population kept busy with preparations for the ceremony. They washed Lalawethika's body and rubbed it with dried dogwood blossoms. They dressed him in a traditional woven shirt under a fringed deerskin frock, a woolen breechcloth, leggings gartered below the knees, and beaver fur moccasins. Around his head, they tied a scarf to cover his blind eye, and ornamented him with porcupine quills, eagle feathers, and bear claw ear bobs.

Meanwhile, a large number of men, including many strangers from different tribes working side by side, constructed a towering pyre. A hunting party killed a wild razorback for the community feast, taking its good luck as evidence that Lalawethika's ghost was already bestowing bounties upon them.

Tecumseh supervised the activities while keeping an eye out for anything that could go wrong.

Around dusk, the sun came out for the first time that day, suffusing the air with golden twilight. The people saw this as evidence of Waashaa Monetoo's presence, who'd come to observe the wake.

Tecumseh cued drummers and summoned the tribes to order by singing:

"Beneath distant skies, across wide rivers,
through lost forests and over high mountains,
our people have strayed and separated,
but always followed by patient Death,
which brings us together again.
So hearken brothers, listen sisters,
To the tales of brave Lalawethika,
the slayer of demons...."

Tecumseh's attendant young women started dancing. The drummers pounded a heartbeat cadence as the first witness stepped forward. Battle Panther wept and wrung his hands as he described how abruptly the devilish fever had seized him, so that by the time

Lalawethika visited him in the sick house, he was already burning with pain but paralyzed in body, kept alive by Mothsee Monetoo to serve the demon's pleasure in torturing him. But Lalawethika took his place and swept Mothsee into a cyclone, where they engaged in violent combat. The next thing that Battle Panther knew, he was sitting, surrounded by his family, fully restored to health. Now, he testified that he felt better than he'd ever in all his life, able to run faster and laugh harder, and his wives raved about his virility!

Next, Lalawethika's wife, Noise Keeper, spoke. Her husband was a very mysterious man, she said through sobs. Unseen monsters tormented him in every moment of his life by haunting his thoughts and filling his heart with dread. If he drank to excess, it was because his burdens were more than any man could endure. Still, he also possessed great powers, and when he fought his ultimate battle, he'd proven his mettle against Death itself. Doubtless his spirit would continue to keep and protect the tribe... just as, incidentally, he would wish for some other man from the tribe to step forward to marry his mourning wife, so that she might be cared for in his absence. Preferably, she added, a man who did not drink.

One after the other, witnesses stepped forward to eulogize Lalawethika with fulsome praise, the recurring theme being how much they regretted that, in life, they'd failed to appreciate his mercy, his goodness, and the potency of his magic.

At length, Tecumseh had heard enough. He raised his tomahawk and belted out a song that he'd composed just for the occasion.

"Open the Earth, lower the sky
to grant passage of a servant
into a gentle afterlife
more suited to his weary soul.
Let fire release him,
may smoke raise his being
into the winds of our minds,
and lift our hearts to heaven."

Some of the young women swooned, overcome by the beauty of Tecumseh's voice. Battle Panther and his brothers approached Lalawethika's body and each grabbed a corner of the mat that had been placed beneath him. They lifted him, crying, "Praise Lalawethika!"

Lalawethika's good eye opened.

Battle Panther and the others panicked, lost their grip, and dropped the body with a thud.

Lalawethika burped when he hit the ground.

Tecumseh rushed to his side, kneeling above him and slapping his face to revive him.

"Ouch," Lalawethika griped. "Brother, what are you doing?"

Every man, woman, and child dropped to the ground and bowed their heads, except for Tecumseh, who replied in a slightly sardonic tone, "You are dead."

Lalawethika shifted into a seated position, looking only at his brother, oblivious to his surroundings and the entire context of where he was.

"Yes," he panted. "Or... no. Myself, I do not know. But listen, brother, a vast distance I have journeyed. How long was I gone? I traveled beyond time. Let me tell of it to you...

"I myself was in a void, floating in dark emptiness between being and non-being, without a body. I was a free soul, like a memory, but with sensations, for this is the nature of the afterlife—eternal, but also suspended in the feelings contained in a single moment. I felt swirling space around me, heavier air turning over lighter air, so that in a whirlwind I drifted. My path took the form of a narrow, spinning tunnel through a dark forest. Furthermore, I was not myself alone. Other souls, from all Indian nations, were with me. Strong breezes compelled us to travel together, as one, toward the same fate.

"At length, we souls reached a fork in a road. To the right, there were three huts on the wayside, while the road on the left went a short distance then vanished into a gray fog. All souls took the path on the right, as did I. Upon reaching the first hut, we found the door wide open. Inside, a woman whom I knew to be a witch warned us that our sins we must confess and repent, or otherwise we would be doomed. This frightened us, so, fleeing that hut, we returned to the fork in the road. Still, rather than go down the fork that led into the fog, we bypassed the first hut where we had been scared, and went straight to the second. There, however, was another witch, this one uglier and more wicked than the first. She too warned us that if we did not repent, we would suffer horribly forevermore.

"Again, in fear we ran from her hut, and found ourselves back at the fork in the road. This time the other souls determined to avoid the first and second huts, and hope for better in the third. But I was becoming wary of that path. I let others pass ahead of me and enter the third hut. I crept close and cupped my hand to my ear, listening, and while I stood just one step outside the door to the hut, I heard the agonized screams of the damned, like the roar of a thousand waterfalls of blood, while all the liars, the thieves, the drunkards, the heretics, the perverts, the hypocrites, the violent, the greedy, the traitors, and the sinners suffered according to the nature of their wrongs. I myself felt a hand pulling at my shoulder, but I broke away and ran, terrified, for in that moment I had experienced hell."

Lalawethika panted and his voice trembled, as if reliving the experience through his words. Focused only on Tecumseh, though, he remained unaware of how his tale held the entire tribe in suspense. His blind eye shed a tear.

"And what happened next?" Tecumseh prodded him.

"This time, alone I walked down the foggy road, and when I took just one step past the edge, I realized that I had chosen the right path, the one that opens into the realm of the Great Spirit. I became a thought in the mind of Waashaa Monetoo, an instrument of His will. Oh, truly, I wanted nothing more for my whole existence than to stay there with Him. But the Creator sent me back to do more work in this world, to warn my brothers and sisters to turn from the wicked doors, to renounce worldly vices and temptations, and to devote their lives only to glorifying Waashaa Monetoo. It is my calling."

The whole story sounded like a drunken delusion to Tecumseh, but listening to Lalawethika's story bought him some time to think. He knew every single person hearing those words believed them to be true. This story would be told and embellished, over and over, by people who were eager to believe in miracles. As a martyr, Lalawethika would have been useful to Tecumseh—and probably more reliable—but, short of that, he quickly formed a plan whereby his brother might actually be of assistance while still alive.

"Brother, indeed you are the *Prophet*," Tecumseh announced for all to hear.

"Why, yes, I guess that... so I must be."

Lalawethika lifted his head and gazed over Tecumseh's shoulders. "But tell me, Brother, why are all of these people here?"

Chapter 11 - October 1805

Owl Creek

"Married life suits Andy Craig," Toby said to Dead Mary and Fog Mother as he led them along the path to Andy and his new wife's cabin.

"How so?" Dead Mary asked.

"They fight between themselves constantly," Toby replied, "which to a man like Andy Craig is as good as living gets. Without conflict, he would have no use for any other person."

"If conflict is what he seeks, I would oblige him gladly," Dead Mary quipped. "That man is such a—" Unable to think of suitable terminology in Algonquian, she switched to English. "—*shit maggot.*"

"Better to say that his personality is akin to a lightning strike in a bog," Fog Mother corrected her. "He is loud, but usually does no harm."

"Even so, he and I, we understand each other," Toby continued. "I take his goods to market. For my services, I accept a fair commission. That is why you were wise to allow me to bring you to him. If the two of you appeared at his cabin unexpectedly, he would shoot at you."

"That is nothing to be feared," Dead Mary mocked. "He is but a poor shot."

"We seek to spread peace," Fog Mother reminded her. "So we must come to him in peace."

At the mention of the word 'peace,' Toby sighed. "There are many visions of peace. To a man like Andy Craig, peace means being left alone to live as he himself pleases. To Indian peoples, peace is a gift from the gods that must be cherished. To the Long Knives, though, peace is something that they themselves believe can be taken by force and kept through fear. My own belief is that the only lasting peace is one which yields benefits that can be shared by many. Sadly, people say that they want peace, but what they truly want is what is best for themselves."

Fog Mother and Dead Mary knew Toby's story, and why his opinions on matters of war and peace carried some authority. As a young man, he fought with the Indian coalition that was defeated at Fallen Timbers. In the dark years that followed, his Wyandot tribe persevered through hard winters, scarce hunting, and poor harvests, to establish a new village on the Sandusky River, north of the treaty line. Toby was not the traditional hunter/provider, though, nor was he eager to practice the agricultural lifestyle that the Long Knives recommended for Indians.

Instead, Toby pursued prosperity through commerce. With extended family across Indiana, the Michigan territory, and even into Canada, he'd exploited his connections to create a network for collecting and distributing various goods. This positioned him to negotiate trade between Hurons, Ottawa, Chippewa, Cree, and Potawatomi, as well as at American, French, and British outposts. Over time, he established partners in diverse locales, enabling him to coordinate complex operations for trafficking supplies including clothing, pelts and furs, salt, flour, spices, whiskey, hog products, and also luxuries like soap, candles, and the Indian jewelry that seemed to enchant the wives of white men.

In Toby's opinion, written treaties were meaningless. He argued that sustainable peace could only come through mutually profitable enterprise. If he'd learned one thing about the Long Knives, it was that they would spend their money on frivolous things. Satisfying their trivial appetites could create an economic peace that might possibly endure.

Though Toby's work kept him traveling most of the year, he returned every winter to his tribe, to be with his wife and children, and to share the bounty of his success with his community. He had been on his way to his village when he visited Fog Mother, and upon her request, agreed to escort her and Dead Mary to meet with Andy Craig. He couldn't refuse; he owed Fog Mother a debt.

As new settlers increasingly encroached upon virgin lands, Andy Craig had moved farther upstream on Owl Creek. Getting there wasn't easy, and only Toby knew the exact location of the cabin where Craig now resided, along with the new wife whom Toby had helped him to purchase. Toby led the two women around pit traps and trip lines, past bear and wolf skulls that had been nailed to tree trunks as warnings, and along stepping stones through a quagmire that could swallow a body whole. Andy's cabin was at the rise of a wooded and briar-covered knoll, between two erratic boulders. It was so well camouflaged that Toby had to point it out to the women, and even then they lost it in the background if they blinked. He cupped his hand over his mouth and emitted a clear, ringing bird call.

Pit-a-tuck-tuck, pit-a-tuck-tuck....

Inside the cabin, there was a sudden scramble, a clatter of pots and pans, followed by two muffled voices cursing. A woman called out from behind one of the boulders, "Be that you, Injun Toby?"

Andy moved to lie flat on the roof with his musket in a sniper position, poised to open fire at the first hint of trouble.

Toby emerged to be seen. "Yes, friends. I have whiskey."

"Ah'm maghty thirsty!" Andy hollered, hopping down.

"Good. We will get drunk. But, before... I've brought two visitors."

"Visitors! Glory!" cried the wife.

"Visitors! Bah!" cried her husband. "Who wants to come visitin' me?"

"Well, Andy, it don't make no difference, do it? Tain't like we entertain company ev'ry night. I'll set out some cornpone for our guests."

"Woman, mind yore place," Andy cautioned her, although she ignored him and ran into the cabin to gather food and plates. Watching until she disappeared inside, Andy shook his fist and assumed a menacing demeanor. "Who'd yah bring to my home, Toby? And why fer?"

Fog Mother stepped around Toby, opening her arms.

"Well, if'n it ain't th'Indian witch. Yah speak'um English? Did yah bring tha' black whore Mary, too?"

Dead Mary had been called worse, but never by a worse man. "Mind yo' tongue, pig. I've done kilt men daid fo' lessah insults."

"Ah thought tha' ah'd killed yah back when ah shot at yah in the springtime."

"Yo' missed."

Andy chuckled. "So be it. Ah don't hold no grudges. Well, yah'll maght jest c'mon inside fer a spell. Mah ol' bitch wife likes company."

Unlike the drafty, single pen cabin where Andy lived previously, this new dwelling was tidy, spacious, and adorned with touches of domesticity, like a bundle of dried flowers hanging above the hearth and a braided rug on the floor. Andy's wife beamed and beckoned them into the domicile, where she showed her guests the skillet cornbread and basket of apples on the table.

She explained, "I growed the corn in my own garden yonder, and those apples are from an orchard planted by that Appleseed feller."

Andy Craig sidled next to her, and the sight of the two of them, man and wife, prompted Fog Mother and Dead Mary to look at each other and shrug. They'd been told that Mrs. Craig was a homely woman—some called her downright ugly, what with her cow neck, thinning hair, and eyes too close together—but paired with leathery, rotten-toothed old Andy Craig, these minor deformities gave her a look of spit and vinegar. She seemed tough enough for him.

"My name is Marge Cuss," she said. "Welcome."

"These folks don't care none wha' yore name is," Andy complained.

"I got a name and I intend to use it. I ain't your property."

"Ah paid twenty good skins to get yah, an' that would've otherwise bought twenty bottles o' good whiskey, what would keep me jest as warm at naght as yah'll do. So don't git so big-headed. An' yore name is *Craig*, not Cuss no more."

"I'll let you know if 'n' when'll take that name."

Fog Mother cut slices of cornpone for herself and Dead Mary. They smiled and nodded while chewing, although the cake was dry and tasteless.

"Thank you," Fog Mother said.

Under the table, she kicked Dead Mary, who added, "Yea, thankee yo'."

"Piss on thanks! Yah'll ain't here jest t'eat cornpone. Wha's yah want to talk wit' me fer 'bout?"

"That ain't no proper way to talk to guests!" Marge protested.

"T'is when they's jest Injuns," Andy countered.

Toby had anticipated the need for social lubrication, so he proffered whiskey.

Andy snatched the bottle and took a slug.

Fog Mother used that interlude to gather her thoughts into English. "Me and Mary, we must go. Not safe here no more. Many devils will come, kill us."

Dead Mary, cringing to listen to Fog Mother struggling to speak the language she hated, cut her off. "She means dat dey'z an evil has come int' d' land. Scouts who set up camps by d' Ko-ko-sing in summer ain't left fo' d' winter. They aim to settle down. Next year, our whole valley'll be filled wit' deyz cabins an' taverns, ain't no treaty line goin' to stop dem. Fog Mother 'n' me, we gotz to get away. Ain't no mo' safe."

"Ah'll stop them!" Andy Craig shouted. "Ah'll kill ever damn one o' them. Twice."

"No!" Fog Mother blurted. "No kill."

Unable to proceed, she paused for a spasm to pass, then addressed Dead Mary. "Please, daughter, translate for them my words, because it sickens me too much to speak in their dog tongue. Explain to them that the white people's migration into our fields and forests cannot be stopped, for it is part of a drama that is playing out among many spirits and souls in worlds beyond ours. As with two winds that blow storm clouds across the heavens from different directions, so do our gods and the white men's gods clash when they drift across the same sky. But we know, too, that storms are part of nature, and after them sunshine and rebirth can follow. There must be peace in both the realms of gods and men. Killing is nourishment only for those with evil hungers. Killing any man—white or Indian—will anger his gods and create thunder in the heavens. Men and gods must thus cooperate, each with one another, none seeking advantage, all desiring only for life to prevail. There is no other way."

Dead Mary wasn't sure that she understood what that all meant, but she tried her best to explain. "She said dat our gods and yo' gods be in d' clouds, causin' storms. Killin' each otha' makes gods angry, tho'. So we gotz to be good wit' each otha. Ain't no otha way."

Andy sat rock still and stared. "Say what all?"

"She speaks of magical things," Toby suggested.

Continuing, Fog Mother spoke in a rising voice. "Peace requires the kind of faith that questions everything. There is more to learn than we can possibly comprehend. Wisdom is not defined by what we know, but by accepting that which is beyond our ability to know. That alone leads to contentment. This is true even among the gods. But there are certain gods, like some men, who hoard knowledge and seek selfish advantage from it. They sing lovely songs and make grand promises, but they always remain in hiding, like shadows that flee whenever there is light. They may call from the other side of a door—*come, join me, let me embrace you*—but they never show themselves. Any person who passes through that door becomes their slave. There is no return."

Dead Mary stared at Fog Mother with a confused look on her face, as if she was scratching her brain with the backs of her eyeballs.

Toby whistled and said, "Those words are deeper than the deepest river, too deep for me."

Andy Craig and Marge Cuss turned to Dead Mary, awaiting translation.

"She said... be wise. Don't ask no questions. Let answers come to yo' on deyz own. Don't listen to no lies, 'specially dem ones that yo' want fo' most to be true. Don't go through no door that yo' can't go back outta."

Andy Craig slobbered, "What the huh?"

Marge Cuss offered, "That makes good sense to me."

"No it don't. If'n it made sense, ah'd tell yah so."

Marge Cuss stuck out her tongue at Andy Craig, who fumed at her, "Do tha' 'gain, an' ah'll cut yore tongue raght off its stem."

Marge Cuss stuck out her tongue at Andy Craig again.

Fog Mother interrupted their quarrel with her final thoughts. "There is still a chance for peace in this land. Humans have gotten the gods' attention. The potential of their grace surrounds us, but it is swirling like golden leaves in a whirlwind, difficult to catch and hold. Every time violence visits this world, the winds will blow more furiously and scatter hope farther from our grasp. But kindness stills the turmoil. Self-sacrifice heals." She inhaled that thought, held it in her mind, and spoke again in English. "You must not *kill*."

"Not nev'r?" Andy Craig whined. "Ah don't see how ah ken *not* have to kill somebody, someday, sooner 'n' later. Lots o' people jest fairly deserve to get kilt."

He reached for the bottle of whiskey.

Toby stopped his hand. "It would be unwise to ignore the Fog Mother's warnings. She works powerful magic."

Underscoring that point, Fog Mother waved her fingers as if casting an invisible spell.

At that, Andy shivered as if something cold had crawled across his shoulders and down his back.

Marge Cuss started laughing out loud. "Hee hah. Don't you worry about this old coot doing no killing. I know how to keep him under control."

"Ain't damn likely, woman."

"Talk, talk, talk. You sure talk loud with whiskey in your gut."

"Dry snatch!"

"Limp cod!"

"Ah'll damn sure make yah beg fer mercy."

"Oh, I will be a-beggin' all right... for you to get stiff, for once."

Andy Craig stood and reached for his belt.

Marge Cuss rose and faced him, eyes full of dare.

Looking away, Toby cleared his throat and said, "Thank you for seeing us." He tapped Fog Mother on the shoulder and gestured with his eyes toward the door. "But we must leave now."

Marge Cuss said, "Oh, ain't no need to leave so quick on our account. This won't take but a few seconds."

Andy Craig brushed them away. "Jest leave the whiskey!"

PART THREE – 1806-1807

"The implicit obedience and respect which the followers of Tecumseh pay to him is really quite astonishing, and more than any other circumstance bespeaks him one of those uncommon geniuses which spring up occasionally to produce revolutions and overturn the established order of things. If it were not for the vicinity of the United States, he would, perhaps, be the founder of an empire that would rival in glory that of Mexico or Peru. No difficulties deter him. For four years he has been in constant motion. You see him today on the Wabash and in a short time you hear of him on the shores of Lake Erie or Michigan, or on the banks of the Mississippi, and wherever he goes he makes an impression favorable to his purposes."

William Henry Harrison, Governor of Indiana,
in a letter to William Eustis, U.S. Secretary of War,
August 1811

Chapter 12 - April 1806

Chillicothe, Ohio

The grayish sandstone statehouse in Chillicothe was square, with a stepped porch, shuttered windows, and a soaring cupola at the center of its steeply hipped roof. Colonel Frank Bantzer couldn't help but stare at the first all-masonry building he'd ever seen. To him, its solid architecture represented that justice and civilization had reached the frontier.

For that day's important meeting, he'd resolved to leave no nuance of his professional demeanor or appearances to chance. He donned his full-dress military attire, a dark blue coatee with gold trim around the collar, herringbone embroidery on the vest, and long tails in back. He wore his plumed shako hat drawn tight around his neck, its brim shadowing his eyes. He'd bathed, shaved, clipped his nails, and oiled his hair and goatee. He'd practiced standing with an upright, disciplined carriage, walking as if his backbone didn't bend, and sitting so stiff that the surface of a drink placed on his lap didn't move. If, when that meeting with the governors was over, he had done nothing more than say, "Yes, sir," at least he would have done so with impeccable posture.

A rather boyish private answered Bantzer's knock on the door, and nearly poked himself in the eye in his haste to salute the colonel. He snapped off, "Welcome to the Ohio statehouse, *sir!*"

Bantzer allowed himself a moment to relish the respect, then said, "At ease."

The private then led him into an antechamber and offered him some tea while waiting.

How genteel, Bantzer thought, although he refused. What he'd have much preferred was a quick pull off the flask hidden in his stockings.

A longcase pendulum clock ticked interminably. Fifteen minutes past the specified time for the meeting, the private returned to inform Bantzer that the esteemed governors would see him. It occurred to the colonel that it might be one of the expectations of powerful men that people should be made to wait for them.

Inside the spacious office, the Governor of Ohio, Edward Tiffin, stood next to his desk, clasping the handle of a teacup with one hand and extending the other in greeting.

"Colonel Bantzer, I am pleased finally to meet you."

On the occasions that Bantzer had heard Governor Tiffin speak in public, he'd listened with feigned interest, all the while thinking *get to the point, already.*

Tiffin was a glib, plump-cheeked man, a physician and a lay preacher before entering public service. People often described him as "charming."

To the degree that charm had no military value, Bantzer was not particularly impressed.

"I've heard good things about your work clearing nuisance squatters and Indians from our state's southeastern districts. For that, the people of Ohio owe you a debt of gratitude...."

As Tiffin spoke, Bantzer noticed that the second man in the room, with his back turned, was looking out the window and turning his head from side to side.

"...as well as for your continued contributions ensuring the peace through your excellent leadership of the local militia."

At this, the man at the window rapped his knuckles against the glass and attested, "So true!" He tugged on his sleeves, offering the colonel his hand. "I am William Henry Harrison."

Bantzer felt his hand being squeezed like a rag as they shook.

"It is an honor, sir," Bantzer said.

Harrison let go and grunted what sounded like, "Of course." His thick brows, sharp nose, and deep-set eyes afforded him a handsomely diabolical look, as befitting his reputation as a fierce Indian fighter, and a no less determined politician.

"You and I are both veterans of the Battle of Fallen Timbers, sir," Harrison said. "I salute your service on that day. Alas, though, we now face new enemies. The cause of freedom calls you once again, Colonel Bummer."

"That is *Bantz*-er, sir, pardon me. But rest assured that you will find me ever vigilant and prepared to answer the call of duty, sir. My lifelong motto is: always be ready, in all ways," he said, proud of himself for having thought that up on the spur of the moment.

"What did I tell you, W.H.H.?" Tiffin interrupted. "Is he not just the man we need?" He pulled out two chairs in front of a small conference table. "Please be seated, gentlemen. We have much to discuss."

Snapping his fingers, he ordered the private to bring the men some more tea.

"Tea?" Harrison scoffed. "Have you no brandy? It is not manly to discuss politics over anything less. Don't you agree, Colonel Bugger?"

Bantzer was so encouraged by this proposition that he didn't bother to correct the misuse of his name. *Bummer? Bugger? So what?* A man had to earn the right to be recognized by the likes of William Henry Harrison. Besides, for a shot of good brandy, he'd have answered to Colonel Boxer, Blizter, Bungler, or whatever the great man wished to call him.

Harrison poured nut-brown brandy in glass snifters, then proposed a toast: "To almighty God, who shall bless and fortify us to slay our enemies, be they savages, Brits, blasphemers, or traitors."

The men drank and chatted awhile about pressing local concerns, like the late spring, George Rennick's cattle acquisitions, road conditions along Zane's Trace, and the outrageous cost of salt. Naturally garrulous, Tiffin played the role of the host by asking questions, agreeing with his guests' points of view, and calling for refills before glasses were empty.

Meanwhile, Bantzer stole several sideways glances at Harrison, trying to guess what he was thinking, but careful not to look him in the eye, lest he appear presumptuous.

At length, Harrison cleared his throat, which seemed to be a signal to Tiffin, who changed the subject in mid-sentence.

"Well then, Colonel," Tifin said, "let's get to the point. As you no doubt realize, despite Ohio's great growth and hopes for prosperity, there remain certain intractable threats to our welfare."

"Indeed."

"Specifically, we are monitoring two situations, one to the east, and the other to the west. I fear that military action may become necessary at either, or both."

"Do tell me of these concerns, sir."

Tiffin paused, summoning depth in his voice. "Having served in Marietta, perhaps you have made the acquaintance of Harman Blennerhassett."

"No, sir, I was not a member of Mister Blennerhassett's society."

"Good for you, because he keeps very dubious company. Twice in the last year, no less a scoundrel than Aaron Burr has visited him. Having fled Washington, Burr seems desirous of establishing a new government in western territories, where he fancies that he would be president. We suspect that he has been building a secret redoubt and armory on Mr. Blennerhassett's island. I have met him—an amiable enough man, with a pretty wife—but while he clearly takes pleasure from arts, letters, and philosophy, he is also a radical with visions of grandeur. Such a man is easy prey to the blandishments of a charlatan like Burr. His island is strategically important for controlling commerce along the Ohio River, and his personal assets could provide revenue for whatever manner of treason Burr is scheming. These circumstances can simply not be allowed to stand."

"Indubitably so, my governor. When do I lead my troops against him?"

"Ah, such zeal for action. That's why I recommended you," Tiffin said. "Alas, would that it was so simple. Since his crimes are against the nation, orders to move against Blennerhassett must come from President Jefferson himself. The local militia is on the ready, awaiting that command, which may come at any time. However, there is another matter that occasions even greater immediate concern...."

Harrison leaned forward, between Tiffin and Colonel Bantzer. "Over Indians," he snorted, finishing Tiffin's sentence. "Even after we defeated them in battle and legally relocated them to reservations, those ruthless savages continue to insult God-fearing Christians in our land. There are new problems with certain Shawnee, who have recently established a large encampment on Ohio's western border, where it is prohibited by the Treaty of Greenville. They claim it as their homeland. This is unacceptable."

"How many Indians, sir?" Bantzer asked.

"Could be five hundred. The population varies, for there are many pilgrims coming and going"

"Pilgrims?"

"So they fancy themselves, although their devotion is clearly madness and deviltry. A self-proclaimed holy man has emerged among the Shawnee, who is attracting disciples from across the Northwest—not just from his own tribe, but others as well. Doubtless he is nothing more than a rabble rouser, or worse, a pawn of British agitators, but, even so, his ministry seems to be thriving among the primitives."

"Who is this so-called holy man?"

"We know very little about him. Gossip suggests that he was the medicine man from a Kispoko clan, whose village along the White River was by blind luck spared from the plague last winter. Now, he boasts that he has magical powers, can perform miracles, talks with God, walks on water, and shits pure gold... it's the usual bunk and piffle that, unfortunately, is quite effective at agitating the barely human Indian mind."

Bantzer pounded his fist against his breast. "Give me two companies of Christian patriots, and I will see to it that this quack gets to meet his god. I would be honored to personally strike my knife through his heart."

"Alas," Harrison continued, "there are three problems with that course of action. First, we do not know the extent to which this faker has won over converts outside of his own tribe. Moving against him could risk inciting a broader Indian retaliation, especially if the infidels are being armed by the Brits. The second issue is that, for these reasons, President Jefferson favors the strategy of softening them up with liquor and bribery, the better to persuade them to sign friendly treaties."

Harrison sighed and shook his head, as if passing negative judgment on that policy.

"And also, sir?" Bantzer prodded. "You said that there was a third problem."

"The truth is that since they began arriving just a few months ago, these Indians have comported themselves in a generally peaceful manner. They claim that they occupy holy ground, and they've done little more than sing their songs and smoke their pipes. Of course, we are still within our rights by treaty to remove them from Ohio. But, lacking any obvious aggression on their part, political considerations hinder us from using force against them. That brings me to the subject of your mission."

"My mission?"

"We need reliable intelligence on this holy man. We need to know his designs. We thus order you to take a regiment of men to the site of old Fort Greenville and establish a camp. Make sure the Indians see you. Put the men through some drills. Fire some cannon shots into the air for good effect. But your real mission is to gather information. We have a spy—a man known to and trusted by the Shawnee—who will infiltrate their settlement and report back to you. As soon as you have facts sufficient to expose this bogus prophet and his dangerous intentions, you will have the honor of leading the charge, and the glory of killing him.

"Do we understand each other, Colonel *Bantzer*?" Harrison asked.

Never had he been so elated to hear his own name. "Consider it done, sir."

After the meeting, Colonel Frank Bantzer felt like shouting "hallelujah" as he strolled through the streets of Chillicothe. While merchants and laborers busied themselves with their toils, women swept their porches and gossiped across picket fences, and children played their cute little war games, Bantzer strode among the citizens with the sense that he was personally responsible for protecting their innocence and happiness.

Upon seeing the colonel in his uniform, a pack of grubby boys broke off their game and flocked toward him. One child asked Bantzer if he had killed any *Injuns* yet on that day.

"Why? Have you seen any?"

The lad looked around nervously, then, realizing that he was being jested, laughed that he had not, but when he did, "Ah'll shoot 'em down daid like skunks." He then fired off several shots with the whittled pole that he pretended to be his musket.

"Someday, son, you will be a fine addition to the Ohio militia."

The boy lit up at Bantzer's praise.

The governor had ordered the colonel to mobilize the troops and march on to Greenville at sunrise the next day. He knew it would be difficult rallying the men for duty on such short notice. Still, this splendid occasion warranted a brief, private moment to pause and celebrate the honor and trust that the governor had shown him. With a taste of brandy lingering on his tongue, Bantzer thirsted for more. He was thinking about the bottle of bootleg grain alcohol he'd hidden behind a loose floorboard in his quarters. He figured that he deserved a few minutes to take off his boots, maybe even his trousers, and relax while savoring a dram or two of the highly potent beverage before dispatching his duty.

Outside his quarters, Colonel Bantzer saw a peculiar man standing by the door, badly playing a tune on a cheap wooden whistle. At first glance, this man looked reputable, wearing a gray frock with a sharp collar, and freshly barbered with hair trimmed above the ears, and just a few days' beard growth. However, beneath the folds of the cape, Bantzer saw that he wore a tattered linsey shirt and coarse pants that were patched at the knees and cut off crookedly at the bottoms. When the colonel noticed that this man was also shoeless, he immediately recognized the hairy feet.

"Appleseed?"

Johnny tooted a note that sounded like, 'hello,' then spoke. "So ye do recall meeting me? However, I would be pleased if ye chose to call me Johnny."

"Even if I had succeeded in forgetting you, I could hardly avoid hearing the stories that folks tell about you from town to town across Ohio."

"Most things folks say about most things are exaggerated, and what they say about me is no exception," Johnny said. "But I am flattered if they think me-self worthy of being talked about."

"They call you a fool."

"As Benjamin Franklin said, 'He is a fool who cannot conceal his wisdom'."

Determined that nothing was going to spoil his mood, Colonel Bantzer continued toward his door, muttering, "Good day," and hoping that would conclude their interaction.

"If I may have a moment of your time, Lieutenant Bantzer—"

"*Colonel* Bantzer. I'm quite busy."

"I shall not detain ye for long. I have a letter from a mutual friend, which I promised to deliver personally."

Frank Bantzer gripped the doorknob. "A letter? Not... from Mona?"

"Why, yes indeed. I visited her in Pennsylvania just four days ago, and I promised to deliver this letter straightaway to ye, although I do confess that I did not follow the most direct route in getting here. After rafting down the Ohio, I overnighted with my good friends Margaret and Harman Blennerhassett at their lovely estate—"

"Blennerhassett! What has Mona to do with him?"

"Why, nothing at all. I was simply explaining to ye the cause of my brief delay in delivering her letter. They are friendly folks, the Mr. and Mrs. Blennerhassett, and the missus is a devout member of me church. I was passing by their island, so I stopped to visit. I have planted a small orchard at one end of their estate. Maybe next year, I shall plant another at the other end."

"Ha. That is unlikely." The idea of thwarting Johnny's plans pleased Bantzer, even more if he could find a justification for arresting him. "But never mind that. Give me the letter."

Appleseed removed a sealed letter from a pocket inside his frock and handed it to Bantzer. He stood by, waiting, as if he viewed his task as incomplete until he'd witnessed Bantzer actually read the missive.

"I hope that ye will find that Sister Mona's letter contains good news," the man said. "Her church is moving into Ohio. She would like to see ye."

"Why, you impertinent hair-brain! Have you dared to read my mail?"

"Certainly not, I assure ye. These are merely things that Sister Mona told me face-to-face, while she was barbering me. Mona is a fine barber, for a woman. Do ye not agree?" Appleseed turned his head from side to side, profiling his recent haircut.

Bantzer ground his teeth at the thought of Mona running her fingers through this scraggly man's hair. "Tell her that it will be a dark day at noon before I consent to see her."

Appleseed said, "Dark day at noon? 'Tis odd that ye should say so, for that very thing is predicted to happen this coming summer. Blennerhassett told me—something to do with the moon passing across the sun. 'Tis written in one of his books of natural philosophy."

Disregarding those comments, Bantzer grabbed Johnny by the shirt and spoke directly into his ear. "Tell Mona that I am married to my duty. I have no need or desire to see her."

"That I cannot do, for I do not know when I shall meet her again," Appleseed replied, and then, with a shrug, he slipped out of Bantzer's grasp. "All summer, I shall be quite preoccupied planting seeds up north. But first, I am going to call upon some of my Shawnee friends. I hear that they have a new Prophet, whose acquaintance I should very much like to make. Adieu, though. I wish ye nothing but the best."

"Be gone now!" Bantzer barked. He wondered how it was possible, in just two minutes, that such an inconsequential dolt as Appleseed could spoil his mood and present him with so many tribulations. First, Mona; then Blennerhassett; and finally, the Shawnee holy man. It was as if Appleseed purposefully wandered the country seeking out everybody whom he wished to avoid, arrest, or slay.

Colonel Bantzer decided that even though Appleseed was a dimwit and a swine's arse, he was also something worse—an enemy.

But Appleseed wasn't quite ready to take leave of him just yet. When Bantzer tried to step around him, he thrust a page ripped from a book into the colonel's hand.

"Here is one last thing for ye to think about," he said. "Fresh news straight from heaven."

Chapter 13 - May 1806

Greenville, Ohio

When he lived among the Shawnee, Stephen Ruddell wore a necklace with a sturgeon jawbone. Conversely, when he passed time in the company of white folks, he wore a crucifix around his neck. It was all pretty much the same to him. He'd tried both ways of life and could get by in either. Ironically, whenever he dwelt with the Indians, after a while, he began pining for the comforts of American civilization, but within a few months of returning to it, he missed the community of his Shawnee brethren. Plus, he liked Indian women better. They could do things that Christian women didn't even know to try.

During all the years that he'd hunted, feasted, danced, laughed, loved, mourned, wept, and worshipped with the Kispoko Shawnee, they'd never made Ruddell feel any less than an equal. Under the new regime, though, he bristled at how people shunned him or gave him hostile looks whenever he came around. Nobody spoke to him about it, but nobody had to. Ruddell understood: there was a new prophet in town.

In the aftermath of his miracle, Lalawethika had proclaimed that he was Waashaa Monetoo's one chosen Prophet, and for anybody to believe otherwise was dangerous heresy. He insisted that he alone could interpret the Great Spirit's commands. So, when he declared that Indian people must renounce the ways of the white race and return to their native beliefs, his words carried divine authority. The Prophet thus modeled himself as an example of Indian virtue through how he'd renounced alcohol, kept only one wife, and repudiated American food and fashions.

In that environment, Ruddell didn't need for anybody to point out to him that, while he might be a citizen of the tribe, he was a white man even more than that. Under other circumstances, he might've slipped away from the tribe until things blew over. Unfortunately, he knew that if he tried to move on, he'd have that damned Colonel Bantzer chasing after him, demanding answers to all sorts of leading questions about the Prophet, such as if he was truly a drunkard, and whether he was receiving illicit supplies from the British. At first, Ruddell had been flattered when Bantzer recruited him to be an "informant" for the government; he'd logically assumed that the job involved reporting "information," which seemed like a downright helpful thing to do.

As it turned out, though, Bantzer was not interested in hearing any news that did not confirm his presumptions of the Indians' ignorance, insobriety, or brutality. Colonel Bantzer refused the truth the way a dog refused vegetables, but give him news that he liked, and he was face-deep chomping like a jackal on red meat.

Not that the Indians were any more open-minded. Lalawethika warned that the Long Knives were soulless dupes of the evil god, Mothsee Monetoo. When the community's braves saw the American soldiers setting up a bivouac near old Fort Greenville, they gathered their swords and tomahawks and vowed to defend their Prophet, unto death.

Ruddell tried to calm his Shawnee friends, explaining that the militia's deployment was nothing more than a show of force; they had no real intention of launching an assault. By saying so, though, Ruddell worried that he was bringing even more suspicion upon himself.

Ruddell could speak freely with only one person. "It's got so bad that I can't tell the truth 'cause nobody believes me, and I can't lie 'cause nobody listens," he griped to Johnny Appleseed, while they dined on a mush of cooked beans, dandelions, and field greens.

"Tell the truth to God, and he will reward ye," Johnny said.

"My problem ain't what to say to God, but what to say to somebody who thinks he's god."

"Tell him he is a fool."

Ruddell stirred his mush and wondered if that was what Johnny really intended to say to the Prophet—that he was a fool. It might get him killed if he did.

Johnny had arrived at the Indians' village a few days ahead of the soldiers, requesting a private audience with the Prophet. He was rebuffed. Undeterred, he'd asked again the second day, and the third, and the fourth.... On each occasion, he was advised that the Prophet's time was too precious to be squandered on anything other than God's business... and on each occasion, Johnny replied by saying that he, too, was doing God's business.

"But I am patient," he'd added.

Downstream and across Mud Creek from where the two men sat, a solider at the militia's camp played taps at the end of the day. Upstream, the assembled tribes likewise chanted and drummed to mark the day's passage.

"Their music mixes together agreeably," Johnny said. "If only they could hear it."

"A regular hoedown," Ruddell agreed.

Three Shawnee riders, led by Battle Panther, appeared at the crest of a hillock behind Johnny and Ruddell. With one hand on the horse's bridle and the other brandishing a spear, he rode into their camp, looked down at the men, and spat into their mush pot.

Johnny opened his mouth to say something, but Ruddell caught his eye and shook his head sideways.

Battle Panther sidled off his mount, lifted his loincloth, and pissed into the white men's fire. While pissing, he spoke to Ruddell. "Tell this stinking imbecile that the great Prophet Lalawethika will see him now."

Ruddell hesitated, unsure about how literally to translate those words, when Johnny piped in.

"Never mind, I understand. Let us make haste." He stood and brushed himself off. "And thank ye, sir, for putting out our fire. 'Tis never a good idea to leave one burning at an empty camp."

In the massive council house, Lalawethika sat in a chair carved of solid black walnut, beneath the roof's highest point, where he imagined that his presence evoked majesty... even though his brother continued to argue and tell him what to do. Despite the affront to his omniscience, he still listened begrudgingly to Tecumseh's advice. It was helpful whenever the Great Spirit was silent in response to direct prayers.

"I do not understand," Lalawethika complained. "I myself can only see with one eye. Why should I not cover the bad one with this fine patch of soft mink fur?"

Tecumseh snapped, "It looks like a rodent is humping your eye socket."

"But my eye is ugly. All my life, I myself have been mocked because of it."

"Listen, brother, once more, while I explain to you how to act like a Prophet. Your clouded eye is a powerful sign. It inspires fear and awe in people. Tell them that with it you can see into their minds. Fix your gaze upon them with the blind eye, and do not blink. Do this, and I swear that those same people who mocked you will bow before you."

Lalawethika liked that idea. Removing the patch, he practiced staring ominously, imagining that he could shoot lightning bolts from his afflicted eye.

Meanwhile, Battle Panther entered the council house and waited to be recognized.

"What do you want?" Lalawethika asked, glaring for good effect.

"I have brought the vagabond white man, as you requested."

"What?," Lalawethika bellowed. "I myself did not grant permission for this filthy scarecrow to stand in my presence."

Tecumseh said to him, "Yes, you did. This man may appear like a tramp, but he travels this country far and wide, and knows it better than any other. I want to hear what words he has to speak. So, too, should you."

Snorting, Lalawethika centered himself in his chair and instructed Battle Panther to, "Let him come."

Accompanied by Stephen Ruddell, Johnny traipsed forward with his frock swooshing, until after just a few steps he realized that he was walking alone. Behind him, Ruddell was bowing, face down.

"Oh, I am sorry," Johnny said. "Was I supposed to kneel?"

Lalawethika ignored the scarecrow, bade Ruddell to rise, and spoke to him. "Tell this vagrant that he must show me the respect that is my due."

Ruddell started to translate, but Johnny abruptly jumped in. *"Waske pakekiliwewa, chena pakekiliwewa wece hipemile, Waashaa Monetoo, chena pakekiliwewa, Waashaa Monetoo."*

Lalawethika rubbed his jaw and wondered whether to be flattered or offended. Before he could decide on a response, though, Tecumseh said, "What you say is true, apple man. The Word is God. The Word is eternal. But how do you know Shawnee beliefs?"

Proudly, Johnny continued speaking in the Indians' language. "That wisdom comes from the white men's holy Book of John, chapter one, verse one. Is it not grand that we ourselves believe the same things?"

Lalawethika protested. "The Shawnee are Waashaa Monetoo's people, and I am his Prophet. Your man 'John' is a demon!"

"Patience, great Prophet, for this man is ignorant," Tecumseh said, laying his hand on Lalawethika's shoulder. Then he turned to Johnny and asked, "How is it that you have come to speak our language?"

"A man like myself who wanders with his ears open acquires words naturally. I spent two moons during the summer last with Black Hoof in Wapakoneta. We smoked many a pipe. He calls me *Olam-a-pies,* the Teller of Strange Stories."

At the mention of Black Hoof, Tecumseh cringed. "Black Hoof's tribe has not accepted the Prophet," he said. "But he will."

"I believe that each person must himself find his own way to God," Johnny affirmed. "This leads me to a question that I have come to ask of the Prophet."

Lalawethika was glad to have the attention return to him. "You may proceed to make your inquiry."

"Does Waashaa Monetoo speak to you directly?"

"Of course. I am His ears in this world."

"Do you hear His voice?"

"As clearly as I hear yours now."

"What does He sound like?"

Lalawethika shifted uncomfortably in his seat. This line of questioning seemed impertinent, especially from a white man. Perhaps he should order that his tongue be cut out. He could do that.

While Lalawethika was thinking, Tecumseh interjected. "The voice of Waashaa Monetoo carries like thunder from beyond the horizon."

Wagging his finger, Lalawethika disagreed. "No, it begins like a distant cry that cracks the air but does not shatter it, and as it builds, it also surrounds, until when Waashaa Monetoo addresses me personally, his voice sends tremors through my bones."

Johnny nodded. "May I ask further, at the same time, does it sound distorted, like a person calling out from behind a closed door?"

"Yes!" Lalawethika cried. Then he aimed his blind eye at Johnny. "But how do you know of such things?"

"Well as a matter of plain fact—" Johnny broke off and swatted at his backside, then glared at Ruddell as if to ask, *why did you do that?*

"I am done with your questions," Lalawethika pronounced "There is no need for any man to ask about the voice of the Great Spirit, for He speaks only to me. I am separate from all other men, just as the light of day is separate from the darkness of night."

"Hmmm." Johnny rubbed his chin and appeared intrigued. "That is an odd statement, for I have learned that very thing will soon happen.

On one fine afternoon later this summer, the darkness will devour the day's light in the middle of the afternoon—"

Johnny stopped talking when Ruddell stomped his heel on Johnny's toes.

"Leave me now," Lalawethika commanded, cupping his ears so that he would not have to listen to any more. "I must rest."

Following Ruddell's lead, Johnny genuflected before leaving the council house.

While Lalawethika closed his eyelids and began napping, Tecumseh followed the two men outside and called for them to wait.

Pointing at Johnny, he said, "Tell me everything that you know about this miracle, when the day's sun will cease to shine."

Johnny obliged.

That evening, the Prophet insisted that everybody in the entire community attend to hear him speak at the dedication of the united tribal council house. The log edifice spanned the length of forty bears east to west, and was as wide as twenty pack horses. By working together, men and women of all tribes in the Northwest—the Delaware, Kickapoo, Potawatomi, Ojibwa, Ottawa, Wyandot, Miami, Sauk, Seneca, and even a few of Black Hoof's Mekoche Shawnee—built the house in just one month. The workers sang plainsong hymns to Waashaa Monetoo while laboring side-by-side to peel the logs, raise the posts, and fasten slabs and thatch to the building's roof. Three rows of hewn beams supported a soaring ceiling. There were entrances at each of four sides, so that people and their spirits from every corner of the universe could come and go as equals. Inside, hundreds of feet had pounded the ground into a hard surface, and parallel rows of logs provided seating that faced the Prophet's fire pit and his chair at the ceremonial hub. As people entered and settled into their places, they lit and passed several *hobocans* containing aromatic *ksha'te,* and as they exhaled, a layered haze of greenish smoke drifted above their heads.

Lalawethika cringed at the sight of Johnny Appleseed and Stephen Ruddell, who stood in the farthest corner behind the last row. The scarecrow, Appleseed, coughed and waved at the smoke around him, and Ruddell, looking as if he feared being scalped at any moment, whispered something into Appleseed's ear. At that, Applseed steeled himself.

Seated in the Prophet's chair, the spiritual center of the assembly, Lalawethika watched and sucked on his own pipe. He'd adorned himself in gaudy but traditional attire, with bronze clasps around his wrists, feathered and jeweled pendants dangling from his ears, and a bright silver gorget around his neck. In the months since receiving his vision, he'd grown a sparse, down-sloping mustache that, matched with his perpetual frown, gave him a look of judgmental severity—at least, he hoped it did. His followers had noted that sobriety had restored a crimson tint to his brow and cheeks, that the white in his good eye was bright, and that even the fluids clouding his bad eye seemed creamier.

Seated next to him, one step lower on the platform, was Tecumseh. "All rise to honor the Prophet," his brother proclaimed.

Five hundred Indians stood side by side, shaking their rattles and beads, pumping their fists in solidarity, amid spontaneous shouts of, "Speak, great seer!" "Lead us, oh mighty priest!," and "Deliver us into heaven!"

The shouts, applause, and stomping of feet felt to Lalawethika like an earthquake beneath his seat.

After a moment, Tecumseh shouted, "Now sit!"

Anticipating the Prophet's words, the crowd quickly stilled.

Lalawethika rolled forward in his seat, opening his arms to take in the adulation. Still, even surrounded by cheers and calls of devotion, he felt, oddly, alone and exposed. In the breathless hush of the crowd, Lalawethika felt his heart throbbing out of control, like an angry beast trying to burst free from his ribs. He'd never imagined himself as an orator, capable of words worthy enough to captivate so large an audience. A nauseous feeling began to crawl up his throat.

He drew an utter blank.

Off to the side and below the line of sight of everybody except Lalawethika, Tecumseh made a fist, with thumb erect, and tipped it, simulating a bottle being emptied.

Ah, yes. Now Lalawethika remembered what he was supposed to say.

"Brothers, sisters, we are all ourselves children of the Great Spirit," he began, a bit jittery. "On the day that I died, I myself was summoned into the divine realm. There, the first dwelling that I encountered was that of an Evil Spirit, who is Mothsee Monetoo. He showed to me a house occupied by all the Indians who had died as sinners and drunkards, whose bodies now had flames spewing from their mouths, and they screamed while dragging their melted intestines behind them across hot coals. Mothsee Monetoo bragged to me that he had fooled stupid Indians into thinking that white man's alcohol made them stronger, braver, more virile... when in truth it robbed from them all dignity and courage. This made plain to me the terrible consequences of drinking white men's poison, how it chokes an Indian's pride and sinks his soul nearer to hell. I understood that the only hope for me and my people was to banish the use of alcohol by all Indians, forever. Yes, I myself confess that before receiving my revelation, I too was a vomiting drunkard."

Lalawethika squeezed his neck and feigned to be unable to breathe. He heaved and panted, making sounds like a dog before it died, in just the manner as he'd practiced with Tecumseh prior to the speech.

Then, he threw back his arms, lifted his chin, and shouted, "But when I battled my demons in the world beyond death, Waashaa Monetoo cured me of my affliction. So too might He cure all Indian peoples."

He paused, allowing the crowd to respond, until Tecumseh cued him to continue by scratching his palm.

"In primitive times, Indian people all glowed with radiance, because we were kept warm by the grace of the Great Spirit. We moved through the woods without leaving footsteps, killing only those animals that gave themselves to be our food. Our corn and beans and squash sprouted from the Earth, and grew large to satisfy healthy appetites. We drank only clear water, as nourishing as the milk of our mothers' breasts. The forests, lakes, and the sky filled us with peace, so that when we listened for the Great Spirit, we heard Him speaking in the sounds made by natural things.

"In those ancient times, we used our voices only to pray to the Great Spirit, or to speak wisely in council, or to say kind words to our children and our elders. No Indian spoke ill to any other. We dwelled near in heart to Waashaa Monetoo in a bountiful land, and we were free to go where the game led us or where the soil was fertile. That was our state of true happiness. We could make everything we needed from trees and plants and animals and stone. We wore only the skins of beasts. We mastered fire for cooking and for making offerings. We learned how to heal with barks and roots, and how to make foods taste sweet with berries and fruits, with papaws and the sap of the maple tree. The Great Spirit gave us tobacco, and asked us to send prayers up to Him in fragrant smoke. We took loving mates, and we lived according to fair laws that gave our people harmony. Our Creator sang to us in the wind and the running water, in the bird songs, in children's laughter, and we made music on drums to please Him. When we were mindful and obedient to Waashaa Monetoo, our stomachs were never empty. That is how we were created.

"But who among us now lives the way that the Great Spirit intended? Nobody! When I died, I saw how living in decadence leads always to torment. The Great Spirit sent me back to warn the Indian peoples, and to lead them into the peace and purity that He intended for them. Who will follow me?"

In vociferous affirmation, the people used every noisemaking device at their disposal—drums, rattles, hands clapping, feet stomping, and a bedlam of voices that included men chanting, women singing, babies wailing, and dogs barking.

After a few moments, when the uproar began to subside, Lalawethika shook his fists, and with that gesture triggered a new crescendo. As Tecumseh has advised him, Lalawethika turned to his blind side and scanned the crowd, intending to mesmerize them with his mystic eye. He felt loved. He felt feared. He felt eager to test his powers.

Tecumseh raised one finger to the air, to remind Lalawethika what to say next.

"Now we ourselves have become weak and afraid, but hear me when I promise that, while a single twig breaks, a bundle of twigs is strong. The Indians must unite again as one people. The property of one Indian must belong to all. We must revive our natural religions. We must believe again that all Indians are people of Waashaa Monetoo, and thus superior to the white men and their evil civilization.

"Today, some Indians have adopted the detestable ways of living of white devils. From this moment forward, let no Indian wear their linens, but dress in the skins of animals. Indians must not eat cattle or sheep, but only native prey. We must never eat bread made of wheat but only of Indian corn. To kindle fires, we must use sticks and rocks instead of flint and steel. Indians can never marry whites, for this practice dilutes the purity of our blood. And by no means drink alcohol. Leave the vices of white men to themselves, for they shall lead to suffering in this life, and then damnation."

The Prophet's speech inspired a chain reaction of conversion experiences. Some men tore off their knit shirts and ripped them into shreds. Others who had been drinking earlier that evening stuck their fingers down their throats to induce vomiting. Women removed their scarves and passed them down the aisles, to be tossed into the fire. Row after row, Indians from all tribes bowed, up and down, again and again, while confessions and testimonies rang out, each trying to be more emphatic to gain the Prophet's attention.

Tecumseh cued his brother to wrap things up by twirling a finger.

"Let me say it plainly. The Great Spirit is Waashaa Monetoo. All others are demons, and those who worship them are witches. They must be uprooted from Indian peoples. I am the one Prophet of Waashaa Monetoo. I will eliminate witches wherever they hide.

"Should any person still doubt my powers, I will prove that I speak truth by delivering a certain sign. Fifty days from this one there will be no cloud in the sky. Yet, when the sun reaches its highest point, at that moment Waashaa Monetoo will take it into his hand and hide it from us. The darkness of night will cover us and stars will shine at midday. The birds will roost and the night creatures will awaken and stir. When this happens, nobody will dare to disbelieve me ever again.

"I promise that if all Indians follow me, we will triumph and be free. Waashaa Monetoo has given us the power to defeat our enemies. We can reclaim the Great Spirit's favor. I am the only Prophet who can make these things come to pass. Believe none but me."

Hearing this, at last, Tecumseh nodded at his brother, indicating that the speech had gone well and it was now time to sit back down.

However, Lalawethika remained on his feet and silenced the multitude by waving his arms criss-cross above his head. Tecumseh glared at him, but he did not acknowledge the look. The lines on his brow narrowed, his nostrils flared, and his blind eye widened in an expression that nobody had ever before seen on his face. Stepping to the fire, so close that he glowed, the Prophet tossed his medicine bag into the flames.

He bellowed in a voice that sounded like a storm. "I have one final command. From this day forward, I am no longer to be called by the name Lalawethika, the Noisemaker. That is the name I once bore in shame. Now, I am Tenskwatawa, the Open Door. Call me only by my new name."

There was reverence and rapture in the screams of, "Tenskwatawa! Tenskwatawa!"

While the cries and accolades continued, Stephen Ruddell nudged Johnny toward the nearest exit. "We'd best be gettin' outta here while we still can," he whispered.

"I do not reckon anybody would mean us harm."

"Are yah daft? Didn't yah hear what he said?"

"Tain't no worse fire and brimstone preaching than what you might get from your average Baptist," Johnny said. "But did ye notice how his voice changed when he spoke those last words. It was not his voice at all."

Flustered, Ruddell pulled Johnny by the collar. "If we don't hustle outta here, it may be the last thing yah hear, period."

"Ye go onward ahead, and I'll catch up by and by."

Ruddell, not needing to be told twice, scurried out.

Johnny stayed behind and listened intently, trying to catch an echo of something that he thought he'd heard cutting through the din, a sound like an explosion in a dream. The dancing, shouting, and pandemonium in the council house overwhelmed his senses, though, and he began to sweat and tremble. Johnny didn't exactly recognize the feeling, but it had all the symptoms of fear. He backtracked until he was out the door, then he started running.

When he was able to think again, the first thought that occurred to him, after all the things he'd just heard and seen, was that he would have to plant a whole lot more apple seeds, if there was ever going to be peace in Ohio.

Chapter 14 – May 1806

Greene County and Greenville, Ohio

Rebecca Galloway sat behind the barn stuffing fabric scraps into her bloomers to sop up the blood that had started leaking from her tweeny. That's what older friends who had lived through this ordeal said she should do, although it felt dirty and uncomfortable. It scratched down there, and after a while the clippings turned into a soup that made it hard for her to walk without it all coming apart. All morning she'd waited, sitting on the porch with her legs crossed, until nobody was looking, then waddled behind the barn to change her stuffing. The dogs followed her, and she worried that one of her snoopy brothers might catch her in an awkward moment. Now she knew why her mother referred to a woman's monthlies as a "curse."

Still, to Rebecca, this was a spectacular menarche, for it meant that now, finally, she had become a *woman.*

It had seemed like a long time coming, for her mother told her to expect it months ago, and she'd begun to think that something was internally wrong with her. Her little breasts were budding, and faint, kinky hairs had sprouted around her girl's crack, but until she'd expressed first blood, Rebecca fretted that her femininity was stunted. The cramps and the mess and the hot shivers were thus a welcome relief. Now, finally, she was mature enough to marry the man she loved with all of her heart.

Chief Tecumseh.

Rebecca remembered the first day he rode onto her family's farm, how he sat tall and bare-chested on his horse, how the wind blew his hair behind him, and how he smiled magnanimously when he caught her gazing at him. Tecumseh carried himself with such gentle dignity, as well as a demeanor of mystery, that Rebecca had to remind herself to breathe in his presence. When she was little, he'd visited the farm often, always bringing her bits of hard maple candy. She picked flowers for him. It did irk her that he was always surrounded by

Indian women who fawned and posed for him, but he seemed indifferent to them, as if he were searching for a different kind of love than they could offer. Rebecca grew up believing that her love for him was pure, and that when she reached the age when Tecumseh was finally able to see her as a woman, he would realize that hers was the love he'd always sought.

Now, just in time, she'd overheard her father discussing with other men that Tecumseh had returned to Ohio. This, Rebecca was certain, was because of her.

"Becky!" her mother called from the cabin. "Where are you?"

Rebecca pulled up her bloomers and dropped her skirts, hastening to answer the summons. Jittery as she was, she still noted the use of her familiar name, Becky. From now on, she wished to be called Rebecca. When, oh when, she wondered, would her family finally get that through their heads?

Rebecca rounded the barn, walking guardedly... until she saw her Aunt Mona standing next to the gate of the pigsty. Instantly, Rebecca sprinted into Mona's open arms. They collided in an embrace that spun them both around.

"By the grace of the Lord, look at how you've grown. You are practically a woman."

Hearing that made Rebecca feel so proud that she wanted to blurt out, 'Yeah, and I'm bleeding now, too.' She guessed that, somehow, as one woman to another, Mona probably knew.

The Galloway family had assembled to greet Mona. The last any of them had seen her, she'd been so heartbroken she could barely finish a sentence without collapsing into tears, and while they were encouraged to see evidence of her recovery, her subsequent declaration that she was now married to Jesus Christ was disturbing in a different way. While the Galloways welcomed her eagerly, they were also unnerved by how, just beyond the fence line of their property, a small wagon with three female passengers, a tethered donkey, and a male escort who remained mounted on his horse, parked and waited. Were they keeping an eye on her? Why didn't Mona introduce them?

"Come'n sit with us for a spell," Mrs. Galloway said. "Will you stay for dinner?"

"Alas, not today," Mona lamented. "We have miles ahead of us. I can stay no more than an hour, but I could not pass without seeing you.

"Then let's go inside for cider and pones."

"Just milk for me."

The Galloways left the chair at the head of the table for Mona, who sat, folded her hands and prayed—out loud—with her eyes closed. For several seconds after crossing herself, even after saying, "Amen," she kept her head down.

Finally, the littlest boy said, "She done said amen. When can we eat?"

"I prayed for al l of us," Mona said. She picked one of the pones from its basket, and spooned gobs of apple jam onto it. After taking a bite, she declared it to be delicious.

This pleased Rebecca. "I helped Mama make the jam. It's from our own apples."

"Were they planted by Johnny Appleseed?"

"He's an oddball," Rebecca offered by way of indirect reply. "But I like him."

"Yes, he is a likeable man," Mona concurred.

Then, the Galloways barraged Mona with questions. Where had she been? Where was she going? How was her health?

Rather than answer those questions individually, Mona began by telling her story from when she left Ohio five years earlier. At the time, she'd sought to convalesce within a spiritual community, while she figured out what God wanted for her to do with her life. She'd planned to travel to Albany, to seek the female preacher, Mother Ann Lee, but only got as far as Pennsylvania, where she fell in with Sister Say and her cohort of United Believers. After living with them for a period of time, she got baptized as a sister in the church, and swore her heart, soul, and body to Jesus Christ, her celestial husband.

"For the Lord, unlike men of this world, is always true, never lies, and will never abandon me."

Upon further questioning, Mona described her life among the United Believers: how they began each day by ringing the Great Bell; then after prayers, every member performed some necessary task meant to synchronize their worldly efforts with God's will. Men and women worked side-by-side, doing physical labor where, sometimes, their bodies brushed against each other, and yet they remained strictly celibate, without even a whiff of lust. Everything they did was for the glory and honor of God Almighty, and thus they kept their minds and their souls free from worldly taint. In return, He blessed them with such joy that, when it seized their bodies, they trembled with ecstasy. Hence the name by which outsiders commonly called them: "Shakers."

Over time, Mona admitted, membership in their community waxed and waned, but overall a core group remained steadfast in their belief that Jesus Christ would come again in glory to judge the living and the dead, just about any day now. Meanwhile, though, the devil had other plans. One of their group, a German gentleman named Fritz, who in fact owned the property where they all lived, listened to the teachings of a false prophet, named Johann Georg Rapp, and was seduced by them. When Brother Fritz abandoned the United Believers to become a Rappite, he evicted his brother and sister church members. God did not forsake them, though, for the spiritual leaders of the Shaker faith were keen to expand into the Northwest. So, along with her devoted sisters, Mona was going to join a new congregation in nearby Turtle Creek.

"There we shall create a village in the image of God's heavenly city, and we will preach His message to all willing to listen with open hearts, even if they be drunkards, mercenaries, or Indian savages."

"Indians! Oh, please, convert Chief Tecumseh," Rebecca begged. "I think that he'd make an excellent Christian."

Mona pressed her palm against her heart and replied, "You are an eager lass, so full of zeal that it sometimes feels like your heart will burst. Am I right about that, Miss Rebecca?"

Rebecca nodded, less because she agreed with the sentiment than because she appreciated being referred to as Rebecca.

"That passion comes from God. Celebrate your youth, but be wary, too, for you are at the age when you are vulnerable to losing your innocence. Be very careful whom you love, for of all human emotions, love is the most sublime, but also the most fragile. You will never forget anybody to whom you faithfully give your heart, no matter how it might hurt."

"How do you know when love is true, auntie?"

"Time, my dear girl. True love proves itself through patience."

Rebecca thought that was the most beautiful thing she'd ever heard in her life. She lunged across the table and hugged her aunt gratefully.

Meanwhile, Mrs. Galloway heard those words and shook her head, while James Galloway groaned, "Love, my arse."

Mona started asking questions of her own. Remembering Rebecca's love of books, she asked her if she'd read the Bible. Upon seeing how robust the boys had grown, she asked them about their schooling and advised them not to neglect their spirituality. She asked her sister and brother-in-law many questions about how their farm was prospering, how the nearby towns had grown, and what religions were the most prominent thereabouts.

As they chatted, the Galloways noticed how Mona invariably commented upon whatever they said with some remark about how God's handiwork was evident in whatever happened, or didn't happen, or should have happened—it always came back to God.

At length, James Galloway grunted and pushed away from the table.

Mona had barely sipped at her milk, when all of a sudden she tilted it back and drained it, announcing that she needed to be getting on her way.

They all embraced and patted each other's backs, and Mrs. Galloway made Mona promise to visit again soon.

"I hope that one day you will join us," Mona said.

"Oh, of course, we'll visit."

"I mean *join* us."

Turning to Rebecca, Mona kissed both of her cheeks. "Mind what I said to you. It is hard to do but... trust me on that subject. You must first love yourself, just as Jesus Christ loves you."

Rebecca stifled tears as her aunt retreated from the cabin to where the church members awaited her.

Mona turned to wave, twice, until finally she reached her people and stepped into the wagon.

Mona sighed as if relieved, tightened her bonnet, and whispered, "Holy Lord, help me guard my heart."

"Amen," Sister Say said as the wagon pulled away. Then she asked, "Did thou fulfill God's will?"

"My first task is done," Mona replied. "But my more difficult one is next."

"Thou are not required to do this."

"I believe it is God's will, so I must."

A few hundred yards down the road, as soon as they were out of sight of the Galloway farm, Mona called for the procession to halt.

The rider accompanying them stopped his horse and grabbed the wagon's reigns out of Sister Say's hands. The brim of his hat covered his eyes when he spoke. "If I dare say so, sister, I am not completely persuaded that what you're askin' is so much God's will as your own."

"The two are not mutually exclusive. By serving my conscience, I am still, ultimately, serving the Lord. Is that not true, Brother Bunselmeyer?"

"I don't cipher matters of faith," Brother Bunselmeyer answered.

Mona avoided his eye as she untethered the donkey from the wagon and tossed a blanket over its back. "God's plan is never simple."

"It will take you the rest of the day's light to reach Greenville. Maybe longer, on that nag. I cannot guarantee your safety."

"But God can."

"Perchance I ought to ride with you. Elder Worley told me clearly to take good care of you all."

"Leave her be," Sister Say interjected. "This, she must do alone."

Mona raised her brows in surprise. As recently as that morning, Sister Say had been opposed to this course of action.

"Do as you wish, then," Brother Bunselmeyer said. "But guard your virtue, sister."

Mona huddled with Sister Say and the Rose and Mary sisters for a prayer.

Brother Bunselmeyer watched them while chewing on his plug of tobacco. After a while, he said, "God is patient, sisters, but I ain't."

Sister Mona stood by the donkey, watching while Brother Bunselmeyer and the sisters proceeded down the road to Turtle Creek and disappeared around a bend. She felt at once alone and liberated, realizing this was the first time she'd done anything entirely on her own in five years. Her determination had grown greater than her ambivalence, though. Her actions this day would be the only way she could understand what was truly in her heart, and the only way she could know whether her faith and character were strong enough to withstand temptation.

Colonel Frank Bantzer waited for his foot massage. It relieved tension, and under the exasperating circumstances of his current deployment, the stress of doing nothing made his heels ache and his arches cramp. Putting the men through their daily drills was a poor substitute for the battlefield action he craved.

When first given this assignment, he'd seen it as an opportunity to demonstrate his mettle and leadership capabilities. Forty-five days into the mission, though, he was growing restless. The "spy" that governors Tiffin and Harrison promised, Stephen Ruddell, had provided no actionable intelligence on the Indians' true intentions. In fact, to hear him tell it, the so-called Prophet and his people were an amiable fellowship of song-singing, flower-picking pacifists who wanted only to be left alone.

Colonel Bantzer, convinced that Ruddell was either lying, duped, or being influenced by the Shawnee women whose company he admitted to frequenting, had sent his own scouts to reconnoiter the Indians' village. Yet despite their stealth and camouflage, his scouts could never creep up on them undetected, and as soon the savages spotted his men, they greeted them by turning around, lifting their loincloths, and showing their heathen arses. They were devious, indeed.

Many of his men, he also suspected, had taken to slinking out of camp at night seeking the attentions of those agreeably immoral Shawnee women. So, Colonel Bantzer marked his time and hoped that, any day, the governors would issue the order to attack.

Meanwhile, he tried to present a positive role model to the men by soliciting only clean, Christian whores imported to the front lines from Dayton. Every other night, he had one delivered to his tent, making sure that the men saw her. He regarded this as an aspect of his duty, while also making a public statement of his virility. Most often, though, the only service that he required from these women was a foot massage, and even then, in his heart, all he truly wanted was to enjoy his whiskey in peace.

After another long day, Colonel Bantzer took of his boots and stockings, lifted his feet onto the chest in front of his chair, and dreamt of having his toes nibbled.

"Permission to enter, Colonel," his personal attendant, Sergeant Work, called from outside his tent.

"Granted."

Sergeant Work presented himself and saluted. "A woman has come into camp askin' to see ya."

"Yes, of course. Show her in, already."

Still at attention, Sergeant Work stuttered, "But sir, there's one thing ya should know—"

"What could I possibly need to know about a common whore?"

As if to answer that question, a woman entered Colonel Frank Bantzer's tent. She wore a gray calico dress that hung to her heels, with sleeves that covered her wrists, a plain white bib over her shoulders and breasts, and her hair bunched under a straw bonnet tied tight around her neck.

Bantzer might not even have recognized her, were it not for the soft but penetrating blues of her eyes.

"My God! *Mona*?" He stubbed his toe on the chest as he lurched onto his feet. He turned to Sergeant Work, looking for somebody to blame. "Who have you brought to me?"

The sergeant shrugged. "She said that she knows ya, Colonel."

Mona said, "I have come a great distance, Frank. I ask only a few minutes of your time."

Confused and alarmed, but at the same time oddly aroused, Bantzer struggled to assess the situation. Mona looked fetching, in a forbidden way. If this had been any normal whore masquerading in a Shaker habit for his pleasure, he'd have jumped her with enthusiasm. But this was Mona—innocent, confounded *Mona*—and she was far too guileless to wear those garments with anything other than complete sincerity. The naivety of her convictions was part of what he'd once found so alluring about her.

"You may leave now, Sergeant," Bantzer said, dismissing the man lingering outside of the tent.

Frank Bantzer and Mona Junkin faced each other in candlelight, and the shadows brought back memories of their last encounter. Bantzer recalled that he'd tried to give her one final kiss goodbye, but her sobbing and pleading had made that impossible, so he merely said, "Duty calls me," and backed away.

When he turned away from her, Mona lunged for his sword—for what reason, he did not know, but Bantzer had suspected that she intended to run it through her heart. He dodged her easily, and left her groveling.

Now, five years later, they countenanced each other like two sad ghosts, each come to haunt the other.

"Were you expecting somebody?" Mona asked.

"A soldier must always expect the unexpected."

"May I sit?"

Bantzer pushed forward his own chair for her, then sat on the chest. "You look well."

"I came to tell you something that I want you to know," she began, then waited until he put on his socks. "I have found the love that you could not give me, in my Lord Jesus Christ."

"Oh, uh, yes, so I had heard, not that I was inquiring, of course, but just through odd gossip here and there. Are you, then, some manner of vestal nun?"

"I am a sister of the United Society of Believers in Christ's Second Appearing."

What a nuisance! Expecting a whore and given a nun!

Even so, the quivering fragility in her voice reminded him of the taste of her lips, and how when she'd finally yielded to him, she gave herself with such rapturous abandonment that no woman since had made him feel more powerful. He couldn't refrain from wondering what her body looked like under that sack of a dress.

Mona continued, "For weeks, after you left me, I was heartsick. I worried that I might be with child, and yet I also wished that it could be so, to bring you back to me. I gave my heart and my body to you, Frank, and you left me with nothing."

"Now, now, Mona, I never made any promises. You knew that my duty came first."

"I didn't come to blame you, Frank. I came for two reasons. First, to thank you. By forsaking me, you compelled me to seek and find God's true love."

Mona folded her hands on her lap, and Bantzer struggled against an impulse to take them into his. "If our, uh, experiences helped to lead you to some contentment... well, you are welcome," he said earnestly. "But what is your second reason for coming to me?"

"I just wanted to look into your eyes once more."

Until that moment, Bantzer had been avoiding her direct gaze, but his reservations crumbled when Mona spoke those words. Searching the depth of her eyes released feelings in familiar channels of his soul: the yearning, the passion, the illicit joy. She did not blink, holding him rapt—inviting him to enter? During the best of their times together, they'd connected through their eyes as much as through their bodies. Bantzer still thrilled at the recollection of how Mona's eyes had sparkled when she achieved her ecstasies.

Now that *is something I'd be happy to see again!*

He reached for Mona's hand. He exhaled and she inhaled....

With a stomping of boots, Sergeant Work called from outside the tent. "Beggin' yer pardon, sir, but yer, uh, appointment has arrived."

A painted floozy strutted into the tent, moving in a way so that her bouffant curls bounced and her ample cleavage, on display below a drawstring neckline, jiggled as if full of strawberry jam .

"Hey, ho, Colonel. Are yah barefoot yet?" she chirped.

The spell was shattered.

"Oh, Frank," Mona gasped.

"No, wait...."

"Pardon me, sis'," the floozy interrupted, looking Mona up and down. "But save yer sermon 'til after we're done."

Mona gathered her equanimity and walked toward the door, while Frank, gone limp, could only manage to sputter the word, "Don't!" He didn't know what to say next.

On her way out, Mona paused and, with back turned, said, "I will pray for you, Frank Bantzer."

To which the amused floozy chortled, "Yeh, do that now, 'cause he'll need it." Then she knelt in front of Frank and tugged on his socks. "Now, let's see those toes, Colonel."

Chapter 15 – June 16, 1806

Danville

"Is it for true that you shit apple seeds?" Millie Blubaugh asked with utter sincerity.

The way his seed bag hung behind his backside, kind of like a horse's turd catcher, made the question seem almost reasonable, at least enough so that Johnny took no offense.

"No ma'am," he said. "I do eat plenty of apples, and a seed or two may pass on occasion, but I purge me bowels the same as any other man... excepting possibly the odor. I eat no meat, so me own droppings do not stink."

"Do tell! That ain't like my Otto. His shit reeks so awful, it chokes flies."

Overhearing their conversation, Otto objected. "Honey doll, don't tell such things. Leave us men t'our'n work."

"I can help some."

"This ain't none fit work for no woman, 'specially in yahr condition."

Millie pulled her blouse tight, proud of her round belly and how high she carried it. "I ain't got no *condition*. It's called a *baby*."

"Still, ah heard tell that a woman wit' child ought not to raise her arms above her head, or else the baby'll slide too far down."'

Millie squealed in exasperation, but before she could argue, Johnny butted in. "I too would prefer if ye left the work to us, my dear, just to be prudent."

"Some folks say you ain't far from a fool, Mr. Appleseed. Others have done told me yar a wise man." Millie shrugged. "But I ain't made up my own mind, yet."

"Please tell me when ye decide. I too am yet to make up me own mind on that subject."

Otto and Johnny resumed their toil.

A deluge of rain had fallen that spring, and the early summer heat was unusually scorching, so by June the whole countryside was a riot of verdant grasses, colorful wildflowers, knee-high fescue, and leafy maples dropping their whirligig seeds everywhere. The acre on Dan Sapp's estate where Otto and Johnny labored was muddy and overgrown with chokecherry, ironweed, and bitter nightshade.

In exchange for clearing this parcel of land along Jelloway Creek, Dan had granted Johnny permission to plant an orchard there. He'd instructed Otto, his hired hand, to lend assistance.

Although Johnny usually worked alone, he found Otto's vigor and work ethic to be heartening, and he also enjoyed Millie's company, for he'd had a soft spot for her ever since the day of the horse race in Newark. Ohio needed more women with her honesty, curiosity, and optimism—qualities that on so fine a summer's day radiated like the warmth from second sunshine.

Around midday, Dan came riding Lulu to survey the work's progress and to bring refreshments to the crew. He'd openly expressed low expectations, as the tract of land was gnarly and possessed poor drainage. Furthermore, he remained wary of Johnny, claiming the stories about him confounded common sense. Still, he'd declared that as a purely business venture, he saw no downside to their agreement, for if Johnny could clear and cultivate an otherwise unproductive corner of his land, and share the proceeds from selling apple seedlings to boot, Dan had nothing to lose and much to gain. In fact, he'd said that was what bothered him. As Dan reckoned it, Johnny was giving up too much, which either made him too charitable for his own good, or the shrewdest flimflammer this side of Washington, D.C.

Either way, Johnny understood that Dan figured it wise to keep an eye on him.

Two slobbering hounds followed alongside Dan and Lulu. After dismounting from his horse, Dan removed a loaf of bread and some dried venison from his pack. "I've brought some lunch." He rubbed his eyes, then shouted, "You fool, Appleseed! You're up to your elbows in poison ivy!"

Johnny chuckled as he heaved the vines into a burn pile. "Never mind. I have thick skin."

"Wash your hands just the same."

Johnny considered excessive hand washing a vanity, but he scrambled down to the creek and began splashing to demonstrate his compliance. While holding out his arms to dry, he noticed that the moisture on his skin seemed sticky and heavy, like evening dew. The sunshine on the ripples in the creek glinted in an unusually orange hue. Behind him, the hounds started to whimper.

"What day would this be?" Johnny inquired.

"Yesterday having been the Sabbath, today is Monday, of course," Dan Sapp answered.

"No, not the day, the *date*."

"I don't know. What's the use of knowing the date?"

"Is this perchance the sixteenth?"

Otto broke in. "Yessuh. Ah know 'cause ah'm countin' days 'til Millie's due-on-date."

Johnny jogged to the center of the open field and bent back his neck so far that it looked like it might snap. He gazed toward the highest point in the sky, with a feeling in his heart that was half like he'd just seen a ghost, and half like he'd just found a pot of gold.

"'Tis happening," he said, pointing heavenward.

"What?" the others asked in unison.

"Behold."

There was nothing to behold, not right away—not that they could see, anyway. Increasingly agitated, though, the hounds nudged at Dan's calves. Lulu flicked her ears, snorted, and danced around her tether. Birds took to the air and began fluttering to and fro', as if they'd lost all bearings.

Johnny, as anxious as the animals, bounced on his tip-toes and began singing softly:

"Of all the ages ever known
The present is the oddest;
For all the men are honest grown,
And all the women are modest."

While calming his horse, Dan Sapp looked up and muttered to himself, "Jesus, Mary and Joseph."

Millie grabbed her husband's arm and asked, "Is there somethin' wrong with the sun?"

Johnny ogled wide-eyed and jaw dangling at the firmament, as if making more room in his head, and he cupped his hands over his ears, straining to catch an echo of something dim and distant.

"Do ye hear the angels?" he asked.

Nobody answered.

The four of them stared toward the fading midday sun. No night ever raced behind the setting sun as quickly as that afternoon's total eclipse devoured the daylight. Steadily, a crescent shape blotted out sections of the sun in a diffuse shadow. Over the next few moments, the mass of the moon advanced across the solar sphere, creating a spectacle at once frightening and majestic. Bats skittered overhead as stars began to glitter around the inky horizons. Venus crowned the tallest of the forest trees.

The temperature fell perceptibly, and moisture beaded in the hairs on Johnny's arms. A pale, copper penumbra covered the contours of the creek, hills, fields, and forests. Finally, the moon's ghost seemed to snap into a niche cut into the globe of the sun, as if it were crafted to fit there. The sun's scintillating corona scattered white flares like cut gemstones on fire.

Nobody breathed. Nobody spoke for the duration of this marvel, yet in their silent awe they shared a moment that would bind them in a rare, collective memory for as long as they lived.

When the moon began slipping over the far side of the sun, Millie said, "It's a sign from God, don't you reckon?"

"It must gotta be," Otto agreed.

"I'd call it a blessing," Millie added.

"'Tis more than a blessing!" Johnny could hardly control his jittering. "'Tis a revelation, says I! At just the same time as this land was eclipsed, so too were heaven and hell. I could hear a hundred voices in both realms, all a-mixing together, but each one as clear and distinct as yours or mine."

"I heard only the whipporwhill," Dan Sapp said.

Johnny dropped to his knees, pounded his chest, and began to rant. "Moses recognized the presence of God in a burning bush. Saint Paul saw a vision of the risen Christ in the skies above Damascus. Swedenborg traveled into heaven and hell to see everything with his own two eyes. For me, revelation comes in sounds. Just now, in heaven, great joy and singing rang out. I heard their choirs. I heard their cheers and trumpets. A multitude of angels and spirits shouted hallelujah. How I wish that ye could have heard, too, my friends.

"But in hell, the suffering damn raised a wrathful clamor. 'Tis almost enough to make a man's ears bleed—a sharp and chilling noise that grew louder as the skies darkened, until at the very moment when the sun was blacked out, I heard the whirling of a tornado and a crash like hell's gates had just slammed down. From the other side came a hissing sound, like from the mouths of a thousand snakes."

Johnny remained kneeling, face down, tears glazing his eyes. "I am grateful that ye were deaf to that particular sound."

If Dan Sapp's expression was any clue, and Johnny figured it must be, then he thought the experience had driven poor Johnny plumb noodles.

Millie buried her face into Otto's chest. Otto ran his fingers through her hair, and cast a worried look in Johnny's direction, as if looking for some confirmation from him that none of this had put any kind of hex upon his wife and their baby.

Lulu stepped loose from her tether, walked up to where Johnny sat hunched over, and pushed the back of his head with her muzzle.

With that, Johnny hopped onto his feet, shook his arms, and said, "It appears that the daylight is a-coming back. We ought to return to work, do ye not agree?"

Mohecan John's Creek

There was a bounty on wolves in Knox County, Ohio: two dollars for the scalp of a gray wolf male over the age of six months, and three dollars for that of a she-wolf. After a week, the land agents who'd organized the hunt calculated that they were paying nine she-wolves for every one male, and by that realization acknowledged that nobody knew for certain how to tell a male from a female wolf just by its scalp. Thus, they changed the bounty to two dollars for all, period.

Normally, Andy Craig would have taken advantage of this opportunity for supplemental revenue, and because he knew where the wolves had their dens and how they migrated across the territory, he figured he could earn a tidy sum. The problem was that the local lands bureau had designated his goddamned older brother, Jim, to serve as the officer in charge of making bounty payments. Andy would rather be shaved and fried in bear grease than accept any money from his hated sibling.

Just as bad, though, was the great hunt's impact upon the tranquility of Andy's world.

Mount Vernon, the largest settlement, rested where Owl Creek spilled from the gap into fertile lower land. There, a man named Gilman Bryant ran a general goods store out of his sycamore cabin, selling powder, lead, shot, traps, axes and knives, corn whiskey, and other essentials. Five miles to the north, in another habitation named Clinton, a certain Samuel Smith operated a business in pelts and furs, with off-the-bone wholesale prices from 25 cents for muskrat to one dollar and 50 cents for beaver. Thanks to the wolf bounty and the market for animal products, hunters now infested the woods, ready to shoot at anything that moved.

Andy fired back every chance he got, but there were lots more of them than there was of him. It was becoming almost impossible for him to get through his day without seeing any other person—other than Marge and baby Andrew, of course, but they didn't count as persons. All he wanted in life was to avoid any goddamned interference from people who couldn't mind their own business, which was just about everybody other than him.

The last straw was seeing his brother in the woods. Andy had been checking his traps in the plains between Owl Creek and Mohecan John's Creek when he practically tripped over a hunting party's trail, so he followed to see what mischief they were up to. In the clearing at the confluence of the Clear Fork and Mohecan John's, perched on overturned rocks with their feet in the water, sat two men, one a thin and long-legged fellow puffing on a pipe, and the other a negro who was playing the spoons and skating with his voice, "Bingo, bango, boingo, banjo, beeedeeedle doo...."

A third man, hidden by hazel shrubs, chortled while taking a piss.

Andy knew that chortle anywhere, though—half a horselaugh and half like the grunt a man made when pushing out a huge bowel movement.

In the next instant, Jim Craig stepped into view. His profile cast a peculiarly long shadow.

Andy hoisted his musket and fired at his brother's head. The bullet ricocheted off the rock on which the man smoking a pipe had been sitting.

"Git on up, Rope!" the negro yelled.

Instead of getting up, though, Mister Rope rolled onto his side and cowered.

Meanwhile, Jim faced the direction from which the shot had come, puffing himself up, shaking a fist, and hollering, "Come'n out 'n fight, yah pink pussywillow!"

Andy ducked behind a tree trunk. His brother's clenched fist brought back painful memories—literally, it hurt Andy to think of them. Beatings were passed down in his family, father to son, eldest to youngest, and Jim had introduced his fist to Andy's jawbone on many an occasion when they were growing up. "Building character," was what Jim called it, not that he needed a reason.

In haste, Andy pulled the rifle's hammer back to half-cocked and primed it, then shifted its butt against his thigh so he could pour powder down the barrel. Fumbling with the ramrod, he missed the barrel and inadvertently thrust it onto the ground, where it rolled into some bushes and blended in with the strange shadows that were creeping over the land.

"Shoot me, suck me, or fight me... which'll it be, yah dang dingleberry!" Jim Craig cackled.

Andy ran. He diverted from the worn path and bushwhacked through the forest in a helter-skelter flight. He did not look back, but even though he could not hear any sounds of pursuit, he sensed danger in the dreadful gloaming that was closing in on him from every direction. With an unnatural night falling fast, Andy figured his sense of time must've gone awry and that he'd run through an entire day and not even realized it. Worst of all, he didn't seem to be covering much ground, and when he passed a grove of tall pines for a second time, he realized he'd been running in circles. Fear felt like a slap across the face.

Coyotes howled in the distance. Andy knew that the eye shine in a tree above belonged to an owl, but still he imagined something sinister watching him, following him, hunting him—perhaps his brother had placed a bounty on *his* scalp. He tangled his feet in a tree root and, trying to extricate himself, he tumbled, rolled down a ravine, and came to rest in a pond where frogs were croaking as if they'd gone mad.

On his back, he watched in dazed, helpless terror as the last sliver of the sun narrowed, engulfed by a void. His stomach seized with a cramp, but still he couldn't look away. The sky seemed to be coming after him. Even figuring that this meant he was doomed, Andy marveled at the beauty. He'd never imagined that dying could be so beautiful.

The moment passed, and the landscape that just moments ago had looked foreign and menacing now resolved into his familiar environs. Andy knew where he was. He waded across the pond, trampled through a patch of vines and briars, reconnected with one of his trapping paths, and hurried back to his cabin.

Marge stood outside, cradling a squealing infant in her arms. "The sky is a-fallin'," she wailed.

Andy wrapped his arms around her and his son. "We cain't stay here no more. T'aint safe."

"Where can we go?" Marge cried.

"Farther," Andy said.

On the Road to Newark

Although he spent a lot of time there, Reverend Copus still didn't much care for the town of Newark. He had an arrangement with Joseph Black to stay for free in a room above the tavern whenever he was in town, which was convenient but noisy. Drinking was not what distinguished Newark, though; it was gambling. The plebs in Newark were uncommonly fond of games of chance, whether faro cards, horse racing, dog fighting, arm wrestling, shooting contests, or random wagers on everything from birth dates to death dates. Theoretically, gambling provided conversion opportunities, for it often happened that the losers in these sports sought redemption through religion. In practice, however, their devotion lasted only until their next turn of luck, at which point they were off to the races again.

Reverend Copus recalled how Johnny Appleseed had once commented to him that Newark was the nearest place to hell on Earth that he knew of. That seemed like a harsh assessment, but Appleseed had intended it more as an explanation than a criticism. "The wicked cast themselves into hell because it suits their disposition," he'd said. "Instead of suffering physical torment for all eternity, sinners are condemned to continue doing evil, and to have evil done unto them for endless time."

On those terms, Reverend Copus knew exactly what Appleseed meant. Having free will, some folks would invariably choose sin; there was nothing anybody could do about that. Copus sometimes wondered if he kept going back there to try to save souls, or if, deep down, he was casting himself into a kind of hell because, at some level, it suited him.

While traveling the road to Newark, Reverend Copus was distracted from his meditations by a sudden feeling of isolation. He'd ridden that narrow, rutted trace many times, usually by himself, but for some reason on that particular day, he felt a palpable awareness of solitude grab hold of his shoulders and shake him. Unnerved, he stopped his horse and dismounted, struck by how the entire landscape seemed faint and unreal, yet his senses felt heightened, his mental outlook crystal clear. His mind went blank, but in that emptiness, he was conscious of being surrounded by some pervasive intelligence.

Just off the road was a beaver pond, its surface smooth and clear as any mirror. He sat on a stump, mesmerized by the details in the reflections of tree leaves, swaying grasses, and dancing wildflowers, and of the color of the sun, so yellow it was almost screaming. It felt like looking through a window into heaven.

That notion made him think of something. He took from his pocket a page of the book that Appleseed had given him, and he read.

> *Spiritual things cannot proceed from any other source than from love; and love cannot proceed from any other source than from God, who is love itself. The sun of the spiritual world therefore, from which all spiritual things issue as from their fountain, is pure love, proceeding from Jehovah God, who is in the midst of it. That sun itself is not God, but is from God, and is the proximate sphere about Him from Him.*

Those words pretty much described Copus's thoughts and feelings at that moment. His lungs were buoyant; his shoulders seemed to be rising over his head; and his fingers and toes felt like they were letting go of gravity. The sky's reflection filled his head. He felt at once the wholeness of his personal being, and also a connection to every little seedhead on every sheath of Indian grass, every petal on every bloom of goldenrod, and every pointed thorn on the wild rose stems. He understood that this sense of well-being was not within him, but encompassed everything surrounding him. Still, he mused that it was all just a reflection of a more sublime reality, which included and transcended everything present in the moment, from the infinite heavens to the drone of one persistent mosquito next to his ear. Everything in all creation was reflected right there in that pond.

The brilliance of the sun's reflection began fading. Reverend Copus blinked and rubbed his eyes, unconvinced that what he was seeing was real. Even at that moment, when he felt his fullness of being most profoundly, he also sensed that he was getting squeezed through a narrow passage, as if the day was collapsing around him.

Had he completely lost track of time? Was it already dusk? In his private reckoning of time, that seemed possible, except that instead of a sunset, there was just a steady darkening.

The leading edge of a crepuscular moon crept across the sun, extinguishing the light of the world in small segments, at a pace synched to the reverend's slow breathing. As shadows engulfed him, he resolved not to avert his gaze from the reflections in the water, for he worried that if he stood up and looked around, the entire experience would disappear in a poof, and life would go on as if none of this had ever happened. He considered the possibility that he might die. It felt like he was inside a swirling funnel, either rising up or falling down, depending on any moment's perspective. Around him, the animals of the night stirred.

When the last piece of the totality slipped into place, Reverend Copus braced himself against absolute night. Yet instead of smothering the sun entirely, the lunar orb fitted precisely in front of it, revealing a dazzling halo. Even at full eclipse, even when he viewed it through a mere reflection, the reverend felt his soul branded permanently by God's shining scepter. He was *not* alone.

All his life, Copus had hoped for a genuine revelation. In the reflection of that infinite pond, he saw his future—a wife and family, a church, and the self-knowledge that came from having a true calling. By degrees, the light returned, bringing with it sad relief. The reverend was glad the world hadn't ended, but also sad with the knowledge that he'd never behold anything so miraculous again on this side of heaven.

With nobody around to confirm what he'd just witnessed, he began to question whether it had really happened. Had God appeared to him alone? If not, what had the miracle meant to other people? In Newark, how had the hell-bound citizens reacted? When things looked darkest, he supposed, many of them would've probably chosen to cast themselves into hell. For some folks, revelation could be a pretty scary business.

Reverend Copus kept riding right through Newark, on to the next settlement upriver, determined to go as far as necessary—until he found the exact place where God wanted him to be.

Black Fork

Toby arrived at Dead Mary and Fog Mother's camp on foot. He'd left his horse in the Lenape village at Black Fork, and snuck out before dawn, so as to leave undetected. He wasn't sure stealth was necessary, but lately so many Indians had fallen under the influence of the Shawnee Prophet, he guarded what he did or said for fear of causing offense. Religion was bad for his line of business.

"Hey, wha's yo' doin' here?" Dead Mary called, suddenly appearing behind him. She only spoke English when she was angry or worried.

He answered her in Algonquian. "I must speak words with you and with Fog Mother. There is danger."

Fog Mother emerged from her wegiwa, followed by a black cat, a white cat, and a cat that changed colors depending on how close it was to the fire. She opened her arms to welcome Toby. "Dear friend, you honor us by your presence. Come to our fire. Sit. Join us in a cup of hemlock bark tea. It gives courage to a person."

Is she able to tell, just by looking at me, that courage is precisely what I lack?

"I cannot stay," Toby said, even though by accepting the cup he contradicted himself.

Dead Mary remained standing beyond the range of the fire's heat. The look in her eyes, with her brows converging, showed that she was still thinking in English.

"Mother, I have fears for you," Toby began. "I come to warn you that before this day is finished, you will be confronted by the Shawnee who calls himself the Prophet. He will demand that you renounce your faith and your powers."

"My faith is in peace and my powers come from love. How could I renounce these things for the sake of appeasing the supposed Shawnee Prophet, called Tenskwatawa?"

"So you have heard of him?"

"Who has not heard of him? The breezes themselves carry stories about him."

"Then you must also know that he is himself coming to the Black Fork Lenape at invitation from their Chief Arm Strong, and to the people he will profess his vision and demand obedience from them. Already, many have converted. Those who follow him come from all tribes. Many have suffered from plague, famine, death, and war, and so were eager to rally themselves behind the hope that he offers to them. Tenskwatawa makes a simple promise: Waashaa Monetoo will watch and care for those Indians who join him. But, for any Indian to deny that he is the one Prophet is to oppose the Great Spirit. Everywhere Tenskwatawa goes, people swear oaths to him. He calls those who resist witches, and forces them to renounce their beliefs, or suffer for their defiance. In the end, almost everyone submits."

Fog Mother gazed into the fire. "People who embrace prophecy out of desperation lose faith just as fast."

"Mother, I myself know that your powers come from the Great Spirit, because you cured my daughter when she was afflicted by the scarlet pox. But this man, Tenskwatawa, will insist that if you refuse to acknowledge him as the Prophet, it is proof that you are a witch. He will ask you to give up your medicine bag, recant your sins, and surrender to his authority. If you do not.... He has vowed that no witch must be permitted to live."

Fog Mother laughed dryly. "I have my faith, which defeats fear. Perhaps I should demand of this Tenskwatawa that he renounce *his* ways and follow *me*."

Dead Mary shook her bow and arrow, declaring, "I will launch an arrow between his eyes. Whether he is a prophet or a fraud, he can be killed either way."

"No, listen to me, daughter," Fog Mother said. "You will do no such thing. When this man arrives, you must hide yourself and remain silent, no matter what is done to me. Swear to this!"

"But Mother, I could never deny you or allow harm to come to you."

"By committing violence, you would do both. Tell me that you will do as I bid."

"Yes, mother." Mary bowed. "But could you not cast a spell to scare this man? A false prophet frightens easily."

Toby offered another solution. "Or why could you not simply fill a medicine bag full of weeds and rocks, and turn it over for him to burn? Repeat whatever empty chants amuse him, but keep your true feelings to yourself. That's what other medicine workers have done, and no injury has befallen them."

"Not to worry." Fog Mother picked up the cat that changed colors, and looked into its eyes. Two more cats came scampering in from the woods and joined the others, like a feline phalanx gathering for a mission. "Whatever should happen to me reveals the true will of the Great Spirit."

When Fog Mother spoke the last word on any subject, her words came out softly but echoed loudly. To hear them was to end all discussion.

Tenskwatawa hated traveling. He slept poorly in unfamiliar surroundings, away from his own straw mattress and feathered pillow. Rising early to break camp vexed him. On top of that, after an hour or so on horseback, he developed internal duress, for a bumpy road shook his kidney stones and stirred the hungry worms in his liver. He had to stop to piss often, even though he usually produced little more than a trickle. Most discouraging, his summer-long tour of the tribal villages throughout northern Ohio wasn't even halfway finished. He'd been quite content for the pilgrims to come to *him*, but Tecumseh had insisted that he carry the message far and wide, to all Indian communities. The people had to hear him and look into his cloudy eye. Flattering as that was, schlepping across the muddy and buggy frontier didn't seem like the proper way for the exalted Prophet to spend his summer.

It helped somewhat that wherever he went, people lauded him as the Prophet, the Chosen One, the Great Deliverer, or—his personal favorite—He Who Speaks with the Master of Life. Even better, he didn't have to share the notoriety with Tecumseh, who was off scheming with Blue Jacket of the Wapakoneta Shawnee, Withered Hand of the Potawatomi, and indirectly with emissaries of the British from Fort Malden. Tenskwatawa was relieved to cede politics entirely to his brother. Worldly affairs bored him. Besides, by agreeing to divide their labors along political and spiritual lines, Tenskwatawa felt he was getting the better of the deal. Nobody bowed to his brother when *he* rode into a new village. He also appreciated being able to interpret the will of Waashaa Monetoo without having to first check with Tecumseh to verify that he got it right.

On that day, the schedule called for the Prophet to speak in a small Lenape community on the Black Fork of the Mohecan River, just north of the treaty line. Their leader was Chief Arm Strong, an elder who walked bent over due to injuries from his warrior days. Tecumseh had advised Tenskwatawa that, like so many Indians who'd endured demoralizing defeats in battle, privately Chief Arm Strong no longer believed in the Great Spirit, even though he still performed the public rituals expected of him. Though Arm Strong himself was perhaps beyond the reach of sincere conversion, Tecumseh had said he would still be a useful ally in the north.

Tenskwatawa shook his head. *I do not care for allies. I care only for followers.*

The Prophet's entourage arrived at the Black Fork just before noon.

The villagers scampered out of their huts and quit their work to line the path into town, eager to see if a halo shimmered around the Prophet's head, and hoping he would work a miracle for them. Hunters heard the clamor from the forest and hurried back. Women washing by the creek came running. Children abandoned their games and dashed to see the cause of the ruckus. Even dogs barked to join the event.

Battle Panther, leading the procession, raised his spear and sang forth at the top of his lungs:

Listen and hear, True Path Walkers,
your Prophet is among you.
He reveals the True Path
that you must follow or perish,
for we all will live or die as one.
You must choose today.

As the company rode into the village commons, the people cheered and formed a semi-circle around the Prophet. Tenskwatawa relished the worshipful attention, but kept a stoic face by biting the insides of his cheeks, lest he betray vanity unbecoming a holy man. Also, he was hungry and wished to postpone his sermon until after a hearty lunch—people fed him well wherever he went, a perk of being adored.

Chief Arm Strong stepped forward and offered his hand to help Tenskwatawa down from his mount. "The Lenape of the Black Fork open their hearts to you, great Prophet."

Tenskwatawa's stomach growled, loudly enough for those nearest him to hear. They oohed and aahed, as if his gastric utterances carried some deep meaning.

"It pleases Waashaa Monetoo that you have welcomed me," Tenskwatawa said. He said this everywhere he went, and meant it sincerely. Whenever an appreciative crowd received him as a Prophet, he truly felt as if his heart would burst with joy. This feeling got better every time. He had come to believe that Waashaa Monetoo ordained all of the mockery and derision he'd suffered in his earlier life, so that he could better savor the love and worship he now received. Humility had uniquely prepared him to be idolized.

Chief Arm Strong, anxious to capitalize upon his people's enthusiasm, cried, "Oh, great Prophet, would you inspire our hearts with a prayer?"

This was a typical request, and Tenskwatawa had a repertoire of prayers for all occasions. While considering which one to use, he felt another pang in his stomach, this one sharp enough to bend him over slightly. Something deeper than just hunger roiled in his guts. He looked around and noticed that the people's brimming expressions of hope and gratitude cast long shadows over their faces. He took a few steps toward the front of the crowd, feeling a bit rickety, when a knifing cramp assailed him, so sharp that it felt like a blade cutting into his bowels. He staggered and began heaving.

"The Great Spirit is coming upon him!" many in the crowd speculated.

Crows cawed and took to the trees. Dogs went into hiding. Crickets chirped. Fireflies came out of the forest and flickered at random.

An audible thought took shape in Tenskwatawa's mind: *"Open the Door."*

The door? Of course, the door! The pain in his guts dissolved like a great gas bubble popping. He remembered what day it was. Hopping onto a stump, Tenskwatawa pointed at the sun.

"Behold, brothers and sisters, the living truth of my prophecy," he shouted.

"For all of my days, doubters have taunted me. They called me He-Who-Makes-a-Loud-Noise, and scorned me as lazy, stupid, drunken, and incompetent. I failed at even the simplest deeds that make a man worthy of a better name. In despair, I gave myself to death. When I died, there was none to mourn me. But Waashaa Monetoo knew that there was courage in my soul, so He showed to me visions of heaven and hell, revealing to me His will and giving to me the powers to deliver Indian peoples from oppression.

"Still, many doubted me. Even when I cured a dying man, they doubted me. Even when I built a community of followers, they doubted me. Give us a sign, they cried. Show us a miracle that will prove to us that you are indeed the Prophet. Until now, I have resisted their demands, for it is better to touch people's heart through faith than to force them to believe through power.

"On this day, though, I will answer all doubters with sure proof that Waashaa Monetoo is the Creator and I am his only Prophet. Let none dare to doubt a Prophet who can remove the sun from the sky!"

The horizons were darkening and a nebulous shape was beginning to cover the edge of the sun. People instinctively huddled closer together, so that when one person gasped or shuddered, everybody felt it.

A man cried: "Spare us, please, great Prophet."

A woman begged: "Bring back the light, and we will serve you!"

Tenskwatawa let go of a sudden impulse to laugh. It felt as if he could make anything that he wished happen by simply thinking about it. He paused to allow the people's awe and fear to deepen while the daylight dimmed, until when he sensed they were at their most vulnerable.

"Hear me, now, and see proof of my powers. I have taken the sun from the sky. Just so, these are dark times for Indian nations, and wickedness has snuffed out the light of our faith. Had we stayed true to the ways that Waashaa Monetoo gave to us at Creation, no evil would ever have befallen us. But across these lands, people who were once righteous allowed themselves to be seduced by the Mothsee Monetoo, and by his evil witches, and by his false prophets. And by his demons, the Long Knives."

At the moment of full eclipse, the people became seized by angst and astonishment, and they abandoned with relief any lingering resistance to the Prophet. The sight was so terrible and beautiful at the same time that strong men fell to the ground sobbing. Neighbors who had not spoken to each other in months embraced. Every person felt an emotion that no individual could process alone; it was something that they could only feel together, as a group sharing a common destiny, over which they had no control or choice other than to trust the Prophet.

"But just as I, once a loathsome sinner, was resurrected by the grace of Waashaa Monetoo, so too can all of the Indian nations return to righteousness..."

Tenskwatawa then rambled into his well-rehearsed sermon about renouncing the ways of the white men, on the racial purity of Indian nations, and on the imperative for repentance, spiritual rebirth, and above all obedience.

As he continued speaking, the darkness began slowly to retreat, and a great passion swelled in people's hearts with the reawakening of day. Unshackled from their indignity, cleansed of their sins, they cheered and lauded Tenskwatawa.

Chief Arm Strong stood upright and took several agile steps, with no visible pain. "I have been cured of my lameness!" he exclaimed. "Hail the Prophet, the Thief of the Sun, lord of Waashaa Monetoo!"

The Prophet continued: "Now you must all yourselves declare your faith! Any who would oppose me, opposes the Great Spirit. They are witches, who must now be judged.'

Hearing this, Chief Arm Strong decreed: "We cannot suffer a witch among us!"

Several returned by shouting: "Fog Mother!"

"Fog Mother is a witch!"

"Death to the witch!"

Chief Arm Strong led the hordes across the Black Fork and along the mossy path to Fog Mother's camp. Throughout, Toby had stood by himself, cautious about getting too close to the madness. When he heard the angry voices demanding a sacrifice, though, he hurried to intercept the mob. As they approached, Toby stood in their way, extending his arms, palms forward, in a defiant gesture.

"Stop! Listen to me…!" he pleaded.

But the people passed through him, as if he was only a ghost.

By the fire, Fog Mother sat cross-legged in meditation, eyes raised toward the sky, her cats rubbing against her side. When she lowered her gaze, the people saw that her pupils were shining and slit like a cat's. She had tied the strings of her medicine bag around her wrists.

"Seize the witch!"

The cats formed a line in front of her, hissing; but when Fog Mother stood and spread her arms, the animals dispersed into the woods. Although the men had brought ropes and were prepared to drag her away, she walked straight into the riot, toward the Prophet. The people parted to allow her passage, but filled in behind her, so there was no turning back.

Tenskwatawa waited for her, his arms folded. He hadn't expected that she would dare to get so close to him, so even while he stood fast, he was on his heels, prepared to bolt in a split second if he sensed danger.

"This woman works bad medicine!"

"She spins witchcraft among our people!"

Hidden in a tree, where she had watched everything, Dead Mary could no longer bear the constraints of the promises that she'd made to Fog Mother. She opened her mouth to protest, but a blast of dry air rose in her throat, gagging her. She tried to climb down the trunk, but the tree would not let go of her. She was powerless to do anything but watch.

Tenskwatawa faced Fog Mother with his blind eye.

"Do you deny that you are a witch?"

"I myself am only a healer and a peace-maker."

"Peace and healing are no good," Tenskwatawa said, "unless done for the glory of Waashaa Monetoo."

When Fog Mother answered "Waashaa Monetoo is but one of many watchful spirits," the people shrieked and cursed.

"You must renounce all other gods but Waashaa Monetoo, and all other prophets but myself."

"I cannot, for you court violence. I have witnessed many kinds of bloodshed, and I know them all by their sources. Prideful violence demands action, but is never satisfied. Hateful violence flares abruptly, but burns slowly. Mob violence blends fear, frustration, fury, and outrage, and it erupts like a great storm through a narrow canyon. It is always evil."

In all of Tenskwatawa's previous confrontations with alleged witches, this was the point where, persuaded by the obvious dangers, they'd relented and turned over their medicine bags. Instead, Fog Mother made a fist around hers.

"I am the Prophet of Waashaa Monetoo," he asserted.

"I am a prophet for *all* of the spirits," Fog Mother replied, with a sarcastic resonance in her voice.

Censure rang from the crowd: "She defies the Prophet!"

"Fog Mother sleeps with demons!"

"Such evil must be destroyed!"

"I warn you." Tenskwatawa paused to consider whether he was serious about this. For the first time since becoming the Prophet, he wished that Tecumseh was there to tell him what to do. "Renounce all other gods and give me your medicine bag, so I can burn it... or suffer the consequences."

"You will have to burn me with it."

Thus Fog Mother left Tenskwatawa with no other choice. As soon as she spoke, some among the tribe began building a pyre of twigs and branches. They then swarmed the self-proclaimed healer and peacemaker, bound her feet and hands to a pole, and, while she still clutched her medicine bag, lowered her onto the combustible heap. She did not resist, but even so, it took four men to carry her. Her face was like a mask made of stone. Battle Panther lowered a torch to the kindling. At first, the flames didn't catch, but once the fire took hold, it exploded.

Not wishing to watch, and with nobody paying any further attention to him anyway, Tenskwatawa backed away to wait until it was over, which he hoped wouldn't take long.

Fog Mother raged with wild laughter as the blaze engulfed her, even louder as her skin began to sizzle, and continued until long after she should have been dead. The smoke of her burning flesh smelt sweet, like wood from the sassafras tree, but as people breathed it in, they were sickened. A miasma hovered over the village for days, like the haze of a troubled conscience.

Chapter 16 – December 1806

Chillicothe, Marietta & Blennerhassett's Island

"Have patience, Colonel, for if you aspire to become a general, you must equally distinguish yourself in duty, courage, conduct, and character."

Had Governor Harrison limited his advice to just that, Colonel Bantzer would not have taken it so hard; but when he added, "Your ambition shows like a hungry bulge in your trousers," that stung. Even more disconcerting to Bantzer was the thought that, perhaps, the governor was suggesting that he might not measure up to those criteria.

He believed he'd managed his disappointment stoically when Harrison ordered him to dismantle the base at Greenville, and leave the Shawnee Prophet's village intact, although to him it felt like craven surrender.

"Leave it to the winter to soften them up," Harrison had explained. "With luck, plague and famine will kill them off and save us the bother."

Thus, Colonel Bantzer could not count his first major command as a success. For six months, he had maintained his troops in a high state of readiness with promises that, when finally ordered to attack, they'd be richly rewarded with plunder and Indian women. Personally, he claimed dibs on Tecumseh's tomahawk pipe and the Prophet's silver gorget.

Every morning, the colonel rose thinking, *maybe today's the day.* He'd go to the lookout rock and watch the Indians conducting their quotidian affairs, as if taunting him with their indifference. He considered ordering his men to provoke even a small skirmish that he could use to justify an invasion. With every new courier, he hoped for orders to finally embark upon an assault. He'd told himself that for as long as he waited, his eventual triumph would taste that much sweeter.

When commanded to draw down, though, Colonel Bantzer's first reaction was to start a fire. He did not want to take anything back from

Greenville, nor did he want to leave anything behind. Fire would take care of that.

Of a mind to celebrate, the men were fain to comply. They consigned everything that they did not wish to pack out to the blaze—general refuse, cracked pots and pans, broken stools and chairs, moldy blankets, leaking bladders, threadbare shoes, splintered hand tools, ripped gunny sacks, stockings with holes in them, and oaken barrels of cider, just as quickly as the men could empty them. The giddy troops danced around the bonfire with the whores they had purchased for the occasion, and everybody tossed something into the fire, keeping the flames stoked long into the night.

Bantzer imagined that the ruckus attracted the attention of the Indians across the valley, and he wondered about their reaction. Were the Indians celebrating, too? Was he the only person saddened and demoralized by this turn of events?

While the men were thus preoccupied, he filled a linen bag with empty brown bottles that he'd stashed in his tent over the last six months. He lugged these down to Mud Creek and broke them one by one against a boulder in the middle of the stream, leaving the shattered mess to be blamed on drunken Indians. Then he returned to his tent and sorted through his personal effects. He was of half a mind to pitch everything into the fire, down to his cotton handkerchief and his wooden fine comb. In the end, though, he carried just two items to add to the fire: the parchment of his original orders signed by Harrison and Tiffin, and a handful of letters that the courier had given to him—not knowing what else to do with them, for they were addressed to the Indian Chief Tecumseh. At first, he'd found these short missives amusing, for a young lass had written them in florid script and, after a page or two of rambling about girlish fancies, like the scent of trillium in the fields, or lamenting that her brothers were so cruel, their author always concluded with an invitation.

Please do come to visit me at my Pa's farm when so ever you can.

Yours,

Rebecca Galloway.

Frank Bantzer thought about Mona as he flipped these letters into the heart of the bonfire. What was wrong with the women in that family, anyway?

For the next two months, he lived in his officer's quarters in the Chillicothe armory, settling into a pattern where he slept most of the days so that when he awakened, it was already a suitable hour to start drinking. His obligations were few, but tedious. When not mixing with influential members of society, performing conspicuous public services, or otherwise posturing to enhance his reputation, he preferred the solace of drink and solitude. Acting his part as an officer sometimes exhausted him, especially under circumstances where he was frustrated and anxious for another chance to distinguish himself. People expected victories from their military commanders, and he worried that those in power still regarded him as unproven in battle.

Alcohol proved good medicine for his sour mood. There was no shortage of taverns in Chillicothe, but he avoided their bawdy conviviality both as a matter of principle and predilection. Plenty of backwoods liquor entrepreneurs were pleased to deliver discreetly to his back door. He managed his comings and goings so that he was always within reach of a bottle.

Once in a while, after the taverns closed and the streets sat empty, he wrestled into a pair of trousers and embarked upon digressive, solitary rambles through the city, taking personal pride in how peacefully its citizens slept. Most nights, though, Bantzer enjoyed simply cloistering himself behind a closed door and drawn curtains, sitting in his under garments with his feet elevated, sipping whiskey or rum for as long as he pleased, answerable to no other person on Earth.

Drinking alone had an almost sacramental quality; the best moment of any day was its first drink, which released a feeling of relief and clarity that nothing else so reliably produced within him. Sometimes, while drinking, he liked to read, for literary company suited him better than that of living persons, and, unlike other people who became impaired, Bantzer was convinced that alcohol sharpened his rational abilities. The news in the *Scioto Gazette* always provided something to amuse, stimulate, or infuriate him. Books were hard to come by, but he kept personal copies of Ethan Allen's *Narrative of Captivity* and Benjamin Franklin's *Autobiography*, which he skimmed for inspiration, and of course, a Bible, which he read toward the end of many a long night, for it put him to sleep.

Then, at last, something happened. On the 2nd day of December, the Ohio Legislature met in special session and drafted a resolution authorizing the arrest of Harman Blennerhassett, for "certain acts hostile to the peace and tranquility of the United States." The complicating factor was that, since Blennerhassett's Island resided within the boundaries of Western Virginia, Ohio enjoyed no jurisdiction. This fact precluded the Ohio militia from apprehending him unless he stepped onto the northern shore of the Ohio River. However, the legislators also sanctioned the state militia to blockade all ships passing Marietta bound for Blennerhassett's Island, and to take lawful possession of whatever contraband they attempted to transport there.

To wit, on December 3rd, Harrison and Tiffin summoned Colonel Frank Bantzer, and ordered him to ride with due haste to Marietta, where he was to raise the local volunteer militia and implement a downriver embargo.

"And should Blennerhassett be so audacious as to venture even a toe onto Ohio soil, seize him pronto."

"Nothing would give me greater pleasure," the colonel said. *Finally!*

Within three days, Bantzer's troops occupied Picketed Point and set up a checkpoint for all boat traffic proceeding downriver. Local folks warned that he was too late, however, for just prior to their arrival, several flatboats full of men and provisions had docked on the island. Bantzer thus presumed that the island dwellers were armed and dangerous.

Three more days passed, during which the only significant contraband that Bantzer managed to confiscate was a case full of three dozen bottles of French wine—which, of course, he retained for himself in a safe place. It tormented him to think of that shameless criminal, Blennerhassett, lording over his little island, so very close yet beyond reach. he imagined heaving a large net across the river and dragging the man back to answer for treason. To the Colonel's further ire, his efforts to raise a local militia equal to the task of raiding the island had been almost equally fruitless. For this failure, Bantzer blamed Lieutenant Clayton Work, whom he'd brought from Chillicothe specifically because he was known and liked by many men in the area; Bantzer expected him to be useful for recruiting purposes. When asked about this matter, Lieutenant Work explained that many people in Marietta were quite friendly toward Blennerhassett, and thus disinclined to take arms against him. Bantzer listened incredulously, but he didn't know if he trusted Work to tell him the truth, or if he wanted to hear it, in any event.

On December the 12th, curiously, no traffic whatsoever drifted on the Ohio River, save for the occasional fisherman in a canoe or booze runner in a row boat. Most days, a dozen or more keel boats passed by, so the abrupt cessation of all river commerce seemed too unusual to be a coincidence. Bantzer inferred that the boats must be getting stopped somewhere upriver, and if that were so, then authorities on the Virginia side must be responsible. That meant just one thing: the Western Virginians were preparing to invade Blennerhassett's Island.

If correct about his assumption, then time was of the essence. Bantzer worried that Blennerhassett, too, might deduce that an assault was impending, and take that opportunity to abscond. Furthermore, he reasoned that these extraordinary conditions superseded his prior orders. It was thus imperative that he muster a militia and seize Blennerhassett's Island as soon as possible, lest the scoundrel get away. The desire for action burned within him like a shot of whiskey poured directly over an open wound.

"Lieutenant Work, come here!" he called. "There's much to be done!"

"Hey up, brodder Apple-tree, yah got bugs in yer whiskas," Little David giggled while tugging on Johnny's beard.

"Since they do not bother me, I do not bother them," Johnny said.

The most charming thing about children was their honesty. The least charming thing about children was that they didn't know when to quit. Johnny was plumb exhausted from having spent the afternoon being jested and molested by his youngest half-siblings.

"Mammy says that yah keep 'em fer food."

Lucy Cooley clamped her hand over little David's mouth. "Land's sake," she cried, "Don't young 'uns say the darndest things?"

"I do not eat bugs, nor any living thing," Johnny replied, not doubting for one second that Lucy Cooley had, in fact, said that about him.

He took some personal satisfaction when his father moved the family to Marietta. He liked to believe that his descriptions of the beauty, freedom, and fecundity of the Ohio countryside had lured them west. It hadn't taken long, though, before he realized that his father was running from debt and looking for a place to hide, where he could start over... yet again. Since the last time Johnny had seen his family, they'd added two more children, five-year old David and Sally, a mere two. Clearly, poverty had not diminished their fertility, nor enhanced their discretion.

Not that he often had second thoughts, but if Johnny harbored any dim longings for a family of his own, prolonged exposure to small children quelled those urges. He couldn't handle children. He doted on them—he knew no other way—so they wrestled him, played with him, piled onto his lap; but eventually they wore him down. His last resort for dealing with children was to give them back to their parents. Swedenborg taught that angels in heaven cared for children who died. Those children continued to grow and develop until they reached spiritual maturity.

Perhaps I'll adopt a dead baby in the afterlife, but in the here and now, I don't have the time.

"'Tis not almost their bed time?" he asked.

"Ol' Lady, put them sprouts to bed," Nathaniel Chapman hollered from his chair.

Lucy Cooley scooped up David and Sally and hauled them, wailing like piglets, up the ladder into the loft.

"Stuff their mouths with rags if'n they won't shut up," he added.

At that moment, for the first time since... maybe ever, Johnny was alone in a room with his father.

Nathaniel hadn't moved from his chair all evening, except to bend over and cough up blood, which he did as nonchalantly as if he were picking his teeth. He claimed to have a chest cold, but Johnny knew what consumption looked like.

"'Tis frigid as a witch's nipple outside," Nathaniel said. "Ye'd be welcome to stay here. We got a spare corner and a blanket."

To Johnny, squeezing into that tight corner would've felt like lying down in a casket. "Thank ye, but no. There are many other places nearby where I can stretch out."

"I reckoned that's what ye'd say," Nathaniel said, hacking up something that had shaken loose in his throat. "G'night, then."

Johnny reached into this pocket and unearthed a handful of coins, mixed with a few seeds, which he placed on the table. He knew the money wouldn't last long, but it probably wouldn't need to.

Before leaving, he said, "When ye get to heaven, father, ye will be out of debt and have all the elbow room that ever ye have wanted." Then, he was gone in a cold gust.

Walking the streets, Johnny contemplated how, despite how often he'd passed through Marietta over the years, he'd probably never bedded down in the same place twice. Marietta took a man on his own terms, welcoming nobody but accepting everybody, and respecting any person's desire to be left alone. Folks didn't so much live in Marietta as they got stuck there. Still, that fostered a kind of knowing camaraderie among transients, who all had pasts they wished to forget, and therefore preferred the hospitality of strangers who knew better than to ask too many questions.

Among the citizens were survivors of the Ohio Company's doomed expeditions, mountaineers from Western Virginia, displaced farmers and tradesmen from Pennsylvania, shipping merchants whose jobs required for them to live there, pockets of French, German, and Irish immigrants, a fair number of escaped slaves, and a handful of Christianized Indians. Because of river traffic, Marietta also hosted a new influx of keelboaters almost every night. While by day these myriad factions mostly ignored each other, by night they gathered as one in the Adelphia Public House, where men accustomed to being avoided could make merry with other outcasts. If any unity existed among the people of Marietta, they expressed it when the Adelphia opened for business, and it vanished by closing time.

More than the usual commotion resounded from the Adelphia that night, so Johnny decided to investigate.

The moment he walked in the door, a man wearing a lieutenant's bars on his great coat pointed at him and called, "Hey, citizen, are ya a private?"

Taken aback, Johnny paused to consider the question. "Well, yes, I reckon that ye could call me a rather private, one might say introspective person, by me nature."

"No, no, no, fool! I mean a private in the Ohio militia."

The notion that he could be mistaken for a soldier struck Johnny as hilarious. "Ha! Me? I have never fired a musket in me whole life, nor shall I ever, says I. The only army I would ever join would be one of puppies and butterflies."

The lieutenant chuckled and shrugged, equally amused and discouraged. Turning his attention to no one in particular, he shouted over the din, "Come now, men, this is yer call to arms. The Governor of Ohio requires yer service. Honor bids you all to do no less!"

Most of the men present were, in fact, conscripted to the militia and thus under legal obligation to answer the call of duty, although they seemed bound by a silent consensus that so long as nobody volunteered to go first, the mission could be put off indefinitely.

"Cain't it wait 'til morn?" many pleaded.

Johnny mixed with the Adelphia patrons, trying to ascertain the nature of the action for which the lieutenant sought to recruit them. Nobody seemed to know, except that it involved the unpleasant prospects of marching forth on that very night, into the dark and cold, and that there was no guarantee that they wouldn't encounter aggression before they'd gotten very far. This news piqued Johnny's curiosity, for despite his neutrality on all military affairs, he'd still been wondering about the purpose of the blockade on the river. Also, he'd overheard the frequent use of the word "traitor" among the barflies. That got him to recollecting some ugly rumors that he'd head concerning Harman Blennerhassett.

Then, he heard a word in his mind—his mother's voice, saying, *"Go!"*—and he knew what that meant without having to think on it.

At that moment, Colonel Frank Bantzer entered the tavern. He stepped onto a tabletop where men were in the middle of playing poker, swept aside their cards with the tip of his sword, and shouted in a voice that rattled glasses, "Soldiers, tonight your country asks for your valor!"

Thinking about the possibility of violence scrambled Johnny's innards, compelling him to do something, *anything*, whatever he could to spare even a drop of blood. Even with a head start, though, he needed time.

He looked around and noticed Mike Fink, his back to the tavern's door, quaffing a tall mug of hard cider. Johnny sidled over to him and said, "Well, hello my good fellow, Mister Fink."

Fink finished his mug and slammed it onto the bar. "Appleseed! Sit yer boney arse down and tell me a story!"

"Oh, me own story is always the same," Johnny said. "But is it true that ye have been ailing?"

"Not Me! I uh ne'er get sick, jest a pinch hung over, t'all. Why? Who says that I uh ain't fit?"

"Nobody in particular, but seeing as how ye have always prided yourself as being able to out-run, out-shoot, out-jump, drag out and lick any man in the country, I was confused, because there's another man claiming the very same thing. So I assumed that ye must've taken ill, if there was another who is better than ye."

"T'aint so, I uh do swear! Why, I uh'm a roarer, a ring-tailed squealer, and a reg'lar rough 'n' tumble red-hot snappin' turtle!" Fink bellowed. "What white-milk drinkin' farm boy done says he ken best me?"

Johnny could not bring himself to speak a lie, so he just pointed to where Colonel Frank Bantzer was barking orders to the crowd.

Fink spat out his chaw. "I uh got me some clobberin' to do," he said, then spun and walked off.

Johnny took advantage of whatever time that would buy him. He snuck out of the tavern and took off running as fast as he could to Blennerhassett's Island.

Harman Blennerhassett worried, as a flotilla of fellow revolutionaries was supposed to have joined him by now. Along with his own men and the dozen boats he'd made ready, they should have pushed off toward Kentucky to join forces with Aaron Burr and his armada. Instead, that scurrilous President Jefferson had issued an arrest certificate for Burr, and with the river blockade preventing reinforcements from reaching the island, along with the distinct possibility that Governor Cabell of Virginia would authorize action against him, Blennerhassett's situation had grown perilous.

How had things gotten so badly out of control? Burr had promised that his campaign would inspire such an uprising of popular support that citizens would line the riverbanks to wish him well when he embarked. Harman had tried his best to muster people's enthusiasm for revolution. He'd published an editorial in the *Ohio Gazette* entreating his fellow Ohioans to awaken to the reality that they could not trust the corrupt government in Washington to manage their local interests, and the only solution was to break from the oppressors and create their own nation. To his consternation, though, his article did not win the expected accolades.

Harman still eagerly wanted to believe that he was destined to become a founding hero of a new country, but as the days dragged on, he was less and less mollified by Burr's continued appeals for patience and to keep his mouth shut. No, this was not at all how he'd envisioned the good battle would begin. Perhaps the populace was even more ignorant than he'd feared.

At least he'd managed to shield Margaret from their increasingly grim prospects—not that she was especially curious, content to be left to her leisure pursuits. Harman paced the floor of the parlor, marveling at how, even while unseen villains conspired against them on every front, she was blithely content playing her pianoforte, with their children listening absently and playing ninepins at her feet. On that chilly evening, a fire twisted and popped to Mrs. Blennerhassett's playing, while Harman fretted about what to do.

Somebody pounded on the Blennerhassett's door, and everything stopped—Harman's pacing, Margaret's music, even the children's game.

Momentarily, two of the island's guards entered, dragging a soaked and shivering Johnny Appleseed between them.

"Beggin' yer lorship's pardon," one of them said. "But this fellah swam to shore sayin' that he has got some urgent news."

Johnny stepped forward, dripping. "Ye must leave! There is not a second to spare! Even now, a militia is forming to seize this island and to arrest ye, Mr. Blennerhassett, for high treason and conspiracy against the United States government."

Harman shrank inside of his clothes. "Arrest... *me*?"

Margaret clanged her hands upon the pianoforte's keys. "Harman, what is this?"

The children, more excited than frightened, began to giggle. Johnny always made them laugh, so the sight of him, wet, promised much more entertainment than a boring game of ninepins.

"Where are we going?" they sang out.

Johnny approached Margaret directly and, removing her hands from the keyboard, held them in his own to stress his seriousness.

"Ye must take the children and hasten to Marietta. There, surround yourselves with your best friends and well-wishers. Tell them that your husband left without a word, to an unknown destination. Deny any knowledge of his political views or of any collusion with Mr. Aaron Burr. So long as ye are viewed as an innocent woman abandoned by her scheming husband, no harm will come to ye or the children."

"Now wait one minute," Harman objected.

"I can do no such thing," Margaret insisted.

"Are we a-goin' for a boat ride?" the children clamored.

Still speaking only to Margaret, Johnny continued. "Ye must leave immediately."

Margaret pressed her palm to her forehead. "I feel a possession coming upon me. I must consult with my guardian angels before taking such desperate action."

"My dear Margaret, the spirits may well love and protect ye, but they can do naught to stop these actions tonight."

"This is my home, where I belong."

"The truth, I am afraid, is that ye may never set foot on this island again."

Margaret gulped at the finality of that statement. Johnny couldn't tell if she was acting of her own volition, or if some divine being had taken control of her, but when the moment passed, she rose and said calmly, "I see."

"But, what am I to do?" Harman asked.

"Ye must get as far from here as the river will take ye. Gather the men and launch your boats to your rendezvous point with Burr, then keep going. They will pursue ye, but if God wills it, ye may escape the government. I shall pray that ye find peace, my friend."

This was what Harman had always feared most. Stunned and shaken, he nodded at Margaret, silently endorsing Johnny's plan.

"Prepare the boats," he said to the guards. Turning to Margaret, he vowed, "I will send for you, when it is safe."

Margaret lifted her chin, forcing him to look her in the eyes. She placed a hand behind his neck, steadying him with loving pity, then kissed him and said, "Leave."

"Can we ride on the deck?" the Blennerhassett children cried.

It encouraged Colonel Bantzer to see the big galoot pushing his way through the crowd toward him. He could use this slobbering behemoth to lead his landing party. So what if the man was more than a bit tanked? That only made him more intimidating.

"Come right here," he waved to Mike Fink. "Let me shake your hand."

Snubbing the colonel's hand, Fink pounded his chest and belched pungent vapors. "Ain't yer a pretty boy, wit' yer polished boots and shiny buttons?" He made a smooching noise with his lips. "But I uh done heard t'at yer fancies yerself able to out-run, out-shoot, out-jump, drag out and lick any man in the country. I uh'm tellin' yer t'at it ain't so, an' I uh'll challenge yah to prove it, 'cause I uh'm Mike Fink, an' thyar ain't a better man than me on neither side 'a the river from Pittsburgh to Saint Looeey."

Colonel Bantzer half unsheathed his sword, a gesture which he hoped would dissuade the drunken goliath from his aggression. To his dismay, though, Mike Fink only guffawed at him, which elicited widespread mirth from the tavern's clientele.

A voice called out, "What so, commander? Are yah as big a man as yer talk?"

Another said, "The colonel wears a skirt 'neath his coat!"

A third said, "He wanked his manhood right off at the stem."

Fink reveled in the jeering. "So what'll it be? Will yah accept a manly challenge, or do yah surrender like some cod slurpin' coward whose momma butt humps scabrous Injuns?"

Bantzer knew he'd never be able to rally the troops to his cause unless he accepted the challenge. Fink seemed dumb, drunk, and muscle-bound enough to be dangerous in a fight, but, judging from the way his head was spinning, the colonel calculated that he had an advantage in any skills competition.

Summoning all of his bravado, Colonel Bantzer declared, "So be it. I choose a marksmanship contest."

The cry rang out. "Here yah! We got us a shootin' fest!"

Never had folks emptied a tavern more quickly for any reason less than a fire. The raucous company repaired to the Mound Cemetery, just across from the Adelphia, the nearest place to safely hold a shooting contest.

A cluster of fellow keelboaters whisked Fink outside.

Bantzer walked with Lieutenant Work, who asked, "Does this mean we won't be raiding Blennerhassett's Island tonight, sir?"

"This won't take but a minute," Bantzer replied summarily, trying to sound like he believed it.

Men drained their bottles hurriedly, so that they could line them up on the fence rail by the cemetery gate, to serve as targets. Somebody marched off forty paces and drew a boot line in the dirt.

Bantzer tried to raise the issue of rules governing the contest, but Fink huffed and said, "We don't need no lad-dee-dah *rules*. Here's how it'll go down. Yer'll shoot. Then I uh'll shoot. First one to miss, loses. Got it?"

Bantzer shouldered his long rifle. "Let us proceed, then."

He primed, loaded and rammed his weapon, lifted it into firing position, selected the centermost bottle in the row as his target, stared, stared, stared, said a prayer... then fired.

When the flash cleared, the bottle had exploded, and Bantzer could not refrain from crowing, "And so! Behold the skills of an officer in the great Ohio militia."

Amid mostly curses and grumbling, some men applauded reluctantly, and a few even whistled in admiration.

Mike Fink scoffed, "Bah!", and asked for a drink. "Watch this," he slurred, licking his chops.

With some difficulty, Fink toed the line. Even dug in, he teetered like a door hanging from a single hinge in a strong wind.

Men to either side of the fence gave him wide berth, for fear he might jerk at the moment of firing, and there'd be no telling where the ball might fly.

Fink allowed a helpful bar wench to load and ready his rifle, then took it from her with a promise to shoot long, straight, and hard, just for her. He seemed more to be leaning on his rifle than aiming it, and by the time he found the trigger with his finger, his head started swaying all over again.

"Hold still, damn yer," he cursed at the bottles, as if they were dancing in front of him. Finally, exasperated, he fired.

The ball hit the fence rail smack where it was nailed to the post. Down went the rail, and all of the bottles with it.

"Lookit! Fink wins!" the shout arose.

Fink, who'd closed his eyes, opened them when he heard the cheering. "I done told yer so. Ah'm the horniest toad in all the land!"

"No!" Bantzer protested. "Such luck I've never seen. This was not done honorably."

"Admit it, dog. I uh bested yah."

"Sir, to quote your very words: you say that you can not only out-shoot, but also out-run and out-jump any man in the country. Therefore, I challenge you to a second match, one where fortune will not affect the outcome—a foot race!"

"Quit yer gripin' an' admit defeat," Fink answered.

However, eager for more entertainment, the crowd applauded the proposal of a foot race.

Fink brightened and snatched a bottle from the hands of a stranger standing next to him, chugged it down, and growled, "Well then... let's uh race!"

The bar patrons measured a track forty yards in length, between the tombstone of Ebenezer Sproat and a well pump handle. Fink and Colonel Bantzer took their positions side-by-side in a starting block that was the butt of a sycamore root.

Lieutenant Work aimed his rifle into the air and called, "Ready... set...."

At the moment when Work fired—perhaps a split second before—Colonel Bantzer sprang out of his crouch and bolted furiously toward the finish line. Halfway there and still accelerating, he sensed by the peripheral space around him, as well as by the moans and catcalls from the crowd, that he was running alone.

Back at the start, Fink had lost his footing at the push-off and landed on his belly. When he managed to right himself, he was facing the opposite direction, but seeing nobody in front of him, believed himself to be in the lead. He broke into a trot and tripped over Ebenezer Sproat's tombstone, at the same moment that Bantzer breezed past the finish line.

Hardly even panting, Bantzer raised his arms in triumph. "Victory is mine!"

The colonel's taunts enraged Fink. "Cheat! I uh'll lick yer arse, fer goddamned sure!"

Fink barreled toward Bantzer with arms outstretched and murder in his eyes.

When he saw Fink coming, Bantzer's hand-to-hand military training kicked in. He assumed a boxing stance, with arms cocked and fists clenched.

Fink stampeded toward Bantzer while hollering, "I uh'll break yer dainty li'l chin, yer bootlickin' rascal!" But he hadn't gone far before laboring to breathe, his stride a rubbery and bow-legged parade.

Bantzer held his position and waited, waited, until just the moment when Fink made his final charge... at which instant he took a deft sidestep.

Unable to brake himself, Fink ran smack dab into the groin-level well handle, buckled over in pain, tumbled to the ground, conked his head against a monument, and did not get up thereafter.

Bantzer walked over to Fink's unconscious carcass and lowered his foot on the man's head. "Now that we've settled that, I repeat the call. Who will join me taking lawful action against the traitor, Harman Blennerhassett!"

To Bantzer, the crowd's resulting murmur sounded not so much like assent, as it did a reluctant consensus that now they really had no other choice. To nudge them over the top, he added, "To every man who joins me now, I promise a free bottle of fine French wine from the traitor's own cellar!"

That tilted the balance in his favor. Within a matter of minutes, the rabid, chanting, torch-wielding militia began its march toward Blennerhassett's Island.

By the time Colonel Bantzer and his troops reached the ferry dock across from Blennerhassett's Island, the Western Virginia militia had already arrived, its soldiers in the process of wholesale looting. The sight crushed Bantzer's morale, and he spat with disgust onto the ground.

Lacking any more convenient scapegoat, he turned to Lieutenant Work and snapped, "This is your fault. If you had mustered the troops when I ordered, we'd have gotten here first, and the glory would have been ours."

Lieutenant Work flinched. "Yes sir. Sorry sir." He then muttered something inaudible under his breath.

With a small detachment of men, Bantzer ferried across to the island.

The Virginians, engrossed in their moonlight plunder, continued to ransack the mansion of its riches, artifacts, contraband, and booze, without acknowledging the latecomers from Ohio.

Johnny Appleseed sat on the dock, dangling his feet and skipping stones. When he saw Bantzer, he remarked, "Unfortunately, Colonel, ye have arrived too late to prevent this tragedy."

Of all the people in the world, the last he'd expected—or would have wanted—to see was Johnny Appleseed. "What do you know of this incident?" he demanded.

"About an hour ago, the Virginians came with legal papers for the arrest of Mr. Blennerhassett, but he was not here. Nobody was. That being the case, they instead took to pillaging his home. 'Tis a sad, sad day."

Bantzer would have enjoyed nothing more at that moment than to strike his blade through Johnny's heart. "And what, pray tell, are *you* doing here?"

"I'm just a-skipping stones. Watch. See that piling over yonder?"

Johnny selected a smooth stone from his kerchief and gripped it with his whole hand, as if it were an apple. He slung it side-armed across the river surface, counting its hops all the way to the opposite shore, where it plinked dead-center on the piling he'd pointed out.

"You are a nuisance," Bantzer groaned. Had he been able to contrive a single reason for arresting Johnny on the spot, he'd have thrown him into the brig with glee, if only for the satisfaction of having something to show for his efforts. Despite his anger and frustration, though, the colonel knew there was nothing whatsoever that he could do.

"If I may, Colonel Bantzer, I would like to take that ferry back to shore. 'Tis late and I am a might chilled."

Bantzer allowed Johnny to pass, then bade Lieutenant Work to go and find the commander of the Virginians, and announce to him that the Ohio militia was prepared to be of assistance, even though he knew they would disregard the offer. While behind him Johnny poled the ferry into the river, Bantzer trudged onto the island, kicking dirt and looking for something to destroy. Near the dock, off a gravel path, sat a small, thatch-fenced garden. There, Colonel Bantzer took delight in personally stomping each of the young apple tree seedlings that Johnny had planted there. As far as he was concerned, if he never ate another apple in his life, he'd be a happier man.

Chapter 17 - March 1807

Turtle Creek, Ohio

When Brother Bunselmeyer pledged his soul to the life of the United Believers, he swore off buggering domestic livestock... and even though he sometimes wavered in that commitment, he always swore off the practice again—just as soon as he was done. He didn't entirely know whether it was a matter of doctrinal necessity. Did the obligation of celibacy extend to dumb animals? Still, he didn't suppose the elders would appreciate his honesty if he asked them for clarification on that point.

He'd long ago sworn off women... which was no huge sacrifice, seeing as how they'd already seemingly sworn off him. He wondered why women found him so loathsome, and decided it was probably because they couldn't see beyond the pox scars on one side of his face. Even so, the ladies didn't respond any better when he approached them from the other side. Fortunately, most women of the Turtle Creek congregation were bossy, ill-tempered, and, well, ugly. They made it easier for him to keep his lusts in check.

The one exception, Mona Junkin, stood out like a flowering dogwood in a burnt-out forest. She was as fair, fragrant, and delicious as a fresh-baked apple pie.

Although Brother Bunselmeyer's instincts invariably failed him around women, it almost seemed to him that, sometimes, she did not treat him quite as shabbily as he'd come to expect from women in general. Her saw her, the barber for the community, once a month for a haircut and beard trim, and she always wished him a "good day" and told him he looked "respectable" when they finished. Once, when he sneezed during a haircut, he expected she'd quit in disgust, but instead she just said, "God bless you," handed him a rag, and kept on snipping. Such gestures of civility encouraged him. It might be possible that Sister Mona was not as innately repulsed by him as all the other women in the world. He even entertained the remote possibility that she was a bit fond of him.

Joining the United Believers, who professed the spiritual equality of the sexes and the sanctity of celibacy, had seemed like an obvious solution for Brother Bunselmeyer. He longed to rid himself of his debased and fruitless yearnings, and he came to the Believers hoping that he could pray those vices straight away.

Toward that goal, he scolded himself mercilessly every time he allowed himself a lingering gaze at Sister Mona. Once, shaken to the core by desire, he pleaded out loud, "You must resist bodily temptations, 'cause they lead to strife, disease, and perdition."

Elder Malcolm Worley had overheard him, and concluded he was sermonizing upon spontaneous inspiration, and urged him to repeat his exhortations at evening prayers.

Whenever the inner needs seized him, his feelings came out in a burning harangue. Since his normal, conversational style was terse and clumsy, folks concluded his tirades were directly inspired by the Holy Spirit. Thus, the men and women of Turtle Creek agreed that Brother Bunselmeyer was a first-rate moral orator, and among the most blessed men in the community.

He tried with all his might to channel his prurient appetites into his homilies. So, every day when Mona had walked by him on her way fetch water from the creek, he slapped his own face to prevent himself from staring at her posterior. Just the bouquet of her passing was almost more temptation than he could bear. He told himself that God's gifts came at a price. This conviction made it much easier for him to think one thing, believe another thing, and yet do something else entirely, all without the slightest sniff of moral compunction.

Then, Johnny Appleseed showed up; something about the man raised Brother Bunselmeyer's hackles. From the moment of his arrival at Turtle Creek—"just visiting old friends," he claimed—Bunselmeyer kept a vigilant eye on him. Of course, he'd heard the stories of the famous Appleseed—how he sprouted apple seeds in his armpits, and how he knew every squirrel in the state of Ohio by its first name. In some respects, the reality of the man disappointed him. For example, although he walked swiftly, he did so awkwardly and often bumped into things. Second, while he remained circumspect about his vegetarian diet, he was rather a glutton when it came to devouring spuds, bread, turnips, and johnnycakes.

Most of all, despite his reputation as being something of a monk, Appleseed spent entirely too much time chatting with Mona Junkin. Brother Bunselmeyer had noticed how Appleseed had a knack for conjuring a smile from Mona when their eyes met. That augured of indecent and licentious possibilities, the likes of which Brother Bunselmeyer believed that he, if anybody, was more rightfully deserving to experience.

Then, one day, Mona walked by in the company of Johnny Appleseed, just two people carrying pails of water. In Bunselmeyer's mind, however, they were flaunting an illicit sexuality that angered him so much, he ground his teeth hard enough to draw blood from his gums.

It ain't right, he decided. *It's downright wrong!*

When Johnny skipped into Turtle Creek wearing the gray frock that she'd sewn for him the previous winter, Sister Mona forgot what she was doing and accidentally snipped off a sizeable chunk of hair on the backside of Elder Worley's head.

"Oh my," she gasped.

Elder Worley, though, had fallen asleep in the barber's chair, so she just kept clipping until she'd removed all evidence of her mishap.

Later, she explained to Elder Worley that he looked much more "dignified" with his shorter coif.

He glanced in the mirror and decided that, if she said so, it must be so.

Sister Mona kept a respectful distance from Johnny all that day, and only smiled at him when Sister Say introduced him as a guest that evening at the communal dinner. All the while, though, she thought about how anxious she was to get him into her chair and barber him up right and good.

That opportunity came the next day when, just as she'd expected, Sister Say directed Johnny to report for a bath, shave and haircut. When he met her, though, barefoot and smelling of spring dirt, the first thing that popped into her mind to say sounded stupid as soon as it came out of her mouth.

"When was your last bath?"

Johnny sniffed his armpits and said, "Ye are a-looking as lovely as spring flowers, Sister Mona." He shrugged and added, "I have not felt the need for a bath since last year."

"Well then, we'd better scrub you clean enough to last another year."

"Thank ye for your concern."

Mona handed him a washcloth. "I am so pleased to see that you are still wearing your frock."

"Oh, yes. 'Tis a mighty handsome garment."

"It's not too heavy for you, is it?"

He paused as if considering it, and replied, "It suits me very fine."

While Johnny bathed in the men's dormitory, Sister Mona tidied herself. She arranged her bonnet so that, while stuffing most of her long hair underneath, she left two wavy locks hanging loose on either side, from the temples to below the ears. She adjusted the neckline of her dress to allow for more breathing room in the front, and crumbled a bit of lavender on the bare skin over her collarbones. She filed her nails and cleaned the dirt from beneath them.

All the while, she sang softly:

In the Lamb's first revelation,
though he sought from east to west,
He could find no habitation.
No abiding place of rest.

Johnny walked into the room and contributed his voice to the song:

Father of the new creation,
once on earth he suffered pain

They concluded together, with joyous enthusiasm:

Now he comes to take possession.
Now the beast has closed his reign.

"That is one fine hymn," Johnny said, clapping. "And ye have a delightful voice, if I may say so, Sister Mona."

"You may not!" Mona snapped, at first more embarrassed than pleased, until she realized that nobody else had heard. "But thank you even so."

With the barber's chair ready for Johnny, They acted as if performing a well-rehearsed routine. Johnny swooped into the chair and raised his chin, then Mona wrapped a sheet around his shoulders and turned it into his collar. His hair, still wet from the bath, hung in tangled strands, impossible to work a brush through. Mona decided right away that all that extraneous length had to go. After cutting through the worst of the knotted tresses, it pleased her to find that the thick hair growing straight out of Johnny's scalp remained as rich and soft as she remembered. She rubbed her fingertips through it as if massaging a furry dog's belly. In doing so, she also admired the smoothness of Johnny's dome, almost like an inverted serving bowl. Surprisingly, he had no dandruff whatsoever.

As his head got lighter, Johnny rose higher in the chair. "I have observed how differently people act toward me after I have been barbered," he said. "I can walk right into any church in Chillicothe, and the preacher will welcome me, the ladies will wave at me, and the gentlemen will make room in the pew for me."

"With a fresh haircut, you look like you could just as well be the governor of Ohio."

Johnny flinched at that suggestion.

"So why not? You are well liked and trusted. You have a thriving business in your apple orchards. There's no reason whatsoever that you could not be as influential as any citizen."

"I seek no honors in this world, although I am indeed flattered that ye think so."

"A man can be humble and ambitious at the same time. I suspect that you have many personal goals."

Johnny nodded. "I believe that a person is either a part of creation or part of destruction. God wishes for us to emulate Him by being creators."

From another man, that would've sounded like puffery, but coming from Johnny, Mona sensed that he was entrusting her with a secret.

"Tell me how," she urged.

"I pondered about this me-self for a long time, until I read in Swedenborg that *the center and expanse of nature are derived from the center and expanse of life, and not the contrary.* To me, that means that life constantly pours forth into nature. When God created this world, He centered life in just one place, the Garden of Eden. I envision the Garden to be a field full of grass and flowers surrounding a warm little pond. Everything that Adam and Eve needed was free and abundant there, but the Earth beyond that place was empty. As life multiplied, creatures pushed farther into those frontiers, and as they spread, the nature of living things themselves changed according to their environments, so that new plants and creatures took shapes better adapted to their own habitats. Creation never stopped. Everywhere under the sun, life is changing always, and if ye look very closely, verily, ye can witness those changes over time. With every shower or gust of breeze, there is the potential for something new to come to life. For example, no two apple trees bear identical fruit. Swedenborg wrote that *Nature is imagination itself.* I do believe that nature, like imagination, is unlimited."

Sister Mona wasn't sure if her own imagination could adequately grasp those concepts, but even so, Johnny's visions moved her.

"Sure enough, there's grandeur to that view of life," she eventually said. "It's as if there is a growth of life, a progression—an evolution, if you will."

Johnny snapped his fingers. "That is the exact truth, says I. 'Tis an *evolution*."

"You really ought to write down these thoughts. They might be valuable someday."

"Oh, no. 'Tis just my own theorizing. I am not smart enough to think anything worthy of being written."

"Well, do you want to know what I think?"

Johnny didn't respond, perhaps because she was scraping a razor across the underside of his neck.

"I think that animals are just as smart as people, in their own ways. If you watch a beaver build a dam or a raccoon wash its hands, you can't think otherwise than that they know exactly what they're doing. Even a spider that hides while waiting for a fly to get caught in its web is working out a plan. The Bible teaches that God made human beings unique, because He gave us souls, but still, we are as much a part of the grand, natural order as beetles, pigeons, frogs, or bears. I wonder sometimes how it is that an animal thinks. It isn't in words, like you and me, but they must have a whole different kind of consciousness. The thing that most impresses me is that animals never make mistakes. Every choice they make is the best that they can in any situation. That ain't so for people. I guess that's what free will is all about."

Johnny patted her free hand. "Mona, I have thought those very same things me-self."

Johnny's touch felt to Mona like an exchange of deep intimacies. She wanted to take his hand and wrap it in her own, fingers through fingers, palms rubbing together... but the thought made her grip on the razor slide a bit, and she nearly nicked Johnny's Adam's Apple.

With another scrape, she was finished, and gave Johnny a towel.

When he'd wiped the cream and stubble from his face, he grinned for her. "How do I look?"

"This world is a better place with you looking your best."

After dinner and prayers, Sister Say summoned Sister Mona to meet her in the kitchen, where she waited with a meat cleaver in hand. Since moving to Turtle Creek, Sister Say had gained weight, and her hair had gone from streaked with gray to as bright silver as a steelhead trout. The look enhanced her gravitas.

Mona entered the kitchen, her bonnet low in front of her eyes. "You wish to speak with me?"

Sister Say took a pinch of salt from a seasoning bag and put it on her tongue. "Come," she said. "Would thee like a small taste of salt?"

"No, but thank you."

"'Tis my medical opinion that salt is healthful for thy kidneys. It makes for bright yellow urine, and relieves cramping during a woman's monthlies."

Mona doubted that Sister Say was still plagued by her monthlies. "Praise Jesus," she said—a safe remark for any situation.

Sister Say kicked a chair toward Mona. "Sit down."

Every time anybody in her life told her to sit down, Mona had always preferred to stand. She was not afraid of Sister Say—not the way she used to be—but still, she took a chair out of respect.

Sister Say slammed the cleaver into a pine chopping block; it lodged there, its handle shaking. "In my experience, the most effective way to solve a problem is to take a cleaver to it. If something is tempting thee, troubling thee, or leading thee astray, the longer thou delayeth taking necessary action, the more difficult it becomes. It is both virtuous and courageous to stand up to the object of thy distress, and hack it off without hesitation, then never to think about it again. That is why I allowed thee to go to Greenville and face that soldier who had long ago trifled with thy affection. I trusted that, by confronting him, thou might finally banish him from thy mind. Is that so?"

"Aye, sister, I no longer think of that man."

"Never? Not even to pity his hell-bound soul?"

"I do suppose that I must have pity for the damned."

Sister Say made a chopping motion with her hand. "Slice those feelings from thy heart. Pity makes thee vulnerable to doubt, to regret, to forgetfulness, and ultimately to future missteps. Thou cannot yield to thy gentle nature, not where men are concerned. Woe will come to any woman who pities a man, for that will just encourage him."

"Concerning that soldier... yes, he is a rogue and a deviant," Mona conceded. "Nevertheless, I do believe that it is possible for some men to live honorably."

"If thee knew men as I know men, thou would not be so sure." Sister Say sighed. "But be truthful, Sister Mona. Thou are referring to Johnny the Appleseed Sower. There's a sparking between the two of thee."

Mona surprised herself with her first instinct, which was to defend rather than to deny. "A spark, yes, but not a lustful one."

"Bah. He is a man, is he not?"

"Is it not possible that he can be fully a man, but still free of degraded carnal desires?"

"I doubt it. There is little that a man does where his true purpose does not involve feeding his sexual perversity. Men have a ravenous monster between their legs, with such an uncontrollable craving that it subdues all decency, morality, and dignity. When under the influence of the throbbing of his phallus, any man becomes possessed by an animal obsession.

"I was married once—indeed, to my shame, *twice*—to men with lewd appetites that I could never satisfy, no matter how often I debased myself. Oh, how brutally they foisted themselves upon me, with their pushing and prodding and ramming and thrusting and digging, digging, digging, until finally with a grunt and a heave, they'd spend themselves entirely, then roll over and fall asleep like sated dogs. The cruelest thing of all was that I could not carry a child, and although I begged them to torment me no longer by spilling their seed inside of me, still they battered me night after night, until God released me through their deaths. So, I personally have scant faith that any man's character is stronger than his hungry beast. Such a man would be no less than a saint."

"Perhaps...." Sister Mona considered what it would feel like to lie down next to Saint Johnny Appleseed, neither of them feeling anything other than spiritual comfort from each other's presence. She wondered, if that ever happened, what they would do with their hands.

"Thou are still a young woman, dear Mona, and while it is to thy credit that thou hath chosen to live pure among the United Believers, there remains a chance that thy body is not as firm in that decision as is thy spirit. Many young women become fickle and backslide, for when they let down their guard, along comes some handsome fellow with clean teeth and sweet words. Before a lass has a fair chance to resist, she has fallen. 'Twould be a poor shame if that happened to thee, Mona."

Sister Mona felt no embarrassment, but thought it would reflect better upon her if she did, so she averted her eyes. When she said "Yes,

Sister, I will keep a proper space between myself and Mr. Appleseed," what she really meant was that she would wait. For what, she didn't know.

A sign, perhaps?

The forbidden nature of the waiting made it possible for her to cling to her fantasies, and to let them go at the same time.

For days, Brother Bunselmeyer tried to avoid being seen, for he worried that something of what he felt on the inside must show on the outside. Specifically, he felt as if being eviscerated through the rectum by a clawed lamprey. His body pulsated with a branding iron-grade fever that burned from his heels to his temples. The last thing that he wanted was for somebody to ask him, "Is anything wrong?" What would he tell them? That he was so backed up with untapped desire that he was afraid that if somebody patted him on the back, he'd cut loose such an explosion that it'd level the forests all the way to the Great Plains? That he felt like a twenty-foot copperhead snake slithered through his intestines, coiling around his bladder, and hissing its forked tongue over his glands? That when he walked, he had to clench his jaws and squeeze his sphincter because he was afraid that with one false step, he would spew bile, blood, jism, and viscera from every orifice? Brother Bunselmeyer had no wish to compound his suffering with shame.

But, oh, to purge everything, fully and completely, would feel so good.

Rarely was Mona Junkin absent from Brother Bunselmeyer's thoughts. Once he'd started paying close attention to Mona, he'd learned that her daily routine and his intersected through a predictable sequence of comings, goings, near misses, glimpses, and sightings from afar. At any moment, he knew where she was, and this knowledge enabled him to visualize what she was doing—her fluid movements, the rise and fall of her breathing, the placid expression on her face while deep in prayer. He could pick out the sound of her sighing in a room full of people talking. He could recognize the swish of her skirts when she walked by. He was able to detect the honeyed scent of her sweat from among the mixed aromas of everybody else in the community, and he could even infer, from their blend, something of her varying moods. When he closed his eyes at night, in the dormitory redolent with the snoring of gaseous men, he visited a realm of blissful, Mona-inspired reverie. The dreams seemed so real that he could feel her presence and bask in her aura, but when he reached to embrace her, she vanished. Even in sleep, his frustration kept building.

Being watchful of everything Mona did, he found especially distressing what he regarded as her questionable conduct in the company of Johnny Appleseed. For the first few days after he arrived in Turtle Creek, Mona and Johnny were often together, collaborating on chores, discussing scriptures over tea, or sharing prayers in the chapel, side-by-side on their knees. Brother Bunselmeyer thought such behavior bordered on scandalous. Then, suddenly, their overt fraternization ceased; probably, one of the elders had said something to them.

This confused and somewhat agitated Brother Bunselmeyer, until, through continued reconnaissance of Mona, he realized that she was not so much avoiding Johnny as she was recalculating more discreet terms of engagement with him. At meals, she sat next to the potatoes so that when Johnny asked for them, she'd be the one who passed them to him. During community song one evening, she came in late, after all the psalters had been taken, and asked Johnny if she could share his. In her own way, she seemed as vigilant of Johnny Appleseed as Brother Bunselmeyer was of her.

This made him angry, but also, oddly, encouraged his desire for Mona, for it made her seem attainable.

Then, over supper that evening, Johnny stood, thanked the entire community for its hospitality, and announced that it was planting time, so he had to depart to tend his orchards. He would leave immediately and travel by night, under the light of the full moon.

"Fare thee well, each of ye," he said.

Mona's face went from buoyant, to punched-in-the-gut shocked, to hang-dog, slack-jawed despondent by the time Johnny finished speaking. Moisture pooled in the corners of her eyes until two plump teardrops formed, one dripping down each cheek. She forced a cough and excused herself from the table.

It seemed to Brother Bunselmeyer that he and Sister Mona were both afflicted with the same variety of raw passion, just not for each other. He presumed that she must ache and burn as ceaselessly as he did. He further supposed that, like him, she'd prayed for relief but gotten none.

Now that Johnny Appleseed was leaving, though, the solution for them both was obvious. Brother Bunselmeyer thanked God for his wisdom and mercy.

When Mona left the supper table so abruptly, Brother Bunselmeyer had a hunch where she would go. Across the hayfield, in a gulley where a brook ran in the spring, beneath a lone willow tree that hung so low its branches swept the ground, Sister Mona had a private place. When she went there, she just sat, completely still, on the hard ground, sometimes for hours. Often, Brother Bunselmeyer had followed her and watched from behind a parked wagon, also for hours.

That's where I'll find her. She's probably waiting for me there.

After the congregation dispersed from supper, Brother Bunselmeyer slipped out the back door of the men's dormitory. To make sure nobody followed him, he took a roundabout way to Mona's hidden place, approaching not through the open field, but from the forest.

She stood in the willow glen, silhouetted from behind, moonlight on her shoulders. Even though he was certain that he hadn't made a sound, Mona turned and called, "Is someone there? Johnny, is it you?"

Brother Bunselmeyer glanced over his shoulder to confirm that he was indeed alone. "Yes'm. No'm. That is, yes, someone would be here, but it's just me."

"Oh," Mona said in a hard breath. "What for?"

What for, indeed?

He blurted out the words he'd rehearsed so fast that he didn't leave enough time to think about what he was saying.

"Sister, the Bible teaches that whene'er a person has got a problem, God will provide a solution if he prays faithfully upon it. I have confessed to God, and now I'm confessin' to you, that I got a real bad problem. There're urges that come with being a flesh and blood man. The thoughts that have took hold in my mind won't go away. I'm much sorry to tell you, Sister Mona, but Satan has done took possession of my body, giving rise to an unholy desire that I just cannot shake myself loose from. I've prayed long 'n' hard for faith, for courage, for strength, for wisdom, and for virtue... but day after day, this pain jus' got worse, so that I started to worry that if I don't get some relief, I might be going to hell when I die.

"I came here tonight, Sister, to confess that *you* have been the object of my sinful imaginations."

Mona pulled her collar tight.

Brother Bunselmeyer continued. "Finally, I asked God, why am I so tempted? What has Sister Mona done to deserve to be thought 'bout in such a foul manner? So I started prayin' for you, instead of for myself. That's when God opened my eyes. Sister, I know that you are ailin', just like me. It's a sickness of the heart, the mind, and the body. I've done been watching you, Sister, and it's obvious that ever since that Appleseed man came to Turtle Creek, you've been all gay one moment, then all woebegone the next. Now, I'll tell you straight: I don't like him none, and it irks my britches that you fancy him so much. But I want to tell you plain that I do know just what you are feeling. When it builds up and up, temptation becomes like a nightmare that you can't wake up from. It's led to the eternal damnation of many a soul. I pray, not ours. For, Sister, God has shown me an answer to our predicament."

He had hoped she would take his pause as an opportunity to ask how, but when she kept staring at the ground, he proceeded.

"You and me are different from the rest of the Turtle Creek Believers. They're all, e'ry one of them, long-lived enough to have left their sinful ways far behind them. Not so, you and me, Sister. We're younger and healthier, with stronger feelings but little knowledge about such acts as what makes men, men and women, women. Without knowledge, we are helpless 'gainst these feelings. We need to confront them to defeat them.

"But that knowledge is dangerous, too. It must be gotten in a right and safe way, lest we take too much pleasure from the act and forget that it is sinful. Don't you think so, too?"

Sister Mona gasped, which Brother Bunselmeyer figured was not so bad as if she'd disagreed completely.

"So, I finally figured out God's plan for you and me. Ain't by no accident that He brought us together. God pities our sufferin'. He revealed to me how we can ease each other's pain. It'll also strengthen our faith, as one True Believer to the other.

"God wants for us to couple, Sister Mona."

"Leave now," Sister Mona said forcefully. "And I shall forget that you were ever here, and we shall never again speak of the disgusting blasphemies which you have proposed."

He'd spent a lot of sweat and mental effort to come to this conclusion, so the finality with which she dismissed him seemed unnecessarily rude. "It ain't because of lust that I say so. I just want to know what it's like. I *need* to know you, in the Biblical sense. And I do honestly think that you need this, too."

"I have no such vile needs. And my desires are between me and God."

He inched closer to her, disappointed, but undaunted. "I sure did hope that you would see fit to cooperate with me on this. But it's just got to be done, Sister Mona, *one way or the other.*"

"No!"

It looked like he'd have to do things the hard way, but... he wasn't exactly sure what doing it the hard way required of him. Based upon his experiences with farm animals, he figured he'd have to engage her from behind, so he needed to get her turned around. With no delicate way to go about doing what had to be done, he grabbed Mona's hips and squeezed, lifted, and spun her 180 degrees.

Mona writhed violently and tried to squirm free, but Bunselmeyer knew that, unlike a spooked mare, she could not kick backwards. The trick was to hold on and get her bent over. He reached around her midsection and applied pressure with his chest against her shoulders. Just when he felt like he was gaining control, she cut loose with a strident, panicked scream. He'd anticipated that she might holler, though, and no sooner than she shrieked, he slapped his whole hand over her mouth, suffocating her shout in his palm.

So far, this had been easier than he'd expected. All at once, though, Mona seized with lightning spasms and thunder convulsions, as if the apocalypse were erupting insider of her. Fits and conniptions in each quarter of her body seemed to pull her in four different directions at once, as though her muscles were trying to break free from her bones. He let go of her, and she collapsed facedown onto the ground with her shoulder blades and hip bones sticking out like a moldboard plough. Her arms and legs had gone rigid as flagpoles, her spine limp. Only a twitching in her cheeks indicated she was still alive. Her condition seemed unnatural, but.... How could he know? Maybe this was normal for women undergoing the horrors of coitus.

During her struggles, Sister Mona had gotten her skirts bunched up above her knees. The sight of her bare calves and the insides of her buttery thighs enticed Bunselmeyer, but when he lifted her dress and pulled down her under garments, revealing the undulating symmetry of her perfect buttocks, it so aroused him that he popped a crotch button. It was the most beautiful sight he'd ever seen, and he'd have considered himself fortunate just to gaze at it for hours, if not for the simultaneous impulses to grab, thrust, push, and probe.

His meat had grown so engorged that he had trouble getting his pants down over it. He poked it beneath and between Mona's buttocks, expecting that it'd find its own path and slide right in. Every muscle in her lower body was stiff and clamped tight, as if a trap door had slammed over her womb. Prying at her nether regions with one hand, Bunselmeyer took hold of his meat with the other and tried to ram it into any available crease or opening. The pressure in his groin kept building, and the sensation started to overtake him. Desperate, he didn't know whether to push or to stroke, but at the absolute worst possible moment, he miscalculated his angle of thrust, bending himself backwards, and then began spewing his milky seed into the air.

"Nooooooo!" he cried.

He dropped onto his knees, even while he continued involuntarily pumping load after load into the grass.

The wind shifted and rustled the willow branches, making Brother Bunselmeyer jump. He felt filthy, and wondered what he must look like to God.

"Forgive me!" he begged the sky.

Then, by the moonlight, he saw a large female form walking across the field, and he judged from her girth that it must be Sister Say. He scampered into the forest, to get away from Sister Mona, from Sister Say, from God, and from himself, in that order.

The community of the United Believers did not appreciate discord, so much so that the preferred method for managing tension was to ignore it. For any person to speak a grievance implicitly violated the principle that a faithful Believer was supposed to be happy and contented at all times, or else that person must be doing something wrong. Most of the time, this worked. Sometimes, though, saying nothing only made matters worse. It was not in Sister Say's nature to overlook the obvious.

For three days after the incident beneath the willow tree, Sister Mona remained in bed, alternately sobbing, screaming, shaking, or sleeping. Sister Say made excuses for her, saying she had taken suddenly ill after being bitten by a hornet. She turned the doctor away, stating her belief that prayer would cure what ailed her. By the weekend, thanks to Sister Say's ministrations, Mona managed to get onto her feet to vomit. She still hadn't spoken a word.

Brother Bunselmeyer asked another brother to ask another brother to inquire as to Mona's health, but the third-hand news that got back to him was worse than he'd dreaded; they whispered that Mona was bleeding from a very bad place. He wanted to send her flowers, but worried it would cast suspicion upon him. Instead, he lashed his own backside with a horsewhip, by way of performing penance.

On the next Sabbath, after breakfast and morning prayers, when Elder Worley made the routine appeal for any announcements or suggestions for the betterment of their community, Sister Say decided to throw down her ire.

"May God cast me into hell if I am speaking falsely," she began, a guaranteed attention-grabber. "But I fear that the most heinous form of sin has taken root here in our midst. There is *lust* in Turtle Creek."

Many in the congregation, mostly men, rolled their eyes in anticipation of another of Sister Say's diatribes. They couldn't help but think, *what is it, this time?*

However, several women perked up to listen, for secretly, they often shared her complaints.

"We Believers commit to a regimen of strict physical purity. Brothers and Sisters alike agree upon this principle. Desires of the flesh are evil, for they consume the mind and defile the body. Each of us, man and woman, swore to celibacy. Why, then, do some of thee menfolk find it so difficult to abide thy own choices?"

Seated side-by-side-by-side in a row, the elders stiffened in their chairs. Elder Worley mumbled, "Well now...."

Sister Say gestured to the women's side of the room. "Am I not telling the truth, sisters?" Nobody answered, although their energized silence motivated her to continue.

"Our faith teaches us that the souls of men and women are equal, and thus we must obey our higher natures in respect to all sexual concerns. My sisters and I keep this vow as naturally as a bird takes to flying, but it is different with thee menfolk. The beast of thy lust is always restless. We cannot tolerate such vulgar and obscene desires in our community of worship. Yet, I despair that our group salvation will be impossible so long as thee menfolk remain enslaved by that hungry, dangling beast which Satan uses to pull thee toward sin."

Their custom forbade Believers from interrupting any speaker during a public commentary.

Still, Elder Worley, becoming visibly agitated, kept sputtering, "Hep... hep... but... now...."

Sister Say ignored him. "Our founder Mother Ann Lee teaches that God is neither man nor woman, but both, at the same time, and so she says we too should live as spiritual equals. But how is that possible? I say that we should look to the example of our Lord and Savior Jesus Christ, the only perfect man ever to walk this Earth, who lived all his life in chaste holiness. How did He do it? How did He escape the carnal ravages that blight the souls of mortal men? I think I know the answer. Jesus Christ was born in the body of a man, but he had the heart of a woman.

"In order for a man to live in a Godly way, he must become a woman. Matthew the Evangelist counsels us: 'If thy eye offends thee, pluck it out and cast it from thee. It is better to enter heaven with one eye than to have two and be cast into fiery hell.' Thus, I say that this community cannot survive if we tolerate lust, And I have the means to do the Lord's work."

She reached under her bib and brandished the meat cleaver she'd brought with her. "I can rid any man of his wicked desires. I was raised on a hog farm, so I know how to do it efficiently. The pain lasts but a moment, the bleeding a bit longer. Within one month, though, the body will heal, as likewise will the man's heart. Doing this will purify our community. Who will go first?"

No man wanted to utter a word for fear of being misinterpreted.

The women felt empowered to sit in silence, rather enjoying the evident masculine discomfiture.

Finally, Brother Bunselmeyer jumped up and declared, "I'll do it! Geld me, Sister!"

With the first words out of her mouth in days, Mona sang out, "Let *me* do it."

Elder Worley stared Brother Bunselmeyer back into his chair, and tried to smooth things over.

"Surely, Sister, you must be speaking figuratively, referring to the use of prayer and piety as a means to 'cleave' through illicit desires."

"If I were speaking in allegory, would I have sharpened my cleaver?"

"What you suggest is mutilation!"

"Talk of mutilation! Thy manhood is a plague. It will wither and fall off in hell, and thy tiny beech nuts will burn like hot coals. Then, thou will beg to have them chopped asunder. Why, 'tis no more mutilation than to pull a rotten tooth."

"Such talk in not Godly, Sister. I implore you to desist."

"I'll ne'er hold my tongue from speaking God's will. However, I can see that thee are too enamored of thy sins to heed my words. Thus, I will leave this place. I refuse to live with such drooling horn-dogs." She faced the women. "And I further beseech all of thee, dear sisters, to follow me. Together, we will create a church of consecrated women, where we will never again be bothered by these male goat worshippers. Come...."

She stormed out the door.

Baffled and verbally castrated, the elders looked at each other as if wondering if they should try to stop her. Before anyone could speak, Sister Mona stood, glowered at Brother Bunselmeyer, and followed Sister Say out the door. Next to leave were the Rose and Marie sisters, and then other women, anxious for liberation and inspired by the vision, fell in with the procession. Before the exodus was finished, half of the distaff population of the United Believers of Turtle Creek had absconded.

From that day forward, among the women who stayed, the mere use of the word "cleaver" was enough to win any argument with a man.

And the women who left never looked back.

Chapter 18 - Summer 1807

Greenville, Detroit, and Chillicothe

In June of 1807, when a British warship fired upon an American frigate off the coast of Norfolk, Virginia, the settlers in western Ohio knew who was really to blame—it had to be the Shawnee Prophet. Folks had long suspected Tenskwatawa of being in cahoots with those dastardly British, and their aggression on the Atlantic coast proved that the British believed a sufficient number of savages would rally to their side, enough to risk provoking a fight.

War would come, for sure. Only one question remained: where would it be fought? Greenville, Ohio seemed as likely a place as any.

Tenskwatawa had amassed a considerable following. Since early spring, Indian pilgrims had taken many routes into the Prophet's village in Greenville. Some estimated that as many as 1000 warriors lived at the site. In May, unknown Indians murdered the family of a homesteader named John Boyer in his cabin near Urbana. The brutes left a tomahawk with black feathers in the poor man's head. While Greenville was over 80 miles from Boyer's cabin, and a hostile band of Ojibwa resided much nearer, most people just assumed that the Prophet's religion had inspired the homicide. Rumors held that Satan himself looked out at the world through the Prophet's blind eye. People said he was able to bring the dead back to life by reaching straight down into hell, pulling their souls out of the fire, and inserting them back into their half-rotten bodies to serve at his command.

The hearsay lacked specifics about the content of his preaching, although folks speculated that it included elements of idolatry, paganism, bestiality, demon worship, and assorted black arts, for the Prophet professed the preposterous notion that Indian races were morally superior to Christians. Clearly, the savages weren't to be trusted, and needed to be put down once and for all.

"Blame not me, for the folly that is being spoken," Stephen Ruddell apologized. "This message I bear with no pride."

"Their ignorance amuses me," Tecumseh said. "But their stupidity is worrisome. Violence is the first resort of idiots."

"So, they fear me greatly, eh?" Tenskwatawa asked, rubbing his hands together.

"Oh yes. In Urbana, citizens have themselves petitioned to the Indian agent at Fort Wayne, a man of the name William Wells, for the militia to take action against you. Wells has himself testified his opinion that you serve the British as much as the devil."

Tenskwatawa said, "This man Wells should be wary, or I might call down a firestorm upon his head."

"Hold your boasting, brother," Tecumseh said. "If truly you possessed such powers, victory would be ours already."

He pivoted to Ruddell and continued. "Is the threat mere blustering, or is there a risk to us?"

"Hard feelings run as deep as the Scioto River. Ohio has a new governor, who says that he wishes for peace, but if war against the British breaks out, Indians will not be spared."

Tecumseh took a long draw on his tomahawk pipe as he pondered these disclosures. Although his brother had won converts from as far as Illinois, Michigan, and Kentucky, he doubted that the union of faith would translate into a strong war alliance. If attacked now, the Indians would do as they always had done—blame, bicker, panic, and fall apart. Furthermore, he was loath to join forces with the British, who in the past had supplied arms and provisions, but invariably left Indians on their own as soon as fighting broke out. He needed time, more information, and to consider all options... and he trusted just one person in all of the Northwest Indian nations for insights on such matters.

"I will ride tomorrow to Blue Jacket's town. I wish to parlay with him, as one war chief to another."

Ruddell asked, "My friend, is that your vision of yourself? Are you a war chief?"

"War?" Tenskwatawa looked worried. "I have not prophesized of war."

Tecumseh responded to both but answered neither of them. "Our people need a war chief for times as fraught as these. A prophet can inspire the people with promises of salvation, but only a war chief can lead them into combat. This is my responsibility. I cannot hide, deny, or refuse it."

"I myself could be a good war chief, too," Tenskwatawa mumbled.

"Here you will remain, brother. Preach and pray to those who are needful of such words, but do not of your own make any decisions. Within two weeks, I will return. Am I understood?"

Tenskwatawa appeared tempted to say "no," but mumbled, "I do of course understand."

Skeptical, Tecumseh glared at his brother, grunted, and turned his back. He said to Ruddell, "But if you, Big Fish, are of a mind to join my traveling party, I urge you to come. It would be pleasing to Blue Jacket to see you. He regards you akin to a son."

"As it should be, since he accepted me into his tribe as an orphaned boy. I know he is now an aged man, unhealthy, and of unsound mind. To see him once again in this world would give me great comfort, but I am called to other tasks. My horse is ready, and I must leave before the setting sun."

"Then let me walk with you to your horse."

Tecumseh and Stephen Ruddell rose together.

Tenskwatawa started to stand, but halfway to his feet, he slouched over in his Prophet's chair and surrendered to a nap.

Outside the Longhouse, Tecumseh slowed his pace to match Ruddell's foot dragging. "Something is troubling to yourself, Big Fish. Speak to me of your concerns."

Crickets chirping in the field filled the silence with tension.

At length, Ruddell reached under the collar of his shirt and pulled out a cross hanging from a twine necklace. "Always, I myself will bleed Shawnee blood, but, from this day forward, I will dwell only with the Christians. I myself have taken a white woman as my wife."

Tecumseh placed a hand on Ruddell's shoulder. "Most of the relationships of my life are defined by conflict. I have warriors who will fight for me, enemies who will fight against me, and women who will fight over me. What I have too few of, are friends. You are one, Big Fish."

"To be and to do as your friend is a proud calling."

"Tell the Christians that I am also open to friendship with them." Tecumseh reached for Ruddell's necklace and took the cross between his thumb and index fingers. "But leave them with no doubt that I am a war chief. Whether to meet me as friend or foe is their choice."

"I will say to them these things, Shooting Star." Ruddell slung his saddlebags over the horse. When he did, one pouch flapped open, and as he re-fastened it, he remembered something inside. "Nearly, I forgot. Last month, I visited James Galloway."

"Is he well? And his family?"

"He prospers, but as I was leaving, his daughter, Rebecca, chased after me and gave to me a letter, which she requested that I deliver straight into your hands."

"The girl? How old is she now?"

"She has blossomed over fifteen summers."

Tecumseh took the letter, and all that he had to do was look at the florid handwriting on the envelope—its voluptuous sweeps and pendulous loops—to guess the general purport of its contents. Initially, the only image he could conjure was of a freckled, stick-skinny, long-necked girl, with dirty knees and elbows. Upon reflection, he also remembered her masses of curly red hair, brighter than maple leaves under the autumn sun. He imagined those crimson waves framing a young woman's face, the faintly-hued hairs on her fair arms and shoulders, and the juicy, fuzzy apricot colors growing around her femininity where no man had hitherto seen.

"Thank you," he said to Ruddell. "If you see him, give Galloway my greetings. And also, his daughter."

In his warrior days, Blue Jacket of the Piqua Shawnee led a confederation of tribes to both their greatest victory and their most devastating defeat. In the cold of November 1791, he'd commanded 1,500 braves in a preemptive assault on the lumbering, artillery-laden troops of General Arthur St. Clair at the headwaters of the Wabash River. Although outnumbered, the Indian forces of Shawnee, Lenape, and Miami surprised, out-maneuvered, and thoroughly routed the Long Knives, slaying hundreds and evicting them from the northern Ohio and Indiana territories.

At that time, the twenty-year-old Tecumseh had felt jubilant. He believed that Indians could compel the Long Knives to dismantle their forts, annul their bogus treaties, and return chastised to south of the Ohio River. In reality, though, the triumph against St. Clair devolved into a series of bloody melees. Battle after battle, the Indians lost their foothold on the land, for what the Long Knives could not take by force they gained through the slow, demoralizing attrition of disease and starvation.

Finally, backed by arms and promises of reinforcements from the British Major William Campbell at Fort Miami, Blue Jacket rallied his remaining warriors to make a stand along the Maumee River. Since General Anthony Wayne's legion outmanned his army four to one, Blue Jacket launched guerilla forays from the relative safety of the surrounding forests. The Indians were winning, until evil Christian spirits intervened against them, for one night a fierce storm ravaged the woods, uprooting many trees and exposing them, which led to the battle that Indians everywhere would remember as "Fallen Timbers."

Wayne had learned from St. Clair's earlier mistakes. Instead of advancing with cannons and heavy equipment, he deployed an infantry with bayonets, and saber-wielding dragoons bent on killing from close up. Those Indians who stood their ground were quickly slain, and the rest fled for their lives. The survivors reached Fort Miami and cried to their British allies to grant them sanctuary, but Major Campbell ignored their pleas and refused to raise the fort's gate. The Americans took the opportunity to massacre the last standing members of the Indian confederation with impunity.

Tecumseh, who had been knocked unconscious by the butt of a militia rifle, awoke in a decimated landscape with corpses piled wherever they had fallen. He shook his fist to the sky and cursed Jesus Christ.

In the aftermath, Blue Jacket had no recourse but to accept the Treaty of Greenville, which banished him and his tribe from their ancestral lands. However, he secretly advised Tecumseh not to sign it, so that when his day came to lead the Indian nations, he would be able to assert that he had never accepted the unjust conditions of the treaty.

For several years, the elderly Blue Jacket had lived in a small village along the Detroit River, where he subsisted comfortably on the annuities provided by the treaty, as well as unspecified other sources of income that were the subject of various rumors. Unlike so many of his brethren Indians, Blue Jacket had not succumbed to alcohol, but reports suggested he had become a Christian, which, to Tecumseh, was even worse—if it was true—so he chose to disbelieve it.

Tecumseh's visiting party consisted of Battle Panther and three other warriors, followed by an entourage of amorous squaws who kept their distance by day, hoping that Tecumseh would favor them by night. They slowed progress, but Tecumseh tolerated their presence more for his men's sake than his own, and because, knowing Blue Jacket, he would expect to be gifted a woman upon their arrival.

Indeed, when he greeted Tecumseh by the village fire, his attention immediately drifted toward the harem, and he pointed. "That one."

Blue Jacket invited the men into his lodge, winking at his chosen squaw as he closed the flap behind them. At over sixty years of age, he had become rotund, looking overstuffed in the namesake coat that he'd worn for so many years. Always fond of ornamentation, he wore gold epaulets on his shoulders, a red sash around his midsection, silver bracelets up and down his forearms, and a medallion the size of a plate hanging from his neck. His eyes sparkled when he showed his guests the rifles, clubs, bows and arrows, and other war memorabilia decorating the walls of his abode. He rolled out mats for the men to sit, while he plopped himself into a wooden chair with a woven seat and rockers beneath the legs.

Tecumseh had never seen such a chair. He lit his tomahawk pipe and passed it to Blue Jacket. "It warms my soul to smoke with you again, great chief. In all the Indian nations, no man knows more about life, death, and war. I humbly seek your counsel."

"Well you might. Many battles I myself have fought. Many Long Knives I have killed. To this day, because of me, General St. Clair limps. Hah! Do you remember that victory?"

"I do, but—"

"And at Fallen Timbers, I continued to fight even as bodies around me fell."

"Your courage is legend. But—"

"Instead of signing that Greenville treaty, I should have slashed Wayne's throat with his quill pen, so his blood would have soaked the paper."

"Of course, but.... To me, the war never ended."

That remark deflated Blue Jacket's bravado. "For me, it is over. Alas, I am old, never again to fight. Now is your time, Shooting Star."

"Is this now my day, or is that day yet to come? That is what I have come to ask."

"Already, I think you know this answer."

"The old war is new again. Between skirmishes of Americans and British, the Indian people are squeezed—hated by all, trusted by none, feared by many, and respected by few."

"Indian nations must stand on their own strong legs. Once, I built a confederacy that I dreamt was invincible. United as one tribe, we ourselves were emboldened to believe that Waashaa Monetoo blessed our alliance." Blue Jacket stopped rocking. "In defeat, we felt betrayed by the Great Spirit. I have now reflected on this matter for many years, and while He bestowed no aid to us in battle, the true causes of our loss are plain and simple. We were too few, too wild, and too weak. In war, such an army will lose always. *Always*."

While nodding in agreement, Tecumseh wondered, "My alliances are built upon the religion of my brother. He calls himself The Open Door. In him, many people believe with their hearts and minds. But I worry. Will they fight for him?"

"They will, but only until the first taste of defeat. Nobody will keep fighting for a losing prophecy. If you need Waashaa Monetoo to win a battle, it is a battle you should not wage."

"I think, then, that my time, my people's time—*our* people's time—is still in the future of several seasons. Our community is growing, but the Long Tongues watch us, and with small provocation will attack us. If they do, we will fall."

"Then give them no cause for aggression. Even if you must bite your tongue, praise them and promise to be good. Fools love to hear such things."

Nothing that Blue Jacket said surprised Tecumseh. What he had to ask next, though, was something that vexed him, for he could ask respectfully, or truthfully, but not both.

"Will you come with me to the Long Tongues' capital and speak to them? Assure them of the Indians' desire only for peace? To you, they will listen. More than me, they will believe you."

Tecumseh didn't add the reason: that they would see in the old man what they approved of—an Indian tamed, compliant, and grateful for whatever pittance he was granted.

Blue Jacket did not acknowledge any irony in Tecumseh's tone. "Yes, I will ride with you into their capital and petition to keep the peace." He rocked as far forward as the chair would go. "But before departing, there is something I wish to show to you."

From the outside, it looked like a traditional long house, but from within rang such a perverse uproar that Tecumseh knew no Indian could be making it. This kind of bedlam ushered from white men when they dropped their scruples and reveled in their true, decadent selves. Blue Jacket steadied Tecumseh against his conflicting instincts of rage and disgust. They entered the building from a side door, and stood behind a bar, along the span of which several Indian men served glasses of liquor to seated white men. They also loaded drinks onto trays carried by Indian women to patrons waiting at tables throughout the building. On a plank stage near the center of the house, an ensemble of Indian musicians played a caterwauling noise using strange instruments with strings, and one even pounded upon the keys of a pianoforte.

Everywhere he looked, Tecumseh bore witness to his brothers and sisters pandering for the entertainment of an exclusively white, male clientele. He wasn't sure who he wanted to kill first.

"What outrage do I see?" Tecumseh bellowed.

"Look twice, and more closely," Blue Jacket replied. "Behind the spectacle you will see that, here, Indians are making profits."

"I see vice and degradation."

"Which is very profitable."

"Explain!"

Blue Jacket whistled, hailing an Indian dressed in a linen shirt and trousers, who was taking money from a queue of white men that, in exchange, left with handfuls of round wooden chips.

"It is a grand night," the Indian said to Blue Jacket. "Our receipts are overflowing."

"Such impertinence!" Tecumseh cried.

"Well might you recoil from such a sight as this, until you understand the nature of our commerce," Blue Jacket said. He wrapped his arm around the Indian in white man's garb. "This is my friend, my partner. He is named Toby, of the Sandusky Wyandots. He has a new plan for peace, also for prosperity, of all Indian nations. Let him speak."

"Only to honor your request will I listen. But, Toby of the Sandusky Wyandots, choose your words with care, for if I hear treachery, I will cut out your tongue."

Unfazed, Toby removed something from his pocket. "Look here. These spotted cubes of bone are called 'dice.' Shake them and drop them. Each time they will land showing different spots. There is no reason. They fall and bounce as do stones tumbling downhill. How they will stop, no one can know. Yet, for the sake of guessing how they fall, white men put their gold on the table, to be taken by whoever's dice land with the best spots showing. To utter chance, they stake their wealth, and in the long run, they always lose. Their losses, though, are our profits. As long as there are stupid gamblers, this house will never lose."

Tecumseh was defensive in his confusion. "What you are doing is beneath the dignity of a warrior."

"I am a different kind of warrior," Toby countered. "Peace can be bought. These men are our debtors, not only of money, but also of their secrets. Tonight, away from their wives, out of sight of their preachers and superior officers, they feel no constraints in what they do, for we ourselves are just Indians, and of what we see or hear, they care nothing. Come tomorrow, though, they will owe us so much that they can never dare risk offending us. It makes for a more certain peace to know a dishonest man's secrets, than to trust an honest man's promises."

"And thus they give us their wealth!" Blue Jacket added.

Tecumseh said, "Does this not debase our people to serve white men's vices?"

Toby responded, "They deceive themselves to think we serve them. All of these things—the music, the women, the alcohol—are designed to make the white men more willing to give up their money. All advantages flow to Indians. We ourselves can achieve a moral victory over the whites that benefits us, while weakening their character, and sending them to hell."

Blue Jacket added, "So now you see why I myself want never again to go to war. This is a much more rewarding kind of battle."

Abhorrent as it was, Tecumseh had to concede that their business model did contain some evident merit. The possibilities caused Tecumseh a brief moment to ponder the means to his objectives. Still, such corrupt cynicism ran contrary to every moral impulse in his character, not to mention a violation of the Prophet's teachings, and the religious movement around which he'd built his entire confederacy.

His only practical option was to take a principled stance. "Those who stand with me, stand for Indian pride and valor." He squared himself. "I see none here."

Toby shrugged. "Still, one day, by chance, you may change your opinions."

The Ohioans had appropriated the name 'Chillicothe' for their capital, which irritated Tecumseh They did not know what it meant. They thought that just one place could be called Chillicothe, but in the Shawnee tradition, that was the honorary name of the home village of the leader of the tribe. One day, still, he hoped that he would establish a new Chillicothe around himself. Perhaps he would name his Indian capital after one of the Americans' false heroes instead—Columbus, for example—just to mock the ignorant white people.

Just three men comprised the Shawnee delegation riding into Chillicothe on that Saturday in September: Tecumseh, Blue Jacket, and the Prophet. They had argued considerably as to who should attend the conference.

Blue Jacket contended that inviting other chiefs like Roundhead of the Wyandot, Withered Hand of the Potawotami, and Black Hoof of the Wapakoneta Shawnee would demonstrate Indian unity.

Tenskwatawa wanted to muster as many of his followers from Greenville as possible, to march as an army, thus making a statement of the power at the Prophet's beck and call.

Tecumseh, however, insisted that they keep negotiations between the three of them and the leaders of the Long Tongues. He wanted to look into their eyes, and for them to look into his, so that both could measure each other's inner resolve. Anything more was grandstanding. The only exception that Tecumseh granted was for select squaws to follow at enough of a distance so that they'd not distract him, but close enough to be available should he need their services.

As the three men approached the courthouse, Tecumseh surveyed the crowd that packed both sides of the street, and he wondered if anyone among them intended to assassinate him. He knew there were many who should wish him dead. Most of those simple homesteaders, though, were probably more intrigued and fearful of his brother, the miracle-worker. As much as that offended his pride, he also saw an advantage in it. He arrived in the white men's capital as a mystery, determined to leave as a war chief.

A lieutenant named Work, clearly nervous about walking with his back turned to them, escorted the Indians across the town square. He took them to the courthouse door, where his superior officer, Colonel Frank Bantzer, relieved him of duty.

Tecumseh immediately recognized this man from having watched him at a distance across Mud Creek, the prior summer when he'd commanded the militia camp at Greenville. Already, Tecumseh knew this man better than he ever could have guessed. He knew that Colonel Bantzer whored, drank heavily, and groaned when he urinated in the morning. He did not interact with his men except to give them orders, and thus they respected his rank more than they did the man. He often sat by himself, running his fingers through his own hair, which is why among the Shawnee he'd earned the epithet Loves-His-Scalp.

Tecumseh allowed Blue Jacket and the Prophet to enter before him, and paused across from Colonel Bantzer, assessing his posture.

The colonel stood rigidly, but guardedly rather than defiantly so. He smelled like a salt lick on a hot day.

If I say 'boo' to him, this Colonel Bantzer might lose control of his bowels. It is tempting.

On a sudden impulse, he stopped and called back to his squaws, signaling the least comely from among them. She bound to his side, and he bent over to whisper in her ear. "That man. Tonight, take him. Please me by giving of your body to him. As you do so, you will take from him a piece of his soul. Make that your own gift to me."

"Be it done," she said and, turning, batted her eyes suggestively at Colonel Bantzer.

He grinned back, clearly feeling flattered.

When Tecumseh entered the courthouse, he felt a dreadful stare upon him. Embracing it, he stared at the panel of distinguished gentlemen in front of him. Introductions were unnecessary, for Tecumseh could identify each of the Long Tongues' leaders from the descriptions of them that Steven Ruddell had provided. The curly-haired man with a face like a shaved bear cub was the scurrilous Indian Agent, William Wells, whose only qualification for his post seemed to be that every Indian of every tribe across the entire Northwest Territory universally despised him. Next to him sat the owl-faced Edward Tiffin, who had previously been the chief of Ohio but was now a liaison—called a "senator"—to the Great Father in Washington DC. At his side sat serpent-eyed Thomas Kirker, the new chief of Ohio. Another senator, Thomas Worthington, wore his dark hair brushed back, exposing a taut brow and exaggerating his pointy nose. Finally, the chief of the Indiana Territory, William Henry Harrison, had the long, rutted face of a knotty pine trunk, with bushy caterpillar brows over eyes that glinted darkly like hardened sap.

Tecumseh hated Harrison most, for it was he who had bribed, defrauded, and coerced a series of illegitimate treaties from toady chiefs across southern Indiana and Illinois. One day, the two of them would face each other on a battlefield, but Tecumseh was not yet ready for that day.

The three Shawnee sat in the first row behind a podium, where, after pleasantries, William Wells began proceedings by recounting several of the concerns of homesteaders from towns near the Indian encampment at Greenville. Pressed into translating for him, Stephen Ruddell could not look at Tecumseh while he related stories that

Tecumseh personally knew to be untrue—of Indians who placed bounties on white virgins, who ate the brains of those whom they scalped, and who kidnapped white children and buried them alive so as to court favors from Satan.

Wells then gave his version of the massacre of John Boyer's family. Even though Tecumseh knew a renegade Ojibwa band had committed that atrocity, and that it had nothing to do with the Greenville Indians, he also understood that most in the audience were already convinced of their guilt, on the grounds that they trusted no Indian and were always prepared to assume the worst from them.

Having thus stated his case, Wells concluded, "The judicious thing for the government to do is reactivate the militia and push the Indians out of Ohio, or destroy them completely if they resist!"

When Stephen Ruddell sputtered repeating that last remark, Wells grabbed him by the collar and demanded that he say it again, louder.

"Or I shall kiss their asses!" Ruddell shouted in Algonquian, with sufficient gravitas that nobody questioned the message, or why the Indians smiled when they heard it.

Next, Thomas Kirker read from a letter written by the Great Father in Washington, Thomas Jefferson. In it, he spoke about his warm affection for the Indians and his ardent desire for peace with them. At the same time, Jefferson cautioned his "Indian children" against the seductions of "an ungodly religion," which he said gave them false hopes. Instead, the Great Father urged them to embrace Christianity as a sign of their peaceful intentions. Beyond that, he reminded them of their "former misconduct," and warned them of being deceived by any empty promises from "bad persons from Canada," for he would treat consorting with the British as aggression against the United States.

Finished, Kirker waved the letter and addressed the Indians personally. "In his wisdom, the Great Father asks me to give you the chance to speak today, to answer his concerns. Now it is your turn."

By design, Blue Jacket spoke first. Every man in the courthouse knew who he was, although some were surprised to learn that he was still alive. As he rose, Blue Jacket exaggerated his frailty, leaning against the podium as if it were the only thing keeping him upright. He ingratiated himself to his audience by stammering, in English, "Me good Indian thank you." Then discoursed in his native tongue about how far he had traveled, and the hardships of such a journey for a man of his years, what with his aching back and a weak bladder. Yet when he'd learned of the seriousness of these proceedings, he knew he must come and set matters straight. In his retirement, he'd had leisure to reflect upon the turmoil of earlier times, and he was now unequivocally opposed to any future conflicts between the Indians and the Long Knives, no matter what the circumstances. In his prime, nobody had surpassed his valor on the battlefield! No doubt, the Long Knives still told stories of his courage and worthiness as an adversary! But... once he laid down the tomahawk, he'd resolved never to pick it up again, like that famous American George Washington, who was also a great warrior before he became a peaceful statesman. Yes, they were very much alike, George Washington and himself....

Blue Jacket continued speaking for several seconds after Stephen Ruddell had ceased translation. He would have continued, had Kirker not intervened. "Thank you very much, honorable Chief Blue Jacket."

"So me no make war, make love peace instead," he finally concluded, in his practiced poor English.

Next to speak was Tenskwatawa. Encouraged by Tecumseh, the Prophet had accessorized his attire on this day, for the white men would see it not as vanity, but as enhancing his ambience of sorcery. He wore a beaver pelt over his shoulders, a profusion of beaded necklaces around his neck, silver bracelets, armbands, and earrings, a bundle of hawk feathers tied in his hair, and wolf fangs dangling from his pierced nose. He shook himself when he stood, allowing his accoutrements to fall into place, and wagged his medicine stick as he began speaking.

"When I myself died, the Great Spirit of all creation revealed for me a prophecy to share with all men...."

As the Prophet spoke, Stephen Ruddell translated from memory, for the night before this meeting, he and Tecumseh had rehearsed it over and over, until he could recite it verbatim, no matter how much Tenskwatawa might sputter. Tecumseh's intent for the speech was to Christianize the Prophet's message as much as possible, to appease, flatter, and somewhat bamboozle the settlers and their political leaders into believing that the Shawnee religion was essentially the same as theirs, minus only Jesus Christ. Thus, Tenskwatawa moralized about the evils of pride, envy, wrath, sloth, gluttony, avarice, and lust, while stressing that path to redemption was through strict adherence to the faith of his forefathers.

For all of his bluster, Tenskwatawa was evidently nervous, and even the white men who understood nothing of what he said could recognize when he stumbled over his words.

More than once, Tecumseh winced inwardly, although, in truth, he felt that his brother's awkward performance was a good thing, for that way the Americans would see him as less of a threat. When he surveyed the faces of the five men on the panel, Tecumseh noted that their expressions ranged from Wells's pout to Kirker's blank look of disinterest. Harrison seemed more intent on watching a fly buzz around the room. Apparently, the Prophet didn't impress them much.

Finally, Tenskwatawa summed up. "We Shawnee are proud and God-fearing. We ourselves wish only to practice our faith in peace, and for peace also to be with you."

Governor Kirker nodded, as if appeased.

One person in the courtroom shouted, "Hallelujah."

Now came Tecumseh's turn to hold forth his views. Dressed in a suit of fringed deerskin, with his long black hair trailing as he marched forward, he firmed his chin, faced the spectators, and allowed a silent tension to build for a few moments. He stood aside from the podium, solid and statuesque, unblinking. In preparing for this, he'd secretly considered shocking everybody by declaiming in English, but he ultimately determined that the mysteries of his own language would serve him better.

"*Howisakisiki,*" he greeted them, making his vowels reverberate.

Ruddell lowered his voice when translating, which afforded a greater resonance to Tecumseh's words. More than just the words, though, his gestures and cadences held the audience spellbound. None of these men had ever seen an Indian in such command of his presence, so that when he clenched his fist it felt like he had them by the throat, then when he opened his hand and spread his fingers, they felt relieved to breathe again. There wasn't a person in the room who did not feel like Tecumseh was speaking to him alone, and not one among them felt unscathed by his fiery eloquence.

He told the white men of the Shawnee people's connection with the land, from which their Creator had fashioned their bones, and from its rivers, their blood. "The sun is my father," he declared, standing in a shaft of sunlight beaming through the windows. He told how, when the white men arrived, *Kakouhthe*, the cyclone, had swept new seeds across that land. What would grow from these, it was impossible to know, for the future was the prerogative of spirit beings, the greatest of which was Waashaa Monetoo, whose will was interpreted by only one man, the Prophet. But as the secular chief of his people, Tecumseh stated that his mission was to ensure the safety and prosperity of his Indian brethren.

Saying this, he raised his head and drew a breath as hard as a knife thrust, while everybody else, including Blue Jacket and Tenskwatawa, looked upwards as if half expecting the roof to open and for him to ascend into the sky.

Tecumseh had saved his bombshell for precisely this moment. "There is a new spirit in this land, one that arrived with the white men. Therefore, my people will go to where we can create our lives anew, in another land consecrated by Waashaa Monetoo. Come the next season, we will depart from our homeland, so that the seeds of our culture may flourish elsewhere. From here, Ohio, we will leave you in peace."

When Ruddell finished translating, he was breathless. Amid widespread murmuring, order broke down.

Tecumseh knew well that the most any of the Long Knives' leaders would have hoped for was a truce, to buy time for making their plans. His concession had been entirely unexpected, yet it no doubt felt less like victory than a gift. Kirker started to say "thank you," but stuttered and stopped. Wells appeared to be trying to think of something to which he could object. Tiffin and Worthington avoided looking at anybody. Only William Henry Harrison showed any suspicion in how he stood and stared at Tecumseh, who half-smiled and stepped down from the podium.

Blue Jacket and Tenskwatawa were likewise flabbergasted, for they'd not been consulted. The Prophet was wide-eyed, confused.

"We will a better place build," Tecumseh said to them when he returned to his seat. "I know a place in Indiana, far from the Long Tongues, along a creek called Tippecanoe. There, we will build the greatest city in all the Indian nations."

"But no. I like my home. I do not so wish to go anywhere," Tenskwatawa complained.

"We will that place name... *Prophetstown*," Tecumseh said.

"Oh. Very well so. That, I like."

There was no need for further deliberation.

The Ohioans wished the Indians safe travels and encouraged them to set about their relocation as soon as possible. By the time they reached the courthouse door, the public was already milling outside, the gossip spreading as fast as people's tongues could wag. Some were ready to celebrate the news that the Indians were leaving Greenville willingly. Even more than that, most in the crowd chattered about this man, Chief Tecumseh, who according to the scuttlebutt had totally enthralled the delegation with his poise and rhetoric. A gallery of onlookers jostled for a glimpse of him.

Tecumseh walked ahead of Blue Jacket and Tenskwatawa. The day was his. He could feel energy pulsing in his fingertips, as if more than his hands could hold. Among the Shawnee, he'd come to expect the people's deference, so that it felt comfortable upon his shoulders. Until this moment, though, he'd not known that his charisma also worked on white people.

Spectators moved out of his path. Men averted their eyes when he passed them. Women lifted children onto their shoulders to see.

Eyes straight ahead, Tecumseh regarded the crowd like a moving background, hazy in its details, flickering in and out of focus.

Suddenly, though, he apprehended a flash of brilliant color. The vivid scarlet and mixed chestnut hues of her hair stood out from the grayish fabric of his peripheral vision like a strike of blood lightning. It filled him with an instant desire, which preceded recognition, but when he stopped to take her in, he realized that he stood face-to-face with the fair Rebecca Galloway. He could hardly refrain from reaching out and grabbing a handful of that rosy, claret, glowing hair, and running it through his fingers. Instead, he reached down and plucked a wild Black-eyed Susan, growing right next to where they stood, and handed it to her.

"T-t-thank you," Rebecca stuttered, shivering with awe.

PART FOUR – 1811-1812

"A volunteer was asked for and a tall, lank man said demurely: 'I'll go.' He was bareheaded, barefooted, and was unarmed. His manner was meek and you had to look the second time into his clear, blue eyes to fully fathom the courage and determination shown in their depths. There was an expression in his countenances such as limners like to portray in their pictures of saints. It is scarcely necessary to state that the volunteer was 'Johnny Appleseed,' for many of you have heard your fathers tell how unostentatiously 'Johnny' stood as a 'watchman on the walls of Jezreel,' to guard and protect the settlers from their savage foes."

A.J. Baughman, "A History of Richland County."

Chapter 19 – June 1811

On the Road from Mount Vernon to Mansfield, Ohio

"There is a variety of muds in Ohio," Johnny said. "There is clod mud, which is the kind that ye find when ye dig deep. There is slop mud, like the milky ooze that fills puddles. Then there is sink mud, the worst sort, what looks like a layer of hard gunk on the top, but underneath there is a pool of mire that can suck the shoes right off your feet when ye try to walk through it. The road to Mansfield is like a pitfall of sink mud."

Reverend Copus thanked Johnny for that information, although he would have preferred that he not share it in front of his wife, Amy, and their three young children, varying in age from infant to four years old.

Mrs. Copus, a Pennsylvania farmer's daughter, had already expressed considerable concern about moving to such a wild and remote place as Mansfield, and Johnny's descriptions of the perilous road there made her toss her hands over her head and moan, "Oh my soul, we shall be swallowed alive by the Earth."

"Not to worry," Johnny consoled her. "The mud will not swallow ye beyond knee deep."

"Knee deep to you is hip deep to me," she countered.

"If ye can spot it, ye can walk around it."

Reverend Copus jumped in. "Do you see, dearest? We can skip right around the trouble spots."

"But it could be quite a bother yet if ye must pull that wagon of yours through a long stretch of sink mud," Johnny added.

"James, we'll be trapped!"

Reverend Copus fired a harsh look at Johnny, who widened his eyes innocently, as if to inquire 'what did I do?'

When one of the horses nickered, Johnny turned and whispered something into its ear. He then clapped his hands and announced, "Very well. It is settled. I shall walk alongside with ye. Might be that I can help if ye get stuck."

Not sure that he approved of this escort, Reverend Copus was nonetheless anxious to get started. He hopped onto the driver's board of the family wagon, tugged on the horses' reins, and whistled to get going.

Moses, the family's sheepdog, ran ahead of the wagon.

For the past two years, while otherwise raising a young family back in Pennsylvania, Reverend Copus had spent parts of his summers preaching along the Mohecan River in a sparsely populated region of wooded hills and plateaus, in a hamlet that folks had started calling Mansfield—named after a surveyor, of all things. There, he intended to contravene the general pattern of settlement by establishing a church ahead of the migration, so that when folks arrived, they'd know that they'd come to a place where God had already set down roots. That way, he hoped to prevent Mansfield from going the route of the more uncouth towns like Newark and Mount Vernon. To demonstrate the depth of his conviction, the reverend had decided to go all in by moving his whole family there.

If this wasn't the destiny revealed to him by his epiphany during the eclipse of 1806, then he didn't know what was.

To Amy Copus, though, Mansfield might as well have been the last stop on the road to the end of the Earth. She sat in the rear of the wagon, looking backwards and, while sighing occasionally, generally left it up to the children to complain.

"Are we there yet?" Sarah, the eldest, child, asked repeatedly.

Reverend Copus invited Johnny to sit with him, but Johnny preferred to walk, "to make it just a wee bit easier on the horses."

They'd loaded the family's Conestoga wagon to capacity, and the two saddle horses pulling it were taxed under the weight. To keep their spirits up, Johnny promised them apples when they reached their destination.

He also chatted with the reverend. "I recall when this road was no more than an Indian hunting path. I was rousting these parts as early as 1801. The land has changed mightily. 'Tis scarce that ye will even see a bear any more."

"Thank God for that!" Mrs. Copus shouted.

Reverend Copus said, "We must make room for progress."

"Bears need room, too," Johnny remarked.

"So? It's a big country, with lots of space for bears, in places where they won't bother people."

"I am not so sure, me-self. There does not even seem to be enough land for all of the people who want to live here. Just ask the Indians."

"There is plenty of room for Indians who have been Christianized."

"Still, it does make me wonder how come, when the Indians lived on this land, there was room enough for both them and bears, not to mention wolves and cougars. Now, there seems not enough room for none but white folks."

"I suppose that is just the way of civilization."

Johnny had no comment, or perhaps that was his comment—no answer.

Either way, the silence triggered a thought in Reverend Copus. "Incidentally, Mr. Chapman—"

"I would be pleased if ye chose to call me Johnny."

"Oh yes, right, *Johnny.* Some years ago, you gave me a page from your holy book, and I chanced to read it on a day and a time when it made a particular impression on my thinking. Ever since, I've been curious for more. What was the author's name—Schwedenbarber? Switzenburger?"

"T'would be the great philosopher and servant of Lord Jesus Christ, Emmanuel Swedenborg."

"I knew it was something similar to that. In any ways, if you have any extra such pages, I'd appreciate one or two more to read."

Delighted, Johnny reached into his kerchief and took out a handful of loose pages. "Pick any one," he said, offering them like a fan of playing cards.

Reverend Copus reached for one that was sticking out, but on a sudden impulse, dug for another one nearly hidden instead. He folded it twice and put it in his pocket.

"Thankee," he said. "I'll read it by and by."

As they proceeded, Johnny frequently strayed ahead of the wagon, taking various side paths that he said were shortcuts. Each time he disappeared, Reverend Copus wondered if he'd seen the last of Johnny, and he wasn't sure if he wanted him to return or not. Amy seemed to appreciate knowing that he was there, but with his incessant chatter, especially with how he greeted passing woodland animals—"Hello, squirrel, is this not a fine day?"—or—"Fly nearer to heaven, dear falcon!"—he could be a darned pest.

Three or four miles into the trip, they came to a bend in the road, with a slightly hidden but distinct side trail.

Johnny waited for them at the intersection. "If ye do not mind, I would like to digress just a bit from the main road. I wish to look in on some good folks who live just down this-a-way." He turned back from the edge of the thicket and promised, "I will meet ye again, farther along." And with that, he vanished into the wilderness.

The first time Johnny saw this high ground above Markley Run, he called it "Amity," because it was so peaceful. He planted a small orchard in the hopes that whoever eventually settled there would be motivated to live up to the place's name. Several years later, when Sister Say and her all-female schism of the United Believers acquired this land for their church, they appropriated that name and added to it, referring to their little cloistered community as "Fem-Amity."

As he approached the compound, Johnny knew he was being watched from the tops of trees and behind bushes. The matrons of Fem-Amity were wary of any man creeping up on them, so they kept constant vigil on all paths leading into their sanctuary, and, as a good many rouges from Mount Vernon already knew, these ladies didn't waste bullets with warning shots.

In the past, the sisters of Fem-Amity had granted Johnny more latitude to pass among them than other men, for he was kind, cheerful, and did useful work tending their orchard. Also, as Johnny was well aware, many of the good Christian ladies considered him harmless in a way that most men were not, for he'd heard them whispering that he was, "As limp as wet laundry hanging on a line."

In general, Johnny didn't mind being gossiped about, for, although he was sometimes tempted to correct certain common misassumptions about his manhood, he also realized that he had no control over the stories that folks told about him.

As soon as Johnny set foot across the property line, rows of women appeared from behind trees and woodpiles, from inside buildings, and from the fields where they'd been working.

They fell into formation behind Sister Say, who accosted Johnny. "Greetings, Mr. Appleseed. What brings thee here today?"

"The Lord Jesus Christ leads me where'er I go."

"As He does us all. But if He led thee here today, it must have been for a reason."

"I reckon that I ought to check on me trees."

"Thou may so do with our gratitude. Afterwards, we will be pleased to share our supper, although we insist that thee eat outside, for no man can sit at our table. Afterwards, thou must take leave before nightfall."

"'Tis fair enough."

The women parted to allow Johnny to pass. He knew it was best to avoid eye contact with any of them, but even so, he couldn't resist scanning their faces out of the corners of his eyes, looking for Sister Mona. In four years, he'd scarcely glimpsed her. If she was anywhere among this group, she'd have stood out like a white swan in a hog wallow. He scolded himself for thinking such things, but Johnny couldn't help but notice that beauty was not a conspicuous feature among the women of Fem-Amity. He even wondered if some of the women were really women, given their burly, fearsome-looking appearance. Knowing how particular Sister Say was about such matters, he did not doubt the rumor that she made them lift their skirts to prove their gender before allowing them to matriculate into the community.

Of course, in such a rugged country, a woman had to be every bit as virile as any man, maybe even more so. Together, without the aid of a single man, they had constructed three main buildings—a long dormitory where they all lived, a circular barn for their hogs and cattle, and a chapel with a real bell. A number of smaller shrines and prayer sheds also dotted the property. The community grew through attraction, numbering around eighty, and adding more all the time. Among the devotees were women from a variety of backgrounds, including some refugee slaves, Indian squaws, former prostitutes, runaways from abusive husbands, and expatriates from sundry lives, loves, and faiths. When they prayed as one, their voices shook the bedrock.

Swedenborg taught that women were vessels of understanding, so, naturally, Johnny was curious about the truths to which these women adhered. When he asked about the finer points of their doctrines, though, Sister Say just shook her head and said, "No man can e'er understand."

The orchard didn't really require much work. Over the winter, the scrub fence of rolled stones, logs, and piles of brush had held together, with minimal evidence of deer incursion. The young trees had fully leafed out, their new branches just barely touching, like school children holding hands in rows. He packed down some mole holes and, after raking the floor, spread some fresh cut grass to reduce weeds and retain moisture, then got down on his hands and knees to slash off suckers growing out of the bases and trunks.

All along, Johnny had the feeling that someone was watching him, perhaps whoever was inside a small, stick-and-mud shed across the creek, at the bottom of the ravine. He waved, just to be friendly, but got no response.

After a couple hours, Rose Mary and Mary Rose came strolling arm-in-arm to inform Johnny that they were about to serve supper. The hunchbacked sister looked fairly emaciated, while the other had gained her sister's weight, and more.

Johnny thanked them and said he was nearly finished. It unnerved him that they stayed, getting in his way, looking at him, then at each other, then back at him.

Finally, one of them said to the other, "Odd, ain't he?"

"Uhm. Just like her told us."

As much as he was used to others talking about him behind his back, Johnny wasn't quite accustomed to them doing it to his face. He decided to take it as a compliment.

"Men of God do tend to be a bit odd," he explained.

"Men are odd, sure, her says."

"Odd ain't always bad, her says too."

"Excuse me, ladies, but if I might ask, who is the person who says these things?"

"Her? Sister Mona, but her don't talk much no more."

"Her just prays."

Johnny stood, dusting himself off. "How is my dear friend, Mona? Would it be possible to speak with her?"

"Her don't speak to men at all."

"'Cept to Jesus."

Although that sounded like a righteous way to live, Johnny felt a twinge of disappointment. "Well, I have not been barbered in four years, and it would surely suit me well if she could do that for me. She would not have even to speak."

Rose Mary and Mary Rose laughed so heartily, they could hardly manage to get their words out.

"Sister Mona?"

"With a man?"

"With shears?"

"Chopping?"

"Hacking?"

"Sawing?"

"Ha ha ha ha ha ha ha ha ha!"

The hunchbacked sister collapsed against the fat sister, who engulfed her with flabby arms, and in unison they chortled and guffawed as if that were the funniest thing they'd ever heard.

Johnny didn't quite see the hilarity of that moment. He wasn't sure if he even wanted to know what the joke was, for there seemed something vaguely mean-spirited in its connotations. There being no further work that required his attention, he decided on the spot that he wasn't hungry and would prefer not to delay his departure by taking supper.

The Rose and Mary sisters escorted him back into Fem-Amity and delivered him to Sister Say.

With apologies, Johnny explained to her that he needed to make haste to re-join his traveling companions on the road to Mansfield.

"As thou wishes."

Johnny could not refrain from adding, "And please give my regards to Sister Mona."

"Good day, Mr. Appleseed."

Johnny knew exactly where to find Reverend Copus and his family. Just south of the Knox/Richland County line ran a low-lying stretch of road, where Honey Creek formed a marsh and mud filled the wheel ruts, so that a driver who didn't know how to handle a loaded wagon would almost certainly get stuck.

Sure enough, Johnny found the reverend up to his knees in muck, digging with his hands, while Mrs. Copus and the children watched from the side of the road.

Moses the sheepdog rolled in pools of fetid slop.

"I wanna go home," Little Sarah complained.

Fortunately, anticipating this eventuality, Johnny had come with reinforcements. He knew that Otto and Millie Blubaugh had a cabin and livery stable less than a mile off the main road from where the reverend's wagon had bogged down, so he'd taken a quick detour to enlist some assistance.

Otto rode a draft horse and led another.

Johnny trotted alongside them.

"Thank God!" Amy Copus sighed upon seeing them.

Reverend Copus, with two handfuls of dripping mud, kicked the wagon wheel and asserted, "I think I almost got it loose."

"Naw," Otto said. "Yahr cain't dig yer way outta this slop. Tha's why fer it's called Honey Creek, 'cause it's so gooey." Perhaps to make the reverend feel better, he added, "But yahr'll ain't the first tenderfoots to git bottomed out here'bouts."

Otto got right to work, collaring and harnessing his draft horses in front of the wagon's team. When they were ready to go, he deployed Johnny and Reverend Copus to the back of the wagon to push, and Amy Copus to take the reins, while he seized hold of the lead horse's bridle and shouted, "Git on now!"

The team broke the wagon loose with a sudden lurch, which caused Reverend Copus, who'd been pushing with all his might, to lunge face forward into the puddle.

Even the horses laughed.

"That'll be four dollars," Otto said.

"Four dollars!" Reverend Copus exclaimed. "Don't get me wrong, son. I do appreciate your service, but that's a week's wages."

"Fer that price, yahr'll can rent mah horses 'til Mansfield. Ain't gonna make it no oth'r ways with jest those two saddle ponies a-pullin' such a load."

"'Tis near larceny." Although Reverend Copus felt obliged to protest, he realized that he was fortunate that Otto rescued them. "How much farther to Mansfield?"

"Twenty-some miles. Yahr ain't gonna git there t'day, fer sure." Otto took the reverend's money, but kept his palm out. "Fer two more dollars, tho', yahr'll can bunk down at our'n cabin tonight. Supper included."

"Yes," Amy Copus interjected.

"So be it." Reverend Copus, perhaps wanting to put a positive spin on the decision, added, "I do look forward to seeing your charming wife, Mildred. Isn't that her name?"

"Tha'd be Millie."

"And by now you must be blessed with children?"

"Tha's a subject yahr ought not 'a mention to Millie," Otto said, spitting into the mud. "Ah guess tha' we jest ain't so blessed."

On the way, Otto told Reverend Copus that he and Millie lived on one of the Dan Sapp's parcels of land in Knox County, which they were purchasing through Otto's work breeding and training horses for Dan. Gradually, they were also clearing acreage for growing corn and pasturing cattle. They'd built one of the larger cabins thereabouts, with three full rooms on the ground level, and a loft with room enough to sleep a whole brood of children, if only God was willing and answered their prayers.

From the distance, Reverend Copus saw Millie working on her hands and knees in the yard; she glanced up when she heard them coming, but did not rise to greet her company.

Otto rode ahead to get to Millie first, hopped down from his horse, and kissed her lightly on the cheek while she stared at the ground. "Look who ah done found on the road," Otto said to her.

"Hello, my dear," Reverend Copus said, waving.

Finally, Millie rose with a labored sigh; if he didn't already know who she was, Reverend Copus wasn't sure if he'd have recognized her. The way she carried herself seemed labored, unlike the effervescent woman he recalled from their previous encounters. Though still young, her beauty was beginning to wear thin, not so much in ways that he could see, like in the color of her skin or the whites of her eyes, but in the way she didn't bother to shoo the flies buzzing around her, or in her evident indifference to Otto's kiss. The reverend presumed that she recognized him, although she gave no acknowledgement.

"Oh," was all she said.

Amy Copus was clearly relieved to see another woman. With a crying baby in her arms and a timid toddler clutching her leg, she said, "Bless you for your hospitality, Mrs. Blubaugh. You're like a guardian angel for us."

"Ain't no angels here, jest ghosts." She turned and indicated with a nod that Mrs. Copus should follow. "I'll put y'all in the loft. Ain't like its otherwise bein' used."

"I'm hungry," Sarah whined.

While the women and children got situated in the cabin, Otto began unhitching the horses. Reverend Copus offered to help, but Otto pushed him aside with the flat of his hand.

"Son?"

Otto stiffened, dropped the holdback straps, and after a long blow, said, "Millie ain't been herself of late. It hardened her heart when our'n second child got born daid. E'er since, we keep a-tryin', but she ain't been able to hold mah seed. It gits lonely, jest us two."

"Trust God," the reverend said, at a loss to say anything else.

Johnny added, "One day, you shall meet those dead babies all grown up and living as angels in heaven." He stated it as confidently as if he'd been predicting the next day's sunrise.

"Tha's like cold comfort compar'd to havin' a real baby in the here-'n-now."

For dinner, they ate spring peas and onions, with a touch of mint, along with hominy and some chunks of cured ham. Millie ate in silence, while Otto chewed sloppily.

Reverend Copus tried to lighten the atmosphere with genial conversation, so he prattled on mostly just to fill the air with sound, not unlike his style of delivering a sermon to a disinterested congregation.

"With God's help," he said, "I plan to bring the Word to pioneers of the new settlement in Manchester. The summer last, I conducted services among them at the blockhouse, where I shall continue to preach the gospel until I can rouse the resources to build a proper church, one that welcomes all people. Of course, I make use of the Methodist liturgy, but even so, the doors to my church are open to people of all creeds, or lack thereof—even Indians, if they are so inclined. In my fondest vision, Mansfield will grow into a thriving city where churches outnumber taverns, where folks tithe more than they gamble, and where goodwill spreads across the treaty lines, all the way to Michigan and the Canadian border, so that barriers vanish as people carry God's love with them into the vast expanse of this virgin land."

"I am in favor of that," Johnny seconded. "Methinks that peace just needs a chance."

James Junior chose that moment to pluck the last morsel of ham off his sister Sarah's plate and stuff it into his mouth.

"Mama! Papa! James done stole my pig! He's a thief, that one. Mama! Papa!"

Her brother responded with a strident, "Nuh uh no! Sarah is soooo bad!"

Not to be ignored, the baby Wesley began wailing and hurling peas across the table. This encouraged the other children to repeat their accusations even more vociferously.

Agitated, Moses the sheepdog started barking.

Millie stood so abruptly that her chair landed on its back. "For Christ's sake, give that girl some ham!" Then, she stormed away, barely making it out the door before tears overtook her.

The bedlam ceased as abruptly as flames doused by water.

Amy Copus cupped her hands over Sarah's ears.

Johnny whistled and said to Otto, "If ye need to leave the table to go have a few words with her, we all will understand."

"Talkin' don't do no good. She jest needs to cry it out. Sorry fer disturbin' yahr'll's supper." He did not seem aware that he was poking the back of his hand with the fork. Finally, he added, "Yahr'll can have Millie's ham, if'n yer want."

Sarah grabbed for the ham, and Mrs. Copus did not even bother to correct her manners.

After a fitful night of half-sleep and uneasy dreams, punctuated by the reverberations of Millie Blubaugh's sobbing into her pillow, James and Amy Copus awakened at first light, hopeful for an early departure. It seemed that Otto and Millie had just—finally—fallen asleep, and they didn't stir when, one by one, the Copus family descended the loft ladder, tiptoed through the room where their hosts slept, and gathered outside.

Johnny, who'd spent the night dozing in a meadow of clover, had already fastened the wagon and fed the horses.

"Would it be impolite to leave without saying goodbye?" Mrs. Copus wondered.

They delayed making a decision by feeding the children breakfast of johnny cakes and apple butter, with fresh milk.

Eventually, Otto came tramping outside, still dressed in his skivvies and nightshirt. "Ah reckon tha' yahr'll be eager to git gone," he said. "Millie is feelin' a might tottery, so she sent me to bid fare-thee-well."

Reverend Copus offered his hand to Otto, but when he took Otto's, it seemed to sift right through his fingers. "May the Lord bless and keep you—"

"N'er mind," Otto broke in. "Jest foller the road an' yahr'll git to Mansfield by night. Put mah horses in the stable. Good luck."

The reverend nodded grimly, loath to leave things like that, but wary of making them worse by saying more. He climbed into the wagon and whistled while tugging on the reigns.

Johnny lingered behind a few moments while the wagon pulled away. He sidled next to Otto and retrieved from his kerchief the bundle of pages, then leafed through them until he found the one he wanted.

"Here," he said, shoving it into Otto's hand. "Here is fresh news straight from heaven, with a message special for you."

Otto's voice cracked. "This won't do me none no good. Ah cain't read."

"Then let me. Listen."

> *'Faith is formed by living according to truths, which are more than merely matters of thought, but matters of will also. He who learns truths and does not practice them is like one who sows seed in a field and does not harrow in it; but he who learns truths and practices them is like one who sows seed and covers it, and the rain causes it to grow a crop and to be of use for food. The Lord says if ye know these things, happy are ye.'*

"Happy?"

"Faith," Johnny said, as he took a step and began skipping. "And then, happiness," he concluded as he hopped away.

In the middle of the afternoon, young Sarah Copus asked for the twenty-sixth time, "Are we there yet?"

Instead of saying, "No," as he had each previous time, her father answered, "Almost."

This quieted her down for a few minutes, until eventually she became restless and tried a new complaint. "I gotta go pee." Five times in the next ten minutes, she repeated that demand.

Each time, Reverend Copus said, "Soon," hoping that she'd forget.

The reverend pulled over when they came to a fork in the road, ostensibly to grant Sarah her request, but actually so that he could consult with Johnny as to which branch to take.

Johnny cleared some overgrown vines from a sign nailed to a tree, down the lesser traveled route. It read:

Do Not Entry

"Ye do not want to go that-a-way," Johnny said.

"Indeed not," Reverend Copus said. "Whose property is this?"

A cottontail rabbit scurried from a thicket down the alternate road, and Moses instinctively gave chase. The dog barked and pursued the rabbit around a corner.

Reverend Copus called, "Moses!"

A shot answered him.

Amy Copus picked up little Sarah where she was squatting, and carried her into the wagon. He then reached for his long rifle.

Oblivious to any danger, though, Johnny walked down the road, past the warning sign, until he vanished, too.

A second shot echoed through the still air.

Several tense seconds elapsed, with the reverend keeping his finger poised on the trigger, praying that he wouldn't have to shoot.

Suddenly, Moses darted back toward the wagon, followed by Johnny, who was accompanied by a shaggy, sneering woodsman with a rifle over his shoulder, a tomahawk under his belt, and a knife strapped to his leg.

"Who're yah?" the man snorted.

"I am James Copus, a man of God."

"Keep yore dog off'n mah property."

The reverend opened his mouth to apologize, but Johnny intervened, "Andy Craig, do ye mean to tell the reverend that ye are the lawful owner of this here land?"

"Ah got me squatter's rights," Andy said.

"But ye do not rightly *own* this land. Do not lie."

"Ah got what's ah got, 'cept ah ain't got no hog-fuckin' paper what says so. No offense, preacher."

"No offense taken, sir," Reverend Copus said. "Andy *Craig*? Are you perchance related to a gentleman named Jim Craig, who hails from Mount Vernon?"

"Mah goat-headed brother ain't no gentleman. He's a damn skunk-swaddlin' rascal what brings shame t'our family name."

"I was merely inquiring, in a neighborly fashion."

"We ain't a-gonna be no neighbors. Outta respect to yore woman and them l'il ones, ah'm lettin' yah go wit' jest a warnin'. But if'n yah'll e'er come down this here road again, ah'll shoot a hole straight up through yore brain. Got tha' straight?"

Sarah Copus whimpered; her little brother covered his face with his mother's skirts; and the baby spat up something yellow. Mrs. Copus tugged on her husband's belt loops, to caution him against whatever he might be thinking about saying.

"Well...." Reverend Copus started.

Before the reverend could complete the sentence, a booming female voice from around the corner interrupted the standoff. "Andy! Whar is you, yah old turd?"

With a walking stick in one hand and pulling an apple cart containing a boy and a girl with the other, Marge Cuss turned the bend, took in the scene, and started laughing. "Wha's this comedy? Andy, have you been threatenin' these folks wit' your usual death and torture?"

"Woman, bite down yore tongue!" Andy shouted.

"Good day, Marge," Johnny said. "My, your children are growing fast."

"Good to see you 'gain, Appleseed. Yep, them l'il darlin's git their fettle from me, and they git their spit from Andy."

The boy picked a bug out of his sister's hair and put it into this mouth.

Andy stomped his feet and slammed the butt of his rifle into the ground. "Shut yore yap, woman!"

Ignoring Andy, Marge Cuss addressed the reverend and Mrs. Copus. "Don't take no danger from this man. He just don't like people creepin' up on him, that's all."

Mrs. Copus brightened. "How old are your children, madame?"

"Li'l Andrew is five an' li'l Marge is three."

"I am pleased to make your acquaintance. I am Amy Copus. My husband is James. And our children are Sarah, who is four, James Junior, three, and the baby, Wesley, is just 14 months. We're moving to Mansfield—"

Andy fired his rifle into the air. "Ah said shut the fuck up! Now yah'll maght be friendly people an' such, but ah insist tha' yah git gone now. Ah'll still shoot yah."

"No you won't," Marge scoffed.

"Yeah so, ah sure will. An' don't be counter-dickin' me in front 'o oth'r people. Yah need to know yore place, woman."

"An' what might my place be? On top 'o yer bone?"

"Underneath an' likin' it!"

"I'll like it when you learn to do it right!"

"Ain't that what yore candlestick is fer?"

"I need somethin' better'n that loose packed sausage of yours!"

"Bah, they's bloodsuckin' bats in yore cave!"

Hearing Marge and Andy's bawdy exchange, Amy Copus dropped her jaw and protested, not to them, but to her husband. "Well, I have never heard such filthy things said between a man and his wife."

Andy and Marge said simultaneously, "She ain't mah wife." And, "I ain't his wife."

"Not married! But with children? Oh my!"

Reverend Copus tipped his cap and said, "God be with you," looking anxious to escape. He then tugged extra hard on the reigns.

The Copus children shifted to the back of the wagon and kept watching as they pulled away.

"I me-self am traveling with them," Johnny said, although Marge and Andy just kept staring down each other.

Unable to divert their attention, he instead handed a page of Swedenborg to their son. "Give this to your parents."

The boy put the paper into his mouth, while Johnny hustled to catch up with the Copuses.

They reached the Black Fork of the Mohecan River in late afternoon. "We're nearly home," Reverend Copus assured everybody.

When Mrs. Copus saw the cabin belonging to Frederick Zimmer and his family, her heart leapt and she bounded up in the wagon, declaring, "Rejoice! We shall have neighbors."

"Yes indeed for certain, ye shall have neighbors," Johnny jumped in cheerfully. "In addition to the Zimmers, there's Martin Ruffner and his family, Peter Kinney, Jean Jerome and his Indian wife. In fact, just a mile across the river there is a Delaware Indian village, which some call Helltown, but most call Greentown. Old Chief Arm Strong is their leader."

"Indians! So close? James, you never mentioned—"

"They are very friendly Indians. Some are even Christian."

"I don't like In-germs!" little Sarah moaned.

"We must be brave when doing the Lord's work, little one," the reverend told the child, although he stared at Mrs. Copus when he said it. "The Lord does not call us to do any work to which we are not equal."

That statement had the immediate effect of silencing the brood, although Mrs. Copus privately wondered about what dangers and hardships, exactly, the Lord considered her equal to.

Johnny Appleseed stepped forward and announced, "Well, folks, seeing as how ye have nearly reached your destination, I am going to take me leave now. 'Tis been a pleasure traveling with ye, but I have work elsewhere to do, and other good people to visit."

Mrs. Copus frowned, having grown fond of the man despite his odd ways. "When will we see you again?"

"Oh, I shall be by and by, most often appearing when ye least expect to see me."

With that, Johnny splashed across the Black Fork and into the ominous forest on the other side.

When he disappeared from sight, Mrs. Copus said to her husband, "That man is not quite right in his head, is he?"

"Being a bit daft suits him," Reverend Copus said. "Sometimes, I wonder how he stays alive. Other times, I think that we'd all be better off if some of his craziness rubbed off on the rest of us. God must have known what he was doing when He made Johnny Appleseed."

The old Greenville treaty line didn't matter much anymore, since settlers ignored it with impunity. By legal edict of the treaty, the village of Mansfield ought not to have existed, as it was situated well beyond the boundary that the government had ceded to Indian nations, "who have a right to those lands, are quietly to enjoy them, hunting, planting, and dwelling thereon, so long as they please, without any molestation from the United States." Because of these shifting barriers between the compartmentalized tribes and the sprawling white civilization, a person who strayed from the main roads could have no way of knowing if he was traversing friendly or hostile terrain.

Johnny presumed that this *terra incognita* was where he'd likely find the person for whom he searched.

For some miles, Johnny had been carrying a bit of a load in his bowels, not so much that it slowed him down, but now that he was on his own, he figured it made sense to unburden himself. He found a moss-covered boulder with a natural seat and basin, undid his trousers, hunched over, and let go of a pattering of pellets. It'd been days. He was surprised at how much had backed up.

"Great merciful Jesus," he sang out.

As he bent forward to wipe himself with the moss, an arrow zipped over the top of his head and twanged in an oak just behind him.

Dead Mary stepped from behind a holly bush. "I ain't decided if it weren't 've been mo' kind to kill yo' years ago, when I firs' had a chance. But I see yo' is still livin' and still full o' shit. Guess dere ain't no sense in killin' yo' now."

"Mary! The very person that I wanted to see!"

"I've done been followin' yo' since Honey Creek an' all dat mud. Don't yo' know dat it's dangerous bringin' mo' settlers int' dis country? 'Specially folks as green as dem ones. When times git hard, dey'll die first."

"They are good Christian people who trust God to care for them."

"Jus' like a mess o' otha dead folks. God must not care fo' me nearly so much, 'cuz I'd be still alive."

"I disagree with your conclusion, but I am glad that ye are alive. I have been worried about ye."

"Worried 'bout me? Now, dere's a story! Ain't nobody cares none 'bout me no more."

Johnny pulled up his pants and said, "That is untrue. I do care. Five years ago, when I learned that Fog Mother had been so brutally slain, I said a prayer for her immortal soul. Likewise, I was concerned what ye would do and how ye would live with her gone. As new people began settling in this country, they told me stories about a wild negro woman who was spawn of a voodoo slave and the devil, who turned into a wildcat after dark and attacked people's livestock, ate their dogs, and stole their children's souls. Some folks said that although she walked on all fours, she could shoot a bow and arrow without ever missing her target. Like most such tales, I figured it for about 90 percent horse feathers, but the 10 percent that was true, was probably about ye."

Dead Mary flashed her fingernails, which were inches long and sharpened to points.

"I might jus'in fact be mo' wildcat than human, but I got no taste fo' dogs. As fo' child'run's souls, I jus' let dem grow up. Grown men and women give away dey's own souls. Yo' is an 'xception, I do think."

"And so are ye, Mary."

"If I do got a soul, it only gives me pain. It's done been so ev'r since dey kilt Fog Mother. I could'a saved her, or at least tried, but she made me swear not to kill no person, not e'en to save her life. It still haunts me, tho. There'd be times when I jus' wants t' kill somebody so bad it makes me wanna scream."

"Why don't ye, then?"

"Kill somebody?"

"No, scream. Just rear back, suck in air, and let fly with a good holler loud enough to strip the bark right off a sycamore."

"Who says I don't? Dem stories tell 'o da wild woman howlin' at da full moon, don't dey? Well, dat's jus' me lettin' go." Mary walked around Johnny and plucked her arrow out of the oak tree. "But dey's more to dat story. C'mon an' I'll show yo' what I mean."

She led him up a steep bluff behind the creek, through clumps of maple, beech, and birch. The canopy had grown so thick, the full sun overhead winked through only for a moment at a time, and the ground lay shadowy and colorless. Ferns brushed against their ankles, fronds getting stuck between Johnny's toes. At the top of the rise, they followed a steep ridge where the clay shale broke off in sheets underfoot. They reached a stream that cut through a clump of hemlock, where shafts of sunshine burst through so that the honeysuckle and lady slippers caught sparks and seemed to dance.

Johnny wanted to ask where they were going, for it seemed that wherever it was, they weren't taking the most direct route. Then he realized that was probably the whole point; Dead Mary didn't want him to know how to get there.

They kept following the stream to where it disappeared, echoing, into a sinkhole. There, Mary pulled aside a heap of branches and scrub that she had piled to conceal the mouth of a damp, chilling cave. The opening exhaled cool air, but was so narrow that the only way for a person to enter was by crawling. On a low-hanging branch above the cave's entrance, an albino squirrel stood on its haunches, guarding the domain.

"Heah's where I live," Mary said. "Dat white, bushy-tailed rat is my friend."

"Once, some years ago, I met a white squirrel. They are very rare. Do you suppose it could be the same one?"

"It might could be, 'cuz dis here l'il squirrel, he cain't die. I done put a spell on 'im to live fo'ever. It's worked so far."

Johnny offered a seed to the squirrel, which snatched it then dashed into foliage. "It would seem that you have gone to great pains to keep your distance from the rest of humanity."

"Dat's 'cuz I needs to. Da things I do, I gots to be alone."

"What do you do?"

Dead Mary reached into a fire pit in front of the cave and scooped out a handful of ashes, which she blew into the breeze. "I aim to fix a spell to bring back Fog Mother's ghost."

"You don't need a spell to accomplish that. The spirits are all around us, always."

Dead Mary pointed a crooked finger at Johnny and snarled, "Some folks say dat yo' talk to da dead."

"When they talk to me, I answer them. 'Tis only polite."

"Po-lite! Das da whole problem wit' da dead. Dey is too polite. If I got kilt like did Fog Mother, I be damn mad."

"The dead can be very patient."

"Yeah, I s'pose so." She turned over a rock covering a hole, in which was hidden a latched box. "What's heah is all dat I got left 'o Fog Mother. I got roots and dried flowers. I got bones and grizzle parts. I got shreds 'o her clothes an' locks 'o her hair. Dese're things fo' makin' a spell what to bring down da spirits in a fog. Much as I done tried, tho', I ain't still got da spell right. Somethin's missin'. Yo' got any stuff good fo' makin' a spell?"

Curious, Johnny reached for the box, but Dead Mary wouldn't let him have it. As for relics, charms, talismans, and various sorcerous conjurations, he was genuinely intrigued and innately respectful, while at the same time wary of their potential for misuse. He untied his kerchief, which carried a whistle, a jackknife, some hemp twine, a haw comb, a tin cup, flint and steel, a wax candle, a water bladder, a pounding stone, tweezers, dried beans, scraps of calico, a ginseng root, one hundred and twenty-three dollars, and a bundle of pages of Swedenborg text.

"This is all that I have got," he said. "Except for one piece of advice."

"Will it make her come back?"

"In my experience, the spirits come when they feel they are needed."

"I cain't need her no mo' den I do now."

"Perhaps your needs alone are not enough."

She pounded her fists into the dirt and shook her head. "Yo' ain't no use to me none. Go!"

"Forgive me for offending you."

"Jus' git be gone."

Johnny stood and tugged on his pants legs. "As ye wish."

"Don' yo' come back, and don' tell no body where I live." She cleared her throat. "But...."

"Yes?"

"If it does happen dat yo' speak wit' Fog Mother, tell her dat I'm a-tryin' as hard and da best way what I knows how. Tell her I miss her."

"She knows," Johnny said, gathering his possessions.

Chapter 20 – July 1811

Prophetstown and Vincennes, the Indiana Territory

In the early days of his prophecy, Tenskwatawa had harbored occasional but nagging doubts about whether he was, indeed, the highest among men, chosen by Waashaa Monetoo to be the vessel of His will. He never questioned the authenticity of his revelation or the veracity of his teachings, but sometimes he just did not feel, in his own heart and mind, like he imagined a genuine messiah ought to feel.

He blamed Waashaa Monetoo for that.

To start, he thought it reasonable that, as a gesture of good faith, Waashaa Monetoo could restore sight to his blind eye. Short of that, Tenskwatawa considered himself entitled to many other divine benefits. The persistent indignity of intestinal distress still assailed him, and his recurring hemorrhoids had flared again, despite fervent prayers for relief. No prophet ought to be bothered by such debilities. Why didn't Waashaa Monetoo fix them?

Those were mostly private matters, however, between himself and the all-powerful but sometimes inattentive Waashaa Monetoo. More puzzling was why He declined Tenskwatawa's specific request to furnish another miracle, to silence his critics. The people's passions of the day when he'd darkened the sun had receded too quickly from their memories, and while he could always answer his skeptics by reminding them of that story, he worried about what he might be able to manufacture as an equally impressive second act.

However, Tenskwatawa could always allay his misgivings by taking a walk through Prophetstown, the great Indian metropolis that his devotees built in his honor. There, folks bowed when he passed, warriors saluted him, and mothers brought him their babies to bask in his aura.

In the rich soils and abundant forests near the confluence of the Tippecanoe and Wabash Rivers, people of several tribes lived, worked, and flourished together. Rows and rows of bark-sided *wegiwa* lined broad lanes along the high ground, overlooking the rivers where women washed clothes and warriors beached their armada of canoes. In fields surrounding the town, the Indian nations grew corn in fertile fields, and they kept horses in a large corral. The House of the Stranger sat across the river, where the Prophet welcomed travelers who could stay for the duration of their pilgrimage, or until they'd settled in as new residents of the community.

Tenskwatawa held court in The Medicine Hut, in the heart of Prophetstown. There, he sat regally in his elevated walnut chair adorned with plumes and feathers, draped with belts of wampum, inlaid with stones, bones, and pieces of silver, and framed by two upright spears with copper tips. Whenever doubts bothered him as to the legitimacy of his prophecy, all he had to do was plop into that chair, and his uncertainties vanished. Seated in his throne, surrounded by his regalia and doted upon by his worshippers, everything felt all right—except, sometimes, in his stomach.

On any given morning, by the time that Tenskwatawa arrived at the Medicine Hut, a line of pilgrims awaited their turns to beseech him for favors regarding whatever difficulties afflicted their lives. Prior to gaining his powers, Tenskwatawa had never considered the great variety of plights that burdened other people's lives—he'd always rather imagined he was uniquely oppressed by unjust fortunes. Yet in his capacity as the Prophet, part of his function was to give comfort and hope to the common Indian lot of abused, diseased, despised, deprived, tormented, and downtrodden, among whom there seemed no end of suffering.

That was the least he could do, and that's what he did—the least.

"Who is first today petitioning my grace?" Tenskwatawa asked his wife, Door Keeper, who managed the queues.

"First is a Lenape delegation from the Black Fork in Ohio lands, the very place where you worked your miracle on the day of the Black Sun," Door Keeper said, fluffing the pelts in his chair so that Tenskwatawa could sit more comfortably. "Arm Strong is their chief."

The mention of that day filled Tenskwatawa with nostalgia. "Ah, well I do remember these people. Waashaa Monetoo selected them to bear witness to my greatest triumph. Bring them forward."

Door Keeper parted the beaded curtains covering the entrance, and gestured for the Black Fork group to advance.

They had slept outside the building all night to be first in line, and although dirty, tired, and hungry, they jumped onto their feet when summoned. Dressed in ceremonial garb, Chief Arm Strong led them, doing his best not to limp despite his evident pain at walking. He was accompanied by two braves with shaved heads and painted faces, and one young woman wearing a deerskin jingle dress. They dropped to their knees in the dirt before the Prophet.

Tenskwatawa left them kneeling for a few moments before he beckoned them to "Speak."

"Oh, Tenskwatawa, great Prophet of Waashaa Monetoo, it is our honor to be in your presence," Arm Strong said, still facing the ground.

"For what reason do you presume yourselves upon my time?"

Chief Arm Strong raised his head to look at Tenskwatawa. "From the day when first you came to our village and worked your miracle, no others in all of the Indian nations have been more devout in your praise and worship. Our storytellers sing of your glory, our women speak your name when they plant seeds, our braves keep your faith in their hearts during their hunts, and our children are taught to pray in the words that you gave us. In body, soul, and heart, we are your most fervent followers."

"It is to your benefit to follow me."

Chief Arm Strong continued above the sighs of his warriors. "In you and your benevolence, we have every confidence. Yet...."

"Speak, but guard your tongue against offending Waashaa Monetoo."

"Hardships have fallen upon us like a gray cloud. During the winter, a killing plague took many of our people. Then last year's corn was meager, and from our hunting grounds, game has all but vanished. More and more white settlers build downstream, crowding us out, mocking us and abusing our women. Despair has led many Lenape back to alcohol and bad moral behavior. Thus do I plead for you to ask that Waashaa Monetoo give my people a sure sign that He has not forsaken ourselves—perhaps a small miracle, such as if a whirlwind were to destroy the white men's village—"

"Enough!" Unable to get comfortable in his seat, Tenskwatawa had been tossing and twisting. He had heard enough, for during his ministry, so many abject wretches had come to him so many times with similarly miserable tales, that they had collectively drained his sympathy. His customary advice in these situations was to pray, trust, obey, and accept.

"Your people have strayed from my teachings," he said. "They must be righteous to expect rewards from Waashaa Monetoo."

"But merciful Prophet, we ourselves were first among Indian nations to embrace your message. We watched when you hid the sun in your hand, and we exalted your name when you restored it to the sky. We burned our witch to prove our loyalty. Even so, these ordeals have visited us, over and again, no matter how hard we prayed."

"Blasphemer! You yourself admit that the people have turned to alcohol and immorality. How brazen of you to beg for mercy. It stings my heart that the same people I chose for my greatest miracle have reverted to vulgarity. Repent, I say. Return to me when you have cleansed your souls."

For dramatic effect, Tenskwatawa leaned forward and ogled with his bad eye.

Chastened, Chief Arm Strong blinked and let go of a sigh.

The two braves with him kept their heads down, although one of them began slowly reaching for the knife tied onto his belt.

At once, the young woman among them spoke, with her head down and her long, loose hair covering her face. "If it pleases the Prophet, may I address you, unworthy though I am?"

Tenskwatawa was curious to see what she looked like. "Show your face, but speak warily."

"My name is Smiling Coneflower...."

When she looked up, Tenskwatawa was glad that he'd granted her permission to speak, for she was so comely that she made him forget about his belly ache—even while, from behind, he could feel Door Keeper bristling.

"By birth, I am Wyandot from Sandusky, but married now to a Lenape brave, I live on the Black Fork with his people."

"Wyandot, eh? That is not to your credit. Your people are disappointing to me, for too few have joined my faith."

"My father is a man of some influence among the northern Ohio tribes, and also the Michigan Shawnee and Potawatomi. He knows little of your religion, I confess, but dearly he loves me, and should I beg him, he would convert to your true faith. As a believer, his example would sway many others."

"Your father is who?"

"He is known as Toby."

"I have heard of him. They say he is a sinner."

"Those who say so know him not."

"And despite his lewd and indecent ways, you fancy that you yourself have the power to compel him to abandon his sins and follow the path of salvation, which leads to me?"

Smiling Coneflower widened her eyes earnestly, with just a trace of flirtation. "I do."

At moments like this, Tenskwatawa had doubts about whether Waashaa Monetoo's prohibition against infidelity and polygamy applied equally to His Prophet as it did to other men. "Very well, I will pray to Waashaa Monetoo to forgive your people, and, if you prove worthy, to remove His curse upon you."

Smiling Coneflower's face brightened.

"But you, young woman, must return to me in six months, to express proper gratitude."

With that, he told the Lenape foursome to leave.

Door Keeper went to admit the next group of penitents, which included an old man with one leg and a fat woman with orange lesions on her face.

Suddenly, some kind of disturbance arose outside, and Door Keeper went to investigate.

Tenskwatawa remained seated, unwilling to commit to moving for anything less than an emergency.

In a few moments, Door Keeper dashed into the hut and panted. "Husband, a circumstance requires your attention. Under a white flag of peace, a group of Long Knives has ridden into camp. They wish to confer."

Tenskwatawa ground his teeth. *What a bother.* Some days, he missed drinking. "Tell the white men to wait, and go find my brother."

For several months, Tecumseh had been in an especially antagonistic mood. It all started with the Treaty of Fort Wayne. Just mentioning it was enough to make him berserk. The chiefs who had signed it—Beaver for the Lenape, Winamac for the Potawatomi, and Little Turtle for the Miami—were sniveling lapdogs for Governor Harrison. Content to grow fat on their annuities, they surrendered lands that were not rightfully theirs, against Tecumseh's vehement protestations. Because of their treachery, Harrison had been able to annex the southern Indiana territory into his empire, and Tecumseh had no doubts that he had further designs on the upper Wabash, including Prophetstown.

Tecumseh responded by redoubling efforts to drum up recruits for his coalition, in many cases bypassing tribal chiefs and appealing directly to younger braves, who joined eagerly, for they saw in him an ideal to which they could aspire—and, possibly, to attract women.

Likewise, the Treaty of Fort Wayne was enough to finally convince Tecumseh that he had no choice but to tolerate an alliance of convenience with the British. On several occasions, he snuck into Canada, where he listened to the promises and blandishments of General Isaac Brock. He did not trust the British, who were proven scoundrels, but neither did he trust most tribal chiefs or his brothers' followers to make good soldiers. Whether he trusted even his brother was a matter he debated with himself.

What mattered, though, was that they all trusted him, and that he trusted himself.

With British backing, Tecumseh began taking small actions to provoke the Long Tongues. In one recent incident, he refused a government annuity, paid in the form of a large delivery of salt. When a merchant boat unloaded it on the riverbank below Prophetstown, Tecumseh stormed to the site, grabbed the boat's captain by his hair, and railed at him that the Treaty of Fort Wayne was illegal, that the government was illegitimate, and that he would not accept blood payment from thieves. Cowed, the captain re-loaded the salt onto his boat and hastened back to Vincennes, where Tecumseh hoped that Harrison would consider himself to have been personally insulted.

Tecumseh's now sat across the council table from the emissaries who had ridden into Prophetstown. "Is this about salt?"

Colonel Frank Bantzer, the leader of this group, clearly heard the venom in Tecumseh's voice, even through Stephen Ruddell's translation. "Your governor has heard disturbing rumors about his Indian brothers. He hopes they are untrue."

"Bah," Tecumseh sneered.

Tenskwatawa tried to say something less confrontational. "We ourselves are your brothers in peace. We live in this holy city, which is named after me, wishing only to worship in freedom and harmony."

"Of course." Bantzer replied to Tenskwatawa while maintaining eye contact with Tecumseh. "The governor congratulates you for your excellent community... but it hurts him deeply to hear that your religion preaches *treason*."

Tecumseh held his tongue and allowed Tenskwatawa to huff. "Treason? Is it treason for Indians to worship their God and serve their Prophet? My people are sober, peaceable, and hard-working. If the governor himself thinks otherwise, he is listening to bad birds."

"The governor cannot help what he hears. Some tell him that your religion promises that one day Indians will drive white men off these lands, even though we have purchased them through fair exchange. Others tell the governor that his Indian brothers have been seen consulting with the British. More troubling to him than these rumors, though, are some of your peoples' actions. When the governor sent a ship loaded with generous provisions, as per agreement, his men were sent back in a rude way."

Tecumseh could listen to no more. "So, this is truly about salt."

Bantzer continued, with Ruddell translating. "That incident confused the governor, for he has come to cherish his Indian brothers as loyal and esteemed friends."

One thing about Long Tongues' diplomacy that Tecumseh truly could not comprehend was the mandate to speak to even your most reviled adversary in syrupy, flattering terms. Still, he'd developed a knack for doing it, so with a cheerful but deprecating insincerity, he said, "Tell the governor the glad news that I myself will go to Vincennes to meet with him in eighteen days. When he and I speak, my words will wash away all of these bad stories that he has heard, and all troubles will be settled in peace and happiness."

The meeting continued for another hour, while Bantzer pressed for details as to logistics, agendas, and accommodations for this proposed conference. Repeatedly, Tecumseh dodged direct questions with sunny assurances that his intentions were benevolent, and he would answer all questions in due time. Beyond that, he deferred to Tenskwatawa, who blathered on and on about the joys of living in Prophetstown. At the point when he caught Bantzer stifling a yawn, Tecumseh cut his brother short and asked the colonel if he had any further questions.

Bantzer replied that he did not, then excused himself by saying that he had to hurry back to Vincennes to convey the news of their conference to Governor Harrison.

As soon as the Long Tongues left the Medicine Hut, Tecumseh opened his mouth to scream, but instead of letting it out, he slammed his tomahawk into the arm of Tenskwatawa's throne. "Never have I wanted to scalp a man more than that one," he growled. "There is something about him that makes insects crawl under my skin."

"Oh, yes, he is a vain and pompous man," Tenskwatawa commented. "But listen, I do not want to go to Vincennes. They do not like me there. Besides, my sores are hurting me too badly for travel."

Tecumseh glowered at Tenskwatawa and shook his head. "I do not want you to come with me. This trip I myself will organize, as a demonstration of Indian might. When Harrison sees our forces, he will take pause in his aggressions. I earn some time for our cause by saying to him what he needs to hear. Afterwards, I will travel south to invite the braves of Creek, Chickasaw, and the Choctaw nations to join us. You will stay here and keep Prophetstown. I will return before first snow....

"But I caution you, brother, do not confront the Long Tongues while I am away. I will return with more followers and a larger army, and then we will finally be strong enough to defeat them. Until such time, I expect no more of you than to hold to our plans. Pray. Be strong. And if you have it in you, a miracle would not hurt, either."

To be in Governor William Henry Harrison's good graces was to be a privileged person in the territorial capital of Vincennes, and Colonel Frank Bantzer relished the perks of partisanship. From the moment he'd first met Harrison, Bantzer recognized him as a dynamic leader to whom he could profitably attach his own ambitions. Thus, over the years he'd seized every opportunity to curry Harrison's approval.

Some fellow officers thought Bantzer was being gallant by accepting a post in remote Vincennes, when safer and more comfortable deployments were available to him in Ohio. After ten years in the military, though, Bantzer had grown impatient, and he sought to further his rank and influence now. In Vincennes, under Harrison's patronage, he commanded nearly 1,000 regular soldiers in the U.S. Army. Every morning, standing in front of the mirror and putting on his uniform transformed Frank Bantzer into the man he wanted to be, and whom he wanted other people to acknowledge.

Soon after Colonel Bantzer returned from Prophetstown, Harrison summoned him to the palatial Grouseland mansion.

A slave let him in and led him to a young woman seated at a desk in the foyer, flipping through the pages in a ledger. Waves and tangles of unruly yet lustrous red hair bobbed across her features as she scanned the pages. She seemed familiar.

"Here is today's entry," she proclaimed. "So you must be...." She traced her finger across the line and read the name, with a slight tremor in her voice. "...Colonel Frank Bantzer."

Unwelcomed recognition is easy to ignore, especially when there is legitimate ambiguity and a will to do so. Bantzer let the moment pass without remark.

Harrison appeared in the threshold of the council room. "Bantzer, please come in."

As soon as the door closed behind them, the colonel asked, "Who is that young woman?"

"Rebecca Galloway? She is a sweet, somewhat impulsive lass. From time to time, she assists with my accounts." Harrison sensed the colonel's arousal. "Aye, she's ravishing and still as pure as a daisy, but mind that she is betrothed to my factor, Millard Doody."

"No, do not misinterpret my query. I knew her when she was a mere stripling child."

"My, those young girls do grow, don't they?"

"When is she to be wed?"

"I don't know. They keep postponing the date." Harrison put an arm around his shoulder, and steered him toward the bureau containing a bottle and two glasses. "Sir, you could have the pick of Vincennes' lovely debutantes. Marriage would suit you. And you could always keep a few whores discreetly on the side."

Even though he knew that people tolerated a soldier's indiscretions in direct proportion to his rank, this subject always made Bantzer uneasy, so he changed it. "I have important news from Prophetstown."

The colonel reported his version of the discussions with Tecumseh on the matter of the contested salt annuities, as well as the allegations—which Tecumseh did not explicitly deny—of clandestine collaborations with the British.

"Our talks were extremely strained," he exaggerated. "Even under the white flag of truce, I feared the savage might jump me and try to scalp me. But I was steadfast when staring into the war chief's eyes, and I swear I made him blink. In the end, he consented to meet with you here in Vincennes. He assured me that he will come in peace."

"But what will we talk about?" Harrison wondered. "After all, we are enemies. I have enough respect for political realities to listen to him, as does he toward me. At the end of the day, though, we will still be enemies. If he had not been born a primitive, Chief Tecumseh could have been a worthy officer. It makes a Christian wonder why God would have wasted his grace on such a hopeless cause."

Colonel Bantzer shook his fist. "It is our manifest destiny to rid the heathens from the length and breadth of this land."

Harrison thought about that for a second, then chuckled. "Bantzer, in my years, I have heard a great deal of puffery and ballyhoo, but you can shovel bull manure as well as anybody. I'd worry if I thought you actually believed it."

That comment made Bantzer cringe, for he'd thought that he really did believe it, or at least that Harrison believed that he did.

Harrison said, "I think we should have a drink. I would like to propose a toast."

A toast was an excellent excuse to start drinking early. Bantzer accepted the snifter of brandy and waited for Harrison to elaborate.

"You've been loyal to me, Frank. I need a man whom I can trust totally. I know also that you are driven and ambitious, yearning for greater rank. I have decided that you deserve to be rewarded with that which you desire."

Harrison handed a small cherry box to Bantzer.

He took it like a child receiving a gift, resisting the urge to shake it.

"Open it, already."

Inside, centered on a tiny, blue silk pillow, lay the single star of a brigadier general.

"I've submitted the paperwork to Washington to make it official, but as the governor of the territory of Indiana, I am asserting my authority to raise your rank in the United States Army."

Harrison lifted his glass. "To you, *General* Bantzer."

General Frank Bantzer's first impulse was to gulp his drink—he had never tasted anything sweeter in his entire life.

After leaving Grouseland, General Bantzer dashed into town, only to find himself confronting a personal dilemma.

On one hand, he wanted to rush into the nearest public establishment and declare today a holiday in the Indiana Territory, and in the festive spirit of the occasion, he'd buy a drink for everybody in the house. He wanted men to shake his hand and raise their glasses in his honor, and for women to sit on either side of him, one to hold his drink, and the other to feed him berries and sweetbreads. At the end of the day, he wanted a grandiose display of pyrotechnics spelling his name across the sky.

On the other hand, he also wanted to relax, sit in his favorite chair, bask in his new status, take off all his clothes, and fondle himself while getting as drunk as he possibly could. Ultimately, he decided that there would be many other opportunities to revel in public accolades, but, now that he was finally a general, his chances to drink as freely he wanted might be fewer and harder to come by.

Thus, he returned to his quarters, shut the door, closed the shutters tight, and sighed happily as he let his pants fall to the floor.

Even if Frank had not seen her niece earlier, it was inevitable he would think of Mona Junkin on this occasion. How he wished he could take this chance to gloat to her.

Over the years, Frank had often revisited the memory of how he'd sworn to Mona that, one day, come hell or high water, he would wear a general's star. At first, she had been thrilled... until he further expounded that this was the obvious reason why he could not marry her. When Frank told Mona he simply didn't have enough time in his ambitious agenda to take a wife, he hadn't intended for her to take that plain fact so personally. He'd merely needed to prioritize and manage his time—not the kind of decision that required any apologies or soul-searching. Granted, maybe he hadn't selected the best moment for making that revelation, seeing as how just minutes before he'd deflowered her. Still, he knew that to achieve his highest calling, he could not afford to be distracted or diverted by any woman's nagging.

Finally, he thought, the events of that day validated his choice in a way that even Mona would have to agree proved that he'd been right, all along.

This line of thinking, abetted by his third glass of whiskey, led Bantzer to consider whether, now that he was a man of sufficient means and prestige, he ought to follow Harrison's advice and take a wife. A dutiful woman could be an asset—not one of the tramps from whom he occasionally purchased affections, but a lady of culture and breeding. It'd be helpful, though not absolutely necessary, if they were also fond of each other. However, she could not cling to him, or expect sweet words, glittery jewels, or complete fidelity.

Where am I going to find such a woman?

Thinking it over with inebriated clarity, he realized that the only woman for whom he'd ever had any feelings whatsoever... was Mona. It was a shame and a pity—even an outrage, when he thought about it—that she'd insisted upon more emotional commitment than he was prepared to allow. Now, after all the trouble that had come from his affair with her, he didn't know if he could still muster sincere feelings for any woman.

That damnable Mona Junkin! She ruined me!

Halfway through a second bottle, Frank no longer drank happily; he was soused with anger and resentment. This made him horny. He told himself he should be able to snap his fingers, and have a woman report, ready to do her duty.

It's my goddamned right! After all, there are plenty of women who would be grateful to spread their legs beneath a brigadier general!

The notion occurred to him that it was not too late to go into town, find a whore, and give her that honor. Lurching to his feet, he brushed his hair and gargled with vinegar. When he pinned his general's star above his heart, though, it stung like a wasp's puncture. He looked at his fingertips and wondered where the blood had come from.

He'd just pinned his general's star to his bare chest, just above his heart.

Rebecca Galloway couldn't help but smile, thinking her day had finally come.

Panicked citizens of Vincennes felt differently. "The Indians are bringing their army!" they cried when they learned of Tecumseh's approaching convoy.

Advance scouts reported that Tecumseh was en route to Vincennes, accompanied by a force of dozens of canoes, and probably two hundred warriors on foot. They came with weapons in hand and their faces slathered with war paint.

Furious, and feeling duped, Harrison placed the citizenry on high alert. Soldiers concentrated gunpowder in the armory. Women and children sequestered themselves in blockhouses.

General Bantzer summoned the militia into active duty, and sent for a brigade of regulars from Fort Knox to reinforce their troops.

The Indians camped at Busseron, just a few miles upriver from town.

Although Tecumseh's men numbered around 400, the anxious citizens of Vincennes believed they were equal in their brutality and bloodlust to the more than twice as many soldiers at Bantzer's disposal. Many feared that, at any moment, the savages would unleash carnage upon their town, and not cease until they'd butchered every white person, down to the last babbling baby.

To Rebecca, though, the arrival of the Indian hordes was as exciting as Indpendence Day, New Year's Eve, and her nineteenth birthday all rolled into one. In her girlhood, she'd always dreamt that one day Chief Tecumseh would come for her with pomp and spectacle, and declare himself to her for the whole world to see.

After three days of negotiations, Tecumseh finally agreed to enter Vincennes with just a few dozen of his men, who armed themselves with tomahawks and bows and arrows, but no firearms. On the day they marched into town, the entire population lined the streets to gawk.

Rebecca stood next to her fiancé, who struggled to hold onto her arm while she bobbed up and down trying to catch a glimpse.

"Simmer down, dear," he said. "It is unbecoming of you to fuss so."

"Pish!" Rebecca grunted.

Millard Doody was such a worrywart, sometimes. Oh, she was earnestly fond of Millard, mostly because among all her potential suitors, only he had the means by which to take her away from Ohio. She didn't feel that she was trifling with his affections, though, for she believed she could marry him, if all else failed.

Still, her heart had never surrendered the girlish fantasy of becoming the Shawnee Chief's queen. Now, with her first glimpse of Tecumseh, that childish dream flooded her anew with a mature woman's sensual longings. "There he is!" She extricated herself from the factor's grip.

She didn't get far before the crowd blocked her way. She pushed and shoved and struggled to break through, in the process nearly knocking Stephen Ruddell off his feet.

"Whoa!" he said. "'Scuse me, misses, but.... Wait. Becky Galloway?"

If she could've feigned to be somebody else and gotten away with it, she would have. She'd always considered Ruddell to be kind of a blowhard, and certainly did not wish to engage him in pleasantries. "Do I know you?"

"Why, Becky Galloway, sure as hogs got curly tails, yah ain't forgot old Stephen Ruddell, have yah? My, ain't yah growed into a beauty."

"I live here now," she replied.

"Yah do, do yah now? Well, I can't say that I envy yah, what with all this fright 'n' commotion in this town. It's a kind o' madness, which I've seen from both sides. Shawnee mothers in Prophetstown tell their children to be good or else a bad white man will bite off their heads, while here in Vincennes there's a saying that every time the trees are full of crows, there's another Indian demon from hell searching for a white soul to steal. It's worse now than ever." Ruddell paused to check if Rebecca was still listening, then shrugged and kept talking anyway. "If I didn't have to be here, I'd be back home with my family in Kentucky. But I got called back, one last time, so said Harrison, 'cause they need for me to interpret for them. Also, Chief Tecumseh trusts me to speak his words."

Rebecca felt a thrill slide up her chest. "Are you Chief Tecumseh's interpreter?"

"To the degree that any man can interpret words that folks refuse to hear, yeah, that's my reason for being here."

"I would like to see him. Will you take a message to him?"

Ruddell gave her an admonishing look. "Say what, Becky?"

Undaunted, she said, "I have news for him... from my father. As you know, they are old friends. I'm sure he'd like to hear what I have to tell him."

Ruddell shrugged and said, "I ain't sure that's such a swift idea, given these circumstances. It might in fact be dangerous. I'm just a-sayin'...."

She made a pouting face.

"But I s'pose that whatever you got to say to him, it's something that Tecumseh will want to hear. I'm sick 'n' tired of bringing bad news back and forth 'tween Indians and white folks. So... yeah, I will."

Rebecca stood on tiptoes and whispered into his ear. She chose the words carefully, but the tone made both of them blush.

That afternoon, Tecumseh and Harrison met in a walnut arbor on the Grouseland estate. The reception was a grand event. On one side, 80 dragoons with pistols tucked into their belts sat on rails, while on the other side, the Indians chose to remain standing with their arms folded. The two men shook hands and exchanged gifts—a Bible for Tecumseh, and a pipe, full of especially pungent *ksha'te*, for Harrison.

The agreed-upon itinerary called for the formal ceremony to lead directly into closed-door discussions in the conference room of the mansion; however, while he had the eyes and ears of those multitudes who had gathered to observe, Tecumseh surprised the governor by requesting the opportunity to make a public speech.

He said, through Stephen Ruddell, that he had words everybody in Vincennes needed to hear.

Harrison's eyes said 'no,' but feeling boxed in, he inflated his chest and said, "I will permit it."

Before he began, Tecumseh pulled Ruddell aside and said, "When you repeat my words, speak them *loudly*."

He then raised his head and parted his arms, as if to gather everybody's attention, and said, "Brothers, I wish you to give me close attention, because I think you do not clearly understand what I have to say. I want to speak to you about promises that the Americans have made.

"Do you recall the time when the Jesus Indians lived with the Americans at Gnadenhutten? They had confidence in the white men's promises of friendship, but the Americans murdered all the men, women, and children, even as they prayed for mercy to their Jesus. Do you remember?

"The same promises were given to the Shawnee at Fort Finney, where my father and his people were forced to make a treaty. Flags were given to them, and they were told they were themselves now the children of the American president. My people were told that if any white person meant to harm us, we could hold up these flags and be safe from all danger. And what happened? Our beloved chief Moluntha stood with the American flag in one hand and a peace treaty in the other, but his head was chopped off by an American officer, and that man was never punished.

"Brothers, after such bitter memories, can you blame me for placing little confidence in the promises of Americans? When we buried the tomahawk again at Greenville, the Americans said they were our new friends, and they would treat us well. Since that treaty, though, they have killed many Shawnee, many Winnebagoes, many Miami, many Lenape, and they have taken vast lands from us. When they killed us or stole our possessions, no American was ever punished—not one.

"It is by such bad deeds that Americans push Indians to do mischief. You do not want unity among our tribes, so you seek to destroy it. You try to make differences between us. Indians, though, wish to unite and consider their land the common property of all among ourselves, but you Americans try to keep us from coming together. You separate the tribes and deal with them one by one, and advise them not to enter into this union. Why? Your American states have set an example of forming a union. Why should you censure the Indians for following that example?

"But, Brothers, I mean to bring all the tribes together. By making your distinctions between Indian tribes and allotting to each particular tracts of land, you want to set us against each other, and thus to weaken us. You never see an Indian come to make the white people divide up their homes, but you are always driving the red people this way! In time, you will drive us into the Great Lake, where we can neither stand nor walk.

"Brothers, what you are doing to the Indians is a very bad thing, and we do not like it. When Indians form our own union, we will destroy the bad village chiefs, by whom all such mischief is done. It is they who sell our lands to the Americans. The Treaty of Fort Wayne was made by men with greedy hearts, but in the future, we are going to punish those chiefs who sell the land that belongs not to them, but to all of ourselves.

"The only way to stop this evil is for all the red men to unite in claiming an equal right to the land. That is how it was in ancient times, and should be still, for the land never was divided, but was given by the Great Spirit for the use of everyone. No groups among us have a right to sell, even to one another, and surely not to outsiders who will not be satisfied until all our land is theirs.

"Sell a country! Why not sell the air, the clouds, and the Great Sea, as well as the Earth? Did not the Great Spirit make them all for the use of his children?

"Brothers, you said that if we could prove that the land was sold by people who had no right to sell it, you would restore it. I will prove that those who sold did not own it. Did they have a deed? A title? No! You say those things prove someone owns land. Those chiefs had only words, and so you pretended to believe them, only because you wanted the land. But many tribes do not agree with those claims. If the land is not given back to us, we ourselves will have a great council, at which all tribes will be present. We will make the case that those chiefs had no rights to the land, and we will decide what to do to those greedy men. I am not alone in this plan, for it is the choice of all the warriors who follow me.

"Brothers, I wish you to listen to me. If you do not wipe out that treaty, we will kill all the chiefs who sold their land to you! I tell you so because I am authorized by all tribes to do this! I am the chief of them all! My warriors will meet with me, and do as I command. If you do not restore the land, we will kill the bad chiefs, and you will have had a hand in killing them!

"I am Shawnee! I am a warrior! My forefathers were warriors. From them I took my birth. The spirit within me hears the voice of the generations, which tells me that once there were no white men on this land, that it then belonged to the Indians, placed here by the Great Spirit who made them, to keep it, to traverse it, to enjoy its yield, all as the same race. Once Indians were happy! Now they are made miserable by the white people, who are always taking from us! How can we have confidence in the white people? When Jesus Christ came upon the Earth, you killed him, the son of your own God. You nailed him up. And only after you thought you killed him did you worship him, and started then killing those who would not worship him. What kind of people is this for us to trust?

"Now, Brothers, everything I have said to you is the truth. I have declared myself freely to you about my intentions, and I want to know your intentions. I want to know what you are going to do about taking our land. I want to hear you say that you will wipe out that false treaty, so that the tribes can be at peace with each other, as you pretend you want them to be. Tell me, Brothers, what you will do for me? I want to know."

When he finished, Tecumseh beat his chest and raised a spear above his head, so that the shadow of its point landed upon Harrison's neck.

A long silence endured among the people of Vincennes. In the breathless stillness, the sound of one person's sniffling and stifled tears turned many heads.

Rebecca Galloway had dropped onto her knees, and now let go a lachrymose cascade that compelled those next to her to move aside to give her room.

Tecumseh saw her, and he knew.

The conference lasted five days, during which Tecumseh and his delegation reported at Grouseland early each morning and left after dinner each night. Since neither camp released any public proclamation regarding the nature of their discussions, or if they'd made any progress, the townsfolk engaged in rampant speculation and supposition. Some conjectured that Tecumseh was merely distracting Harrison, while British troops were secretly advancing, intent upon taking Vincennes and declaring it for the King. Other opinions held that the shrewd Governor Harrison was plying the war chief with liquor and women, and when all was said and done, he'd have fooled him into signing a new, better treaty, exiling the Indians to the God-forsaken wildernesses of Wisconsin.

Everybody agreed upon one thing: talking was better than fighting. Many of the citizens of Vincennes said that, for all they cared, they could just keep talking until Indiana became a state, and then it wouldn't matter anymore.

"I believe the governor is looking for a justification to kill that mad Indian," Millard Doody opined to his fiancé.

Each day, Rebecca Galloway waited near the gate to Grouseland when the Indians arrived in the morning, and returned when they departed in the evening, hoping to catch Tecumseh's eye. She worried that Ruddell had reneged on his agreement to deliver her message to the chief. Likewise, she worried that he had delivered it, and that Tecumseh had been unmoved by it.

On the third evening, over dinner, Millard Doody asked her, "Are you ailing, my dear. You look a bit pale and pekkid."

She responded by breaking into tears, leaving both her dinner and Millard at the table to get cold.

By noon on the fifth day, word began to spread that the conference was done, the Indians were leaving, and there was not going to be war. Other than that, details were scarce, but just that much news did much to relieve tension. Even before the Indians had left, the taverns in Vincennes began filling up.

Rebecca knew that now was time to execute her plan. Complaining about a headache, she informed Millard that she wished to lie down, and asked that he please not disturb her. In her room, she hastily packed a small case with her hairbrush, some parchment paper, a silver spoon she'd taken from her mother's best dinnerware, a book of common prayer with a dried Black Eyed Susan pressed between its pages, and comfortable underclothing—she'd always heard that Indian women wore none. She then slithered out a rear window.

Her message to Chief Tecumseh had been simply to meet her at a downstream bend in the Wabash, as soon as his business with the governor concluded. She had tied a fancy ribbon to a cottonwood trunk to mark the spot.

He was not there when she arrived, so she sat on a log and waited...

And waited...

And waited...

In her fantasies about this long-anticipated rendezvous, she'd never envisioned so much dull time spent just waiting. She sifted sand from one hand to the next. She skipped flat stones against the water. She blew puffballs into the air. She knelt above a shallow pool and sighed to her reflection.

"I'd sooner die than go back."

Tecumseh had been there the whole time, hiding at the edge of the woods, watching her, fascinated and aroused by her every movement. When she broke off a flower and put it behind her ear, he stared at her earlobe, its curve and its fleshy delicacy. When she sighed wistfully, he felt the longing in his chest, but when he heard her say aloud, to nobody, that she preferred death to going back, he could stand down no longer.

At that moment, Tecumseh revealed himself. Shirtless, draped in beads and feathers, he emerged with his arms folded, but slowly separated them so that Rebecca would know what to do.

"I love you," she cried, throwing herself into his arms, pressing her hands to either side of his head.

Tecumseh filled the space between their gazes with his lips. They kissed while the world spun around them like a dust devil in the middle of a prairie.

He lifted her and whooped jubilantly. He'd never wanted a woman that he could not have, and as a result, over time, he'd stopped wanting any. Just when he'd come to believe there was nothing new in the entirety of womanhood for him to experience, he was enthralled by Rebecca Galloway, with her skin as fair as morning dew on white magnolia petals, and hair the color of flames, fruit, and blood. He felt a thrill he'd almost forgotten—lust for something forbidden. He became ardently excited by thoughts of her naked, and wondering what shades of red hair adorned the slopes and crevices beneath her skirts.

In English, he said, "I will make you first among my women."

"And I am yours. I can wait no longer."

He lifted her into his arms, carried her across the river, and lay her in a field covered with clovers and wildflowers. In the back of his mind, he wondered how long it would be before somebody realized she was gone and organized a search party. As he untied his loincloth, he placed his tomahawk within reach, just in case he needed it in an emergency.

Chapter 21 - Autumn 1811

Tippecanoe Creek, Indiana Territory

Tenskwatawa cursed his brother for leaving him with so many problems. While Tecumseh stumped through the Mississippi Territory in search of recruits and converts among the Choctaw, the fragile détente he'd fashioned at the conference in Vincennes deteriorated quickly, owing in large part to his absence. Throughout Prophetstown, fearful rumors spread that Governor Harrison was preparing to attack while the war chief was away. His actions seemed to support that supposition.

In September, Harrison amassed all soldiers within his jurisdiction, including eight hundred regulars from the Fourth Regiment, another four hundred Indiana militiamen, and a couple hundred ass-kicking Kentuckians who were always spoiling for a rumble. Under the command of Brigadier General Frank Bantzer, this formidable army marched up the Wabash and constructed a new fort—christened Fort Harrison—on disputed high ground along one of the major routes into Prophetstown.

Tenskwatawa's scouts saw the sizable American forces and said extra prayers. Upon returning to Prophetstown, Battle Panther told Tenskwatawa, "We need for you to petition Waashaa Monetoo for another miracle. Without one, we have little chance in a fight against so large an army."

Although Tenskwatawa faulted his brother for having abandoned him at such a precarious time, he still resented it when the people openly wished and even prayed for Tecumseh to hurry home. They almost seemed to mock the Prophet when they asked, "Why can you not ask Waashaa Monetoo to find him wherever he is, snatch him off the ground, and bring him back to us?" In his speeches, Tenskwatawa reminded the people that Waashaa Monetoo, not Tecumseh, was responsible for protecting them. He scolded them for their sinful doubt. Nobody overtly challenged the Prophet's authority, but even so,

Tenskwatawa knew he needed more than words and promises to allay the people's uneasiness.

Now, more than ever, he needed to produce some manner of divine assurance.

Every day, the Prophet sequestered himself for hours in the Medicine Hut, praying in multiple ways and positions—on his knees, flat against the ground, standing on tiptoes, even upside down while holding his breath—but despite trying every method, his supplications had proven ineffective, and he began to feel bereft and overwhelmed. Where was the Master of Life who had appeared to him in his dreams on the night he died? When, oh when, would He reveal his true intentions... with instructions? The misgivings that Tenskwatawa harbored in his own heart upset him even more than those of his followers.

If Waashaa Monetoo was testing his faith by making him wait, Tenskwatawa figured that his best strategy was to stall for time. In his public proclamations, he told his people that the Great Spirit demanded that they guard their faith and be patient, for He would surely give them a sign at the right time, and tell them the right thing to do. In his own prayers, though, the only sign he asked from God was for Him to bring Tecumseh back, and release Tenskatawa from the burdens of having to make such fateful decisions.

Around dawn, General Frank Bantzer climbed into the sentry's turret at Fort Harrison to watch the sunrise. He could envision his men armed and positioned along the perimeter of the upper wall, steeling their nerves while awaiting his orders. Then, with a clamorous outcry, hordes of fearsome Indian warriors would charge from the surrounding woods, wave after wave advancing in a hellish onslaught, determined to battle unto the death.

Steady, he'd tell his men, even as arrows began raining down on them. Steady, steady, steady... *now, FIRE!*

The Indians' front line would fall, nary a single soldier's bullet missing its mark. General Bantzer would pick out a hostile, take dead aim, and shoot. The bullet would strike the brute's heart with blood-spraying precision. Fire, reload; fire, reload; fire, reload—Bantzer would methodically drop every Indian upon which he drew his sights. At last, finally, he'd spy the war chief, Tecumseh, riding into the fray with spear held high, and the general would feel the hand of God Almighty fall upon his shoulder as he squeezed the trigger. The shot would land straight between the chief's eyeballs, splattering his brains. Seeing their leader slain, the surviving savage combatants would flee panicking into the woods, dispersing in terror, never to pollute American territory with their presence again.

That day, when it came, *soon*, would belong to God, to America, and to General Frank Bantzer.

"Good mornin'," Colonel Work said, breaking the general's reverie.

"Yes, it'd be a grand morning to kill some Indians, wouldn't you say?"

Work shrugged. "As yah say, sir."

"Are preparations finished for Governor Harrison's arrival?"

"Aye sir. The men's boots will be polished and the fort will be battle ready."

"Good. I wish for the governor to be favorably impressed," General Bantzer said, for he presumed that the point of Harrison's trip to the fort was to inspect it. At least that is what he hoped.

Privately, he worried about Harrison's visit creating confusion among the men concerning who was in charge. He had advised Harrison against making the trip, contending that the situation with unruly Indians in the vicinity was too dangerous. If that was so, the governor wrote in his response, then he needed to come as soon as possible. So now, Bantzer had to make it seem like he had everything under complete control, even while being at high alert due to imminent danger. Inwardly, he felt more threatened by Harrison's presence than he did over any peril posed by the Indians.

In reality, the state of affairs at Fort Harrison had been routine, almost dull. Entire days passed without anybody sighting a single Indian. The only incident in a fortnight had involved a party from a local Delaware tribe who came bearing gifts to welcome the soldiers, and to assure them that they were not allied with the Prophet, so they would appreciate it if the soldiers would kindly refrain from killing them, strafing their village, and raping their women. This had disappointed Bantzer, who would have preferred that his men practice some live-action war games against an easy opponent prior to marching onward to Prophetstown. Perhaps, he encouraged himself to believe, Harrison was coming to authorize him to lead the troops northward, toward glorious destiny.

"Carry on," General Bantzer said to Colonel Work—meaning, *go away*.

For the remainder of the morning, the general busied himself with symbolic tasks associated with his rank, like watching the men perform their drills and take target practice, while making it a point to select at least one man for praise and another for rebuke, to serve as examples that he was capable of both. He took his lunch alone in his quarters, washing down his bread and salted pork with a tall glass of cow's milk. Since assuming command of Fort Harrison, he'd abided by a regimen prohibiting alcohol prior to dinner. He had to admit that he felt better—so much so, in fact, that he embarked upon an unprecedented fourth straight day sober. After finishing his meal, though, the notion occurred to him that, with his additional stresses and worries related to Harrison's coming, he could excuse himself for lapsing just this once. With his hand on the liquor cabinet door, his will teetering....

A sentry called out from the tower, "Boats are coming!"

Taking that as his answer, Bantzer dashed off to the riverbank.

Colonel Work mobilized the entire contingent of Fort Harrison into two formations, from the entrance of the palisade to the river docks.

General Bantzer proceeded between the lines to meet the governor's boat.

Several soldiers and attendants disembarked first, and the last to step off was Harrison, grinning like a man who hadn't a worry in the world.

Bantzer noticed that the governor was wearing two stars on his blue coatee.

"Good day, Bantzer," Harrison said. "Would you be so kind as to show me my fort?"

Words stuck in his throat, so Bantzer merely gestured for Harrison to follow.

They walked slowly through the center of the lines of soldiers. Harrison meandered from side to side, saluting, slapping backs and chirping words of encouragement in a way intended that every man should feel like he'd been personally recognized. Together, the two generals toured the high ground and its fortification. Harrison commended everybody within earshot for the industry that they'd demonstrated in clearing this land so quickly, and building a stalwart base of operations. While Harrison did all the talking, Bantzer followed like a guest in his own home.

Meanwhile, more boats stocked with provisions arrived at the docks, and as the men unloaded barrels of whiskey along with crates of supplies and heavy artillery, gossip spread among them that this was it—they were about to go into battle.

Back in the sentry turret, the last stop of their tour of the fortification, Harrison and Bantzer watched as the men unloaded the flatboats. At length, Harrison remarked, "Tonight, leave the men to drink and defile themselves however they wish, for tomorrow, we march onward to Prophetstown."

"Sir? We?"

"Of course. We must solve our Indian problem. The eventual statehood of Indiana depends upon defeating the Shawnee Prophet." Harrison's vaporous breath made Bantzer's eyes water. "Because this mission is so critical, I have elected to command the campaign myself."

Bantzer felt like a man with a noose around his neck, waiting for the gallows trapdoor to drop beneath him. "I do not...." He did not... *what?* Bantzer wasn't sure.

"I know that this may seem a blow to you," Harrison said, in a voice that conveyed not an iota of empathy. "But, politically, for the good of Indiana, this is the best decision."

"But when you awarded me my star, you said you trusted me."

"I also said that I appreciated your loyalty. That is what I need from you—nay, *command* from you. Remember that you are indebted to me."

"I do." Bantzer sighed. "I am."

Pleased, Harrison laughed. "Be glad, Frank, for being second in command at the ultimate battle in the Indian wars will be an honor. Why don't you join the men in celebration tonight?"

Without another word, Bantzer descended the ladder, leaving Harrison alone in the tower. Rather than mingle with the men as Harrison had suggested, Bantzer hastened to his quarters, eager to escape behind a closed door where he could release his disappointment and disgust.

What a villainous backstabber Harrison is, not to mention conceited, grandiose, treacherous, unscrupulous, scurrilous, and megalomaniacal.

It made him choke to think of how they'd so recently toasted to their partnership, Bantzer calling Harrison "wise," and Harrison flattering Bantzer as "brave." Now, it was obvious that Harrison had used Bantzer, lied to him, and played him for a fool. Bantzer slapped himself for having believed anything Harrison had ever said to him. Indeed, the life lesson in this turn of events was that he ought never again trust any other person, nor delude himself into thinking that anybody cared about anything except his own best interests.

Bantzer grabbed a bottle of bourbon by its neck and tilted it six inches above his mouth, pouring it into his mouth in a long, glugging arc. After so many years of allegiance to the United States Army, he would no longer serve it.

No, the army will serve me.

For Tenskwatawa, the worst thing about not knowing what to do was that everybody told him to do something different, and they all sounded equally convincing. In the first week of November, Harrison's forces established camp on a plateau above the creek, from where they could see and be seen in Prophetstown. Many of the Prophet's people urged him to evacuate women and children from town and to deploy a front line around the perimeter, in preparation for an assault. A few proposed inviting Harrison for dinner and a smoke, to show their peaceful intentions. Some of the more radical factions agitated to attack first, suggesting that if the Indians succeeded in killing Governor Harrison quickly, the whole army of the Long Knives would scatter like frightened birds.

Listening to so much conflicting advice made the Prophet's head throb. More than anything, he wished that either God or Tecumseh would make these decisions for him.

Prophetstown's entire population gathered and chanted Tenskwatawa's name outside the Medicine Hut, as he sat in his chair and closed his eyes, wishing his troubles would go away. When Battle Panther kicked him in the shins, the Prophet blinked and grimaced.

"You must speak to the people yourself," Battle Panther said. "Or else, their faith in you will waver."

"Leave me to pray for guidance from Waashaa Monetoo," Tenskwatawa grumbled, throwing his medicine bag at him. "I will speak to the people only after He has spoken to me! Now, be gone, for your presence makes aching in my head!"

He heard the roar that arose from the crowd outside the tent when Battle Panther told them what the Prophet had decreed. Now he'd done it; he'd backed himself into a corner with no way out, unless Waashaa Monetoo provided him with one. In better times, Tenskwatawa had been confident enough in his role that he felt comfortable directing the day-to-day affairs of the community without seeking input from the

Great Spirit. In these more trying times, though, he felt as if Waashaa Monetoo were rudely neglecting him. Tenskwatawa reassured himself that it was not his fault, for he was doing his part through prayer, piety, abstinence, and public ritual. He remained ready to listen whenever Waashaa Monetoo felt like speaking. He could wait no longer, though. On that night, he needed for the Great Spirit to intervene, or... he feared he would lose all credibility.

"Why do you taunt me, Creator?" Tenskwatawa wept. "I do all the work, but you get all the credit. When you fail, though, I myself get the blame."

Then Tenskwatawa had a frightening realization: the magic of his prophecy was gone. He felt no enchantment in the Medicine Hut, no spiritual presence around him. Perhaps, he mused, he needed to alter his consciousness, thus making him more receptive to Waashaa Monetoo's transcendent message. After all, the first time Waashaa Monetoo had revealed Himself to Lalawethika, that revelation came amid an alcohol-induced trance. Attaining divine wisdom might require a little boost. Besides, Tenskatawa was getting thirsty.

In his efforts to keep Prophetstown dry, Tenskwatawa had confiscated and dumped hundreds of bottles of every manner of potent beverage. Still, he kept a personal reserve about which nobody knew, just in case of emergency. This was an emergency.

That night, Tenskwatawa broke five years of sobriety, with the very best of intentions. The fate of his whole race of people depended on his ability to interpret God's will, so if he had to drink in order to gain access to the divine world, then it was his moral duty to do so. With the first sip, he absorbed a pervasive sense of well-being. His skin tingled with relief and anticipation. With the second, heartier swallow, he braced himself against the sensation of sudden motion around him. Seated, he felt as if being lifted, his soul breaking through the confinement of his body and rising toward a blessed realm. This was the feeling of confidence that he'd lacked; this was what had been missing from his ministry. This was what he needed. After just a few chugs, he felt as if being pulled through a door into the supernatural realm, where his Higher Power awaited.

"I am here," he cried into the heavens. "Are you?"

With another drink, the buzzing in his ears resolved into a harsh, dissonant voice, which spoke two words. *"Believe. Do."*

He did... and did.

Tenskwatawa woke up when Doorkeeper dumped a pitcher of water on his face.

"Rise, husband," she said. "It is morning, and the people are anxious to hear their Prophet speak."

Tenskwatawa felt blood rush to the pain centers in his brain. "I was not sleeping. I was praying."

"Tell that to your people. They themselves have kept vigil outside the hut all night. Under the yellow moon, they could hear you raving and shrieking. They said, 'Our Prophet is possessed by spirits.' They believe that last night you spoke with Waashaa Monetoo. Today, they wait for you to reveal to them what He said."

"I did! I heard His voice surrounding me, like the howling of a strong wind but on a breezeless day. He told me what to say. He told me what to do."

"Then you must so tell the people, and hope that they still believe."

Tenskwatawa felt wobbly on his feet, but when he staggered outside the Medicine Hut, everybody turned their heads toward him, stifled their conversations, and ceased doing anything that might distract them. The entire community stilled its breath with anticipation. Instinctively, he looked for his brother, and even though he knew Tecumseh was not present, he'd needed to confirm it. Tecumseh's absence, as much as Waashaa Monetoo'spresence, gave him more faith in what he was about to say.

One man called out, "Has Waashaa Monetoo revealed His will?"

Another said, "The Prophet looks drunk."

Several people at once cried, "We are doomed!"

Inspired by faith, or by the fear of failure, or both, Tenskwatawa dropped his shoulders, allowing the blanket draped over him to fall to the ground. He unstrapped his leggings and kicked them aside. Finally, he untied his belt and let his breechcloth fall to his feet. Naked, he spread his arms and legs; the more the people stared in shock, the more energized he felt. The only way he could actually be doing this, he thought, was because Waashaa Monetoo gave him the strength to do it.

"We all must stand naked ourselves before the Master of Life. I myself have bared my soul to Waashaa Monetoo, and now He knows all of my being, and I know what He requires of me. Today I bare my body to you, so there can be no doubt or confusion. I am clothed in only the word of Waashaa Monetoo. Here is what he told me.

"The Long Knives intend to kill us, but Waashaa Monetoo has revealed to me a plan for our salvation, if we execute it exactly as He has foretold. Today I will send Battle Panther under a white flag into their camp. He will greet them warmly and invite them to enter Prophetstown, to confer with me and settle all misunderstandings. So that we might have time to prepare to receive them, Battle Panther will ask the Long Knives for twenty-four hours, then to come into our village to meet with us under the next day's sun.

"But that is a trick. Never again will I pretend to make peace with the Long Knives. They seek nothing other than to destroy Indians. So must we first destroy them. Tonight, in the long shadows before dawn, while they sleep, we will attack them! They will be so surprised that they will not know what to do. Our warriors will spare no quarter against them. We will infiltrate the Long Knives' camp and kill their generals. Once we have slain their leaders, the rest of the Long Knives will flee like scared dogs.

"Some of you may worry that the Long Knives have greater numbers and more deadly weapons, but Waashaa Monetoo has promised to protect and watch over our warriors. Every Indian will have a spirit fighting with him, giving him the strength and courage of ten men. The Long Knives will be unable to see in the darkness, but to the Indians, it will be as the light of day. Though they will try to fight back, their gunpowder will turn to sand, their bullets will pass right through our bodies, and their knives and bayonets will bend backwards against our ribs. We will attack relentlessly, while their defense will be chaotic and disorganized. Their blood will soak the Earth, so that next year, crops will grow tall in the spot where they fall."

Two beautiful Potawatomi women broke from the crowd and prostrated themselves at Tenskwatawa's feet. Unfazed, he continued. "Today, I speak to each one of you. Every man has a duty to perform."

He gestured at the women. "And so does each squaw."

Squaring himself, he added, "As for myself, tonight, when the battle begins, I will remain here, praying, in constant communication with Waashaa Monetoo." Then Tenskwatawa concluded by using the oratorical technique that had always worked best for him—telling his audience exactly what they wanted to hear. "We will force them off our lands, so that all Indian tribes will be free. It is our destiny. Waashaa Monetoo has spoken!"

Pandemonium erupted among the confederated tribes of Prophetstown. Spontaneously, men and women began stripping off their clothing in ecstatic emulation of the Prophet. There was hugging, chest-thumping, and jumping up and down, mixed with loud ejaculations of joy and thanks.

Tenskwatawa wished things could just end, right at that moment, so that they could avoid the nuisance of fighting a battle altogether. After all, Waashaa Monetoo could do that for him, couldn't he?

General Harrison was speaking, but all Frank Bantzer could hear was *blah, blah, blah.* He'd already heard enough, and all the excess verbiage just seemed like piling on. Bantzer nodded and intoned, "Yes sir, right away sir," then turned to Colonel Work and instructed him to do whatever the governor had just commanded.

As a result of not paying attention, later that afternoon, Bantzer went looking for his tent in the camp headquarters, which he naturally presumed would be next to Harrison's.

"Sir, did'ya forget? You're responsible for overseeing defense of the northwest flank," Colonel Work said.

"I knew that," Bantzer replied summarily, all the while thinking to himself how far it was beneath his rank and dignity to be charged with so middling a task.

The flank was surrounded by dense forest and an understory of stinging nettles. Bantzer scouted for trails but, finding none, convinced himself that the woods were impassible, so the camp would be safe and secure. At ease, he sat on a rock and tilted his flask above his mouth. He wondered if anybody would miss him if he took a quick nap. Closing his eyes, he drifted.

Suddenly, he heard a rustling sound and sensed a presence upon him. Were it a hostile, he'd be a dead man. He turned and braced himself to fight or to flee, but what he saw elicited an entirely different response. Two of the loveliest Potawatomi maidens that he had ever beheld stood behind him. When Bantzer rose, they gasped and clutched their breasts, but did not back away. Looking them up and down, he let his gaze linger on their voluptuous cleavage.

One of them spoke in broken English. "You are great leader?"

The other added, "Handsome man, oh yes."

This was not the kind of ambush he'd expected. Bantzer not only dropped his guard, he shoved it aside completely. "I am Brigadier General Frank Bantzer of the United States Armed Forces," he said, pointing to his star.

"Ooooh," the women oozed.

With the flask already in hand, he offered the women a drink.

Giggling, they accepted. "Drink is forbidden," one said, and the other finished, "But we like."

It occurred to Bantzer that if he ripped off their clothing, tied them up, and ravaged them on the spot, his conduct would be acceptable under the generally understood rules of warfare—but he got the impression that such drastic measures would not be necessary.

"What are you doing here?" he asked the women.

"We are gift."

"From the Prophet."

Two women? Banzter had been the recipient of this peculiar but very welcome custom of Indian diplomacy before, but... *two women!* Imagining the possibilities made him nearly burst out of his trousers. However, guessing that Harrison might frown upon his second-in-charge engaging in carnal fraternization with enemies, Bantzer had to think fast.

"Come with me." He led the women around the rear of the flank, urging them to stay low and keep quiet, until they reached the back of his own tent. He took out his knife and cut an opening large enough for the women to slip inside. Pressing a finger to his lips, he whispered for them to, "Go in. Be silent. Wait for me."

The women reclined onto a mat and started undressing each other.

Propelled by the kickback of his erection, Bantzer scampered around the perimeter of the camp, slipped in behind the horse tether, and nearly broke into a gallop hurrying to get back to his tent.

Colonel Work spotted him and called, "Whoa there, general. Where're ya going?"

Bantzer skidded to a halt, but did not turn to face Work for fear that his tumescence would be obvious and thus raise suspicion. Instead, he answered over his shoulder. "I am tired. I wish to bed early this evening."

"Without supper?"

"Yes, without supper. As I said, I must rest."

"But sir!"

"What *is* the matter, Work?"

"I'm a bit worried about the security of the perimeter," he said.

"Not to worry. I've inspected it myself. Kentuckians are watching sentry all night. We are as safe as if we were home in Vincennes."

"Even so, sir—"

"I said not to worry, colonel!" he snapped. "That is an order."

"Yes sir," Work retorted, but he did not salute.

Bantzer guessed by the disapproving expression on his face that Work could smell the alcohol on his breath.

So what? "And please see to it that I am not disturbed."

Three hours before dawn, the Americans' camp lay still and hushed—precisely why Colonel Work woke up. It was too quiet. Leaving his tent, he found fires dying and the sentries sound asleep, wrapped in blankets, bottles at their feet. The camp had an ambience closer to the dead-drunk dormancy of a tavern after closing time than a military regiment deep in enemy territory.

Work's first responsibility was to awaken General Bantzer and inform him of the sorry condition of the troops. Outside the general's tent, he called, "Sir."

Whispered female voices came from inside, as well as Bantzer's cannon-fire snoring.

Indignant, Colonel Work tossed aside the flaps to the tent, and two naked Indian women passing him in haste nearly knocked him down.

"What the...?"

His thoughts shifted abruptly at the sound of a twig breaking somewhere in the forest. He grabbed his rifle, ran to the camp's edge, and began kicking the sentries to awaken them. The woods were as dark as a cave, but he fixed his gaze at the point from where he'd heard the sound, and even though he saw nothing more clearly than a ripple in the black emptiness, that was enough to raise every alarm in his body.

Colonel Work hoisted his weapon and fired the first shot of the Battle of Tippecanoe.

The Indian forces had been watching, waiting, and studying their adversaries while the Americans' fires burned lower and they sank deeper into slumber. Deployed at positions to strike with three rapid, coordinated offensives, the Indians' plan was to launch the first sortie at the vulnerable northwest flank. Their objective was to surge through the flimsy perimeter defenses and straight into the center of the camp, where Harrison himself was the primary target. The warriors were coiled, ready to pounce, and had that first shot not rang out, Battle Panther would have shouted the order to "Charge!" within seconds anyway. Thus, the element of surprise remained almost entirely intact.

The first wave of combatants mowed over the American sentries and dragoons guarding the flank. By the time most of the regular soldiers rolled out of their sleeping bags, the Indians had already overwhelmed a quarter of their brigade, and were advancing.

Battle Panther led the natives' attack, barreling toward the Long Knives' camp headquarters, swinging his tomahawk and screaming, "Hail, Tenskwatawa!"

He proceeded through a fiery spray of bullets, undaunted and untouched, as if to fulfill prophecy. Behind him, some fell, but Battle Panther did not look back, drawing a bead on the pants-less General Frank Bantzer, who had just appeared, dazed, from his tent. Battle Panther raised his tomahawk, closing to within a few steps of bringing it down between General Bantzer's eyes....

A bullet smote the charging Indian warrior in the heart, and he collapsed just two steps short of General Frank Bantzer. Colonel Clayton Work had fired the deadly shot, and he now glared back at the trembling Bantzer, and spat at him.

A chaotic orgy of malice, violence, desperation, and bloodlust ensued. The soldiers scrambled to rally and recover their bearings, while many Indians appeared shocked that their comrades were dying when shot, as if they should somehow be immune to the bullets.

Aimless, mindless shots blasted in all directions, taking lives indiscriminately, while those who did not fall to gunfire had no other choice but to engage in hand-to-hand combat unto death. The militia's first defense crumbled, but the second line of regulars, marshaled on the spot by Colonel Work, held its formation despite mounting losses.

When Harrison rode into the fray, his horse was shot out from beneath him. Still, he coolly directed reinforcements into position, and although many Indians broke through the line with the singular intention of killing the governor, none could make it that far.

Just when the momentum seemed to have shifted to the Americans, the Indians initiated a second ambush on the camp's southern flank. A crossfire melee erupted wherein arrows and bullets flew so randomly and in such quantity that the only strategy that mattered was numbers, and that factor favored the Americans. The wails of the wounded and dying on both sides, punctuated by constant, crackling gunfire, filled the sky with such agony that the reverberations seemed to shake the clouds loose from the sky. Rain fell, a cold, heavy drizzle that soaked every man body and soul.

As the Indian casualties diminished their ranks, they regrouped deep in the woods. Not a brave among them still believed that Waashaa Monetoo was fighting alongside them, so they scrapped as if they had no Great Spirit, no soul, and no fate available to them but to fight unto meaningless death. Still, they continued attacking in columns, thrusting as far toward the center of the Long Knives' formation as they could, until the last among them perished, and then came the next column, and the next... until they could not muster enough men to prolong their assault.

They retreated, despondent, into the woods. As the first lights of a leaden dawn filtered over the horizon, an American Colonel led his soldiers into the forest and flushed out the surviving braves. Those who tried to surrender were executed despite their pleas.

As war waged, Tenskwatawa had remained behind, rapt in prayer. When reports of the conflict's grim toll reached his Medicine Hut, he screamed at the men to return to the battlefield, and to keep the faith, for at any moment the Master of Life would surely intervene. But when he saw the Americans advancing closer and closer to Prophetstown, he conceded to the logic of retreat. The remains of his forces had scattered so far and wide that there was hardly anything left to pull back.

With the women and children, and the few braves who had survived and remained loyal, he embarked on a journey north, unsure of his destination, with nothing but what little faith remained in false promises and unanswered prayers.

A month after the sack of Prophetstown, Tecumseh re-joined what was left of his people—hungry, disheartened, and near death—outside of Blue Jacket's village on the Detroit River. It was far worse than he'd feared. While journeying in the south, Tecumseh had seen a brilliant comet in the sky and felt tremors of an immense earthquake underfoot, and wondered what these omens signified. On his return travels, he'd heard various accounts of the debacle at Tippecanoe Creek, for there were as many versions of what happened as there were tongues to tell them. Some tried to hearten him by pointing out that the Long Knives suffered a greater number of casualties, and that many Americans condemned Harrison for courting the terrible confrontation. About such things, Tecumseh cared not. The only thing that mattered to him was that Prophetstown had fallen, his great Indian coalition had disintegrated, and all of his work had been for nothing.

This, he could not abide, but facts were facts, and given the choice of responding through despair, surrender, or retaliation, he chose the latter.

Declining Blue Jacket's offer to stay as an honored guest in the village, Tecumseh established a base upriver, where he and a few selected men intended to weather the winter at a distance. Only one woman remained in his company, and Tecumseh told Rebecca Galloway that she, too, must leave him, to spend the winter with Blue Jacket's tribe, for her own safety.

"But you promised!" she objected.

"I promised nothing, other than the truth."

"You cannot quit on me."

It annoyed Tecumseh that, despite his better judgment, he still desired Rebecca Galloway. "When it is safe, I will send for you. Now, go."

Rebuilding his forces would be daunting work, and although in his mind Tecumseh had already begun to prioritize next steps, there was one piece of personal business that he could not avoid.

"Find my brother. Bring him to me," he ordered his men.

Tenskwatawa had awaited this summons, unsure and fearful of what it boded. Already, his prestige among the people had plummeted, despite his labored rationalizations of what had gone wrong and why they should still trust him. He no longer even knew what *he* believed. Having secluded himself in a hut on the fringes of the village, Tenskwatawa filled his days with ardent prayers for atonement from Waashaa Monetoo, and with petitions for sympathy from the people.

When the braves came for him, he asked for a moment to dress himself in his Prophet's regalia. It was the first time he'd worn the red scarf and feathered headdress since the day of the great battle. He told himself he would stand proud before Tecumseh, unbowed in defeat, still a holy man.

When he entered Tecumseh's *wegiwa* and saw his brother's yellow, burning eyes, all he could do was drop to his knees and blubber, "Woe to us."

Tecumseh boxed his ears viciously. He poked his pinky finger in Tenskwatawa's good eye. He pinched the ring dangling from Tenskwatawa's nose and twisted it. He yanked on the scarf wrapped around Tenskwatawa's torso so hard that it spun him like a top. Then Tecumseh dug his fingers deep into his brother's hair, made a fist, and pulled backwards so hard that the skin on his forehead nearly split.

"I should scalp you," Tecumseh sneered.

"Please, oh please, brother. Nothing was my fault."

"I left you with just one command—do not provoke the Long Tongues. So, what did you do?" He spat in his brother's face. "Ambush them?"

"I had no choice."

"You told the people that you could work a miracle."

"It was not my fault."

"Who else is then to blame?"

Actually, Tenskwatawa had given this question considerable thought, for while he recalled his revelation that night as a profound experience, it puzzled him why Waashaa Monetoo had failed to provide support as promised. At length, he had figured it out, but resisted speaking, until under the threat of decapitation, he squealed, "It was the fault of my wife. She interrupted my prayers."

"Bah."

"I swear to this truth, for she was afflicted by her monthly menses, which of course offended Waashaa Monetoo and polluted my prayers."

"What kind of a man blames a woman for his disgrace?"

Tenskwatawa sputtered, "A woman can rob any man of his better judgment." Sensing that Tecumseh was taken aback by that remark, he followed it with an accusation of his own. "You know that is true, do you not, my brother?"

"Mind what you say."

Tenskwatawa saw that he had struck a nerve. "Even though I have preached Waashaa Monetoo's command regarding the separation of white and Indian races, you have committed forbidden intercourse with the flame-haired girl!"

Tecumseh bellowed, "What I do is neither your concern, nor Waashaa Monetoo's!"

Tenskwatawa freed himself from his brother's grip. "I then leave that matter to your conscience."

"Go away. Never again cast your shadow in my presence."

Alone, Tecumseh clawed at his clothing and pounded his head against the wall. Guilt was a new feeling to him, in some ways sharper than the sting of a bayonet. He had never wasted time distinguishing between what he wanted, what he believed, and what was right. He knew that he could not achieve glory if he allowed himself to doubt.

The waves of emotion that Rebecca Galloway aroused in him were unprecedented, as troubling as they were irresistible. Perhaps she *was* a witch. What other explanation was there?

Tecumseh hurried out of his *wegiwa* and pointed at the first man he saw. "You, come here. I have a task for you. Go find the white woman with the hair like sunrise. Tell her I sent you to take her to a safe place. Bring her to the American fort in Detroit. Leave her there. Tell her—" For a man who had never regretted anything he'd done in his entire life, this was hard. "—that I am sorry."

Chapter 22 - July-August 1812

Mansfield, the Black Swamp, and Lake Erie

Nobody knew what to call this war. Since the enemy was the same as the last war, some folks referred to it as the "second war for independence," but that seemed fairly uninspiring—who wanted to fight a second war against the same enemy for the same reason? Everybody agreed in principle that it was primarily a war against the British, but most on the frontier believed it a better goal to rid their lands of Indians, once and for all. They could then call it the British and Indian war, but that sounded too much like the earlier French and Indian war, in which the British fought against the Indians. Now the French were on the Americans' side.

The whole business was just too confusing. So, from the get-go, many people started calling it the War of 1812 and trusting that eventually somebody would come up with a better name for it.

Sergeant Jim Craig didn't care what it was called, so long as he knew who to kill. He'd been a proud member of the Ohio militia for two years before the war broke out, at which time his superiors promoted him to sergeant. Craig's first duty was enlisting new recruits and punishing deserters, and since any able-bodied man who refused service was a de facto deserter, the job had a simple logic that he appreciated.

Although based in the Mount Vernon militia, Craig's orders were to aid the citizens of the nearby hamlet of Mansfield, who were eager to bolster their local defenses. His task, then, was to round up as many volunteer soldiers as he could find between the two settlements.

"Count me out of any war," Johnny Appleseed said to Jim Craig. "I get me own marching orders from a higher power."

"Ah'm the highest power that yah'll see t'day."

"Oh, I do not actually *see* the Lord God. Few indeed are so blessed. But I do hear His words, spoken directly to me by spirits of the heavenly realm."

"Yah hear things, do yah? What do them voices tell yah?"

"The Scholar told me that, 'Those who trust in the Lord find peace.'"

"Tha's 'xactly so, 'cause God is on our'n side."

"God is on all people's sides."

"Now, sayin' such things is jus' foolishness, 'cause God clearly chooses Christians o'er savages."

"Only God can look into a man's heart and know his inner self."

Jim Craig had no patience for such theological nonsense. "So which is it, Appleseed? Will yah fight, or won't yah?"

"I will not."

"Ah could shoot yah now an' say yah was a traitor," Jim Craig said. "But ah do believe the militia is better off without yah. Now go git gone, 'fore ah change mah mind."

"Good day, then," Johnny said.

He waved and darted into the woods, leaving Jim Craig to comment out loud so that his men could hear, "If'n that man weren't so crazy, he'd have died a long time ago."

An unknown number of rural homesteads sat at various locations off the road between Mount Vernon and Mansfield. Jim figured he could smoke out a batch of new recruits along the route. Most householders had either already enlisted or been conscripted, so as he encountered them at their residences, he merely checked his ledger to confirm they were on record for active duty, and ordered them to report to the blockhouse in Mansfield within a week. In the process of tracking various side paths and kicking in a few doors, he also unearthed several shirkers and malingerers, whom he immediately drafted, registered, and commanded to present themselves for duty, or suffer the consequences.

Upstream past Honey Creek, he came upon property with a cabin, a small garden, and a horse barn, all listed as belonging to Dan Sapp who lived in Danville. Evidently, somebody else was living there.

"Thar," Jim Craig called, pointing that direction.

At the end of the road was a young lad shoveling horse manure. He leaned his shovel against the barn and went to stand by his wife, who was on her knees, weeding the vegetable garden in front of the cabin.

"Greetin's, young man," Jim Craig said. "And what maht be yore name?"

"Otto Blubaugh. What ken ah do fer yahr?"

Craig spoke down to him from horseback. "How come ah don't see yore name in this registry fer military service?"

"Ah ain't none a-feared to fight..." Otto gave his hand to his wife and helped her onto her feet. Standing upright, she rubbed her pregnant belly, while Otto continued. "But mah wife Millie is a-carryin' a baby. Ah jest cain't leave her now."

Among the excuses that Jim Craig had heard for ducking military service, this was better than most. It wasn't that he had no sympathy at all, just that if he allowed exclusion from service for every man with a pregnant wife, there'd be none but sodomites left to fight.

"When is yer wife due?"

Millie answered, "This baby'll come in late-wise September."

"Then yah'll still got two whole months. Why, by such time, this war could be ended."

"If that's the truth, I don't see why you'll need my husband's help."

"Listen, ma'am, thar's babies get born ev'ry day, an' most o' the time, their pappies ain't nowhar near to be found."

Otto winced. "Mah wife needs special care," he objected.

"Well why did yah not say so? Hah. We'll jest ask the Injuns to cancel the war, so as yer woman can git some o' tha' *special care."*

Otto lifted his shovel and brandished it with both hands, as if he were contemplating whacking Craig across the face with it.

Millie interceded. "I'll be fine," she assured him, adding, "Lover Boy."

Smiling weakly, he relented. "What'er yahr say, Baby Lover."

Now Jim Craig felt nauseous. "Quit all o' that sweet talk an' stuff. Young man, git on to Mansfield within the week. Once thar, yah'll git yore orders."

He turned his horse, and, without bidding them adieu, left Otto and Millie locked in a trembling embrace.

A bit farther down the road, the troops stopped at a juncture. "No sense goin' down thar," Sergeant Craig said. "Ain't nothin' but ladies livin' thar."

Craig didn't say so, but it unnerved him to know they were probably already being watched by armed women hidden in trees and behind bushes. If what he'd heard was true, he figured some of those virile ladies would make formidable soldiers—they were reputed to be especially adept with the use of knives. Personally, he didn't believe those stories about witchy women casting spells to make a man's member turn into a snapping turtle head. The only thing about which he was certain, was that he did not want to encounter a certain farmer's daughter who nursed a grudge against him and was now living there.

Later in the afternoon, round a rutted and overgrown bend in the road, the company staggered to a halt upon encountering a 300-pound black bear ripping the mast from the trunk of an oak tree. It slogged out of their way, but otherwise ignored the men, as if hoping for the same courtesy from them.

Jim Craig dismounted, drew his rifle, took a good long time to savor the kill shot, and then fired right into the beast's neck. It dropped, but rolled and managed back onto its feet, raising its front paw to take a swipe. Several men responded with a salvo of follow-up shots that destroyed the animal for good, and Craig ordered the men to hack off the bear's head and pack it up for him.

"This here's a prime trophy, 'cause it maht jest as well'a been the last bear in Ohio," he bragged.

With that, so far as Sergeant Craig was concerned, he'd done enough work for one day. The company set up camp and feasted on bear meat that night, while one of the men, a free negro named Heck, entertained the troops playing his guitar and singing both traditional songs and original compositions.

All was merry.

A sign nearly hidden by vines next to a fork in the road, itself barricaded with slash and scrub, read: "Do Not Entry." Those words rang vaguely familiar to Jim Craig, though it took some thought to recollect why. His sniveling little brother used to cry those words when he hid in the root cellar and barred the door, thinking he could avert a beating.

Jim Craig consulted his ledger, which indicated only that "wild squatters" resided in these parts. He led the men down the trail about a mile before two dirty children sprang out of the woods, pointing sharpened sticks at the solders while hollering, "Mammy! We got tresser-passers!"

Jim Craig eyed the urchins with an urge to slap them. Dressed in tatters and with long, stringy hair in their faces, he couldn't tell if they were boys or girls.

One, with a boy's voice, said "He looks like a cod sucker," to which the other blurted in shrill girlie tones, "More'n looks like a horse fucker."

"Why you impert'nent l'il elves...." Jim Craig snarled, reaching for his horsewhip.

A woman stepped from behind an ash tree with a rifle under each arm. "I got a bullet fer each one o' yer balls," she snapped. "Nobody threatens my young'uns."

"Ah was jus' reachin' fer some candy," Jim Craig lied. "Them is some spunky children yah got. They look familiar to me, tho'. It's possible that ah maht jest know thar pappy."

"Ain't likely. He don' know nobody, an' he likes it that-a-way."

"Never-the-less, ah would like a word wit' him."

"He ain't here."

"Whar might he be, then?"

"How in the hell ought I to know? He comes and goes like he sees fit."

"Pappy's fishin' Clear Fork," the boy helpfully elaborated, before the woman clamped her hand over the lad's mouth.

"Fishin', eh? Maybe me 'n' mah men oughtta go to Clear Fork. Maybe we'd find him."

"The boy don' got no sense," Marge said. "Ain't that so, son?"

"No sir, nuh huh. I'm dumb as a jackass."

"Ah don't doubt yah'll are dull, but ah'm doin' the busy-ness of the Ohio militia. In case yah ain't heard, we're at war."

"Really? Against who?"

"Against our damn enemies. Thus and so it is the duty o' ev'ry man o' sound body to fight. That means yore husband...."

"I ain't married!"

"...or the children's pappy, either way, is hereby by commanded by the authority placed in me by his honored Return J. Meigs, gov'nuh of Ohio, to report to the Mansfield blockhouse fer militia duty within one week, or be liable to arrest as a traitor. He could get hanged."

"Ain't you heard nothin'? I don' know where he is. We don't care 'bout no war." She pointed her rifles defiantly. "Now get off'n my land."

Jim Craig briefly wondered if he shot her, just in the leg, as a warning, would the men think he'd gone too far? It might be worth it to flush his brother out of the woods, so he could shoot him, too.

"All right, ma'am," he slurred. "But tell Andy Craig that his brother was a-lookin' fer him.

As ordered, the men of the newly mobilized Mansfield militia descended upon that town and, while awaiting their orders, had absolutely nothing to do. This motley assemblage included friends and enemies, debtors and debtees, cuckolded husbands and their rivals, fugitives and bounty hunters, neighbors who'd never met and some who wished they'd never met, and other categories of common riffraff united only by the sentiment that nobody wanted to be there.

Everybody approved of the war, so long as it stayed at a distance. So far, none of the major battles had taken place anywhere near Mansfield, and while the locals had some concern about British and Indian forces gathering on the Canadian side of Lake St. Clair, they trusted that the American stronghold at Fort Detroit provided sufficient deterrence against aggression. That being the case, the men made the best of their situation by carousing, gambling, and getting into fights while they waited for a person in authority to tell them what to do.

After a couple of rowdy days, somebody heard somebody tell somebody else that the new commander was finally going to speak to his charges at Beam's Mill that Saturday evening at 7:00 pm. As rumors about him spread, the men disliked him right off the bat. One tale held that their new leader was an erstwhile high-ranking officer from Indiana who'd been dispatched to the backwoods of Mansfield as punishment for gross insubordination. That sounded as good a reason as any why a military officer would accept a position in Mansfield. With low expectations, the men gathered at the mill at the prescribed time. Many had decided that, if no ranking officer showed up, they were just going to go back home.

A few minutes after 7:00, two riders appeared on the opposite side of the Rocky Fork and led their horses across the narrows. One was Jim Craig. The other wore a cocked hat over a jumble of hair hanging to either side, framing a bearded face that also sported what looked like a very recent scar under his left eye. He wore a captain's bars on the shoulders of his blue linen shirt.

From horseback, he addressed the crowd in a gritty, possibly drunken voice. "What a stinking degenerate lot of inbred cretins I see before me! Listen closely, because I only give orders once.

"Refer to me as Captain Bantzer, sir. I will not reply to anything else. I will not reply to just Captain Bantzer, nor will I reply to just sir. *Captain Bantzer Sir!* I am your captain, and you will obey me. That is your duty. My duty is to ensure that you do your duty. Is that simple enough for your little green pea brains?"

The response came back a mixed: "Yes, Sir!" "Yes, Captain!" "Yes, Captain Bantzer!"

"Apparently that was too complicated for you cattle. Try again... and any man who gets it wrong has to polish my boots with his tongue!"

Appropriately motivated, the troops boomed, "Yes, Captain Bantzer, sir!"

"Finally! Maybe among the lot of you there's half a working brain. The first thing you need to know is that if you do not do exactly as I say, you will die. We are at war! You may think you are safe in this dreadful town in the middle of nowhere, but no more than two days' march from here, battles have raged in Indiana and Michigan. From Canada, those treacherous Brits are staring down at Ohio, and they have armed thousands of soulless Indians who will do their bidding. We will only keep them at bay if each and every one of you does exactly what I say. If you fail to follow my orders—mark my words—if the enemy does not kill you, *I will*. In my militia, it's kill or be killed. Now, how many among you have never killed another man? C'mon, I need to know."

Several of the men started to raise their hands, but waited for others to do so first. Some raised their hands, but then, on second thought, brought them back down. Just one hand in the back went up and stayed up—waving, actually, as if to be acknowledged.

"Who's back there?" Captain Bantzer shouted.

The men to either side of him parted, And Johnny Appleseed stood alone.

Captain Banzter laughed and scowled at the same time. "Ho, look here! We've got the famous Appleseed amongst us."

"Hello... *Captain* Bantzer, sir, now, is it? 'Tis good to see ye again."

"I've always heard that you're shy about killing, Appleseed."

"I am prohibited by God's sixth commandment. 'Tis quite clear where He says, *Thou Shalt Not Kill*."

"Everybody knows that does not include killing during wars. Otherwise, how could we know that God is on our side in battle?"

"I do not trouble me-self with such theological questions. 'Tis much simpler just to draw the line at killing, period."

"Then you are a coward!"

"Begging to differ, Captain Bantzer, sir. I would take a bullet for any man here, but I will not fire one. I believe that if every man in every army just put down his arms, we would all very soon find out that nobody really wants to fight. It could be that simple to put an end to war. If men disarmed and chatted amongst themselves, they would likely make a few friends."

More unnerved than he wished to show, Bantzer tried to mock Johnny. "And perhaps they will settle their differences over a tug-of-war, eh."

"That would be an excellent solution!"

This wasn't working. Bantzer said, "You will fight, if you are threatened. Any man will. Killing is natural. War is natural. And lower your fuckin' hand, you moron."

"Thank ye, Captain Bantzer, sir. I am at ease, then? Is that how soldiers say it? I like that phrase—'at ease'—because, in all honesty, I believe that is how God means for us to be. Life ought to be easy. Fighting is a lot harder than not fighting. Wars do not work. Even if ye win, there is no victory for the dead, or their families, or their friends, which is just about everyone. A better way to manage conflict is by ignoring your enemies. Do not return hostilities. Sit right down and refuse to move. Maybe sing a song or two. I do believe that if just one person does this, others will join him, and before ye know it, peace has broken out."

"So you think you can end war through, what-so-you-call-it—*non-violent resistance*?"

"Oh, I do not call it anything in particular. I just think that 'tis a matter of making love, not war."

Hearing that was the last straw. "Maybe you'll change your mind after I've flogged you."

Johnny gulped. "I would rather that ye not," he said. "But even so, I shall never fight."

This gave Bantzer an idea. Flogging Johnny might encourage sympathy for him, but he still felt the necessity of making a firm example of the consequences of disobedience. "Maybe not. But how about if I flog somebody else, in your stead?" He barked to Jim Craig, "Do we have anybody in the brig?"

"Captain Bantzer, sir, we ain't got no brig in Mansfield."

"Oh, bother. What kind of a low, retarded place is this?"

"But we do got a drunk tied up in the hog waller."

"That will do. Bring him here." Bantzer pointed at Johnny. "So you say that you cannot allow harm to come to another man, but that's exactly what you're doing. I will flog this drunk, as many times as it takes for you to swear that you will obey my orders and kill when I say so."

"Please, no...."

It took four men to carry the half-passed-out drunk, two lifting his arms and two his legs. They dropped him in front of Captain Bantzer.

"Leave me alone," the man moaned. "I'm sick."

"If you think you are sick now, let's see what a few lashes do to you. What is your name, you disgusting pig?"

The man pushed himself onto his knees. "My name is Philander Rope. I ain't done nothin' wrong."

Jim Craig differed. "He got noodled an' exposed his cod to Reverend Copus's wife."

"A teeny misunderstanding, is all it was," Rope complained. "Can't whup a man fer that, now, can yer?"

Bantzer said, "How disgraceful. That is worthy of ten lashes, by itself. Are you listening, Appleseed? You can put a stop to this!"

There was no answer.

"So be it. Tie this drunken lecher to the flogging post."

Jim Craig said, "Captain Bantzer, sir! We ain't got no floggin' post in Mansfield."

"None? This is surely the most vulgar bog anywhere in Christian civilization. Strap him to that tree. Who has a bullwhip? Please tell me that somebody here at least has a bullwhip."

"Now wait jest a minute!" Mister Rope squirmed. "Yer ought to whip my partner, 'stead o' me. He didn't stop me from a-slingin' my cod outta my trousers. He was sober and shoulda known better. Plus, he's a... *nigger.*"

It wasn't hard for Captain Bantzer to identify the man to which Mister Rope was referring, since there was only one dark-skinned man in the mob. "Him?"

Heck slapped at the men who tried to grab him. "Get on down! Hey yo', Rope, what fo' yo' give me up like dat? I always done guarded yo' back!" Rope would not meet his eye, so Heck turned to Captain Bantzer. "I am free man an' I demand my raht to legal trial by a jury o' my peers. Oh, wait, ain't none o' my peers here. I guess den dat means I cain't be whupped."

"Ain't nothin' personal," Mr. Rope explained. "After the beatin' is done, I'll buy yer a drink an' we'll have us a laugh o'r the whole thing."

Captain Bantzer stomped his feet. "Now let me get this straight. The drunken pervert whom I'm flogging instead of Appleseed wants me to flog his darky companion instead of him. What a hive of cowards! The fairest solution is to flog both of them."

Mister Rope and Mister Heck both screamed, "Nooo!"

The townsmen, confused and impatient, were glad finally to have clear orders upon which to act. They dragged Heck and Rope to the tree, bound them to it side-by-side, and ripped off their shirts.

Mister Heck bore scars on his shoulders from a previous flagellation.

"I shall do this myself." Bantzer took a bullwhip and snapped it a few times. "Are you watching, Appleseed? Say to me, 'Captain Bantzer, sir, I will kill anybody upon your command,' and you can spare these men the bite of my lash. Appleseed?" He searched the crowd. "Where are you?"

Everybody looked at the men to their left and their right, but Johnny Appleseed was nowhere.

"He's disappeared," somebody said.

When Captain Frank Bantzer looked at Mister Rope and Mister Heck tied to the tree, in his mind he saw Johnny Appleseed, grinning back with those dirty teeth.

"So be it!" Bantzer then smote Mister Rope and Mister Heck with criss-cross slashes across their backs. He screamed with every lash, almost as loud as they did, again and again... and, like his victims, when the captain was finished, he collapsed, exhausted.

Johnny needed some time alone. Most often, he was alone anyway, so he seldom acknowledged any particular need or desire for solitude. Pressed by the threat of impending war, though, he struggled to unclutter his mind. How could he think straight when everybody around him was frothing at the mouth with bloodlust? Johnny wanted to act in service of peace, which he believed was best done by example, but, although he wasn't the most socially savvy man in Ohio, even he could tell when people were treating him like a fool. Furthermore, Johnny had not heard from any of the Voices for many days, as if the drumbeat of war was silencing or deflecting their words. He hoped a few days by himself in the wilderness might restore and refocus his wits, because, otherwise, he didn't have any notion as to what God wanted for him to do next.

If anybody wanted to be alone, the best place to go in Ohio was the Great Black Swamp. In the northwest part of the state, between the Maumee and Sandusky Rivers, all the way to Lake Erie, the marsh forests and wetland prairies were unexplored and inhospitable to settlement—the joke among Ohioans was that God had created it to keep out Michiganders.

Even so, Johnny found the Black Swamp to be kind of pleasant—apart from the clouds of mosquitos and the fumes of stagnant, algae-choked water—for in his travels through the wasteland, he had found a couple of dry, elevated moraines where basswood and hickory trees grew. Camping there was like being on his own private island.

For several nights, Johnny moved from one hummock to another, by day foraging for seeds, nuts, and berries, and by night praying as hard as he'd ever prayed in his entire life. The better to induce a mystical experience, he resisted sleep. Kneeling before an erratic boulder in the middle of a bog, Johnny prayed in every way he knew how. He prayed with his eyes open, staring into the darkness until his pupils hurt from stretching so far. He prayed with his eyes closed, watching afterimages under his eyeballs dance and churn. He prayed on his knees, until it felt like his kneecaps would break. He prayed standing up, as if a pole had been driven down the length of his spine. He prayed with his hands folded, clenched so tight that his knuckles bulged and his fingers turned purple. He prayed with his arms open, as if ready to catch the whole sky if it happened to fall. He prayed until it made him sick, dizzy, sweaty, achy, giddy and groggy, and he kept on praying past the point where his heart started fluttering and the air he breathed burnt like it was on fire. He prayed to God the Father, Jesus Christ, the Virgin Mary, the Arch-Angel Gabriel, Emmanuel Swedenborg, Abraham, Moses, Solomon and Zephaniah, John the Baptist, each of the twelve Apostles, Mary Magdalene, Saints Peter, Paul, Catherine of Siena, Francis of Assisi, Thomas Aquinas, and James the Lesser, Martin Luther and John Wesley. He even sent out an invocation to Waashaa Monetoo.

Then, exhausted, he put his hand to his ear to listen.

The swamp teemed with the noises of bugs, frogs, birds, and creatures breaking the surface of the water and scurrying through brush, but nary an audible Voice from on high. Nature had never seemed so lonely and disenchanted to Johnny. He figured that if silent prayer weren't enough, he'd try speaking out loud.

"What am I to do? Sometimes, it feels like faith is not working for me. God, I know that ye created human beings in your image, but also made them mortal and full of sins. And Jesus, I believe that ye suffered and died to redeem the human race of those sins. And I know that every one of ye angels listening in heaven began as a regular people on Earth. And, Philosopher Swedenborg, I know that ye have spoken the eternal truth to me plainly from your own mouth. But I do sometimes wonder what good it does me to know these things.

"I try. I do my best. I plant natural seeds without any concern about how the growing trees will benefit me. I have not ever had a bad word to say about another human being. So long as there is somebody else who has no shoes, I will just as soon go barefoot, me-self. Wherever I see beauty, feel happiness, or breathe in the joy of being alive, I tell people. And yet, most folks just ignore me, some dismiss or scorn me, and others make jest of me.

"God, why did ye make me such a peculiar man? I know many people think I am as crazy as a squirrel that fell from a tree. I sometimes believe they are right, but that does not explain the things I have heard. Everything I know, I learned straight from the angels' mouths to me own two ears... but the one thing that makes no sense is: why should I be the only person that hears these things? I do not have the power to make folks believe in things they cannot hear. I worry that I am a poor messenger for your Word. Lord, I could not blame ye for giving up on me."

The wind in treetops sounded to Johnny like God sighing.

"But what about ye, Mother?" he called in desperation. "I know ye can hear me. Are ye going to leave me in dreadful silence, too?"

Johnny's heart leapt when he heard a sudden movement in the weeds behind him. He turned, half expecting to find his angelic mother standing there with her wings spread, eager to embrace him. Instead, there were just trees, vines, and swamp. Frustrated, he kicked at a soggy, rotten trunk near where he'd heard the noise. By doing so, Johnny carelessly uncovered a coiled copperhead snake, which lunged and sank its fangs into his leg just beneath the bottom of his shredded trousers. Without a conscious thought, Johnny snatched the snake by its tail and started whipping it furiously against the boulder that he'd used as his altar—it became an unintentional sacrifice.

When he realized what he had done, Johnny dropped the serpent's body. Shocked, he began pounding his forehead against the rock until blinded by his own blood. He had taken the life of another living creature...

The realization of the evil he'd committed spread across his body like a hungry disease, devouring his skin and digging into his flesh. Through the pain, though, he felt disoriented energy, and it occurred to him that if he was damned, then he was also finally free.

"Forgive me!" he howled, "or don't! But let me know, one way or the other."

Johnny didn't know if it was God's will or his own that had brought him to this moment in this place. In a feverish reverie, Johnny saw himself switching lives for another—one more settled, even normal—where he might've turned into something better than a poor, unloved vagabond, ridiculed as crazy, dying by himself in the Black Swamp, his body left to be picked apart by turkey vultures. He recalled how John Young had once told him that, cleanly barbered and well dressed, he could've passed for a lawyer.

Well, maybe so, and why not?

He imagined himself working in an office in a stately building, maybe in Cincinnati, where he'd dispense legal opinions in accord with both human and God's laws. He'd wear a pair of fine leather shoes, wool stockings, suspenders to hold up his pants, and a top hat.

Why should he have to wait until death for his reward? Swedenborg promised that: *After death, a suitable wife is given to a husband, and a suitable husband to a wife, and they enjoy delightful and blessed communications....* Still, it didn't seem fair to Johnny that he should die a virgin in this world.

He imagined himself strolling arm and arm with a bonneted Mona Junkin, nodding at their friends and neighbors in town, pausing to make amiable conversation, on the way back to their modest but well-kept estate, where their children would be waiting to greet them with cries of "Mommy!" and "Daddy!" He saw his blessed family going to church together, where they'd all read from their prayer books: "Thank you, God, for the gifts that you have given us."

At night, he and Mona would lie down together on a mattress stuffed with down feathers, covered with linen sheets and a homespun quilt to keep them warm on even the most frigid nights. They'd face each other and whisper their good nights in a soft kiss, and fall into a contented sleep holding hands. Every day would be a repeat of this bliss. Those things could have been his—*should* have been. If God was a giver, then He was also a thief. Life shouldn't have to be painful to be beautiful.

Johnny felt his chest cramping as the poison flowed into his heart. There was nothing to do but suffer it out. If he died, he'd have no choice but to cast himself into hell. If he lived...well, he didn't know for sure.

When he woke up and wasn't dead, Johnny guessed that either God wasn't done with him, or He'd left him alive to work out things on his own. Whichever the answer, he wouldn't find out in the Black Swamp; but where could he go? He decided against returning to Mansfield, in the event that Captain Frank Bantzer still bore a grudge against him. Instead, he headed north toward Lake Erie. Near the mouth of the Huron River were small settlements called Huron and New Haven, and Johnny headed there, eager to share a few friendly words with another human being.

That afternoon, on the fringes of the Black Swamp, he happened upon a Wyandot hunting camp. To his own surprise, his first inclination was not to stroll into their midst proclaiming glad tidings and thanks for God's love, as was his usual wont, but instead he had an intuition that he should stay hidden at a circumspect distance.

About a dozen Indians feasted and celebrated around a recent kill and a roaring fire. Although he could not make out precisely what they were saying, he discerned that their gleeful spirits were due not only to their hunting success, but even more to some fortuitous turn of events involving a military victory at Fort Detroit. They whooped and hailed the name of "Tecumseh!"

Thinking better than to ask them for clarification, Johnny kept moving.

Tracking the west bank of the Huron, he passed by slate ridges and through hardwood forests to reach the dunes of Lake Erie. The rush of breezes across the great lake always seemed to lift Johnny off the ground, and even though he knew it was a landlocked body of water that, if he could walk on it, he could traverse in one day, it still inspired in him a sense of limitlessness. He'd never seen the ocean shores, but it was hard to conceive of them evoking a more overwhelming sense of the grandeur of open spaces. Of all the Earth's surfaces for walking, hard sand was his favorite, so he dug his toes into the shoreline, listening to the battering of wind, the screeching of gulls, and the rhythmic splash and retreat of waves. The mixing of sounds mesmerized him, crowding out his thoughts, as if filling his whole head with the sea.

He wasn't sure if he heard it, felt it, or thought it, but some force reverberated like thunder from the unseen, other side of the water, and stopped him in his tracks. He put his hands to his ears and waded into the surf, straining to hear, but only the beat of wind and waves resounded. As soon as he exhaled, though, he heard it as clear as a church bell.

The Voice was harsh, yet subdued, like an angel in pain.

"Go through the door."

Johnny heard it only once, and then a hard gust came and blew every echo of it into a whirling distance. Something popped between his ears, and when he looked up, Johnny blinked and rubbed his eyes. He could make out dark shapes in the distant water, which, as they approached, he realized were boats. From behind a grassy dune, he watched and counted nine schooners, bearing in the direction of the mouth of the Huron River. He figured there might be as many as a thousand men on them, but who? The only answer that made any sense sent a shiver of terror through his body. It had to be the British invasion that everybody had been so dreadfully worried about. The war had come to Ohio!

Johnny didn't waste any time thinking; he fled for his life and the lives of others, back upstream, through a gap in the forest, which presented like an open door into the wilderness.

Johnny jogged into the village of New Haven, shouting at the top of his lungs, "Flee, all of ye God-fearing Americans! The British are landing at Huron!"

Villagers spilled out of their cabins and came in from their fields when they heard Johnny's cries. He was leading a contingent of a couple dozen settlers that he'd rounded up in Huron, and they were heading south. Heeding Johnny's warning, these nervous homesteaders dropped whatever they were doing and commenced evacuation procedures. They gathered essential household goods, loaded their horses and wagons, herded their cattle, and rendezvoused at a prairie outside of town.

There, they compared Johnny's eyewitness testimony with second-hand reports that they'd heard regarding the fall of American troops at Fort Detroit. If the British had indeed made landfall in Ohio, the Indian armies would not be far behind, which led them to conclude that they were smack dab at the vanguard of a Canadian attack upon the United States of America. The settlers were too few to counter with any effective resistance. Flight was their only recourse. They set out immediately, even though night was falling.

"To Mansfield!" Johnny urged them, that being the location of the nearest militia.

Refugees flooded onto the narrow path along the Huron River that connected them to the settlements on the upper reaches of Mohecan John's River. The going was arduous due to recent heavy rains. The Huron swelled over its banks, so in places where the path had washed away, they had to wade or even swim. The men formed a human chain so that the women and children could cross the rapids one hand at a time. Several cattle drowned or were abandoned in the effort. The whole time, the men guarding the rear kept looking behind their backs, afraid that at any instant the enemies would catch up to them.

By dawn, the group still hadn't reached the East Fork, so even though they were drenched, hungry, and exhausted, they could ill afford to pause for rest. When they finally made it to the state road, they warned the inhabitants of the isolated cabins along the route, who likewise packed their possessions and joined the caravan.

That next evening, they came scrambling into Mansfield bearing machetes, torches, and rifles, screaming "Sanctuary!" They headed straight for the blockhouse.

Inside the fortification, Captain Frank Bantzer had already retired to his quarters and his bottles. He'd left instructions not to be disturbed for anything less important that the Second Coming, but Sergeant Jim Craig saw the approaching commotion and decided that was close enough. Fortunately, it was early in the evening, and Bantzer was still awake and sober enough to answer the knock on his door.

Jim Craig apprised him of the situation as best he understood it.

"The sheepish fools," Captain Bantzer sneered.

He stomped out in stocking feet to address the crowd. The citizens from Huron and New Haven, combined with nearly the entire population of Mansfield, gathered outside of the blockhouse. The din suggested utter confusion. Some, in favor of fighting, were already collecting firearms and gunpowder. Others argued that they should abandon the town and continue onward to Mount Vernon, with its larger militia. Either way, most lamented that the likeliest outcome was that they were all about to die, and the best they could hope for was that it'd be quick.

When Bantzer appeared on the steps of the blockhouse, he calculated that the only way he could get their attention was to fire a shot into the air, which he did.

"Shut your cowardly yawps!" he bellowed. "People, compose yourselves! The story that you've heard is but a false alarm! Earlier today, I received reliable dispatch from a rider who informed me that, contrary to the hysteria you are promulgating, the boats seen landing on the shores of Lake Eire are *not* an invading force. Yes, it is true that Fort Detroit has fallen to the British—*surrendered,* no less, by that spineless poltroon General William Hull, without a single shot being fired. However, those ships contained good and true Americans who'd been released as part of the surrender agreement. There is no imminent danger. You should all go home."

Before anybody left, though, Captain Bantzer asked one question: "Who told you this dangerous nonsense?"

Numerous voices replied in unison. "It was Appleseed."

"Appleseed!" Bantzer snorted. "That felon! Where is he? I will have him hog-tied for this outrage!"

Everybody in the crowd looked at everybody else, but nobody saw Johnny Appleseed.

Chapter 23 – September 1812

Mansfield, Ohio

Trusting God wasn't always easy, but Reverend James Copus had learned over the years that if he didn't want to do something but did it anyway, it usually proved for the best in the long run. It sometimes seemed that God's will and his own desires stood categorically opposed to one another. Still, concerning the task that Captain Frank Bantzer had forced him to perform, Copus had serious reservations. Not only did he not want to do this, it felt like something of which God would disapprove strongly.

Reverend Copus did not like Bantzer. It seemed contradictory, but even in those perilous times, having a local militia commanded by an experienced military officer made him feel *less* secure than before, when they relied on only themselves to protect the people of Mansfield. He didn't approve of the way Bantzer treated people.

Many times, Copus had watched uneasily while Bantzer put the men through their daily drills, barking at them to "scalp, slash, rape, and rampage!" He told his soldiers that they had to turn their fear into hatred for the enemy, and he didn't' mind if they hated *him*, too. Thus, he insulted the men as "bloody arseholes writhing with wormy shit," and "diseased faggots with scabby rotten peckers." He warned them that their enemies were cunning and ruthless, so that the sound of a twig breaking in the middle of the night might be the last thing they heard before getting tomahawked between the eyes.

It was no wonder, then, that people were jumping out of their boots every time somebody sneezed in Mansfield. For that, Copus blamed Captain Frank Bantzer.

On spiritual grounds, Reverend Copus was excused from military service, but Captain Bantzer still insisted that even a conscientious objector was obliged to perform certain duties in support of the war efforts. It didn't take him long to call in that favor. One evening, when

Bantzer came knocking on the Copus family cabin, the reverend shooed his wife and children into the loft and answered the door with a heavy sense of foreboding.

"I trust that the Lord finds you well tonight," Reverend Copus said as he let Bantzer into the home.

"The Lord does not listen to me, anyway," Bantzer replied. He sat at the family table and helped himself to an apple from the fruit bowl. It was bitter, but he seemed to like it that way.

"Some folks say that you're an Indian lover, Copus."

To the degree that epithet was invariably attached to any minister who preached to Indians, he took it as a backwards compliment. "So?" he asked.

"They say that you come and go among the Delaware Indians on the Black Fork like a regular guest of theirs."

"I have always been welcomed into their village. I consider Chief Arm Strong to be a friend."

"Hah!" Bantzer slapped his knee. "A Christian cannot be an Indian's friend! That's like cozying up to a bear. It may eat out of your hand, but when you turn your back, it'll maul you."

"I believe that God created Indians out of love, too."

"That's good, because if you really believe that Indians have any justification for the air they breathe, then you'll do this small job that I've come to ask of you."

The more he heard, the less he liked of what Captain Bantzer had to say.

"That sorry band of Indians living in that filthy little ghetto called Greentown make the good people of Mansfield fearful and nervous... and with good cause, I daresay. As gullible as they are, these brutes could be agitated into joining Tecumseh's coalition, thus bringing the war to right onto our very doorsteps. That is just plain unacceptable. Simple prudence suggests we should repatriate the whole lot of them to someplace where they can do no mischief. For that reason, I am ordering the militia to round up and forcibly evict the entire community. Still, I would prefer to conduct this as an orderly, peaceful operation, with minimal casualties."

He leaned across the table into the reverand's space. "That's where you come in. I want you to convince them to leave obediently."

Reverend Copus shook his head. "I do not approve of this. The Delaware are a proud but downtrodden people. They have had enough of war. I believe that some of them may be receptive to turning Christian."

"Even if Christian, they are still Indians, beyond the reach of human decency. The only good Indian is a dead Indian."

Appalled, Reverend Copus said, "God have mercy!"

"If you truly believe in mercy, then do what I say. My solution is merciful, for the alternative is to compel them by force. Mind you, I've no qualms about doing just that, but it would be bloody, and to my way of thinking, that blood would be on your hands, if you refuse."

"Is there no other way?"

Bantzer sucked on the sour apple and let its taste spread across his cheeks. "There are many ways, but only one allowable outcome. Those Indians must be eliminated. But I'm not unreasonable. Tell them that this is just a temporary measure. They may return in the future, when tensions have eased." He stood, leaving the half-eaten apple on the table. "Either way, though, my militia will move against them at dawn in two days. You have until then to gain their acquiescence, or ensure their destruction."

The next morning, when Reverend Copus tucked his Bible into his travelling bag and trudged toward Greentown, he felt torn between what he believed in his heart that he should do, and what he knew in his head that he must do. For inspiration, he took out his Bible, flipped to the Book of Matthew, and started reading.

He was moved to speak out loud when he came upon a particular line: "Come to me, all you who are weary and burdened, and I will give you rest. Take my yoke upon you and learn from me...."

From over his shoulder, a response came. "For I am gentle and humble in heart, and ye will find rest for your souls."

Reverend Copus spun around, half expecting to find Jesus Christ standing there. Instead, he gazed upon Johnny Appleseed. "Chapman? What are you doing here?"

"Begging your pardon. I did not mean to interrupt your prayers."

"I'm surprised to see you. I thought you'd left Mansfield." Copus exhaled heavily. "The interruption is welcome, though, my friend."

"Maybe I ought to have stayed away," Johnny replied. "But lately, I have been feeling sort of stuck, like God wants me to be here, but I don't know why."

"I know that feeling."

"I do no envy ye for what ye have to do, but perhaps I can be of assistance."

Reverend Copus wanted to ask how Johnny knew about his task, or how he expected to help, but, grateful for the moral support, even of a mad man, he thanked Johnny and invited him to walk with him.

Cawing crows followed the men into the village, as if announcing—or warning—of their arrival.

Chief Arm Strong was splashing and playing with his grandchildren in the river. Seeing them, he said, "You hang your head like a bad dog that has been punished."

Reverend Copus admitted that he had some urgent news that concerned the entire tribe.

Chief Arm Strong ordered the elders and leaders of the group to gather for an immediate conference at the long house. Setting aside whatever they were doing, they came, although in no hurry, as if expecting bad news.

Johnny and Reverend Copus were surprised to see Toby the Wyandot among the Greentown Indians.

He'd painted his face, red for rage and black for grief. He approached the two men and stood across from them, eyeing them up and down as if checking for weapons, then finally asked, "Are we still friends?"

"Of course," said Reverend Copus.

"Friends until death, and beyond," said Johnny Appleseed.

"If so, then you are the only white men whose friendship I will now accept. I am ruined, thanks to white men. The same Americans who had patronized my business in good times, now call me a demon and vow to kill me. After Fort Detroit fell, they raided my establishment, stole my money, killed many Indians, and burned everything to the ground for good measure. One of the men who died that day was the husband of my daughter. I have come to be with Smiling Coneflower so that we may grieve together. Now she has a new name—Weeping Coneflower. I worry that whatever news you bring at the behest of American soldiers, more malevolence shall visit Indian people."

Reverend Copus put his hands on Toby's shoulders. "Stay strong, my friend. Now, I must tell you, and Chief Arm Strong, and everybody gathered here, news that weighs heavily upon my mind. Will you translate for me?"

Addressing the tribal leaders, Reverend Copus did not try to conceal his disdain or reluctance to repeat Captain Bantzer's orders. As

Toby translated, several braves shouted angrily, but among the voices of defiance and outrage, others expressed sadness and resignation. Some stoked themselves up to fight, while others argued that they should negotiate. The eldest and world-weariest among them cautioned that it was better to submit and survive for another day.

Chief Arm Strong summarized the only thing upon which they all agreed. "There will never be peace, so long as the white men resent Indians just for living."

Toby stood in front of Copus and exhorted the tribe in their native language first, then translated for the reverend. "There is another way. Instead of allowing the white men herd us like sheep to someplace where we have no ancestors, we can all of us join forces with the war chief, Tecumseh. His numbers are growing."

Reverend Copus did not understand any of those words, except the one, 'Tecumseh.'

"If you try to escape," Copus warned, "Captain Bantzer will hunt you and kill you. But if you leave willingly, he has given me his word that you will be allowed to come back after the war is over."

Chief Arm Strong shook his head, lamenting, in English, "What shall we do?"

"May I offer a humble suggestion?" Johnny Appleseed said.

Of all the men gathered in the long house, he was the last that anybody would have expected to speak on matters of war.

Nobody objected, so Johnny continued. "Resist, but do so agreeably."

"What does this mean?" Arm Strong asked, throwing up his arms. "Is this a riddle spoken by those Voices that only you can hear?"

"No, fact of the matter is that I have heard not a word from the spirits for many weeks, and I started fretting why that was so. Then I heard something that scared me, and I acted in fear instead of with faith. Now, I have come to understand that God wants for me to do the thinking for me own self. But to answer your question...."

Johnny plopped onto the ground and sat cross-legged. "What I am saying is that when the soldiers come, you should all just sit down and ignore them. Do not move. Do not fight. Just sit tight, pray, and wait for them to go away."

Toby erupted. "That it foolish! The soldiers will rope us and drag us away."

"They may try, but 'tis a mighty lot of work to pull an entire tribe against its will. They may just give up and leave instead."

"They will beat us and shoot us!"

"Well, they could do that anyway, but I know that most of those men have mothers who taught them not to start a fight with somebody who refuses to fight back. The way I see things, doing this cannot be worse than any other alternatives, and it could be better. Taking that chance makes good common sense."

"There is no dignity in surrender," Toby objected.

"It is not surrender. It is giving your enemy a chance to make peace."

"Leave us now," Chief Arm Strong said, waving aside Johnny and Reverend Copus. "We have many things among ourselves to discuss."

Otto Blubaugh hadn't realized how long it'd been since he'd fired a rifle, until Captain Bantzer gave him one and said, "Never shoot, unless it is to kill." Accordingly, the captain ordered the soldiers to take target practice at a stuffed effigy called "Chief Shoot 'Em Up," which had a head made of balled-uprags covered by a turkey-feather headdress. It was propped against the whipping tree.

"Every shot goes either through the heart or between the eyes," Bantzer said. "Or I consider it to be a miss."

Rusty with his firearm, Otto not only missed, but sometimes he couldn't tell just where his shots landed. He warned his fellow soldiers that, if they ever got into a battle, they'd be safer staying behind him.

"If we gets us into battle, I will sho' be keepin' way far back," said Heck, who shared Otto's tent with him.

In the mornings, Otto and Heck would lie on their bedrolls and chat while waiting for Sergeant Craig to rouse the troops by blowing his slobbery version of reveille. Seldom in their regular lives did they ever enjoy the leisure of sleeping in, but, despite what they'd heard about military discipline, rising early was not part of this unit's regimen.

Captain Bantzer himself was rarely seen before the sun had cleared the treetops, and he never emerged from his quarters before someone brought him coffee, sometimes several refills.

"Do yahr reckon we're gonna see any action t'day?" Otto asked, as he did every morning.

"None fo' me, please. Tha's jus' an 'xcuse to start killin'. I know how it does go: my black ass'll be the firs' to die."

"Ah got yahr back, Heck."

"Jus' watch yo'self, boy. Yo' got to keep alive fo' that wife and yo's baby tha's comin'."

While Otto and Heck talked, Sergeant Craig began trumpeting; he got mixed up, though, and started playing taps, until he realized his mistake and made up for it by practically screaming reveille into his horn. Finally, he dropped the trumpet and hollered at full lung capacity, "Git yer lazy pussy willow arses outta bed."

Despite Sergeant Craig's bluster, the first drills of any day were casual, requiring the men to do little more than report and rattle off their names, sleepwalk through some easy exercises, then line up for their breakfast rations of stale bread and salty gruel. That morning was even less strenuous than usual, since Sergeant Craig, profoundly hung-over, was winded by the fifth deep knee bend and released the men early.

Taking this as a hopeful sign for light duty on that day, Otto, Heck, and several other men sat around the breakfast table and kept up lively chatter to help the watery porridge go down. As they enjoyed the crisp, early autumn morning, with a crystal blue sky, the conversation turned to what they would be doing on such a day, were it not for being at war instead. Fishing seemed the most popular choice.

Captain Bantzer stomped into the mess tent and, not liking what he saw, put an end to the banter by firing a shot low over the men's heads. The captain was fully uniformed, with his bayoneted rifle by his side, a saddle pistol in his belt, a saber in a scabbard hanging over a shoulder, a knife strapped to one ankle and a tomahawk to the other, and a rolled bullwhip fastened to his hip. There was dried blood around the scar on his face.

"Today, your duty calls!" he bellowed. "If you do exactly as you are ordered, there's a fair chance you will still be alive at sundown." With that, he commanded Sergeant Craig to ready the troops to march.

"Git on up," Heck half sang. He picked up his guitar, strummed a few chords, and then strapped it over his shoulder.

"Yahr goin' march with yore git-tar?" Otto asked.

"Don't go nowhere wit'out Miss Lucille. She keeps me safe better'n any rifle."

The Mansfield militia marched from the blockhouse in rows of three. Captain Bantzer instructed them to make as much noise and possible, leading them in a chant to inspire the proper mood:

Right, left. Left right.
Fight by day. Fuck by night.

Hit 'em low. Hit 'em high.
Scalp 'em raw,
Rape their squaws.
Sound off:
Kill, kill, kill
Kill, kill, kill... Injuns!

Nobody knew exactly where they were marching, or what they would do when they got there. A couple of miles into their journey, Otto pointed out that the only place ahead of them on the path was the Delaware Indian village on the Black Fork. The consensus among the men was that the Greentown tribe consisted of the dullest and most domesticated Indians anywhere west of the Appalachians. Still, their proximity unnerved some folks. Most of the soldiers guessed that the troops were going there to make a show of force, demand obedience, and then go home.

Until that time, Philander Rope, marching near the front of the troops, had kept uncharacteristically silent. Ever since the public flogging, Rope had acted like a sycophant for Captain Bantzer, so when he casually mentioned, "Ah done heard tha' we're gonna move them Injuns outta here an' escort them all the way to Urbana," the men presumed that, if he was spreading a rumor, it must have come straight from Bantzer. It sounded like a long, dreary march.

"I got no grievance 'gainst no Indian," Heck said to Otto. "An' I don' wanna kill none, neither."

"Hush," Otto scolded. "Captain 'll whup yah if he hears such talk."

To everybody's surprise, when the troops rounded the bend in the Black Fork that spilled into the clearing where the Indians dwelt, the entire tribe had already assembled, waiting for them. The braves stood in a semi-circle around the open commons, with their arms akimbo and their legs locked at the knees, while the women and children behind them carried on with the routine work and play of any normal day. At the forefront, Chief Arm Strong and the tribal elders passed a smoking pipe, while Johnny Appleseed tooted merrily into his whistle.

Captain Bantzer surveyed the scene from his mount and said to Jim Craig, "They are unarmed." He then ordered his men to fan into a crescent formation, so that they lined up almost man-for-man across from a specific brave on the other side.

Otto watched in amazement as Bantzer dismounted in front of Johnny Appleseed. Half mumbling, half whispering, the captain said to

Johnny, "I always knew you were an Indian-loving traitor. You will share their fate."

Johnny tooted a single note in his whistle.

Chief Arm Strong bowed to Bantzer and spoke in practiced English. "We welcome friends. We are good Indians. Come, smoke with us."

"We have work to do," Captain Bantzer answered. He spoke over Chief Arm Strong's head, addressing the entire tribe. "By the authority of the governor of the state of Ohio, and under the rules of war established by the United States of America, I hereby order all Indian persons residing here to vacate these premises, taking only such possessions as they can carry, to be relocated to a safe location until the government determines that they may return."

Bantzer paused here, as if expecting disturbance—maybe hoping for an excuse to fight.

Instead, the Indians did not react at all. It was as if he were speaking to the target practice dummy.

He unsheathed his sword and waved it to so that its sharpened edge caught a glint of sunshine. "You have one hour to prepare for your journey. Any resistance will be answered with force."

Chief Arm Strong kept an impassive look on his face. "No thank you. We like peace. We are good Indians."

"This is a command. You will obey, or suffer the consequences."

"No thank you." With that, Chief Arm Strong turned to his tribe and gestured for them to sit.

They did as commanded, one by one, each man in the front row lowering himself into a cross-legged posture on the ground. Then the women followed suit, taking the time to brush off the rocks or stumps upon which they sat, and finally the children, who dropped next to their mothers or onto their laps.

"We will sit," Chief Arm Strong explained.

"What nonsense is this?" Captain Bantzer howled in confusion. "You will not sit! This is no time for sitting!"

"No thank you."

Bantzer pointed his sword at Johnny. "Appleseed! What have you to do with this deceit?"

Johnny kept his eyes closed, and if he heard, he showed no sign of it.

Bantzer thrust the tip of his sword beneath Johnny's chin. "I could run you through."

Johnny flinched, but in response to a gnat lighting around his temple, rather than to Bantzer's blade.

Huffing, the captain turned to Chief Arm Strong, who was still smoking his pipe, and for lack of anything better to do, kicked him in the ribs.

The chief took a deep breath, but then exhaled with a dense cloud of smoke and said, "No thank you."

Otto let an inadvertent giggle escape.

"Who dares?" Bantzer snorted. He called forth for Sergeant Craig.

The sergeant replied with a, "Yes Captain Bantzer, sir!" that contained what Otto, and no doubt many of the other men, perceived to be just a hint of sarcasm.

Standing nose-to-nose with Craig, the captain snapped, "Order the soldiers to force these people onto their feet."

"Yes,sir, but... how?"

"Beat them. Drag them. I don't care. Just move them."

Sergeant Craig shrugged and motioned at the men in his first line. "Yah heard the captain! Force these Injuns onto their feet."

The men looked at each other, then each at the Indian across from him, envisioning the maneuvers required to execute that order. Finally, following Sergeant Craig's lead, the soldiers began wrestling with their opposites, attempting to lift them by their arms or to roll them onto their sides. Despite these efforts, the Indians would not budge.

"Shall we flog them all, sir?" Sergeant Craig asked.

"The cowards!" Bantzer shouted, his voice breaking with frustration.

Even though the braves all wore blank expressions, behind them, many of the women trembled and stared at the ground.

"Perhaps if they are too craven to fight, we should seize their women for ourselves." Bantzer waved forward a dozen of his men and, strutting in front of them like a cock in a hen house, said, "There are some lovely cunts, men, and they're all yours. Their husbands won't raise a fuss. Feel free to rape them with abandon." When the men didn't move, he insisted. "Get your cods out! And they'd better be stiff. That's an order!"

Sergeant Craig inquired, "May I, too, sir?"

"Be my guest."

Captain Bantzer went straight for a woman who may have been the most appealing of the whole lot.

Toby watched as Weeping Coneflower's eyes swelled at the sight of the captain striding straight for her. She locked her ankles and dug her fingers into cracks on the stone upon which she was sitting, but couldn't control the look of fear that washed across her face.

"I choose this one," the captain announced. "I shall bend her over this stone and ream out her bung hole so hard that she will never again move waste without thinking of me."

Until that instant, Toby had remained sedentary, but seething. When Captain Bantzer began groping for Weeping Coneflower's cleavage, Toby emitted a furious cry, lowered his head, and charged toward the captain like an angry bear.

Bantzer froze.

When Toby got within a step of him, though, Sergeant Craig pounded the butt of his rifle against the soft spot below the back of his skull. Blood sprayed from his mouth when he hit the ground.

"Ha! Tie him up, so he can watch me rape his woman," Bantzer gloated.

Chief Arm Strong rose. "No!" He faced the sky and wailed in his language, "Have we ourselves not suffered enough to satisfy your lust for vengeance, Mothsee Monetoo?" Then he addressed Bantzer, in English. "We will go. We are... good Indians."

With stifled grunts and muttered curses, but also with some sighs of dismal relief, the men of the tribe allowed themselves to be herded into a pack, while the women scurried to grab as many of their belongings as they could in the few minutes allotted to them.

Chief Arm Strong carried the tribe's ceremonial tomahawk pipe, but Bantzer snatched it from his hands and broke it over his knee.

As a precaution, the soldiers tied every man, woman, and child of Greentown to a tether around their waists, so they tramped along in a roped chain of misery.

"Move them out!" Bantzer cried when the last two, Toby and Weeping Coneflower, joined the maudlin procession.

As they departed, many glanced over their shoulders for one final look at their homes, but just as many kept staring at their feet, unable to muster the resolve to look either forward or backward.

Alone, his eyes still sealed, the mad man Appleseed remained unaffected by and unresponsive to the tumult all around him. He hadn't moved a muscle during the entire evacuation. Surveying the now empty village, Captain Bantzer walked around Appleseed and wondered if he'd drifted into some kind of trance. He snapped his fingers in front of the man's eyes, but got no reaction.

"So, Appleseed, I think you shall finally be of no further annoyance to me," Bantzer said, not to Appleseed, but so that his men could hear.

When the last of the Indians turned the bend, the men of the unit's rear guard waited for Captain Bantzer's orders to join the march. Instead, the captain cleared his throat and directed his soldiers to, "Burn this hellish place to the ground."

The plodding Indians had marched no more than a quarter mile, barely past their tribal burial grounds, when they noticed the smoke rising from their village.

"They lied!" somebody screamed. "They are burning our homes!"

Even bound and unarmed, this was a greater outrage than the braves in the tribe could endure. Several struggled to break free from their tethers, dragging others along behind them into a human knot. Some tried to run back to defend their village, only to get their feet entangled and fall. Others reached for stones and began chucking them in the direction of the soldiers.

Unrest swarmed, and the orderly march turned into an unruly mob.

Toby, who had hidden a small knife in his leggings, slashed his and Weeping Coneflower's restraints. "Hurry," he pleaded, and led her into the brush.

Then, somebody fired a musket. Its ball whizzed by Sergeant Craig's ear, so that when he pivoted to return fire, he caught just the briefest glimpse of the ragged white man, on the opposite bank of the Black Fork, who had taken the shot at him.

"Come back and fight!" Jim Craig yelled. "Andy, yah hog wipe!"

In the melee, soldiers guarding the perimeter were wary of starting a crossfire, but even so, they wanted desperately to shoot something, so they fired into the ground, the forest, the river—gunshot was contagious, but arbitrary. The agitated Indians became even more tangled in their bindings as they fought to escape, but in the process, several soldiers got ensnared in the ropes, too. Amid so many flying elbows and shoulders, several men, both Indians and whites, got jabbed and pushed to the ground, and with all the bullets slicing through the air, nobody could tell who'd been hit and who hadn't.

Among these faux casualties was Philander Rope, who reached behind his neck, pulled back his bloody hand, and cried, "I'm bleedin'!" He collapsed into a fetal position, groveling and begging for mercy, but by doing so left himself vulnerable to being kicked and trampled by Indians who saw him as the nearest scapegoat upon which to vent their fury. When his real blood began flowing, his cries for mercy were to no avail.

Swords drawn, Captain Bantzer and Sergeant Craig galloped toward the uprising to restore order. They left behind the half dozen soldiers in the rear guard who had executed the torching, and who were now suddenly on their own with no authority in sight.

Included in this group were Otto Blubaugh and Mister Heck, who had the exact same thought at the exact same moment. Heck dropped his rifle, centered his guitar on his back, and said to Otto, "I sho' 'nuff ain't staying heah."

"Are yah talkin' 'bout desertion? Yahr cain't do that. We're at war."

"War? Huh? What it is good fo'? Absolutely nothin.'"

"Yahr'll can say that again."

"Freedom is dat way," Heck said, looking north. "Maybe dem Brits in Deee-troit will like my music better'n da Americans." With that, he vamoosed into the wilderness.

For Otto, freedom beckoned in the opposite direction. He lifted his head, as if hearing something faint, then said Millie's name out loud and wiped a tear from his eye. Without haste, Otto just walked out of town, past the still-sitting Johnny Appleseed, and waded across the Black Fork on his way home.

Captain Bantzer and Sergeant Craig led torch-wielding reinforcements back to the scene of the disturbance, and attempted to squelch the rebellion by setting Indians' clothes on fire. When these ignited belligerents dropped and rolled to extinguish their flames, they pulled everybody attached to them into a squirming mass, thereby giving the soldiers room to regroup and surround them.

"Shouldn't we jus' let 'em burn?" Sergeant Craig asked.

Before he could answer, Captain Bantzer spied movement on the crest of a hill above the road. "Somebody's getting away," he shouted, riding off in pursuit.

"They went that way!" Captain Bantzer hollered, pointing the way with his sword.

Toby pulled Weeping Coneflower by the arm, leading her down a steep slope, into a ravine where a braided creek flowed through a mossy field. She tripped, crying that she could go no farther, but still Toby encouraged her to keep moving by explaining that, if they could make it into the deeper woods beyond the plateau, they had a chance of escaping and getting home to the Wyandots.

But the pursuit was closing in, and when he heard the horses snorting behind them, Toby stiffened and planted his feet as if he had no intention of ever taking another step in his life. He pushed Weeping Coneflower into the creek, and when she caught her balance on the other side, her eyes met his.

"Go to the high ground. Stay off the trails. Return to our people. Tell them what happened here today," Toby said. When she did not move, he added emphatically, "Now!"

She fled, too terrified to do otherwise.

Toby kicked off his moccasins and sat on a rock, with his feet in the cool water. His rigid features showed no fear, except for a single tear that filled the corner of one eye, but did not fall.

Followed by half a dozen men, Captain Bantzer rode into the hollow and pulled up abruptly when he found Toby waiting there, washing his feet. Bantzer gestured for the soldiers to hold back, then hopped down from his horse and walked around Toby, humming as if deciding what to do.

Then, he abruptly grabbed Toby by his long hair and demanded, "Where is your whore squaw?"

"She is my daughter," Toby replied.

Hearing Toby's declaration of paternity somehow changed Captain Bantzer's opinion of him. He felt a quiver of sympathy for the father's desire to protect his daughter, which tugged upon some alien, gut-level emotions in him. Toby's devotion caused Frank Bantzer to realize that he would never, himself, have a daughter, or anybody else that he could possibly love enough to risk his life for. It angered Frank that he should envy the love of a bestial, sub-human savage.

"She's still a whore," he said.

"So, too, is your mother," Toby answered him.

Bantzer let go of Toby's hair, slowly removed the tomahawk from his belt, pounded it a couple times in his palm, and then reached back as far as he could.... He emitted a scream while slamming the blunt end against the side of Toby's skull with all of the malice he could muster. Dark, almost purplish blood sprayed them both, like a wave hitting rocks. The impact snapped Toby's head backwards and drove him to the ground. He landed on his back, smacking his head upon a rock. Brighter, redder blood began to bubble up and pool in the basins of his temples, eye sockets, and throat.

Through a gory mask and with fading eyes, he glared at Captain Frank Bantzer, defiant, and although choking, cursed at him in his native tongue.

"Your head will be a fine trophy," Bantzer said.

He turned his tomahawk so that its sharpened end pointed down, whirled it above his head a couple of times, then whacked it into the bridge of Toby's nose and out through his jaw, splattering bits of bone and brain, along with a shower of fluids that splashed him and his men. Twisting, pulling, and hacking, the captain removed a bowl-shaped portion of the poor man's cranium and held it like a trophy for everybody to see.

"Finally!" Bantzer reveled. He removed a flask of whiskey from his coat pocket and poured a cupful into the fragment of skull. Long, bloody strands of Toby's hair dangled in front of Bantzer's chest as he sipped from this gruesome chalice.

"Who wants a drink?" he asked, wiping his mouth.

In response, the captain's men vomited on him.

That evening, the citizens of Mansfield had planned a public pig roast and cider quaffing contest to celebrate the removal of the Black Fork Indians. As news spread about the violence that had transpired during the mission, however, their mood swung from merry to apprehensive. The Indians' unexpected resistance had raised concerns that the savages still had some fight left in them. Would there be retaliation from another tribe? With half of their militiamen gone, overseeing the Indians' long march to their new reservation in Urbana, the townsfolk knew they were vulnerable to a revenge attack. Instead of a feast, they wanted answers, explanations, assurances.

Captain Frank Bantzer, though, determined for festivities to proceed uninterrupted, summoned the people to the blockhouse and, from the porch outside his quarters, entreated the people to, "Drink to victory! Drink to glory! Drink to the death of the last Indian! Just drink!"

To show them how, he chugged several mouthfuls of a potent brand of corn whiskey known to the locals as "sudden death." Brown liquid trickled from the corners of his mouth as he boasted, "Today, we achieved a great victory! Notwithstanding a few complications, we accomplished our goals exactly as planned. Our troops suffered just one casualty, a man named Rope—a criminal, by the way—who was unfortunately caught underfoot of a mob and crushed to death. Burning of the Indians' village was necessary to disabuse them of any notion that they can ever return, never mind what they may have wished or heard to the contrary. This is war, after all, so any means are moral and justifiable in service to greater objectives. So be glad, Christians!"

Reverend James Copus covered his ears. He couldn't bear to her that voice, those words. In the aftermath of the conflagration of

Greentown, Copus wanted revenge. Outrage boiled his blood, while guilt twisted his guts, and try as he might to pray them away, one vicious thought kept returning to his mind: kill Frank Bantzer. He'd given his word to Chief Arm Strong that his people could return one day, but Bantzer had not even had the decency to wait until they were out of sight to commence burning the village to the ground.

He had been duped by Bantzer... but he also knew in his heart that he'd allowed himself to be used. No more wicked a deception visited a man than when he convinced himself he had no choice but to do what he knew in his heart to be wrong. From the start, it'd been obvious folly to trust that Bantzer would ever have allowed the Delaware to return to their homes. By telling them otherwise, Copus felt as culpable as if he'd lit the torches himself—not only in his own eyes, but in those of the Indians, and of God.

That evening, Reverend Copus went back to the smoldering ruins of Greentown. Chief Arm Strong had told him that a witch's sinister spirit lingered in those woods, and he'd often wondered why, if they believed that, they didn't just leave. Now, he thought he understood, and he was prepared to face the severe judgment he deserved.

Instead, though, he found Johnny Appleseed, still sitting in the same spot where he'd started the day, although now playing a plaintive tune on his whistle. He stopped when he saw Reverend Copus approach.

"This did not have to happen," Johnny said.

"I am greatly to blame," the reverend confessed.

"No sir. Nothing that ye could have said or done would have made a difference. Do not lose faith."

"Faith is insufficient."

"Not so. There's an evil Voice that influences all men, whether they hear it in their ears, ponder it their mind, or just react to it by instinct. It is relentless. No person lacking faith can resist it."

"If only all men believed with as much conviction as you—"

"Belief is not the same as faith. Today, I tried to show my Indian friends a way to defeat evil. They believed, but they did not have faith, so they faltered. Faith cannot be altered or shirked, not even when it conflicts with desire, duty, fear, or common sense. All of me life, I have had faith in the Voices that speak to me, trusting that their word is closer to God's than me own thoughts. I am coming to realize, though, that real faith enters a man at a deeper level than thought. Faith is something that cannot be told, or even heard. It must be put into practice."

Reverend Copus didn't quite understand what Johnny meant, but still found solace in his words. He sighed and said, "Perhaps you are right."

Johnny resumed playing his whistle.

The reverend listened for a long time, then returned to his home.

For the next couple of days, Reverend Copus was the most popular person in town, as folks whom he'd seldom seen on Sundays were suddenly anxious for him to conduct worship services, lead them in prayers, and plead with God to safeguard them from their enemies. He, too, was worried for his family's safety, so the reverend moved them into the blockhouse. After a peaceful week, though, most of the settlers wandered back to their homesteads, and instead of thanking God for deliverance, they thanked Captain Bantzer for his wisdom and valor in managing the Indian insurgency.

The Copus children were anxious to return to normal play, and even Mrs. Copus, who was otherwise terrified of red-skinned heathen, longed to go home now that it was safe.

Despite the sense of foreboding that still haunted Reverend Copus, he forced himself to resume ordinary life, and because it was harvest season, he was able to occupy his body, if not always his mind, with the chores involved in gathering and keeping his crops. It had been a good year with a bountiful yield, a sign of God's providence, or so he would have liked to believe. Yet, one morning when he rose earlier than anybody else and went on a walk among the tall corn stalks, he noticed one plant that was broken and drooping. He tore off an ear and shucked it... then dropped it in horror when he saw that it was rotten, covered with maggots and what looked like blood.

The curse on this land was still not satisfied, nor had it followed the Indians in their flight. Now, it was his.

A few days later, while Reverend Copus was cutting hay, Sergeant James Craig and a handful of soldiers visited his home. Craig informed him that two armed Wyandots had been seen in the vicinity of Zimmer's mill, so they were advising everybody who dwelt in the area to be on alert.

"Zimmer was supposed to meet me today, but did not show up," Reverend Copus said.

The group decided to ride together to Zimmer's cabin, a mile upriver, and check on his welfare. They arrived around suppertime, but spotted no movement within, and the door was ajar and swinging in the breeze.

Reverend Copus pushed it open warily. Afraid to look straight ahead, he cast his eyes down and saw blood pooled on the floor. The reverend recoiled, retching, and spun away from the gruesome scene.

Sergeant Craig continued into the cabin and found Zimmer's, his wife's, and his daughter's scalped and mangled bodies piled on top on each other in front of the hearth. A broken crucifix lay on the floor.

"The damned brutes!" Craig snorted.

"We must get back to my family!" Reverend Copus cried.

The men rode with haste back to the Copus homestead, where Amy was singing *Row, Row, Row Your Boat* while watching her children play hopscotch on a court drawn in the hard dirt next to their cabin's porch.

Reverend Copus met Amy in a desperate embrace and hurried the family inside, followed by the soldiers, and last by James Craig, who fired a shot into the woods for no particular reason.

"We'll have to stay here," Craig said. "It's gettin' on toward night, an' it'd be too dangerous to try to reach the blockhouse after dark."

"Oh, James, will we be alright?" Amy Copus sobbed.

The Reverend replied, "My darling, God will watch over you, and the children, too."

They barricaded the doors and boarded the windows, while Amy and the children retreated into the loft, praying through tears. The men sat on the floor with their backs to the walls and their rifles on their laps, eyes fluttering but awake. Every time they started to relax, the repeated barking of Moses the dog, left in the yard to keep watch, jolted their nerves anew. Eternal minutes and hours dragged on, punctuated by creaks in the wood, deep sighs and cracking knuckles, and shadowed by the dimming of candles as they burned down. Over the long ordeal of that night, Copus thought about how he had responded to his wife's question, and begged God not to make him a liar.

James Craig kept watch all night through cracks in the boarded windows, and Reverend Copus looked out, too, but could see nothing—absolutely nothing, just a dome of darkness. He asked the sergeant if he wanted anything to eat or drink.

Craig, clearly thinking about something else, remarked; "Y'know, reverend, all of this trouble started wit' jest one shot. And it weren't no Injun who fired, neither."

"Oh?"

"It's somethin' personal," he said. "If I live through this night, I'm a-gonna settle tha' score, once and fer all."

Reverend Copus reflected on how a man's thoughts strayed into strange places when he faced a reasonable chance of dying soon. He sat at the supper table and put his head down, not to sleep, but to shut out the world. Half-dreams drifted into his consciousness. He glimpsed distorted images of the times and places in which he'd lived, details he'd never had any occasion to recollect. It surprised him that they surfaced now—things like sitting in the tub scum of his bath in Bourbon County, and the egg-rotten scent of Reverend Otis McDonald's breath, and the buzzing of a mosquito in his ear when he'd stopped to rest on the day of the eclipse. He wondered about whether he had done any real, enduring good in his life.

In this world, how can a man ever truly know?

Eventually, birdsong filtered into Reverend Copus's dreams, and when he looked up, an inner cascade of relief poured over him. The first glimmer of dawn showed through the cracks of the boarded windows.

He called to Amy and the children, "Praise God, it's a new day."

Sergeant Craig grabbed his musket. "I'm gonna take a couple men and go scout 'round. Stay here, reverend. Don't move 'till I say so."

Amy Copus descended from the loft and put out a plate of cakes and jam for breakfast.

The reverend peeked through the window cracks, trying to follow where Sergeant Craig was going, but in the narrow field of vision he soon lost sight of him. Turning away from the window, he said to his wife, "It won't be long now."

Then a piercing scream assaulted them from outside.

A sudden instinct possessed Reverend Copus that he'd never known before. While everybody else inside the cabin listened breathlessly for whatever would come next, Reverend Copus grabbed one of the soldier's rifles right out of his hands, ran to the door, and kicked it open. A painted Wyandot with a firearm on his shoulder stood no more than twenty paces in front of him.

The two men shot at each other simultaneously. Both dropped.

The soldiers who'd stayed behind dragged Reverend Copus inside and returned fire, scattering the rest of the Indians back into the cornfields.

Amy Copus rushed to her husband and lifted his head, wailing inconsolably.

The shot, it seemed, had penetrated his heart. As he died, Reverend Copus pulled his wife close to him and whispered, "Have faith."

The last thought that flashed through Reverend James Copus's mind was that death was somewhat like watching the sun going dark at midday—as beautiful as it was frightening.

Everybody knew that Captain Frank Bantzer did not suffer bad news gracefully. Thus, nobody wanted to be the person who told him about the massacres at the Copus and Zimmer cabins. In all, eight people were confirmed dead, and Sergeant Craig remained unaccounted for. The soldiers who had remained inside the cabin with Mrs. Copus and the children, however, had successfully defended it through an assault that lasted all morning, until the Indians abandoned the scene for reasons unknown. The survivors then made their way back to the blockhouse just as another anxious evening set upon the town. Somebody had to tell the captain, who'd been alone in his quarters since midday, presumably drinking, of the tragedy and the peril that still faced them all.

Mrs. Copus, distraught with grief, but also furious, did not care about the captain's wrath. She pushed her way through the crowd and banged on the door to his quarters with both fists, shouting, "Come out! This is your fault! Now you must answer for my husband's blood!"

Onlookers felt emboldened to add their voices to hers. "Come out! Show yourself!" And as soon as one person uttered the word "coward," it became a chant. "Coward! Coward! Coward!"

Amy Copus pushed the door with her shoulder, but it didn't budge.

Several of the townsmen hoisted a log and used it as a battering ram. With a single blow, they knocked the door backwards, and it crashed to the floor inside the captain's room. Amy Copus was the first inside, followed by as many people as could squeeze through the threshold. They looked around in empty confusion.

Captain Frank Bantzer was gone. His uniform, shredded into rags, hung on a peg above his bed.

The people of Mansfield grew agitated by their desire for vengeance, addled by their sense of helplessness, panicked with fear of an imminent attack, and desperate for lack of anybody with authority to take control of the situation. Families abandoned their homes, farmers and millers from remoter areas came with their wagons full, and even the hunters, trappers, and moonshiners from the hinterlands joined the refugees amassing at the concourse around the blockhouse.

Of the few militiamen who remained, there were no officers, nobody of suitable rank, training, or temperament to assume charge of operations. Thus, the defense of Mansfield rested in the hands of a few green soldiers, old men unfit for duty, and shady characters that nobody knew or trusted.

Furthermore, the nature and degree of the threat were unknown. Nobody could say how many Indians had been involved in the massacres, if they acted alone, or if they were merely the advance scouts for a full-fledged attack. Doomsayers took turns imagining ghastly fates that awaited them.

"We're all going to be killed!" one cried.

"We're all going to be tortured and killed!" the next despaired.

"Our children will be kidnapped, our women will be raped, and then we'll be tied, tortured, and killed!" yet another bemoaned.

That silenced the blubbering for a few seconds, until somebody topped it by wailing, "And then we'll all get carried into everlasting hell by demons with talons!"

Into this pandemonium, Johnny Appleseed came skipping. Appearing from the depths of the forest, he moved swiftly, with apparent purpose, and in that milling, disoriented crowd, there was a natural tendency to make room for anybody who seemed to know where he was going.

Everybody knew Johnny. Some mocked him as a fool and an imbecile. To others he was just weird. A few considered him a kind of holy man. Most everybody agreed that, whatever he was, he wasn't completely right in the head. However, in the midst of crisis, somehow just seeing him provided a moment of distraction—a comfort, even. Maybe a situation like this called for a madman to tell them what to do.

Johnny hopped onto the steps outside the blockhouse and called out, "Friends, listen to me."

Somebody shouted, "We must run for our lives!"

Johnny shook his head and raised his voice even louder. "No. 'T'would be futile. 'Tis near darkness. There are too many of us. The

Indians move through the woods like wildcats. We cannot outrun them. 'Tis best to stay put."

One of the soldiers called out, "Then here's where we'll make our stand!"

"'Tis the surest way to get everybody killed. Friends, just look around at yourselves. We have not got a snowball's chance in hell if it comes to battle."

An old man hollered, "Then what, Appleseed? Give ourselves up?"

"The only thing to do is wait, pray, and keep your faith. Band together, friend to friend, neighbor to neighbor, Christian to Christian—heart to heart, body to body, and soul to soul. Let your serenity be your shield. Meanwhile, I'll go fetch help."

Calls of "How?" and "Who?" and "From where?" rang out.

Like a practiced orator, Johnny made his points by counting them off on his fingers. "The first thing I am a-going to do is say a very special prayer to God, to speed me along me way. Second, I am a-going to race down the road to Mount Vernon and warn all of the settlers along the route to take shelter. I will travel on foot, because I know shortcuts where no horse can go. Third, when I get to Mount Vernon, I shall ask the militia to send reinforcements. If I start promptly, I can be there by sunrise. Help will arrive by this time tomorrow."

There were no further questions or comments. By their silence, the people concurred that believing in him seemed their best bet. So, when Johnny started slowly sweeping his eyes across the crowd, they followed his gaze, taking a good, hard look at their neighbors. It was true what he'd said: they only had each other. Nothing else mattered. There was no purpose to harboring grudges or distrust. Nobody was stronger or weaker than anybody else. Even people who didn't care for each other still felt glad for their presence. Together, they just might have a chance.

Johnny pushed off the top step and broke into a trot, while folks stepped aside to allow him to pass.

"Godspeed, Johnny Appleseed. Our fate travels with you," Amy Copus cried.

Scattered hands clapping caught on quickly, and by the time Johnny had jogged to the edge of town, he was followed by a vigorous ovation.

Chapter 24 – September 1812

On the Road from Mansfield to Mount Vernon

As soon as he was out of sight of Mansfield, Johnny doubled back through the ashen ruins of Greentown, vaulted across the Black Fork, and ascended a steep ridge onto the plateau, following instinct more than memory. The forest canopy blacked out the starry sky and the pale sliver of a crescent moon, save for sporadic flickers. Such darkness engulfed the ground that Johnny could not make out forms or shapes, only areas of greater or lesser density, and the occasional glint of some animal's eyes.

He'd only been in this particular territory once before, and on that occasion he'd been following a guide who purposely took a circuitous path. The way Johnny figured it, his only chance of finding his destination was by first getting lost, then trusting God to point him in the right direction. The most important thing was to keep moving, because he realized that time was slipping away.

Johnny had always heard that the first sign of woods madness was when a person started seeing things. This worried him somewhat, because his eyes were beginning to play tricks on him, creating sudden brain flares when he blinked. To concentrate better, he closed his eyes and gathered his senses in his toes and fingertips, trying to feel his way through the gloom. Low branches brushed his face. More than once, he stepped in a hole or on a rock, nearly twisting his ankle. He eventually caught a sensation that started out as a tingling in his nose hairs, a vaguely chilled air that opened new passages in his sinuses.

It was the Earth breathing.

It grabbed him by the face and turned him around. He made several false starts, walking a couple hundred yards before losing the trail, and each time he found it harder not to panic. Finally, he realized the sensation felt stronger near the ground, so he crawled as fast as he could go on all fours. At length, he felt the slap of a distinctly subterranean breeze that could only be coming out of the mouth of a cave. Even then, he would not have known for sure that he'd reached his destination, had it not been for the ghostly albino squirrel sitting above the grotto's entrance.

Johnny called inside. "Mary, come out. I need ye."

Dead Mary spoke with the voice of the cave. "What fo' do yo' need me?"

"I need for ye to bring down a fog. I need to be able to move through it, everywhere that it covers, all at once. Many people depend on me for their lives."

Preceded by a flurry of bats, Dead Mary egressed from her sanctuary. "What fo' should I care?"

"Fog Mother trained ye to do this. She would have wanted ye to help."

As if she could see perfectly in the dark, Dead Mary peered at Johnny. "I always s'posed dere was some reason what fo' I didn't kill yo' when I had my chance. Maybe dis is it."

"If ye do this for me, I shall never bother ye again."

"I ne'er done worked Fog Mother's spell. It's real powa-ful. I don't know if I can make it work right."

"Please, try."

When Dead Mary raised her arms, the beads on her bracelets jingled. "We'll need to make us a fire."

Johnny couldn't exactly make out what she was doing in the darkness, but when he heard her snap her fingers, sparks shot out of her long nails. The dry leaves and twigs in front of her quickly caught fire, and the cave's breath fanned the flames to a rapid blaze.

Dead Mary arranged four quartz-flecked stones, which she took from the cave, at the compass points around the fire. Sitting cross-legged, she opened her medicine bag on her lap and arranged its contents in several small bundles. Then she said, "Dey's a right way an' a wrong way to ask da spirits to bring down a fog. Is yo' heart pure?"

Johnny put his hands palms-down in the flames and held them there, testifying. "I am pure."

"Best be so, 'cuz dis spell 'll kill yo' if not."

"Proceed."

Dead Mary pinched a bit of powder between her fingers, sprinkled it into the fire, and said, "Dis is some black cohosh, dried, ground an' pounded. It eases a person's way through life's hard passage ways. I offer this to da spell fo' bringin' serenity."

Next, she grabbed a handful of desiccated spikes. "Dese cattails come from da Black Swamp, a scary place, where nary nobody who goes ev'r comes out da same, fo' bett'r or worse. I add dem fo' courage."

Dead Mary took a root, cut it in half, and squeezed a drop of reddish liquid from it. "Dis juice o' bloodroot is poisonous, to remind us dat we must gotta suffer in life, an' da best we can hope fo' is to die well."

With every offering added to the spell, the fire's color changed subtly, from bright yellow, to orange-red, with sharp blue tongues. When Dead Mary broke open a packet of grass stalks and cast them into the flames, they fizzled and gave off a florid scent. "Sweet grass fills da air with perfume. It gives us compassion."

Leaning forward, Dead Mary began to gently rock back and forth. "Now, I gotta pray in da spirits' own language."

Whatever it was, Johnny had never heard the language that Dead Mary commenced reciting. Within a few moments, voices other than her own started coming out of her mouth. She seemed to be shrinking inside of her loose garments, her arms retracting, her neck recoiling. The process seemed interminable, yet Johnny also had a sense that no time was passing. Patience was a kind of prayer, Johnny told himself.

Finally, Dead Mary gasped and returned to her body. "Now, da spirits are listenin'." She nodded at Johnny. "An' now, yo' too gotta add somethin' sacred to da spell."

Over the many miles he'd traveled across that country, Johnny had handed out page after page from his copy of the Philosopher's great book. He had only a single page left in his possession:

> *It has been shown that in the heavens there is a sharing of all with each and of each with all. Such sharing goes forth from the two loves of heaven, which are, as has been said, love to the Lord and love towards the neighbor; and to share their delights is the very nature of these loves.*

"I've got this," Johnny said, showing her the page.

"Is dat sacred?"

"'Tis fresh news straight from heaven." Johnny unfolded the page and held a corner into the fire, so that it burned slowly, releasing those words into the sky.

Dead Mary stood, a bit unsteady and hunched, her hair now streaked with shocks of smoky grey, as if the task had aged her. "We is done," she announced.

"That is it? Did it work?"

A faint smile cracked the corners of Dead Mary's mouth, but the answer to Johnny's question came not from her lips, but from a sudden roar resonating from the bowels of the cave. An eerie fog began pouring out of its mouth, spreading out and covering the earth and every living thing above and below.

It lifted Johnny off the ground....

They would have treated Tecumseh like an honored guest, had he chosen to share British officers' quarters inside of Fort Detroit, but he preferred to camp with his people outside its walls. He didn't like the British much. Their fancy dress, rigid protocol, and pompous way of talking to him all seemed insincere, barely masking condescension. They vowed to him that, after sweeping the Americans entirely out of the Northwestern territories, they would establish a permanent Indian homeland. Possibly, they even believed what they were saying, but....

Tecumseh doubted that in the future they would consider themselves bound to such situational promises. It seemed just as likely to him that, one day, he would have to lead his forces against those same British, struggling to wrest the same rights and freedoms from them as from the Americans, once the British were no longer allies.

None of that mattered, for if they were using him, he was using them, too. After the debacle at Tippecanoe, he'd needed their alliance to re-energize his coalition. And... it was working. Indian warriors had taken Fort Dearborn and laid siege to Forts Wayne and Harrison. Now, Tecumseh had turned his attention to his homeland in Ohio, which after the fall of Detroit was unprotected from a northern invasion. He was eager to lead his forces down from Michigan, pillaging the small towns along the way—Huron, Mansfield, Mount Vernon, Franklinton—adding warriors to his army as they advanced, until finally reaching his birthplace of Chillicothe, where he would overturn every brick the white men had laid there.

"Go ahead," the British commanders had encouraged him. "We will be right behind you."

That's what Tecumseh told his men, even though in his heart he knew better. "Our brothers the British support our quest!" he'd shouted at that evening's war council.

The chiefs and all of their tribesmen greeted this pronouncement with riotous acclamation. The braves were giddy from the successes fighting in Indiana, and aching for more. Somewhat unexpectedly, they actually seemed empowered by the prospects of going to war with no expectations that Waashaa Monetoo would protect them in battle. Finally, Tecumseh assured them, this was their chance to fight for themselves, not for a Great Spirit. They would launch their forces at dawn.

After the rally, while the camp rocked with the snoring of six hundred braves resting up for battle, Tecumseh walked alone through a grassy prairie, consulting the night sky for omens. Not that he necessarily believed in them, but ever since defeat had revealed the folly of Tenskwatawa's religion, he felt liberated to seek private comfort from his own spirituality. Named after a shooting star, he felt that part of him soared across the sky; the sight of a comet or some other cosmic signal of good fortune always gave him confidence.

The sky that night had nothing to offer him, though, for the air grew mistywith a settling fog. It was peculiar, because unlike the typical fogs that rolled in from the lake at this time of year, this one seemed to creep in from all sides, like a cloud that had gotten lost from the sky. As omens went, a fog did not seem particularly helpful. The warm, damp air seeped into his body like a soft caress. For a moment, it reminded him of the feeling of lying with Rebecca Galloway.

Something moved behind him.

He pivoted and instinctively reached for his tomahawk. "Who goes this way?"

When he turned, an undulating wave of fog brushed Tecumseh's face, like the fine spray of a distant waterfall. Compared to the drenching Lake Erie fogs, this nimbus mist had flowing veils of texture and glimmered with green phosphorescence. It danced and billowed despite the almost still air. Tecumseh's eyes watered as well, further distorting his vision.

From the opposite direction, he heard what sounded like a very swift animal running through tall grass. Tecumseh dashed to where he thought he'd heard it, but when he reached that spot, something moving in the trees at the prairie's edge diverted his attention. Then, almost simultaneously, he heard something whistling to his left and something whispering to his right. Feeling surrounded, yet alone, he didn't know where to look.

Waving his tomahawk, Tecumseh stiffened his back and called straight overhead. "Show yourself."

Across the field, Tecumseh thought that he could make out a stick figure, which might've been a dead tree, except that its branches were swinging from side to side. He rubbed his eyes, but only smeared his vision. The same instinct that compelled him to stare also arrested him where he stood. When the vague figure lifted legs from the ground and started to walk, he dropped his tomahawk and felt his shoulders go slack. A shadow, a wraith, a specter—whatever it was, it accelerated into a loping, skipping, twitching stride, while rolling its arms in a "come along" gesture.

Tecumseh had only known one person to move with that particular gait.

"Appleseed?" he called.

As quickly as he could speak the name, the figure vanished, absorbed into the fog. Immediately, Tecumseh wondered if he had really seen anything, or merely imagined it. Whichever it was, he knew it was a revelation nonetheless, but had no idea what to do with it.

He remained standing in the hazy prairie long into the night, dreaming awake in the layers a fog that he now believed was from the Great Spirit, not nature.

The sign nailed to a tree at the crossroads read "Do Not ~~Entry~~ ENTER," with the correction in a different handwriting. Despite that warning, Johnny could see that somebody else had come down this trail recently, maybe just a matter of minutes ahead of him. Whoever it was had taken out unholy wrath on the new split rail fence that had been constructed along the roadside, knocking over its posts and heaving the rails into a ditch. The soft ground preserved fresh, heavy, heel-first footprints.

This was not the way that a person with congenial intentions came a-calling.

With the fog at this back and under his feet, Johnny felt as if he were flying. The terrain passed in a blur, as if he were swooshing along at such an accelerated pace that the wake behind him tugged at the surfaces of solid objects. Likewise, he felt as though the sound of his voice was both amplified and stretched out. When he called, "I am the herald of the Lord! Pray to God! Help is on the way!" he imagined his words soared far and wide, gaining volume as he approached, then fading slowly in case somebody listening didn't make them out the first time. It felt like the fog permeated his whole body, so that he was everywhere that it was.

As he approached Andy Craig's cabin, though, Johnny's instincts compelled him to slow down and keep quiet. Like tiptoeing along a steep ledge, he feared one false move might trigger a landslide. He stayed in the brush, aware that he was following close behind some unknown trespasser, and wary of that person's intentions.

When he reached the narrow glen where Andy and his family lived, Johnny pushed aside some branches and saw Jim Craig, his musket in his hand, shirtless over suspendered trousers, trundling toward the cabin.

"Hoo haw!" Jim Craig shouted as he kicked in the door.

Johnny heard a shriek and a curse from inside. He ran into the clearing, unsure about what to do next, when a sudden cloudbank flowed around him. The fog, it seemed, wanted him to remain concealed, so Johnny crept around the side of the cabin, clambered up a woodpile, hopped onto the roof, and listened through the chimney.

The door had thudded flat on the floor when Jim Craig burst through. "Whar's mah skunk-fuckin' brodder?" he hollered.

The children screamed and Marge Cuss pushed back from the table. "I ain't no skunk," she retorted.

Andy, who'd been whittling in a corner, stepped between his woman and his brother. "If yah got some grievance wit' me, yah scabby shithole, let's us take it outside."

"Andy," Marge said, "how's 'bout if ah hold 'im while yah beat on 'im?"

"Naw, hon', this here's mah fight alone."

The moment they stepped outside, Jim tried to sucker-punch his brother, but Andy ducked. Regaining his balance, Jim put up his dukes. "Fight fair, yah weasel dick." He lunged again, missing once more. When he righted himself again, he reached for his rifle. "Then ah'll have to shoot yah."

Marge, watching from the threshold of the cabin, grabbed Andy's rifle and tossed it to him.

The two men faced each other staring down the barrels of their weapons.

"This ain't gonna work," Jim said. "Let's do this like a proper gentlemen's duel."

"Like countin' off paces and firin' at each other?"

"Tha's what a duel is, ain't it, shit-fer-brains? We start back-to-back an' count off thirty steps, then shoot at the same time."

"How 'bout twenty steps?" Andy countered.

"Nuh uh. The rules o' duelin' say it's thirty. An' we keep on duelin' 'till one is dead or maimed too bad to keep on."

Andy faced Marge and mouthed, *I Love You.*

"Huh?" Marge asked.

"Nev'r mind. Keep dinner warm."

"Aim for his crotch," Marge said. "If yah miss, yah still got a better chance of hittin' him somewhere on his body."

The men squared their shoulders and began pacing off the requisite number of steps, counting as they did. At thirty, they turned and raised their rifles.

Jim did not hesitate to fire....

On the roof, Johnny felt a sudden, icy shiver, like cold lightning knifing through the mist.

At the instant he pulled the trigger, Jim seemed to feel it, too, for he twitched ever-so-slighting upon firing, and his shot flew above Andy's head. He dropped his rifle, trembling in disbelief.

Andy seemed to be taking his own sweet time to draw a perfect beat on his target, but it was hard to see, at the distance of sixty paces, through the shroud rolling and twisting between them.

While Andy was taking aim, Johnny selected a sharp, disc-shaped skipping stone from his kerchief, and gripped it with all five fingers. From his vantage, above the dense layer of ground fog, he could look down on the two men and not be seen. He could tell by the sound of Andy's breathing when he was getting ready to pull the trigger. He, too, figured Andy for a poor shot.

In a split second before Andy fired, Johnny hurled the stone side-armed, flicking his wrist so it spun as it flew hard and true. While Andy's bullet whizzed harmlessly into the woods, Johnny's stone slashed Jim on his bare chest, in the flabby pectoral just above his heart, breaking the skin and cutting into muscle.

Jim collapsed and started writhing on the ground. "Goddamn yore slimy nuts, Andy. Yah done shot me. Ah'm bleedin' from the heart."

Approaching, Andy Craig squinted at the wound. "It jest looks like a flesh wound to me."

"Horse turds! Yah shot me wit' a bullet. Yah gotta take it out an' bandage me up."

"Marge has took a few bullets outta mah hide o'er our years. She maght could fix yah." Andy furrowed his brows. "But why ought ah save yore stinkin' arse?"

"We is brodders. Ain't that reason 'nuff?"

"Yah done beat me an' mocked me all mah life. An' jest now yah tried to kill me."

"Well, ah didn't, right? Maybe ah didn't really wanna. Besides, yah cain't leave me to bleed out like a wild hog."

"Ah could do so. Ah'll hang yah upside down, so's the blood can drain out faster." Andy tossed Jim a rag. "But answer me one thing."

"This ain't no time fer riddles!"

"How come yah done always hated me so much?"

Jim Craig heaved a weary sigh, as it apparently settled in that he would have to answer Andy's question. Finally, he blurted, "Hate jest comes natural to me."

"Even so, hate needs some reason."

"Ah don't rightly know. Pap got drunk and whupped on me, but left yah alone 'cause yah was littler. So who else was there fer me to take it out on? Somebody had to toughen yah up. Now, look, yah got a wife 'n' kids, while ah ain't got none o' those things." As soon as he'd spoken those words, Jim Craig made a face like tasting shit in his mouth. To cleanse his palate, he spat out, "So ah reckon tha'd mean ah'm sorry."

Andy extended a hand to help his brother up. "Tha's all tha' ah ev'r wanted to hear, Jim."

Meanwhile, Johnny Appleseed rolled off the roof and skittered into the woods, borne aloft by the fog, resuming his mission.

Johnny trekked mostly along the main road, diverting where footpaths or natural clearings provided a more direct passage, or when doing so brought him into proximity with a greater number of homesteads. He proceeded on his way proclaiming, "Hear one, hear all! I am the messenger of God, alerting ye that the enemy is nigh! Seek refuge in love! Pray for salvation! God will not abandon ye!"

His words carried over the stillness of the night, reverberating in the crystal fog like echoes shouted into a canyon. Everybody who heard him might well have thought he was right outside their doorsteps, for the pitch of his voice carried across distance without losing any intensity. Jolted from their repose, folks reacted to his voice as if it were a prophecy straight from on high. They gathered with family, friends and neighbors, hunkering down and praying as intensely as if God Almighty was looking over their shoulders. Even their horses, hogs, and dogs sought shelter when they heard Johnny's cries.

Scampering over rocks and potholes, hurdling bogs and brooks without breaking stride, Johnny kept up his incessant calls. "Heed my Alarm! I am God's helping hand!"

"Help!" a man shouted in response. "We need help right heah!" His cry was followed immediately by a wail of gut-wrenching agony that sounded like a bombshell had just exploded in somebody's stomach. The clamor came from Otto and Millie Blubaugh's cabin.

Johnny switched direction and hustled to where he'd been summoned.

The cabin's door blew open ahead of him, as if pushed by an invisible hand. Inside, Millie Blubaugh lay flat on the bed, a blanket covering her splayed legs, and her bare, veined belly protruding from her pullover nightdress. Her knees were shaking, and her toes, sticking out beneath the blanket, looked twisted and cramped. Brownish sweat drenched the pillow beneath her head. Making fists with both hands, she pounded the headboard.

"Oh my burnin' cunt!" she howled. "Here comes 'nother horrible ache!"

Otto stood squirming by her side with a slack jaw and desperate eyes. When he saw Johnny, he exhaled so hard that his trousers nearly dropped. "Oh praise the Lord, Mist'r Appleseed, yah gotto help! This baby is a-comin' early an' ah don't know what to do."

"Yah shoulda thought o' that before yah dicked me!" Mille screamed.

"Please, Mist'r Appleseed," Otto begged. "She ain't of her raht mind."

Although Johnny was mostly speculating on this matter, he nevertheless assured Otto, "That is altogether normal." He added, by way of explanation. "'Tis the curse of Eve."

Millie grimaced so hard that her cheekbones nearly split the skin, and she howled through a spasm. "It's *you* that I curse, Otto Blubaugh!"

Otto winced away his tears. "Thar, thar, baby lover...."

While Millie scowled and threatened to ream Otto's colon with a fireplace poker, Johnny pulled him aside and whispered, "Did ye not plan for this moment?"

"Yessuh, we did, but she ain't actin' like we done planned. Soon as her pains started, ah was all set to ride an' fetch the midwife in Fem-Amity. But Millie grabbed me and wouldn't let me go, jus' a-whining that she needed me an' didn't wanna be left alone. Next thing ah knew, she's a-gettin' all purple and bent, cussin' me out worse'n some drunk keelboater. Ah done foaled many a colt, but gettin' a baby out seems a whole lot more harder. Ah didn't 'spect nothin' like this."

"Ye cannot heed what she says in the throes of her labor. Be strong. I will stay with her, while ye go and bring the midwife. Go now!"

Otto objected only mildly. "It don't seem fair."

Millie screamed, "Fair! What'd be fair is if I rolled your balls on a grindin' stone!"

"Awww, sweet cakes, yah don't mean that."

When Millie roared, "Ah'll dip yah face down in the outhouse!" Otto became convinced of the wisdom in Johnny's advice. He nodded to Johnny, promised to return within the hour, and absconded into the night.

Although glad to have gotten Otto safely out of the way, Johnny felt some immediate trepidation, for upon giving the matter some thought, it occurred to him that he didn't know anything more about child birthing than hearsay from old wives' tales. Mostly, what he'd heard was that men should never, under any circumstances, be present, because they could not be depended upon to keep their wits about them. Sometimes, he'd heard tell, there was cutting involved in places on a woman's body that he'd never even seen in his entire life. On the other hand, he was encouraged by stories of Shawnee women who, when their time came, excused themselves to wander down to the creek, where with nothing more to assist them than running water, they had their babies alone, and were done in time to cook dinner.

That sounded improbable, but it gave Johnny an idea.

Fortunately, Otto had had either the foresight or the blind luck to heat a large pot of water above the fire. Johnny poured it into a tub and tested its temperature with his finger. It was a bit less than scalding, which he figured was just about perfect.

"Now," Johnny said, lifting the corners of Millie's blanket, "If ye don't mind me presumption, I need to have a peek down there to see what is what."

Far beyond modesty, Millie kicked the blanket onto the floor and spread her legs as wide as Owl Creek in August.

Johnny took in the sight, squinting with one eye while gawking with the other. It wasn't as awful to look at as he'd supposed. Millie was extremely hairy down there, with thick, wooly tufts from below her belt line, sprouting in the hollows between her pelvis and legs, and bunching like pillows along her pubic arch. A man could lay his head there and fall asleep. In the middle of all the shag, Millie's womb was bright pink, lipped with a dewy dampness and parted like magnolia blossoms. About the only thing Johnny could see that looked problematic was that her hip and thigh muscles were tighter than fiddle strings. If a baby was going to squeeze through, Millie needed to relax.

"May I touch?" he asked.

"Push, pull, poke, twist, shake... do whatev'r yah gotta do! Jest make this pain go away. Oh glory, here comes another stab!" Millie's legs started quaking from heel to hips, and she passed an eruption of rancid gas.

Undaunted, Johnny began rubbing his palms into her thighs, digging in with his thumbs. "This is a good method for massaging a charley horse. Try to let yourself go loose."

Through clenched teeth, she whined, "Loose? It feels like a damn bull rampagin' through my innards!"

Johnny climbed onto the bed and knelt between her legs, kneading her thigh muscles with his fingers while using his elbows to soften her belly. He tried to speak as though he knew what he was doing. "It might help, too, if ye remembered to breathe. Listen to me. Breathe in.... Do it, now. Breathe in...."

Millie practically sucked all the air out of the room.

"Now, breathe out."

Millie exhaled so hard that Johnny had to hold onto the bedpost.

"Ye are doing very well. Breathe again, this time less hard."

Johnny opened his palm upside down and raised it slowly, while Millie inhaled at the same pace. He then turned his index finger once, and she let a short breath escape, then again, and again, and gradually the relief started to show on her face.

"Thankee," she said. "How much longer, d'you reckon?"

For her sake, Johnny hoped not long... and for his own sake, too, because his schedule hadn't allowed any spare time for delivering babies. He considered the mechanics of what had to happen, and it made sense to put gravity to work.

"Let us see if we can hurry things along," he suggested. "Do ye think that ye can stand?"

"Stand? On my feet?" Millie sounded pessimistic, but when Johnny urged her once more, she threw her legs over the side of the bed and planted her feet on the floor.

"What now?"

"Can ye squat above this here tub, with one leg one each side?"

"Squat?"

"Yes, I figure it will help the baby drop down."

"Squat?" The word sounded ungainly when she said it, like something that, under other circumstances, she might have slapped his face for asking her to do. Still, holding her hand, he helped her find her center of gravity while straddling the tub. Steam rose between her legs. "Ummmm, that hits the spot," she said. "What am I s'posed to do now?"

"Just stand there, while I crawl underneath and see if I can see the baby.'

Flat on his back beside the tub, looking up the way a man might lie beneath a wagon when he was fixing its axle, Johnny peered into Millie's depths.

Despite herself, she giggled. "Mister Appleseed?"

"Yes, Millie dear?"

"Please don't let nothin' happen to this baby. I couldn't bear to lose another."

Johnny had always said he believed that, with prayer, anything was possible. Now was the time to prove it. "In heaven, God leads the angels in the Lord's prayer every day," he said. "So pray with me, Millie dear. *Our father....*"

"Who farts in heaven," Millie continued, as best she knew.

"That is, who *art* in heaven."

"Art in heaven? Like paintings and such?"

"Just repeat after me...."

They continued in unison until finished, then started over again. On the third repetition, another vicious cramp seized Millie, and she made a sound that sounded to Johnny as if a serrated iron spear had punctured her body through the belly button.

"Yyyyyyyeeeeeooooowwww!"

"Remember to breathe, in and out."

"I quit! I cain't do this no more!"

"Not yet, my dear." Beneath her, Johnny sat up for closer inspection. "I think I see the baby's head."

"I feel like I gotta push!"

Sure enough, the baby's spongy head crowned, bulging from Millie's womb in a way that reminded Johnny of a timid turtle peeking out of its shell, then when the spasm passed, it sunk back inside.

Johnny rolled onto his feet and took Millie's hands. "Ye are almost done. Listen, now: I want ye to sit in the tub, all the way down into the water."

Millie wondered why, but was too far gone to argue about it. She lowered herself into the tub, buttocks first, then plopped down with a splash. The water was so hot that it seemed to absorb her pain. She lowered herself to the chin and shoulders, her nipples just above the surface, and her legs dangling over each side of the tub.

Kneeling at the front of the tub, Johnny rolled up his sleeves and reached into the water, his hands in a ready position. "If ye feel like pushing, let it rip."

"I feel something like a wave comin' down from my middle parts. I'm bearin' down now." She took a deep breath and held it while grimacing and thrusting with all her strength.

"I am a-holding the baby's head," Johnny announced. "Another strong push ought to bump the rest out of there."

"I can't see. Everything's all black...." Millie tensed, gritted her teeth, and concentrated the energy in every bone, fiber, and viscera in her body into a final, cathartic thrust. "Wait! Now I see colors!" Then she released. "I got nothin' left," she gasped.

Johnny bent over the tub, concealing what he was doing from Millie.

She heard the sucking and splashing noises. "What's wrong?"

Johnny hunched down farther, still with his back turned to her, so that all she could see was a flaccid umbilical cord hanging over his shoulder like a lasso.

Millie started weeping.

Then, with a burp and a gurgle, the baby began to cry, too.

Johnny turned, cradling the infant in his arms. "'Tis a girl," he said, handing her to Millie. "I have always wanted to say that."

Sitting up, Millie opened her arms and took her daughter against her breast, allowing the moment to sink in as long and as deep as it could. "Thankee, Mister Appleseed."

"Praise the Lord," Johnny said.

As promised, Otto returned in just under one hour, with the midwife from Fem-Amity riding beside him. When he saw the tub full of bloody, foul-smelling water outside the door, he gripped himself and felt a gag reflex in his throat. He ran into the cabin, fearing worse than the worst.

Millie was sitting in bed, covered with a blanket up to her breasts. The baby was lying on her belly, swaddled to its neck, while nursing as vigorously as a snake swallowing an egg. Its cord was still attached to the afterbirth, wrapped in rags and put in a bucket on the floor.

Johnny was playing a tune on his whistle.

"Honey cakes, lookit. We got a daughter," Millie said, as calmly as if she was reading poetry from a book.

Otto swooped across the room and smothered Millie in a clumsy embrace. "Oh joy! Ah cain't believe it," he blubbered. "How...?"

Johnny lowered his whistle and answered. "It was not as difficult as I had thought t'would be."

"I helped some, too," Millie added.

Otto kept whimpering. "Are yah okay, sweet buns? An' the baby?"

"They are both healthy," Johnny said. "Thank the Lord."

Not wanting to dislodge the baby from her breast, Millie sat up higher to give Otto a better look. "Ain't she the purtiest thing?"

Otto petted the baby's head. "She's as purty like her momma."

"I was thinkin' that, on account of how he done helped give her birth, we oughta name her... Johnny."

Otto blinked. "Yah did say tha' she's a girl, raht?"

"E'en so, she could be named Johnny, couldn't she?"

"Ah don't know...." Otto twitched his ears while he thought. "Ah do agree wit' the sentiment, but ah ain't n'er heard tell o' no girl named *Johnny*." He snapped his fingers. "How's 'bout Appleseed?"

"Naw, that won't work no better. Appelina, maybe?"

"What about Johanna?" the midwife volunteered, as if anxious to make some contribution.

"Tha's it!" Otto and Millie sang in unison. "Johanna Blubaugh."

"Baby Lover!"

"Lover Boy!"

Johnny interrupted by clearing his throat and handing Otto a pair of linen shears. "I left it for ye to cut the cord."

Otto took the shears with one hand, and extended his other to shake with Johnny, but that just didn't feel like enough, so instead he reached all the way around Johnny's back and gave him a suffocating hug.

"What yah done is a miracle, Mist'r Appleseed," he said. "We'll tell this story fer the rest o' our'n lives."

Hearing Otto say so confirmed it for Johnny. "Yes, I do agree that we saw a miracle here today, but I must be on me way. I still have far to travel before dawn. And, who knows, there may be some more miracles in the works before this night has finished."

"I'm plumb tired of dancing with other women. I'd rather dance with a real man whose got muscles, hair on his back, and sweats under his arms."

Sister Mona pressed a finger to her lips and shushed her niece. "Refrain from such talk. Sister Say might hear. Besides, your fellow Sisters here have plenty of hair and muscles. And, my, they do sweat."

"'T'aint the same," Rebecca said. "Real men got hair all over and knots in their shoulders, and when they sweat, it's got a woodsy smell. When I'm dancin', I like for a man to toss me off the ground and catch me." She crossed her arms and squeezed her shoulders, as if giddy just imagining the moment.

"But, unlike men, your Sisters will never drop you," Mona said. "Have you already forgotten the condition you were in when we took you in?"

"As if I could forget! You remind me near every day. Oh, I do admit that at first I was a blubbery heart-broken lapdog. 'T'aint that I'm not grateful...." She lifted the corners of her lips. "But I'm all over it now, and ready to get back onto the horse."

"At the time, you said you could never love again."

"Might be so, but how can I know if I don't try? Oh, I 'spect it won't be easy. Some women say that once you've gone red, you'll never be satisfied with a white man again."

"That'll be enough! 'Tis sinful for a lady to speak of being, as you say, *satisfied.*"

"What do you know about such things?" Rebecca snapped. "You're nothing but an old nun who ain't never been in love."

Mona shielded her eyes and lowered her head, wounded by memories of a distant feeling, while at the same time jealous of her niece's naïve resilience. When she was young, she never worried about going to hell, even though she was probably heading in that direction. Ironically, now that she stood on solid spiritual ground, she often questioned whether she was truly worthy of heaven. Sometimes, in private moments between prayers, she wondered if giving in to temptation once or twice was not worth the risk. If it was a sin to think such things anyway, what would be lost by actually doing them?

"I am sorry," Rebecca said.

"Don't apologize. I am what I am, and probably all that I ever shall be." Sister Mona straightened her back and reached to brush Rebecca's hair out of her eyes. "But I do understand that not every woman is meant for the life of the Sisterhood, especially one as young and lovely as you, dear girl. I will write to your mother and tell her that you're ready to go home. She and your father will rejoice to have you back. You can still have any life you want—with a man, if that's your choice. Even a fallen woman can live in a Godly way."

Rebecca clapped her hands. "Oh thankee, Aunt Mona. And bless you, too."

"Yes, well, speaking of blessings, go now and join the Sisters in the grand hall for evening worship. Say nothing to them of what we've discussed."

"Aren't you coming, too?"

"No. I am going by myself to the prayer hut. I need some time alone with my Lord."

"Is that a good idea? It's mighty dark and foggy out this night. There might could be Indians lurking."

"I will be as safe as if God were right there with me." Sister Mona pulled a shawl over her shoulders and hooded her head. "Tell the Sisters not to wait for me. I will join them later."

"If you say so." Lighthearted, Rebecca skipped off to join the Sisters of Fem-Amity. "I do look forward to a good, healthy shaking, even if it is only with other women as my partners."

Mona watched her niece leave, admiring her zeal, and, she admitted to herself, envying her possibilities. Having acknowledged these thoughts, though, Sister Mona knew she had to pray them away. This wasn't new to her; she did it almost every day. Maybe, someday,

God would see fit to remove those longings from her. Until such time, though, she had a place, if not a home; a role, if not a calling; and acceptance, if not happiness. She never prayed for anything more. Rather, she prayed that would be enough.

When Sister Say rose from her chair, it was time for the evening ceremony to start. The women of Fem-Amity believed that every task each one of them did from the moment they awakened and throughout the day, if done with pure intent, was devotional in nature. Right-minded work yielded a credit of spiritual energy, which they then spent collectively during their communal worship. Some women prepared by cooking, some by cleaning, some by gardening, some by tending animals, some by keeping watch, and some, even, by disposing of wastes.

Sister Say generally spent her days sitting, idle only to unenlightened appearances, for in fact she was immersed in meditative commune with God. The women understood that her role was to process all the spiritual capital that the other women accrued through their labors. Thus, when she stood up, she was effectively signaling that she'd accumulated a sufficiently critical mass of everybody's earned grace to conduct a proper liturgy.

Sister Say enunciated so loudly, and with such panache, that it sounded as though she were singing, even though she wasn't really. She quoted from the Book of Ruth:

> *Entreat me not to leave thee, or to return from following after thee: for whither thou goest, I will go; and where thou lodgest, I will lodge: thy people shall be my people, and thy God my God: Where thou diest, will I die, and there will I be buried: the LORD do so to me, and more also, if ought but death part thee and me.*

This was one of Sister Say's favorite Biblical passages, and every time she broadcasted it to the Sisters, they cheered and testified "Hallelujah," then started dancing. The ritual began with two rows of women facing across from each other, in the fashion of a line dance, but with ever louder shouts of "Glory!" and "Hosanna!" from one side to the other. After each couple took a turn stepping between the lines, the formal choreography broke down into what might've looked to an observer like an old-fashioned country dance, minus the men. Partners were thrown and dotesy-doed, while Sister Say, like a traditional caller, urged them. *"Turn, turn again, my daughters!"*

A creamy fog rolled through the doors and windows of the grand hall and began swirling along with the dancers.

This is an enchanted night, Sister Say thought. She hopped down from her platform and began stomping and swinging right along with the other sisters. The floorboards shook when she landed, like the ground tremors that preceded an Old Testament prophet's proclamations.

"Hearken and heed me words!" a frantic voice from outside carried over the din. "I am the courier of the Lord!"

To the last woman, the Sisters of Fem-Amity froze mid-step, planted their feet, and turned to see who was making such claims. Four women—the community's night watchers—accompanied Johnny Appleseed into the grand hall. The entire assemblage of women gathered to either side of Sister Say, making a show of force.

Other men had shriveled with terror when confronted by such a phalanx of estrogenic ferocity. Not Johnny. "God has blessed me with alacrity," he said, "so that I can race faster than Satan!"

Sister Say advanced and faced Johnny incredulously, so close she could smell apples on his breath. "Chapman? What madness possesses thee?"

"Madness? Yes! I am full of God's fervor!"

"So I can see."

"Tonight, I am called by the Lord God Almighty to bear witness to this truth: Evil is near, gathering, preparing to strike! The enemies will slay your bodies to rob your souls! But, rejoice, for the Father has bestowed upon us the means for salvation. My friends—ladies—I beseech ye to *pray*!"

Sister Say had seen enough lunatics to know what they looked like. Men who'd lost their grip on reality could look you straight in the eye, but not see you when they did. That wasn't what she saw in Johnny's features, though. Indeed, it was quite the opposite; he looked her in the eye, and it seemed like his thoughts were entering her head.

"We *are* praying," she replied. "This is how we pray."

"God is great! May I ask: what are ye praying for?"

"For? The usual things—health, strength, to give thanks."

"May I beg of ye, then, to pray for one other thing tonight?"

"Perchance, what favor do thee ask of us?"

"'Pray for peace, Sisters. Pray for harmony. Pray for—"

"Amity," Sister Say finished for him.

"Yes, exactly so!" Johnny affirmed gleefully. "Well, I must make haste, for I have many stops to make tonight. But, before leaving, may I ask for just one word with Mona? I have a particular message, for her alone."

"Sister Mona?" Considering Mona's history with men, Sister Say was reflexively inclined to shoo him away, but something whispered in her mind that whatever he had to say to her, Mona needed to hear it. She looked around. "Where is Sister Mona?"

"She went to the prayer hut," Rebecca Galloway piped up.

"Alone? On this night? Someone should go fetch her."

Johnny did not hesitate. "I will find her," he said, scurrying out of the grand hall, followed by a pinwheel of mist.

Mona knelt in front of a rock altar and large wooden cross in the prayer hut. When saying familiar prayers, she closed her eyes, but when praying really hard, reaching outward as well as inward, she kept her eyes wide open and tried not to blink. She knew she was praying in the best way possible when the images in her eyes all converged and began melting, while visual blobs of consciousness flowed from her head all around her, surrounding her with cloudy tranquility. This was when she felt truly in the presence of God.

"Mona."

Sounds, too, mixed and blended into the amorphous background of her being, like ripples and vibrations amid the smoothness of her reverie.

"Mona, listen to me."

Mona blinked, and her senses retreated. She felt herself being shaken.

"Mona, come to your senses!"

The voice sounded stern, like she imagined God's would be, but breathless and impatient. She rubbed the phantasms out of her eyes and re-focused.

She gasped, faced by a surreal vision of what she'd always supposed the Angel of Death would look like.

The demon manifested himself like an Indian warrior adorned for battle, his body clothed only by a scant, ragged breechcloth. His arms and chest were smeared with dried mud, and his face was colored with blood red ochre in his eye sockets and white ash rubbed into his forehead and cheeks. Around his neck, he wore a band spiked with porcupine quills, and crow feathers so black they glimmered. A cracked human skull hung from a braided necklace around his neck.

Mona breathed in a scream, but her lungs collapsed and she could not get it back out. Was this how death came to a Christian woman?

"Mona, compose yourself. I travel in the guise of my enemy, to gain his powers, but don't be alarmed. It is still just me. Look...."

She took him in with wide eyes. Beneath the mud and the paint, she recognized the angular vanity of those features, the jaw that was always clenched, the raised chin, and the cheekbones that cast shadows. But it was his voice that smote her memory with an unmistakable pain, the same voice she had come to associate with sweet promises and cruel lies.

"Frank?"

Pleased to be recognized, Frank Bantzer beat his fists against his chest. "God spoke to me. He led me to you, Mona. At first, I resisted, for I felt duty-bound to stay and fight, but, the more I listened to the Voice, the more I came to realize that these trivial battles between men do not concern me. My destiny is greater. I have the intellect and courage of the Christian, as well as the skills and senses of the Indians. Everything I have ever wanted can be mine. All that I have to do is take it."

Mona remained on her knees, somehow feeling safer that way. "You cannot be here, Frank. Please go. I'll pray for you."

"Don't you see? I am the answer to your prayers. Years ago, I quit you, but you stuck a curse on me, didn't you? You knew that one day I would have to come back. Well, here I am. This night is mine. It is ours. The fog brought me here unseen. So shall we leave, unseen, together."

"No, no, no... no... *no!* Oh, Frank, I confess that, once, I wanted nothing more than to follow by your side wherever you went. But I didn't know you then, not as well as I know you now. You're frightening me, Frank. You must leave me to my keep my vows."

"I've broken vows, Mona, and let me assure you, it makes a person feel much lighter. I know why you're afraid, though. Even though your curse has cost me everything I once wanted in life, still, I can forgive you. But you must swear yourself to me, forever. That much, you owe me."

Rising, Mona said, "Your conscience is your curse, Frank. Are you surprised to learn that you have one?"

"Not anymore!" Bantzer kicked over the cross, which broke into two pieces. "I will take what I want. You will come with me, or I must kill you. Either way, this story ends tonight."

Mona started to run, but Bantzer snagged her by the wrist and pulled her toward him. With his hands around her neck, he growled, "Which will it be? Love or death?"

Mona paused, hoping for God to answer, since she was unable. And He did....

Simultaneously, from the top of the ravine across the creek, from the canopy of the woods surrounding them, and from just down the path behind them, Bantzer and Mona heard the call. "Fear no evil! Trust in the Lord!"

Johnny Appleseed appeared at the head of the path.

When Bantzer turned to confront him, Mona slipped away and dashed behind Johnny, clutching his shirt while squealing, "Please help me."

Chortling, Bantzer brandished the two halves of the broken cross like weapons. "Ho, if it isn't Johnny the Appleseed. Do you fancy yourself a hero?"

"I am just a humble servant of the Lord," Johnny answered.

"Then serve him with your death!" Bantzer attacked.

Johnny stood fast.

Wielding the boards of the broken cross like jousting lances, Bantzer charged until just before colliding with Johnny, then smashed them, nails pointed outward, against both sides of Johnny's head. Patches of skin on his cheeks and temples ripped open, one of Johnny eyes swelled and blackened immediately, and dark blood spurted from his nostrils. Still, he remained standing in his place.

"You cannot harm me. I trust in the Lord," Johnny said.

Bantzer reared back and punched Johnny on the chin, so hard as to snap his neck backwards between his shoulders with an awful cracking noise. He followed by kneeing Johnny in the stomach, which made him fold nearly in half.

"At least defend yourself!" Bantzer screamed.

Bent over, Johnny spat out a tooth and replied through bloody gums. "I cannot do violence."

"I yield," Mona entreated. "Please stop, Frank. I will do as you say."

But, on the brink of triumph, Bantzer would accept nothing less than submission or death from Johnny Appleseed. He reached both arms around the surface of the rock altar and, grunting, hoisted it over his head. Summoning all the hateful fury within him, he pounded the rock down upon the soft spot at the base of Johnny Appleseed's skull....

...and it passed right through his body, like a breeze through fog.

The force of his lunge made Bantzer stumble, and he fell face-forward onto the ground behind Johnny and Mona. When he pushed up, prepared to counter attack, he was slammed upside the head by a wrought iron frying pan. It made his eyeballs rattle. Bantzer's head whirled, and when he cupped his ears to steady himself, the only thing he could see in his entire field of vision was Sister Say. She boxed his nose, twisted his earlobes, and kicked him in the spleen. Reeling, Bantzer saw that he was surrounded by a gang of torch- and pickaxe-carrying women, whose faces showed utter contempt.

Groveling, he begged them, "Please have mercy."

"Shall we chop him?" Rose Mary called out.

"I have the butcher knife," Mary Rose proposed.

Sister Say pulled Bantzer up by the belt of his breechcloth, then, with a jerk, snapped it clean off. "Bah. Behold this fool. He's got a withered stick and hardly any balls worth chopping." Scouring deep in her guts, Sister Say hocked up a phlegmy wad and spat it directly between Bantzer's eyes. "Go back to thy slimy pit. And if thou ever cometh here again, we'll rub all thy body holes with honey and stake thee to an anthill."

Whimpering like a piglet, Frank Bantzer ran naked into the wasteland of the rest of his life, a mad hermit's lonely existence, absent from even the memory of love.

Heedless of the blood in his eyes or the pain pulsating in his brain, Johnny limped to Mona and took her hand. "Are ye well?"

"I am." She removed her bonnet and wiped his face with it. "Thanks to you, my hero."

"I am no hero, just a man doing God's will."

Face to face with each other, their breaths merging, mere inches between their mouths, Johnny felt sparks firing in his skin and blood surging from his heart into every quarter of his body. Every pore was aroused. Desire pulled them closer. If any moment in his life had ever called for a kiss, this was the very moment God had given him to do so.

"Well, kiss her already," Rebecca Galloway said.

Even Sister Say stood back to allow this to happen.

Johnny closed his eyes and felt his lips growing plump. He shivered gently as the distance he and Mona shrank to less than a breath....

Johnny, it can never be.

As quick as that, the sound of his mother's Voice pulled the moment right out from under him. It was gone.

Johnny took a slight step back. "I, uh... I am grateful to ye, Mona, but...."

Mona steadied Johnny's head between her hands and directed his eyes into hers. "I heard it, too. I understand."

Johnny backed up and kicked the dirt, not knowing why, but doing so elicited a sigh and a moan from nearly every woman who'd been watching. He addressed them all. "I had better be on me way. I still have many miles to go before dawn."

"Thou are always welcome here, *Brother Chapman,*" said Sister Say.

"So, I am off." Johnny took three steps, then stopped abruptly and snapped his fingers. Fishing through his pockets, he retrieved a single seed, which he handed to Mona.

She examined the seed, which he'd picked out just for her. It was a perfect oval, smooth, almost polished, with a fleck of golden color. Mona pressed it against her breast.

"Plant this in a place where ye will see if often. I hope it causes ye to think of me, once upon a while."

With no further hesitation, he jogged down the path and vanished into a cloud of fog, but he heard her calling behind him, "If not in this life, perhaps the next!"

Postscript - December 1823

Danville, Ohio

"Johnny rambled into Mount Vernon at dawn," Dan Sapp said, "just ahead of the roosters' cock-a-doodle-doing. People scampered outta their homes still wearing their bedclothes, and followed him to the town square, where they listened, downright amazed, as he told all 'bout the terrible things that had happened in Mansfield. But what people later remembered most about that morning was how the fog just faded away, like the memory of a dream, at the very moment that Johnny stopped running.

"Within the hour, the Mount Vernon militia mobilized and went marching off to the aid of the good folks in Mansfield. When those reinforcements arrived that evening, they were greeted with jubilation and gratitude. 'We are saved!' the people cried. As one, they joined in a chant of 'Hail, Johnny Appleseed! Hail, Johnny Appleseed! Hail Johnny! *Hail Johnny!*' He was the champion and the hero of the town. 'May his name ne'er be forgotten,' was what they all said.

"The peculiar thing, though, was that the attack they had so desperately feared never took place. For some reason—nobody knows why, exactly—Tecumseh changed his plans and did not lead his warriors into Ohio that night, nor, for that matter, did he ever again set foot in the state where he'd been born. A year later, he died in battle, way up in Canada. It almost seemed as if he'd given his ultimate gift to Ohio, by leaving it in peace.

"Even after all the distance that he'd run, and the adventures he'd had that night, Johnny still didn't stop when he got to Mount Vernon. He needed to spread his message to one more town, so he kept going all the way to Danville.

"Johnny was weary and hoarse by the time he got to his last stop, which was right here at the farm. He just about collapsed when he staggered through that door, his legs gone limp and his voice reduced to wheezing. Me and Missus Sapp were just sitting down for breakfast, so we invited him to the table and served him hotcakes smothered with apple butter. After he had a chance to catch his breath and eat a bit, I asked him, 'Where in tarnation have you been all night?'

"Johnny told the tales of his night of tragedy, faith, thrills, miracles, and redemption, praising the Lord and swearing it was all true, every last word of it. I was skeptical at first, but I know for sure that while Johnny is a strange man with many uncommon ideas, he ain't no liar. So, I hope you've been listening good, young 'uns, 'cause these stories are too good to ever be forgotten."

"I won't never, ever, ever forget, Uncle Dan," Johanna Blubaugh promised. "Mister Apple is my very own godfather, ain't that right, maw?"

Millie exchanged a knowing glance with Otto, then answered, "You know perfectly well that's so, 'cause we've done told you around eleventy-ten million times."

"But I like hearing it again and again!"

Just as they had every holiday season for the last ten years, the Blubaugh family and the Sapp family had gathered together for Christmas dinner. Over those years, both clans had gotten bigger. The Sapps added Gregory, Stephen, Bobbie Jean, and Little Laura. After the birth of Johanna, Otto and Millie were blessed with two more girls, Joy and Faith.

"Ah ain't gonna quit tryin' 'til ah get me a son," Otto often said.

Earlier that evening, they had feasted on turkey with chestnut stuffing, baked acorn squash, mashed potatoes, turnips, hominy pudding, spiced peaches and mincemeat pie. After dinner, as they did every year, Dan Sapp pulled up a stool next to the fire and the children sat on the floor around him, while he regaled them with stories about Johnny Appleseed—the same stories each year, which the children never tired of hearing, and which Dan never tired of telling.

"Where is ol' Mister Apple these days?" Johanna asked.

"He comes 'round every so and such. He's got some land here 'n' there, but he don't keep it up very well. I've heard that he spends most of his time near Perrysville. He wanders, though, so I wouldn't be surprised none if one day, when we least expect it, he will come a-knockin' on my door. He knows that he is always welcome at the home of Dan Sapp."

"Maybe he'll come this night?"

Millie laughed, "Not t'night, Baby Doll. Everybody knows that Christmas Eve is when Santeclaus comes."

Johanna made a pouty face. "Santeclaus ain't real!" she protested.

"Mind what you say, Baby Doll!"

"But Johnny Appleseed, *he's* real."

Dan Sapp sat up higher on his stool. "He's as real as you'n me. So, maybe, you all would like to hear another story about ol' Johnny Appleseed?"

"Yes, please!" the children cried in unison.

"Well, did I ever tell you 'bout how Johnny Appleseed could talk to the animals? Yeah, he spoke with my ol' horse LuLu, and she spoke with him. It was back in 1805. There was a huge horse race in Newark...."

Book Club Guide

1. Most people have heard of Johnny Appleseed. What are some of the stories that you've heard, and/or impressions that you had about Johnny Appleseed, prior to reading *Fresh News Straight from Heaven?*

2. By all accounts, Johhny Appleseed was a peculiar person. In the first chapter, he does several things to reinforce that reputation but throughout the novel, he introduces himself by saying, "Me name is John Chapman, a sower of seeds. I would be pleased if ye chose to call me Johnny." What does this tell you about how he viewed himself, and how he wished to be viewed by others?

3. Johnny, Dead Mary, and Andy Craig each lived in the remote frontier by choice, but for different reasons. What was the attraction of the frontier for each of these people? What kinds of life did they hope to make for themselves in such obscure locations?

4. In chapter one, Johnny encounters an albino squirrel, which later reappears at various times in the novel. What are some of the possible symbolic meanings of this creature?

5. When Johnny sees three Indian canoes crossing the river to intercept him, he waits patiently for them. What does his encounter with the Shawnee, and their chief, Tecumseh, suggest about Johnny's relationship with Indians? How do they treat him? What questions does he ask, and what does Tecumseh ask about him? What does the interpreter, Stephen Ruddell, add to their interactions?

6. Lieutenant Frank Bantzer dislikes Johnny from the moment he first sees him. Why?

7. Dead Mary is devoted to Fog Mother, in some ways as a daughter to a mother, in others as a student to her master. Discuss how each of their stories contributes to the complex dynamics of their relationship. How does each of them view the threat of encroaching settlement, and how the problem should be handled?

8. Christian camp meetings such as the one described in chapter five were common at that time in the Ohio territory. What were some of the social, economic, and cultural functions they served? Discuss how the characters of Reverend Copus, Colonel Bantzer, Otto and Millie, and Johnny Appleseed act at the camp meeting? When Johnny jumps onto the stage and declares, "Look at me, sir. Here I am. *Here* is your primitive Christian!"—what does he mean by that?

9. Many fringe religions thrived on the frontier. In chapter six, Johnny meets a group of schismatic Shakers. Describe each of the characters' motives for joining the order, and how Johnny gets along with each of them. What are some of the things Johnny contributes to the community? Consider Sister Mona's questions to Johnny, and how he answers them—what do they suggest about a subtle attraction between the two? Although Sister Say finally asks Johnny to leave, do you think he would have stayed otherwise?

10. Historians are uncertain about how Johnny Appleseed came to accept the Swedenborg religion. In *Fresh News Straight from Heaven*, he experiences his religious conversion in the Pittsburgh Point Brewery. As he reads/hears Swedenborg's words, he becomes convinced of their truth. Why? What are some of the elements of Swedenboriaism that appealed to Johnny? Later, how does his meeting with Margaret Blennerhasset reinforce his convictions? During his night on Blennerhasset Island, Johnny is visited by several angels. The last voice cries out, *'I am the Door. Meet me on the other side.'* Whose voice was that, and what does that mean?

11. Describe the significance of Reverend Copus's opening prayer during the great horse race in Newark, both in terms of what it meant to him, personally, but what he wanted to convey to his audience.

12. In chapter ten, the drunkard Lalawethika experiences his own religious conversion. Describe the elements of his dream, and what it meant to him and his people. How does Tecumseh react? Why are the people so quick to embrace his revelation? Consider ways in which Lalawethicka/Tenskwatawa's ministry is similar to or different from other apocraphyl religons, both historically and in the present day.

13. What does Fog Mother mean when she says, "As with two winds that blow storm clouds across the heavens from different directions, so do our gods and the white men's gods clash when they drift across the same sky. But we know, too, that storms are part of nature, and after them sunshine and rebirth can follow. There must be peace in both the realms of gods and men...." How do her actions support that belief?

14. In the rally at the council house, Lalawethika goes off script when he declares that he has changed his name and will henceforth be called Tenskwatawa, or The Open Door. What does this new name signify? What does it suggest of how he saw himself, and how he wished to be seen? Why did it inspire fear in Johnny?

15. In chapter fourteen, Sister Mona has two awkward but pivotal encounters. One is with her niece, Rebecca, who has grown into a young woman since their last meeting. Discuss the meaning and intent behind her advice to Rebecca: "True love proves itself through patience." Second, Mona seeks a meeting with Frank Bantzer. Why? What does she hope to accomplish? What happens, instead?

16. The total solar eclipse of 1806 is a true historical event. Discuss how it was perceived and understood by each of the characters in this chapter. What changes after the event in each of their lives?

17. Fog Mother refuses to defend herself against Tenskwatawa's accusations. When she is burnt at the stake, "The smoke of her burning flesh smelt sweet and drifted in its own wind. It hovered over the village for days, like the haze of a troubled conscience." What did her execution signify to Tenskwatawa, to Dead Mary, to Chief Arm Strong, and to Toby?

18. In chapter sixteen, readers glimpse Johnny's family life and upbringing. What can you infer about his relationships with his half-siblings, his father, and his stepmother? How might these relationships account for aspects of Johnny's life, such as his faith, his generosity, and his solitariness? When he leaves his family, he embarks upon a mission to save the Blennerhasset family. Compare and discuss how his attitudes toward his family might have affected his actions on behalf of the Blennerhassets.

19. Shaker community members practiced strict celibacy. Discuss the social and power dynamics between the men and women of the Turtle Creek village. How are these tensions expressed through Sister Say's story, through Sister Mona's dalliance with Johnny, and then through her traumatic experience with Brother Bunselmeyer?

20. Consider the elements of Tecumseh's strategic diplomacy. How does he exploit Tenskwatawa's religion? Why does he seek Blue Jacket's advice? Why does he agree to a summit with the Americans? How are his words and actions received by the Americans? Why, ultimately, does he agree to leave Ohio?

21. Why, after delivering the Copus family to Mansfield, does Johnny seek Dead Mary? Why does she allow herself to be found? What's the point of Johnny's advice to her: "The spirits come when they feel they are needed."

22. Tecumseh's speech to the Americans in chapter twenty is based upon the actual words he spoke at the historical meeting in Chillicothe. Why did he bring an armada with him to Chillicothe? Why leave Tenskwatawa behind? What are his demands, his key points, and his accusations? Why does it fail to satisfy the Americans? How did his visit to Chillicothe, and his blunt ambitions, reinforce Rebecca Galloway's feelings for him, and his for her?

23. In the Battle of Tippecanoe Creek, the Americans had greater numbers of casualties, and the Indians regrouped to fight in the War of 1812. Why, then, was it widely viewed as an unqualified success for the Americans? What did it mean for Tenskwatawa, for Tecumseh, and for General Bantzer?

24. Confused and distraught by the violence all around him, Johnny escapes to the Great Black Swamp to pray for guidance. The epiphany he receives is not what he'd expected. Discuss the significance of his actions and visions.

25. There were many victims at the Copus Massacre and the events that led up to it. Consider ways in which each of the main characters were literally or symbolically victimized.

26. Why did Frank Bantzer flee his position after the Copus Massacre? What does it mean when he reappears, dressed like an Indian warrior?

27. Consider the stops Johnny made during his midnight run, and what he accomplished at each of them, both for other people, and for himself.

28. Why does Johnny's mother say to him, "It never can be" at the end? What does it mean that Sister Mona heard those words, too?

Interview with the Author

Q. What is it about the lore and history of Johnny Appleseed that inspired you to write *Fresh News Straight from Heaven*?

A. Childishness, mostly. Johnny's innocence, idealism, benevolence, sense of adventure, and unalterable faith are attributes that I tend to associate with youth. That's probably why Johnny is such a popular character in children's literature. I know that, when I was a kid growing up in central Ohio, I read about Johnny, and no doubt I was also influenced by the Disney short movie, "The Legend of Johnny Appleseed." Whenever I saw an apple tree—even a crabapple tree—I'd ask my parents if it was one that had been planted by Johnny. In sixth grade, for a history assignment to write a short biography of some famous Ohioan, while everybody else chose athletes, astronauts, inventors, artists, or presidents, I picked Johnny Appleseed. I think of *Fresh News Straight from Heaven* as a continuance of that assignment.

Furthermore, it is high time for an adult book about Johnny. His values matter to grownups, too. Of course, I acknowledge that the characteristics traditionally ascribed to Johnny are part of a folkloric tradition, and thus no doubt have been exaggerated and hyperbolized through many, many a retelling. That's okay. The lore of Johnny Appleseed speaks to a deeper human longing than any facts ever could.

Q. How historically accurate is your portrayal of Johnny?

A. Who knows? That's the beauty of a character like Johnny. Since most of what is "known" about him comes from oral traditions, I felt considerable liberty to create an interpretation of him that served my own literary objectives.

Was Johnny mad? Some historians think so. The one thing that everybody agrees upon was that he was unkempt, a vagabond, and incredibly eccentric. Still, he came to own quite a bit of land, and must've possessed some fundamental business acumen. In *Fresh News Straight from Heaven*, Johnny has audio hallucinations. Did he really hear voices? I can't say—well, probably not—but as a devoted Swedenborgian, he would have believed that angels not only existed, but could communicate conversationally with human beings. I don't think it is too much of a stretch to suggest that, for a man who spent a lot of his life alone in the woods, he might've chatted with spirits from time to time.

Many of the stories about Johnny in *Fresh News Straight from Heaven* are historical, or modeled after actual historical events. He was reportedly a guest on Blennerhasset's Island, although whether he ever met Aaron Burr there is probably questionable. Once, he did in fact hop onto the stage at a Christian rally and declare himself to be a "primitive Christian," although it actually occurred later in his life than the events in this book. And, he did make a midnight dash from Mansfield to Mount Vernon, although I took the liberty of inventing a few stops that he made on the way.

Q. What other characters in *Fresh News Straight from Heaven* are real historical persons?

A. Several of the characters are real, although, as with the character of Johnny, I embellished aspects of their stories. Obviously, Aaron Burr and William Henry Harrison were real enough, and they did visit some of the places and do some of the things that I recounted in this novel. The same holds true for Tecumseh and the Prophet, Tenskwatawa, and while the nature of their relationship and ambitions is not precisely known, I did not stray too far from most scholarly interpretations in depicting Tecumseh as the mastermind, and Tenskwata as having issues that would have qualified him for therapy.

Other characters from history include Reverend Copus, Andy Craig, James Craig, Toby, Mike Fink, Stephen Ruddell, Rebecca Galloway, and the Blennerhassets. Frank Bantzer is based upon a composite of a couple of villains who were implicated in various atrocities. Sister Mona is also fictional. Alas, there's little evidence that Johnny ever had a love interest in his life. There are stories that he once had a girlfriend back in Massachusetts, but after she broke his heart, he swore to love no other. Other sources claim that Johnny chose to remain celibate in this life, anticipating his spousal reward in the next. Still, this story needed Sister Mona, and her various trials and experiences were probably not uncommon for women in that age.

Q. What about the events—which are historical, and how accurately are they depicted?

A. Some writers of historical fiction take extreme pride in their scrupulous attention to even the smallest of details. I am not one of those writers. While I salute their fastidiousness, I have to admit that I think it is rather affected, and perhaps even distracting to readers. Personally, I would suggest that any work of the ilk of *Fresh News Straight from Heaven* is, by necessity, an *interpretation* of history. Furthermore, I don't see how it could be any other way when the main character's whole identity is the creation of folklore, anecdotes, and popular media. Thus, my first commitment is to telling good stories.

Still, I felt an obligation to honestly convey historical cultures and situations with clarity, empathy, and general accuracy concerning cause and sequence. Tenskwatawa's conversion, the raid on Blennerhasset Island, the total eclipse of 1806, Tecumseh's meetings in Chillicothe, the battle of Tippecanoe, the Copus Massacre, and of course Johnny's midnight run, all really happened, but artistic license applies to the details of what certain characters did, said, or felt. For readers who'd like the straight history, I refer them to the various sources mentioned in the Acknowledgements.

Q. What's next?

A. My next project is a mostly satirical novella that takes place over 24 hours in a pay-it-forward chain, in the drive-thru at a donut shop in Columbus, Ohio. Tentatively entitled *#FeedtheDeed,* I should have it done in 2018. I'm also putting the final touches on a poetry anthology, *Sonnets About Things That Most People Don't Think About.* Finally, although I intended *Fresh News Straight from Heaven* as a stand-alone novel, I have a lot more material about Johnny Appleseed that I hope to use in a sequel, or a prequel, or both.

Acknowledgements

While *Fresh News Straight from Heaven* is entirely a work of fiction, I endeavored to make it plausible and in general accord with actual people, places and events. Thus, I invested hundreds of hours of research in primary and secondary sources to convey the life and times of Johnny Appleseed. The following are some of the key resources.

For a general, contemporary, one-volume history covering the period and places where Johnny Appleseed lived, R. Douglas Hurt's *The Ohio Frontier: Crucible of the Old Northwest, 1720-1830* is probably the best. One of the joys of researching this novel, though, was the discovery of how much fun it is to read many of the early histories of some of the important locales in Johnny's life. Among those were Henry Howe's *Historical Collections of Ohio,* Banning Norton's *History of Knox County, Ohio from 1779 to 1862,* A.J. Baughman's *History of Richland County,* N.N. Hill's *History of Coshocton County,* Isaac Smucker's *Centennial History of Licking County,* and Isaac Finley and Rufus Putnam's *Pioneer Record and Reminiscences of the Early Settlers and Settlement of Ross County, Ohio.* Finally, I was inspired by and borrowed from various works by Allan W. Eckert, especially *A Sorrow in Our Heart* and *The Frontiersmen.*

The definitive scholarly biography of Johnny Appleseed remains Robert Price's *Johnny Appleseed: Man and Myth.* A very readable and popular recent biography is Howard Means's *Johnny Appleseed: The Man, the Myth and the American Story.* A new study looking at Johnny from the perspective of his socioeconomic influences is William Kerrigan's *Johnny Appleseed and the American Orchard: A Cultural History.* And, of course, there are a great many articles, reports, essays, literary works, and various expositions about Johnny Appleseed, beginning, significantly, with the famous 1871 *Harper's New Monthly* article by W.D. Haley, "Johnny Appleseed: A Pioneer Hero."

For broad historical coverage of the Native Americans in Ohio and Indiana, I consulted Jerry Clark's *The Shawnee,* C.A. Weslager's *The Delaware Indians: A History,* Colin Calloway's *The Shawnees and the War for America,* and the more scholarly *A Spirited Resistance: The North American Indian Struggle for Unity, 1745-1815* by Gregory Evans Dowd. The primary book I used for reference regarding Tecumseh was *Tecumseh: A Life* by John Sugden, and for Tenskwatawa was R. David

Edmunds' *The Shawnee Prophet.* A recent book that lends further insight into the battle of Tippecanoe is Adam Jortner's *The Gods of Prophetstown.*

Numerous patient and helpful librarians, researchers, and museum curators who provided valuable assistance include good folks from the Johnny Appleseed Museum at Urbana University, Ohio Historical Society, Indiana Historical Society, Knox County Public Library (especially the Danville Branch), Licking County Historical Society, Ross County Historical Society, and Chillicothe Public Library.

Finally, on a personal note, there are certainly numerous people whose support and encouragement contributed to this book. Most of the same people whom I mentioned in the acknowledgements of my first novel, *Dollarapalooza,* deserve thanks this time, too. (Those who do not—well, you probably know who you are.) I'd like to give an extra mention to Bill Dobbins, who provided the soundtrack. Dave Lane (aka Lane Diamond) performed the truly Herculean task of editing this book. The cover art is by Richard Tran. Thanks to the members of the Friday afternoon Darwin Club, who have been asking me when this novel would be finished for the longest time.

But I want to elevate one person to a category of special thanks....

I know I am deeply flawed, often incorrigible, occasionally petulant, and sometimes hypocritical, and I recognize that I am wholly responsible for so many brain-dead mistakes and unmitigated screw-ups that it's a wonder, truly, that I am still breathing. Many, many people I've known over the years ultimately decided that I'm just not worth the frustration. In fact, there's really only one person who has seen the worst that I can dish out, and still stuck with me. I am in awe of the love that my wife, Beatrice, has given me. After all the good times, hard times, and downright awful times, she has been my constant. At this point in my life, I do not take a single moment of being with her for granted. *Je t'aime.*

About the Author

Gregg Sapp, a native Ohioan, is a librarian, academic administrator, and a Pushcart Prize-nominated author. Having written over 60 academic articles and some 300 reviews, Gregg published his first novel, *Dollarapalooza* (or "The Day Peace Broke Out in Columbus") in 2011 with Switchgrass Books of Northern Illinois University Press.

Since then, he has published humor, poetry, and short stories in various literary journals, including Defenestration, Imaginaire, Kestrel, Zodiac Review, Marathon Review, and Writing Tomorrow, and he's been a frequent contributor to Midwestern Gothic.

For more, please visit Gregg Sapp online at:
Personal Website: www.GreggSapp.net
Publisher Website: www.EvolvedPub.com/GSapp
Goodreads: Gregg Sapp
Twitter: @Sapp_Gregg
Facebook: Gregg.Sapp.1
LinkedIn: Gregg-Sapp-b515921b

What's Next?

Gregg Sapp is hard at work on his next novel, which we anticipate publishing in the not-too-distant future. Please stay tuned to his page at our website, inserted below, to remain up-to-date.

www.EvolvedPub.com/GSapp

CPSIA information can be obtained
at www.ICGtesting.com
Printed in the USA
LVOW13s0350090118
562337LV00002B/3/P

9 781622 535071